A HIGH S
SEDUCTION

BY
JENNIFER LEWIS

WITHDRAWN

MILLS & BOON

All rights reserved including the right of reproduction in whole or in part in any form. This edition is published by arrangement with Harlequin Books S.A.

This is a work of fiction. Names, characters, places, locations and incidents are purely fictional and bear no relationship to any real life individuals, living or dead, or to any actual places, business establishments, locations, events or incidents. Any resemblance is entirely coincidental.

This book is sold subject to the condition that it shall not, by way of trade or otherwise, be lent, resold, hired out or otherwise circulated without the prior consent of the publisher in any form of binding or cover other than that in which it is published and without a similar condition including this condition being imposed on the subsequent purchaser.

® and ™ are trademarks owned and used by the trademark owner and/or its licensee. Trademarks marked with ® are registered with the United Kingdom Patent Office and/or the Office for Harmonisation in the Internal Market and in other countries.

Published in Great Britain 2014
by Mills & Boon, an imprint of Harlequin (UK) Limited,
Eton House, 18-24 Paradise Road, Richmond, Surrey, TW9 1SR

© 2014 Jennifer Lewis

ISBN: 978-0-263-91481-8

51-1014

Harlequin (UK) Limited's policy is to use papers that are natural, renewable and recyclable products and made from wood grown in sustainable forests. The logging and manufacturing processes conform to the legal environmental regulations of the country of origin.

Printed and bound in Spain
by Blackprint CPI, Barcelona

Jennifer Lewis has been dreaming up stories for as long as she can remember and is thrilled to be able to share them with readers. She has lived on both sides of the Atlantic and worked in media and the arts before she grew bold enough to put pen to paper. She would love to hear from readers at jen@jenlewis.com. Visit her website at www.jenlewis.com.

EDINBURGH LIBRARIES	
C0046555161	
Bertrams	01/10/2014
	£5.49
CH	DO NOT USE

For Dwnell

ACKNOWLEDGMENTS

Many thanks to my editor Charles Griemsman.

One

"Just get rid of her as quickly as possible. She's dangerous."

John Fairweather scowled at his uncle. "You're crazy. Stop thinking everyone's out to get you."

John didn't want to admit it, but he too was rattled by the Bureau of Indian Affairs sending an accountant to snoop through New Dawn's books. He glanced around the grand lobby of the hotel and casino. Smiling staff, gleaming marble floors, paying customers relaxing on big leather couches. There was nothing he didn't love about this place. He knew everything was aboveboard, but still…

"John, you know as well as anyone that the U.S. government is no friend of the Indian."

"*I'm* friendly with them. They gave us tribal recognition. We ran with it and built all this, didn't we? You need to relax, Don. They're just here to do a routine audit."

"You think you're such a big man with your Harvard degree and your Fortune 500 résumé. To them you're just another Indian trying to stick his hand in Uncle Sam's pocket."

Irritation stirred in John's chest. "My hand isn't in anyone's pocket. You're as bad as the damn media. We built this business with a lot of hard work and we have just as much right to profit from it as I did from my software business. Where is she, anyway? I have a meeting with the contractor who's working on my house."

The front door opened and a young girl walked in. John glanced at his watch.

"I bet that's her." His uncle peered at the girl, who was carrying a briefcase.

"Are you kidding me? She doesn't look old enough to vote." Her eyes were hidden behind glasses. She stood in the foyer, looking disoriented.

"Flirt with her." His uncle leaned in and whispered. "Give her some of the old Fairweather charm."

"Are you out of your mind?" He watched as the woman approached the reception desk. The receptionist listened to her, then pointed at him. "Hey, maybe that is her."

"I'm serious. Look at her. She's probably never even kissed a man before," Don hissed. "Flirt with her and get her all flustered. That will scare her off."

"I wish I could scare you off. Get lost. She's coming over here."

Plastering a smile on his face, John walked toward her and extended his hand. "John Fairweather. You must be Constance Allen."

He shook her hand, which was small and soft. Weak handshake. She seemed nervous. "Good afternoon, Mr. Fairweather."

"You can call me John."

She wore a loose-fitting blue summer suit with an ivory blouse. Her hair was pinned up in a bun of some kind. Up close she still looked young and was kind of pretty. "I'm sorry I'm late. I took the wrong exit off the turnpike."

"No worries. Have you been to Massachusetts before?"

"This is my first time."

"Welcome to our state, and to the tribal lands of the Nissequot." Some people thought it was cheesy when he said that, but it always gave him a good feeling. "Would you like something to drink?"

"No! No, thank you." She glanced at the bar, looking horrified, as if he'd just thrust a glass of neat whiskey at her.

"I mean a cup of tea, or a coffee." He smiled. It would to be quite a challenge to put her at ease. "Some of our customers like to drink during the day because they're here for fun and relaxation. Those of us who work here are much more dull and predictable." He noticed with chagrin that his uncle Don was still standing behind him. "Oh, and this is my uncle, Don Fairweather."

She pushed her glasses up on her nose before shoving out her hand. "Pleased to meet you."

Don't be so sure, John wanted to tease. But this was a business meeting. "Let me take you up to the offices, Ms. Allen. Don, could you do me a favor and see if the ballroom is set up for the Shriners' conference tonight?"

His uncle glared at him, but moved off in the right direction. John heaved a sigh of relief. It wasn't always easy working with family, but in the end it was worth the hassle. "Let me take your briefcase. It looks heavy."

"Oh, no. I'm fine." She jerked away as he reached toward her. She was jumpy.

"Don't worry. We don't bite. Well, not much, anyway." Maybe he should flirt with her. She needed someone to loosen her straitjacket.

Now that he'd got a better look at her, he could see she wasn't quite as young as he'd first assumed. She was petite but had a determined expression that showed she took her job—and herself—very seriously. That gave him a perverse urge to ruffle her feathers.

He glanced at her as they headed for the elevators. "Is it okay if I call you Constance?"

She looked doubtful. "Okay."

"I do hope you'll enjoy your time at New Dawn, even though you're here to work. There's a live show in the Quinnikomuk room at seven and you're most welcome to come see it."

"I'm sure I won't have time." Mouth pursed, she stood and stared at the elevator doors as they waited.

"And your meals are on the house, of course. Our chef used to work at the Rainbow Room, so our food here is as good as any fancy restaurant in Manhattan." He loved being able to brag about that. "And you might want to reconsider about the show. Tonight's performer is Mariah Carey. Tickets have been sold out for months."

The elevator opened and she rushed in. "You're very kind, Mr. Fairweather—"

"Please call me John."

"But I'm here to do my job and it wouldn't be appropriate for me to enjoy…perks." She pushed her glasses up her nose again. The way she pursed her lips made him think how funny it would be to kiss them. They were nice lips. Plump and curvy.

"Perks? I'm not trying to bribe you, Constance. I'm just proud of what we've built here at New Dawn, and I like to share it with as many people as possible. Is that so wrong?"

"I really don't have an opinion."

When they arrived at the floor with the offices, Constance hurried out of the elevator. Something about John Fairweather made her feel *very* uncomfortable. He was a big man, broad shouldered and imposing, and even the large elevator felt oddly small when she was trapped in there with him.

She glanced around the hallway, not sure which way to go. Being late had her flustered. She'd planned to be here half an hour early but she'd taken the wrong exit ramp and gotten lost and—

"This way, Constance." He smiled and held out his hand but withdrew it after she ignored him. She wished he'd turn off the phony charm. His sculpted features and flashing dark eyes had no effect on her.

"How do you like our state so far?"

Again with the charm. He thought he was pretty hot stuff. "I really haven't seen anything but the highway medians, so I'm not too sure."

He laughed. "We'll have to fix that." He opened the door to a large open-plan office space. Four of the five cubicles she could see were empty, and doors stood open to the offices around the walls. "This is the nerve center of the operation."

"Where is everyone?"

"Down on the floor. We all spend time serving the customers. That's the heart of our business. Katy here answers the phones and does all the filing." He introduced her to a pretty brunette in a pink blouse. "You've met Don, who's in charge of promotion and publicity. Stew handles building operations, so he's probably out there fixing something. Rita is in charge of IT and she's in Boston looking at some new servers. I handle all the accounting myself." He smiled at her. "So I can show you the books."

Great. He shot her a warm glance that did something really irritating to her stomach. He was obviously used to having women eat out of his hand. Lucky thing she was immune to that kind of nonsense. "Why don't you hire someone to do the accounts? Aren't you busy being the CEO?"

"I'm CFO and CEO. I take pride in managing all the financial aspects of the business myself. Or maybe I just don't trust anyone else." He flashed even white teeth. "The buck stops here." He tapped the front of his smart suit with a broad finger.

Interesting. She felt as if he'd thrown down a gauntlet and challenged her to find something wrong with the books. She liked that he took personal responsibility.

"It's a family-run business. Many of the people in the office are tribal members. We also outsource to other local businesses—printing, web design, custodial services, that kind of thing. We like to support the whole community."

"Where is the community? I booked a room at the Cozy Suites, which seemed to be the nearest motel, but I didn't see it as I drove up here."

He smiled. "The nearest town is Barnley, but don't worry. We'll set you up in a comfortable room here. We're booked to capacity, but I'm sure the front desk can figure something out."

"I'd really rather stay elsewhere. As I said, it's important to be objective."

"I can't see how where you stay would affect your objectivity." Those dark eyes peered at her. "You don't seem like the type to be swayed by flattery and pampering. I'm sure you're far too principled for that."

"Yes, indeed," she said much too fast. "I'd never let anything affect my judgment."

"And one of the nice things about numbers is that they never lie." He held her gaze. She didn't look away, even though her heart was thudding and her breath getting shallow. Who did he think he was, to stare at her like that?

She finally looked away first, feeling as if she'd lost a skirmish. Never mind, she'd win the war. The numbers themselves might not lie, but the people reporting them certainly could. She'd seen some pretty tricky manipulations since she'd gone into forensic accounting. The BIA had hired her accounting firm, Creighton Waterman, to investigate the New Dawn's books. She was here to make sure the casino was reporting profits and income accurately and that no one had skimmed anything off the top.

She braced herself to meet his gaze again. "I specialize in looking beneath the shiny rows of numbers that companies put in their annual reports. You'd be surprised what turns up when you start digging."

Or would he? She was looking forward to getting her fingers on last year's cash-flow data and comparing it with the printed reports. She wouldn't have time to look at every single number, of course, but she'd soon get a sense of whether there was fudging going on.

"The Nissequot tribe welcomes your scrutiny." His grin did something annoying to her insides again. "I'm confident you'll be satisfied with the results."

He gestured for her to walk into one of the offices. She hurried ahead, half-afraid he was going to usher her in with one of his big hands. The office was large but utilitarian. A big leather chair sat behind the desk, and two more in front of it. A New Dawn wall calendar was the only decoration. Annual report brochures from the last three years sat on the big, polished wood desk, and filing cabinets lined one wall. A round table with four chairs sat in one corner. The realization crept over her that this was his personal office. He pulled open a drawer. "Daily cash register receipts, arranged by date. I add up all the figures myself first thing every morning."

He rested a hand on the most recent annual report, fingers pressing into the shiny cover. Such large hands weren't quite decent. He certainly didn't look like any CFO she'd encountered. All the more reason to be suspicious.

"Make yourself comfortable." He looked at the chair—his chair. She had to brush right past him to get to it, which made her skin hum and prickle with an unpleasant sensation. Worse yet, he pulled up another chair and sat down right next to her. He opened the most recent brochure, which had a picture of a spreading oak tree on the cover, and pointed at the profit data at the top of the first page. "You'll see we're not kidding around here at New Dawn."

Forty-one million in net profits was no joke, for sure. "I've seen the annual reports already. It's really the raw data I'm interested in."

He pulled out a laptop from the desk drawer and punched up a few pages. "The passwords change weekly, so I'll keep you posted, but this account information will get you right into our daily operation. You should be able to look up and analyze any data you need."

Her eyes widened as he clicked through a few screens and she saw he was letting her peek right at the daily intake and outflow.

Of course the numbers could be fudged. But she was impressed by how quickly he could click from screen to screen with those big fingers. They were large enough to hit two keys at once. Was he wearing cologne? Maybe it was just deodorant. His scent kept creeping into her nose. His dark gray suit did nothing to conceal the masculine bulk of his body, which was all the more evident now that he was sitting only inches from her.

"These documents here are monthly reports I do of all our activities. If anything unusual happened, I make a note of it."

"How do you mean, unusual?" It was a relief to distract herself from noticing the tiny dark hairs dusted across the back of his powerful hands.

"Someone winning a suspiciously large amount. Anyone who gets banned, complaints from the public or from staff. I believe in paying close attention to the small details so the big ones don't take you by surprise."

"That sounds sensible." She smiled. Why? She had no idea.

Just being professional. Or so she hoped. He'd smiled at her, flashing those dazzling white teeth, and her face had just mirrored his without her permission.

She stiffened. This man knew he was having an effect on her. "Why do you produce annual reports when you're not a public company?"

"I don't answer to investors like a public company, but I have a greater responsibility. I answer to the Nissequot people."

From what she'd read on the internet, the Nissequot tribe was mostly his immediate family, and the entire reservation was a creative interpretation of local history for the sole purpose of pursuing a very profitable business venture. "How many of you are there?"

"We've got two hundred people living here now. A few years ago, there were only four of us. In five years' time I'm hoping we'll number in the thousands." There was that smile again.

She jerked her eyes back to the screen. "It probably isn't too hard to persuade people to come when you're offering a cut of forty-one million dollars."

His silence made her look up. He was staring right at her with those penetrating eyes. "We don't give individuals any handouts. We encourage tribal members to come here to live and work. Any profits are held in trust for the entire tribe and fund community initiatives."

"I'm sorry if I offended you." She swallowed. "I didn't mean to." She felt flustered. The last thing she wanted to do was put him on the defensive.

"I'm not offended at all." He didn't smile, but looked at her pleasantly. "And maybe we could build the tribe faster if we just handed out checks, but I'd rather attract people more slowly and organically because they want to be here."

"Quite understandable." She tried to smile. She wasn't sure it was convincing. Something about John Fairweather rattled her. He was so…handsome. She wasn't used to being around men like him. The guys in her office were mostly introverted and out of shape from sitting hunched over their computers all day long. John Fairweather obviously spent a good amount of time at his desk, judging from all the material he'd showed her, but somehow—tan and sturdy as the oak tree on the cover of his annual report—he looked more like someone who spent all day outdoors.

"Are you okay?"

She jerked herself out of the train of irrelevant thoughts. "Maybe a cup of tea would be a good idea, after all."

Constance lay in her bed at the Cozy Suites Motel, staring at the outline of the still ceiling fan in the dark. Her brain wouldn't settle down enough for sleep but she knew she needed to rest so she could focus on all those numbers at the casino tomorrow. She wanted to impress her boss so she could ask for a raise and put a down payment on a house. It was time to move out from under her parents' wing.

It was one thing to move back home to save money after college. It was another entirely to still be there six years later, when she was earning a decent salary and could afford to go out on her own. Part of it was that she needed to meet a man. If she was in a normal relationship with a nice, sensible man, a practiced charmer like John Fairweather would have no effect on her, no matter how broad his shoulders were.

Her parents thought almost everyone on earth was a sinner who should be shunned. You'd think she'd told them she was planning to gamble all her savings away at the craps tables the way they'd reacted when she announced she was going to Massachusetts to look into the books of a casino. She'd tried to explain that it was a big honor to be chosen by her firm to undertake an important assignment from a government agency. They'd simply reiterated all their old cautions about consorting with evildoers and reminded her that she could have a perfectly good job at the family hardware store.

She didn't want to spend her life mixing paint. She tried to be a good daughter, but she was smart and wanted to make the most of what natural talents she had. If that meant traveling across state lines and consorting with a few sinners, then so be it.

Besides, she was here to root out wrongdoing at the casino. She was the good guy in this situation. She shifted onto her side, trying to block out the thin green light from the alarm clock on the bedside table. If only she could get her brain to switch off. Or at least quiet down.

A high-pitched alarm made her jump and sit up in bed. Something in the ceiling started to flash, almost blinding her. She groped for the switch on her bedside light but couldn't find it. The shrieking sound tore at her nerves.

What's going on? She managed to find her glasses, then climbed out of bed and groped her way to the wall light switch, only to discover that it didn't work. The digital display on the clock radio numbers had gone out.

A jet of water strafed her, making her gasp and splutter. The overhead sprinkler. A fire? She ran for the door, then she realized that she needed her briefcase with her laptop and wallet in it. She'd just managed to find it by the closet, feeling her way through the unfamiliar space illuminated only by the intermittent blasts of light from the alarm, when she smelled smoke.

Adrenaline snapping through her, Constance grabbed her briefcase and ran for the door. The chain was on and it took her a few agonizing seconds to get it free. Out on the second-floor walkway of the motel, she could see other guests emerging from their rooms into the night. Smoke billowed out of an open door two rooms away.

She'd forgotten to bring shoes. Or any clothes. She was more or less decent in her pajamas, but she could hardly go anywhere like this. Should she go back in and get some? Someone behind her coughed as the night breeze carried thick black smoke through the air. She could hear a child crying inside a room nearby.

On instinct she yelled, "Fire!" and—clutching her briefcase to her chest—ran along the corridor away from the fire, pounding on each door and telling the people to get out. Had someone called the fire department? More people were coming out of their rooms now. She helped a family with three small children get their toddlers down the stairs to the ground floor. Was everyone safe?

She heard someone calling 911. She rushed back up the stairs to help an elderly couple who were struggling to find their footing in the smoky darkness. Then she ran along the corridor and banged on any doors that were still closed. What if people were still in there? She hoped that the sirens and lights would have flushed everyone out by now, but…

A surge of relief swept over her as she saw fire engines pull into the parking lot. It wasn't long before the firemen had finished evacuating the building and moved everyone to the far end of the parking lot. They trained their hoses on the fire, but whenever the flames and smoke died down in one area, they sprang up in another.

"It's a tinderbox," muttered a man standing behind her. "All that carpet and curtains and bedspreads. Deadly toxic smoke, too."

Soon the entire motel complex—about twenty rooms—was ablaze and they had to move farther back to escape the heat and smoke. Constance and the other guests stood there in their pajamas, watching in stunned disbelief.

At some point she realized she'd put her briefcase down while helping people out, and she had no idea where it was. It had her almost-new laptop in it, her phone and all the notes she'd made in preparation for her assignment. Most of the information was backed up somewhere, but putting it all back together would be a nightmare. And her wallet with her driver's license and credit cards! She started to wander around in the darkness, scanning the wet ground for it.

"You can't go there, miss. Too dangerous."

"But my bag. It has all my important documents in it that I need for work." Her voice sounded whiny and pathetic as she scanned the tarmac of the parking lot. The fire glowed along almost the entire roof of the motel, and acrid smoke stung her nostrils. What if she didn't find her bag? Or if it got soaked through?

"Constance."

She jerked her gaze up and realized John Fairweather was standing in front of her. "What are you doing here?"

"I'm a volunteer firefighter. Are you cold? We have some blankets on the truck."

"I'm fine." She fought the urge to glance down at her pajamas. How embarrassing for him to see her in them, though it was pretty selfish and shallow of her to be thinking about how she looked at a time like this. "Is there anything I can do to help?"

"You could try to calm down the other guests. Tell them

we'll find room for everyone at the New Dawn hotel. My uncle Don's driving over here in a van to pick everyone up."

"Oh. That's great." She'd made quite a fuss about not staying there. Now apparently she would be anyway.

"Are you sure you're okay? You look kind of dazed. Maybe you should be treated for smoke inhalation." His concerned gaze raked over her face. "Come sit down over here."

"I'm fine! Really. I was one of the first ones out. I'll go talk to people." She realized she was flapping her hands around.

John hesitated for a moment, then nodded and hurried off to help someone unfurl a hose. She stood staring after him for a moment. His white T-shirt shone in the flashing lights from the fire trucks, accentuating his broad shoulders.

Constance Allen, there is something very, very wrong with you that you are noticing John Fairweather's physique at a moment like this. She picked her way barefoot over the wet and gritty tarmac to where the other guests stood in a confused straggle. One little girl was crying, and an older lady was shivering even under a blanket. She explained that a local hotel had offered them all rooms and that a bus would be coming to fetch anyone who couldn't drive there.

People realized they'd left their car keys locked in their rooms, and that started a rumbling about everything else they'd lost and only intensified Constance's own anxiety about her briefcase and all her clothes, including a nice new suit she'd just bought. She tried to soothe them with platitudes. At least no one was hurt. That was a big thing to be grateful for.

Still, she didn't have her car keys, either. If she'd flown

here and rented the car she could have just called the rental agency. But she'd decided to be adventurous and driven her own car all the way here, so now she couldn't even get into it. She was starting to feel teary and pathetic when she felt a hand on her arm.

"I found your bag. You left it at the bottom of the stairs." John Fairweather stood beside her, holding her briefcase, which dripped water onto the tarmac.

She gasped and took it from his hand, then noticed with joy that it was still sealed shut. "You shouldn't have gone back over there." The fire was now out, but the balcony and stairs were badly damaged and collapsing.

John's T-shirt was streaked with soot. "You shouldn't have brought it with you. We firefighters hate it when people retrieve stuff before escaping."

"My…my laptop." She clutched the handle tightly. Tears really threatened now that she had her bag back. "It has everything on it."

"Don't worry, I'm just teasing you. I'd have a hard time leaving my laptop behind even after all the training I've had." His warm smile soothed the panic and embarrassment that churned inside her. She felt his big hand on her back. "Let's get you back to the hotel."

Her skin heated under his unwelcome touch, but she didn't want to be ungracious after he'd found her bag and offered her a place to stay. The flashing lights from the fire trucks hurt her eyes. "My car keys are gone."

"We'll get you another set tomorrow. I'll drive you back in my car." His broad hand still on her back, he guided her through the crowd toward his vehicle. *Oh, dear.* Even amid all the chaos, her skin heated beneath his palm as if she was still too close to the flames.

And now she was going to be trapped in his glitzy hotel in nothing but her pajamas.

Two

"We were lucky the motel had a good fire alarm system." John steered his big black truck down a winding back road. "It went up fast. Everyone got out, though."

"That's a relief. I'm glad the firefighters got there quickly and had time to check all the rooms. How long have you been a volunteer?"

"Oh, I joined the first moment they let me." He turned and grinned. "More than fifteen years ago now. When I was a kid I wanted to be a firefighter."

He should have become one. Much better than a gambling impresario. On the other hand, her strict upbringing had formed her distaste for gambling, but now that she was here it didn't seem so different from any other business. She admired how John had pitched in and done anything and everything he could to help. He was thoughtful, too, talking to the other evacuees and reassuring them that the hotel staff would help them track down car keys, clothes and things like that in the morning. There was certainly no need for him to have offered everyone rooms at the hotel. He was being very generous. "What changed your mind?"

He shrugged. "I discovered I had a head for business. And at the time I was glad to leave this quiet backwater behind. I got seduced by the bright lights of the big city."

"New York?"

"Boston. I've never lived outside of the great state of Massachusetts. After a while, though, I started to miss the old homestead. And that's around the time I cooked up the whole casino idea. But when I came back I signed right on with the fire department again." His disarming grin cracked her defenses again. "They missed me. No one can unfurl or roll up a hose as fast as me."

"I'm sure they appreciate the help. But there don't seem to be too many people around here." They were driving through dark woods, not a house in sight. The area around the casino was very rural.

"Nope. That doesn't seem to stop fires breaking out, though. Last week an abandoned barn caught fire out in the middle of nowhere. We had to pump water from an old ice pond to put it out. Could have set the whole woods on fire, especially right now when everything's so dry."

It was early summer. Not that she really noticed the changing seasons much from the inside of her pale gray cubicle.

As they continued driving, she could see the pearl-white moon flashing through black tree branches. The woods were beautiful at night.

"I think it's nice that you find the time to volunteer when you're so busy with the casino." There. She'd said it. She'd been a little short with him this afternoon and now she felt bad about it.

"I enjoy it. I'd go crazy sitting behind a desk all the time. I like to have my hands on as many things as possible."

One of those hands was resting on the wheel. For one breath-quickening instant she imagined it resting on her thigh.

She crossed her legs and jerked her gaze back to the moon, only to find it had disappeared behind the trees altogether. What was wrong with her? His hand was filthy from fighting the fire, for one thing. And she would rather die than let a business client touch her.

Not that he'd want to anyway. She'd seen the gossip-column pictures of him with all those glamorous women. A different one every week, from the looks of it. He'd hardly be interested in a frumpy accountant from Cleveland.

She let out a sharp exhale, then realized it was audible.

"Fires are stressful, but don't worry too much. Everything you lost can be replaced. That's the thing to remember."

She turned to him, startled. She hadn't even given a thought to all her burned-up stuff. Clearly she was losing her mind. "You're so right. They were just things."

They drove in silence for a minute.

"It's a shame you missed Mariah Carey. She was awesome." He turned and smiled.

"I'm sure she was." She couldn't help smiling back. Which was getting really annoying.

"What kind of music do you like?"

"I don't really listen to music." She shifted in her seat. Why did they have to talk about her?

"None?" She felt his curious gaze on her. "There must be some kind of music you like."

She shrugged. "My dad didn't allow most music in the house."

"Now that's a crime. Not even gospel music?"

"No. He thought singing was a waste of time." She frowned. Gaining maturity had given her a perspective on her father's views that made living in the house difficult. What was wrong with a little music? He thought even classical music was an enticement to sin and debauchery. Sometimes her friend Lynn drove them both to lunch and they listened to the radio on the way. She was surprised by how some tunes made her want to tap her toes.

She noticed with relief that they were pulling into the casino parking lot.

"So what did your family do for fun?"

Fun? They didn't believe in fun. "We didn't have too much time on our hands. They run a hardware store, so there's always something to do."

"I guess organizing rivets made accounting seem like an exciting escape." He grinned at her.

She bristled with irritation, then realized he was right. "I suppose it did." He pulled into a parking space in front of New Dawn, then jumped out of the car and managed to open her door before she even got her seat belt undone. There was no way to avoid taking his offered hand without being rude, and she didn't want to be obnoxious since he was going out of his way to help her. But when she did, his palm pressed hotly against hers and made all kinds of weird sensations scatter through her body.

Get a grip on yourself! Mercifully he let go of her hand as they paused at a back door to the hotel block and he unlocked it with a key. She was grateful not to have to walk through the glittering lobby in her pj's.

Then he put his arm around her shoulders.

Her skin tingled and heated through the thin fabric of her pajama top. What was he thinking? He was talking and she really couldn't hear a word. He probably thought this was a warm and encouraging gesture for someone who'd been through a traumatic experience. He couldn't have any idea that she hadn't had a man's arm around her in years and that the feeling of it was doing something very unsettling to her emotions.

His arm was big and heavy. He was so much taller than she that he simply draped it casually across her shoulders as if he was resting it. Then he squeezed her shoulders gently.

"Right?"

"What?" She had no idea what he'd just asked.

"You still seem kind of dazed, Constance. Are you sure you didn't get concussed or something?" He paused and pulled his arm from around her shoulders so he could peer into her eyes. "You look all right, but these things can sneak up on you. Maybe we should call for the nurse. We have one on staff here, to look after any guests who need attention." They were standing next to an elevator and he pressed the button.

"I'm fine, really! Just tired." She spoke a bit too loudly, then peered imploringly up at the digital display, only to find that the elevator was three floors away.

"No problem." He pulled a phone from his pocket and made a call. "Hi, Ramon. Is six seventy-five ready yet?" He nodded, then winked at her. *Winked?* It was probably just some friendly indication that the room was indeed ready. Her social skills were rather limited, since she only interacted with accountants. Still, it made her heart start racing as if she'd run a marathon.

She didn't know why, either. Yes, he was handsome. Tall, dark, all the usual stuff. But right now she was tired and stressed out and if she was anywhere near as dirty as he was she must look very unattractive, so he certainly wasn't flirting with her.

The elevator doors opened and she darted in and pressed the button for six. He strolled in after her. She focused her gaze on the numbers over the door as the elevator rose. He didn't say a word, but his very presence seemed to hum. There was something…unnerving about him, something that made her hyperaware of his presence.

When the elevator doors opened, she leaped out and

glanced about, trying to figure out which way to go. She jumped slightly when she felt his fingers in the hollow of her back.

"This way." He guided her down the hallway. She walked as fast as she could and his fingers fell away, which made her sigh with relief. He didn't mean anything by it; he probably didn't even notice he was touching her. He was one of those overly friendly types who hugged everyone—she'd noticed that after the fire. All she had to do was get into her room, shower, get some sleep and she could deal with everything else in the morning.

He pulled a key card from his pocket and unlocked the door. The spacious hotel room beckoned her like an oasis—crisp white sheets, closed ivory curtains, soothing art with images of the countryside. "This looks amazing."

"I'll need to get your clothes from you so we can wash them."

She glanced down. Her pj's were smudged with soot. "I'm going to need some real clothes for tomorrow."

"What size are you? I'll have one of the girls find something for you."

She swallowed. Telling John Fairweather her dress size seemed dangerously intimate. "I think I'm a six." And what would he tell them to buy? "Something conservative, please. And I'll pay for it, of course."

He grinned. "Did you think I'd ask them to pick out something racy?"

"No, of course not." Her cheeks heated. "You don't know me well, that's all."

"I'm getting to know you. And I'm getting to like you, too. You stayed calm during the fire and were very helpful. You'd be surprised how many people lose their heads."

She fought a burst of pride. "I'm a calm person. Very dull, in fact."

His dark eyes peered into hers. "Don't sell yourself short. I'm sure you're not dull at all."

Her mouth formed a silent *oh*. Silence—and something bigger—lingered in the air. Panic flickered in her chest. "I'd better get some sleep. I have a headache." The lie would probably give her a forked tongue, but she was on edge and John Fairweather was not helping her sanity.

"Of course. You can leave your clothes outside the door. There's a laundry bag in the closet."

"Great." She managed a polite smile, or was it a grimace? Her body sagged with relief as his big, broad-shouldered presence disappeared through the door and it closed quietly behind him.

Constance showered and washed her hair with rose-scented shampoo. The luxurious marble bathroom was well stocked with everything she needed, including a comb and a blow-dryer. She dressed in the soft terry robe with *New Dawn* embroidered in turquoise on the pocket. She'd put her dirty pajamas in a laundry bag outside the door for the hotel staff to pick up. Her briefcase had mercifully kept her laptop and important papers dry, so she'd emptied it and put it on a luggage rack to dry out. There was nothing more she could do for now. Hopefully she could relax enough to get some sleep.

But as soon as she laid her head on the cool, soft pillow, she heard a knock on the door. She sat up. "Coming." It was very late for someone to knock. Maybe the hotel staff had a question about the bag she'd left outside the door. Or maybe they'd already found her something to wear tomorrow?

She took the latch off the door and opened it a crack… to reveal the large bulk of John Fairweather blocking the light from the hallway.

"I brought you some aspirin." He held up a glass, then opened his other palm to reveal a tiny sachet of some pain-killer that actually wasn't aspirin at all.

"Oh." She'd forgotten about her "headache." With considerable reluctance, she opened the door wider. "That's very kind of you." She took the pills from his hand, making sure not to touch him.

"And I brought you some clothes from the gift shop downstairs. It's lucky we're open twenty-four hours." She noticed a shiny bag under his arm.

"Thanks." She reached out for it, only to find that he'd already walked past her into the room. She shook her head and tried not to smile. He wasn't shy, that's for sure. Of course, it was his hotel.

"Did you find everything you need?" He put the bag down on the desk and turned to her with his hands on his hips. "It's not too late for room service. There's someone in the kitchen all night."

"Thanks, but I'm not hungry."

John had also showered and changed. He wore dark athletic pants and a clean white T-shirt that had creases as if it was right out of the package, except that the creases were now being stretched out by the thick muscles of his broad chest. His dark hair was wet and slicked back, emphasizing his bold features and those penetrating eyes.

She blinked and headed for the shopping bag. Before she got there, he picked up the bag and reached into it himself. He pulled out a blue wrap dress with long sleeves. It looked like something she'd wear to a cocktail party. "We don't really have office attire in the guest shop."

"It's lovely and very kind of you to bring it." *Now please leave*.

"And we found some sandals that almost match." He pulled out a pair of dark blue glittery sandals and looked at her with a wry grin. "Not exactly the right look for the office, but better than being barefoot, right?"

She had to laugh. "My boss would have a heart attack."

"We won't tell him."

"It's a her."

"We won't tell her, either." He looked at her for a moment, eyes twinkling, then frowned slightly. "You look totally different with your hair down."

Her hands flew to her hair. At least she'd blow-dried it. "I know. I don't ever wear it down."

"Why not? It's pretty. You're pretty."

She blinked. This was totally unprofessional. Of course, nothing about this situation was professional. She was standing here in her bathrobe—in his bathrobe—in his hotel that she'd explicitly said she wouldn't stay in. And now he was giving her gratuitous compliments? "Thanks."

She felt that stupid smile creeping over her mouth again. Why did this man have such an effect on her? *Think about computational volatility in Excel spreadsheets. Imagine him cheating on his taxes. Imagine him...*

Her imagination failed her as his mouth lowered hotly over hers.

Heat rushed through her, to her fingers, which were suddenly on the soft cotton of his T-shirt. She felt his hands on her back, his touch light and tender. His tongue met hers, sending a jolt of electricity to her toes. *Oh, goodness.* What was happening? Her brain wouldn't form thoughts at all, but her mouth had no trouble responding to his.

The stubble on his chin scratched her skin slightly as the kiss deepened. His arms wrapped around her, enveloping her in their embrace. As her chest bumped against his, her nipples were pressed into the rough texture of the bathrobe and sensation crashed through her. She dug her fingers into the roping muscle of his back, plucking at his T-shirt as their mouths moved together.

A humming sound startled them both and they broke the kiss. "My phone," he murmured, low. He didn't reach for it. Still frowning slightly, he raised a thumb and smoothed a strand of hair from Constance's cheek.

She blinked, wondering what had just happened. And why? "I really must…" She wasn't even sure what she really must do. Go to bed? Take a cold shower? Throw herself out the window? Heat darted through her body, and she didn't know how much longer her knees would hold her up without his strong arms around her.

"Take your aspirin. I'll see you in the morning." He hesitated, phone still vibrating in his pocket. An expression of confusion crossed his face and he shoved a hand through his wet hair. "I'll call a local dealership about replacing your car keys first thing."

"Thanks." The word was barely audible, but it was a miracle she managed to force it out at all. He walked backward a couple of steps, gaze still riveted on hers, before he nodded a goodbye and strode to the door.

As it slid quietly shut behind him, she stood there, mouth open, knees still trembling. Had he really just kissed her? It didn't seem possible. Maybe she'd imagined it. In fact, maybe she'd dreamed up this whole crazy scenario while sleeping fitfully in her lumpy bed at the Cozy Suites Motel. A fire and a kiss in one night? Impossible.

She pinched herself and it hurt. That wasn't good. Maybe she *should* throw herself out the window. A desire to gulp in cool night air made her hurry to it, but it was one of those big modern ones that didn't open.

Probably a good thing. She looked out and could see nothing but dark woods barely illuminated by a cloud-shrouded moon.

She'd grabbed him, fisting her hands into his T-shirt, and clawed at his back. Had she totally lost her mind? Her breath came in heaving gasps and blood pounded in her veins.

It had been a very long time since she'd kissed anybody. Since anyone had kissed her, or even shown the slightest interest in doing so. Her one and only boyfriend, Phil, had broken up with her right before they graduated from college. Four years together, sustained by promises of marriage and family and happily ever after, and he'd simply told her that he wasn't ready and he was moving to Seattle without her. Her parents would die—or they'd kill her, or both—if they knew she'd given Phil her virginity outside the sanctity of marriage. They'd blame her for throwing herself away and point out that of course he wouldn't want to marry a woman like that.

The pain and shame of it all was achingly fresh even after six years, so she tried not to think about it.

And now something like this? She could taste John's lips on hers, his tongue winding with hers, and the memory made her heart pulse harder. She couldn't even blame him. She couldn't swear that he'd even started the kiss. It had just happened. And it had happened all over her body, which now hummed and throbbed with all kinds of unfamiliar and disturbing sensations.

She'd lost her clothes, her car keys and now her mind. How would she ever get to sleep now?

Three

"Thanks for picking everyone up last night, Don." John leaned back in his chair in the hotel restaurant and brushed croissant crumbs from his fingers. "I know I interrupted your hot date."

"Anything for you, John. You know that." His uncle sipped his coffee. "Though why you feel the need to help a bunch of total strangers, I don't entirely know."

John shrugged. "Nowhere else for them to go. And Constance Allen was with them." His lips hummed slightly at the sense memory of their kiss. He hadn't planned it, and the chemistry between them had taken him by surprise.

Don put his cup down with a bang. "What? I didn't see her."

"I brought her in my car." He schooled his face into a neutral expression.

"So she's here, right now, in the hotel?" His uncle's eyes widened. "And you didn't even tell me?"

John sipped his coffee. "I'm telling you right now."

Don's long, narrow mouth hitched into a half smile. "Did you put a move on her?"

"Me?" He raised a brow noncommittally. He didn't want to give Don the satisfaction of knowing. And he hadn't kissed her to please anyone but himself.

Don laughed and slapped his hand on the table. "You

kill me. I bet she'll look like a startled rabbit today. Heck, she looked like one yesterday."

John frowned. "You need to stop making assumptions about people, Don. I'm sure she has a lot of dimensions you know nothing about. At the fire last night, for example, she kept her cool and was very helpful. Nothing like a startled rabbit."

Don cocked his head. "If I had half the charm you do I'd never be lonely again."

"You're not lonely all that much now, from what I can see."

"The money from this place doesn't hurt." His uncle laughed. "I was lonely a lot before. I didn't have the knack for making bank that you were born with."

"It's not a knack. It's called hard work." He kept checking the door, waiting for Constance to show up.

"All the hard work in the world doesn't help if you aren't lucky." Don took a bite of his eggs. "Luck is our bread and butter."

"You make your own luck." John scanned the dining room. Had he missed her coming down? He wanted to see her. "Statistics are our bread and butter. Anyone dumb enough to rely on luck will lose it all to the house sooner or later."

"Unless they know how to game the system."

"Impossible." John drained his coffee. "I personally make sure it's impossible. I'm going up to the office. Don't forget to send out the press release about the new lineup of shows. I want press coverage."

"I know, I know. Who booked them all?"

"You did. And Mariah Carey was amazing last night."

Don grinned. "I love my job."

"Me, too." John slapped Don on the back as he headed out of the dining room. His uncle could be a pain in the ass, but underneath all the bluster he had a good heart and put a lot into making the entertainment here as much of a draw as the gaming tables.

But where was Constance? She wasn't in his office. He'd tried calling her hotel room, but no one picked up. He didn't want to knock on her door again. That hadn't gone entirely as planned last time.

He strolled across the lobby.

"You seen Constance Allen?" The staff at the front desk shook their heads. He would have to go up to her room again. He took the elevator to the sixth floor, excitement rippling in his veins. Why had she let him kiss her? In retrospect, it surprised him. She'd seemed so uptight and buttoned-down, but she'd opened like a flower and kissed him back with passion.

He couldn't wait to see what would happen this morning. Of course he probably shouldn't be entertaining lustful thoughts about the accountant investigating their books for the BIA. On the other hand he knew she wouldn't find anything wrong, so what did it really matter? No one would ever know but the two of them.

He knocked on the door. "It's John."

He heard some rustling, and cracked his knuckles while waiting. The door opened a crack and a pair of bright hazel eyes peered out at him.

"Good morning." A smile spread across his mouth. Chemistry crackled in the air again. Which was odd, really, because by any objective standards he wouldn't have thought they'd be a match. Maybe it was that opposites-attract thing.

And she was pretty.

"Um, hello." The door didn't open any farther.

"Can I come in?"

"I don't think that's a good idea." He saw her purse her pretty pink lips.

"I promise I won't try anything," he whispered. "In fact I'm not sure what happened last night, and if an apology is in order then I offer one." Not that he was sorry.

The door still didn't budge. Now she was biting that sensual lower lip. Which had an unfortunate effect on his libido.

"I called the dealership about your car. They're going to program a new key and bring it over here before noon."

"That's great. Thanks."

"Don't you want to come up to the office and look through the books?"

She blinked rapidly. "Yes. Yes, I do."

"All right then. I won't come in. You come out instead."

The door closed for a moment and he heard some rattling, then she appeared again, carrying her bag. "I just had to get my laptop." She opened the door and stepped out into the hallway, looking self-conscious—and very lovely—in the blue dress he'd found for her. He wasn't sure whether to compliment her or not, and decided not to. He didn't want to make her feel any more uncomfortable.

Her hair was fastened back up into a tight bun that showed off her pretty neck. As usual she wore no makeup, and the freshness of her clear skin was heightened this morning by an endearing flush of pink on her cheeks.

"I hope you managed to get some sleep after all the excitement of last night."

Her pace quickened as she headed down the hall toward the elevator. He'd meant the fire, but he realized she'd thought he meant the kiss. The memory of it flashed through his brain, firing all kinds of inappropriate impulses.

"I slept fine, thank you." Her words were clipped and

terse. "I'd like to look at the receipts from your first two years of operation this morning."

"Of course." The temptation to touch her was overwhelming. Normally he'd probably have done it without even realizing, but everything about her energy warned him to back off. "Have you had breakfast?"

"Perhaps I could grab a roll or something from the dining room before I head up to your office."

"No need. I'll have some food brought up." He reached for his phone. "Tea or coffee?"

"Neither, thanks. A glass of water would be fine."

He sneaked a glance at her as she pressed the elevator button. Shoulders tense and bag clutched in her hand, she looked as if she might explode. She probably didn't want to risk ingesting stimulants. He could think of a few ways to help her relax, but none of them was appropriate in the circumstances.

Maybe later, though.

As they got on the elevator, he told one of the new kids who was interning for the summer to bring some eggs and toast and fruit up to the office. And a roll. And some juice and water. But even as he concentrated on ordering the food, he noticed how the enclosed space of the elevator felt strangely tight this morning, the atmosphere abuzz with…something.

He followed her off the elevator, admiring the way she carried herself as she walked across the floor to his office. Then she stopped and frowned slightly.

He gestured for her to open the door. "Head in and make yourself comfortable."

"Is there another office I can work in? I don't want to inconvenience you."

"The only way you could inconvenience me is by making me carry all the files out of my office and into another one." He shot her a glance. "So you'll do me a favor by working in here. I have things to do anyway, so I won't be around much." He hoped that would put her at ease.

She put her bag down on the round table in the corner. "When did you say my car keys would be ready?"

"Noon. And I'll drive you over there to retrieve it."

"Again, I don't want to put you to any inconvenience. Is there someone less…important who can drive me?" She was avoiding his glance as she moved toward his desk.

"We're all important here. It's how we run the place. Every Nissequot has a crucial role to play and would be missed as much if not more than me. The cashiers will be hustling today, as we're expecting twenty buses of retirees visiting from Cape Cod this morning."

"Oh." Her brow wrinkled slightly as she reached for the pile of folders she'd pulled the day before. She bumped her elbow on a jar of pens, accidentally scattering them across the desk. He grabbed one just before it flew over the edge.

Their fingertips brushed as he handed it back to her. Her hand flinched away as though she'd been stung. Somehow that only increased the tension snapping in the air.

He shouldn't have kissed her. She was here on business and was obviously very reserved and proper. She wasn't looking to get her hands on him.

Quite the opposite.

Was that why he'd been irresistibly drawn to her? Was it the challenge of the seemingly unobtainable? There was something more, though. An energy that drew him to her. Something deep and primal. And when she'd folded into his arms and melted into the kiss…

John turned his attention to the filing cabinet with the receipts she wanted. Something had happened between them and he didn't know why. Unplanned and inappropriate, it had stirred his blood and left him wanting more.

Just get rid of her as quickly as possible. His uncle's words simmered in his brain. Sensible advice, under the circumstances. The way her movements snapped with precision and anxiety right now—fingers tapping on her keyboard and eyes darting across the rows of numbers on the papers she'd pulled from the files—she was rushing to get out of here.

So it was all good, right?

John frowned. Was he really the player the Massachusetts press made him out to be? Maybe he was. "Let me know if there's anything I can do for you." The innuendo wasn't entirely intentional, but he enjoyed her hot-under-the-collar reaction. Shifting in her chair and fussing with her bag, she seemed tense enough to burst into flames.

He'd be happy to help put out the fire. "The food should be here any minute, but maybe I'd better get you some water right now."

"Just some peace and quiet will be fine, please," she muttered, without looking up. She pushed her glasses up on her nose with a fingertip. He noticed she wasn't wearing nail polish.

A smile sneaked across his mouth. He liked that she wasn't afraid to be rude. A lot of people were intimidated by him, especially now that the millions were rolling in. It was refreshing to find someone who treated him as though he was a regular guy. "I'll make myself scarce."

"Good." She still didn't look up.

He chuckled as he removed himself from his own office. He could still taste that kiss on his lips. Constance had a surprising well of passion beneath her prim exterior, and he looked forward to tapping it again—whether or not that was a good idea.

Constance couldn't wait to get her car back. Right now, sitting in the grand lobby of the hotel, she felt like a prisoner in John's luxurious den of vice. Dressed in a silky garment she'd never have chosen, surrounded by people laughing and talking too loud and drinking before it was even lunchtime, she felt totally out of her element.

Maybe her family was right and she should have tried to refuse this job. On the other hand, building a career depended on taking assignments that would enhance her profile in the company, and a contract from a big government agency was a feather in her cap. Luckily New Dawn's files were well organized and the information straightforward, so she'd probably get her work done and be out of here within a week.

She heard her phone chime and fished it out of her bag. The display revealed that it was Nicola Moore, her contact at the Bureau of Indian Affairs.

"Hello, Nicola. I'm sitting in the lobby of the casino right now." She glanced about, hoping the woman wouldn't ask a lot of probing questions that would be embarrassing to answer right here.

"Excellent. Are they allowing you access to the books?"

"Oh yes, Mr. Fairweather—" even saying his name made her blush "—has given me carte blanche to go through all the files in his office. He has the original cash register receipts for every day since the casino opened."

"Do they seem legitimate?"

"The receipts?" She glanced around, hoping no one could overhear their conversation. "They do. So far everything looks good."

There was a pause at the other end. "They think it's a routine audit, but the reason we sent you is that we have good reason to suspect fraud. They may be giving you falsified documents."

Constance bristled. "I have considerable experience in examining retail operations. I know the warning signs, and rest assured I will closely examine anything that looks at all suspicious."

"John Fairweather has a reputation for charming everyone. Don't be fooled by his suave manner—he's a very sharp and cunning businessman."

Constance fumbled and almost dropped her phone. Could Nicola Moore somehow know that John had…seduced her last night? Impossible, surely! "I'm aware of his reputation," she whispered. Where was he? She felt as if he was going to materialize beside her at any minute. "I am completely immune to charm and focused entirely on the numbers." At least she certainly planned to boost her immunity to his charms from now on. That kiss last night had caught her completely by surprise, when she was overwrought and exhausted and emotional from the evening's turmoil.

"Excellent. I look forward to hearing an interim report. The New Dawn has attracted a lot of negative attention since it opened. You may have read some of the commentary in the press. We've been hearing plenty of whispers about their operation. No one can figure out how they managed to open without taking on massive debt, or how they're operating with such impressive profits. It doesn't match the other models we've seen. Frankly, we're assuming that something untoward is going on. Those numbers just can't be real."

Constance frowned. She didn't like that Ms. Moore already assumed a crime was in progress. She'd been surprised by the negative slant of some newspaper articles she'd read about the Nissequot and the New Dawn, too. John and the tribe seemed to attract the kind of backbiting usually reserved for successful celebrities. So far she hadn't seen any evidence of wrongdoing at all. Of course it was only her second day, but still…. John seemed to be a concerned and thorough businessman and she was beginning to get annoyed by the relentless negativity about his success.

Not that she had any interest at all in defending him, of course. That would be highly unprofessional. She prided herself on complete objectivity. But maybe everyone should be a bit more open-minded about the New Dawn's management.

She tensed as she saw John striding across the lobby toward her. You'd think an expensive suit would conceal the raw masculinity of his body, but it didn't. Something about the way he moved made her pulse quicken and her brain start scrambling. Ridiculous! She was far above this kind of girlish reaction. She muttered quickly into the phone that she'd report back as soon as she found anything. Guilt made her fingers tremble as she ended the call.

She stood and clutched her bag to her chest. "Ready?" Her voice sounded a little too perky.

"Yup. A rep from the dealership has dropped off the new key, so you'll be a free woman again in no time."

She smiled and carefully took the key he dangled from his fingers, without letting her skin touch his. "Thank goodness."

"You're welcome to stay at the hotel, of course. There really isn't anywhere else that's convenient. The Holiday Inn is at least twenty minutes away, and that's with no traffic."

"That will be fine." Her words sounded clipped. Thank goodness there was another hotel! Staying here had proven to be an even worse idea than she'd suspected. Hopefully they could both forget completely about that insane lapse of judgment last night and get back to business.

His gaze hovered over her mouth for a moment, and her lips parted. She sucked in a hasty breath. "Let's go."

"Of course." He held out his arm.

She ignored it, gripping her bag tighter.

He pulled his arm back with a rueful glance. Was he really flirting with her? He must be doing it to toy with her. She wasn't stupid enough to think that a man like John Fairweather could actually be attracted to and interested in her. It must be a game for him, to see if he could get the prim little accountant all hot under the collar.

She'd rather die than let him know how well it was working.

In the front seat of his big sedan she pressed her knees together and forced herself to focus on the road ahead. Nothing good could come of watching his big hand on the manual gearshift, or noticing the subtle shift in his powerful thigh muscles as he pressed his foot on the pedals.

"What a beautiful day. I can't believe I lived in the city for so long and didn't even think about what I was missing." His low voice rumbled inside the car.

Constance tugged her gaze from the smooth surface of the blacktop and tried to appreciate nature. Trees crowded the road on both sides, filtering the sun. "How come it's all wooded? Why aren't there farms, or, well, anything?"

"Around the turn of the last century, this was all farmland, but it wasn't close enough to the cities or fertile enough to be profitable, so it was all abandoned. So far suburbia hasn't reached out here, either. If it wasn't for the new highway exit, we'd still be in the middle of nowhere."

"But you grew up here?"

"Yup." He smiled.

She squeezed her knees tighter together. It was just a smile, for crying out loud. No need to get all excited.

"I couldn't wait to get away. I thought this was the dullest place on earth. We had fifty dairy cows and I had to help milk them every morning and evening. Makes tabulating columns of figures look really interesting, let me tell you."

"You've got to be kidding." She couldn't imagine him milking a cow. "I thought that was all done by machines these days."

"It is. But someone has to hook them up to the machines."

"Do they mind? The cows, I mean."

"On the whole they're pretty enthusiastic about it. I guess it feels good to lighten the load."

"And now you milk people foolish enough to gamble their hard-earned money." She looked straight ahead. "You help lighten their heavy wallets."

He turned and looked at her. "You think what we do is wrong, don't you?"

"I'm hardly unusual in that."

"It's entertainment. People have free will. They can come and gamble or they can go do something else."

His calm response only prodded her to goad him more. "Do you gamble?"

He didn't say anything. Silence hummed in the air until she got curious enough to turn and look at him. "No. I don't."

"See?"

"See what?"

"You're smart enough to know it's a bad idea."

"I'm smart enough to know it's not for me. Believe me, it's already a gamble opening a big casino and hotel in the backwoods of Massachusetts when it seems like the whole world wants you to fail."

"I notice that you get a lot of negative press. But I don't suppose it hurts that much, considering the money you're making."

"You're right about that." He shot her another warm

smile that made her toes tingle. She cursed them. "So far we've proved everyone wrong and I intend to make sure it stays that way."

"Why does the BIA want to investigate your accounts?" Was she allowed to ask that? She wanted to hear what he thought.

He shrugged. "Same thing, I think. If we were deeply in debt to a bank in Dubai or the mob, or asking for a government bailout, no one would be surprised. They can't accept that fact that we're successful and prospering all by ourselves. It makes people suspicious."

"Why didn't you need to borrow money?" There probably would have been no shortage of offers. Everyone wanted a piece of this juicy new pie.

"I prefer to be in charge of my own destiny. I sold my software company for eighty million dollars. I'm sure you read about that."

"Yes, but why would you risk your personal fortune?"

"It's an investment, and so far it's worked out fine." She managed not to turn and look at him, but she could see his satisfied smile in her mind. It was really annoying how likable he was. And he didn't gamble? She was having a hard time finding reasons to hate him. And if he wasn't cheating, it made her job harder, because it sounded as if her contact at the BIA wouldn't be happy until Constance found something.

She'd expected them to return to the burned-out motel, but instead he pulled into a restaurant parking lot. Her white Toyota Camry sat off to one side, sparkling clean.

"I had them wash it and bring it here. I didn't think you'd want to see the wreck of the motel. It's a mess over there."

"That was thoughtful." She sneaked a glance at him but

he was getting out of the car, not paying attention to her. "But why did they bring it here instead of the New Dawn?"

Unused to the sandals, Constance stepped out onto what felt like shaky ground. At least now that she had her car back, she could go buy some more sensible clothes and book a room somewhere else. This time she might ask some pointed questions about fire safety. She didn't know what would have happened if the motel hadn't been equipped with alarms.

"I made us a reservation for lunch here."

"What?" She glanced at the restaurant, which—with hanging baskets of lush flowers and elegant striped awnings—looked upscale and expensive. "No! I couldn't possibly. I need to go buy some…toiletries, and clothes. And I want to get more work done back at the office today."

The last thing she needed was to sit opposite John Fairweather over a delicious meal. She'd surely lose the last shreds of her sanity. And really, he had quite a nerve even suggesting it. She should report his behavior to her BIA contact.

Except maybe she'd leave out the part about the kiss.

She climbed into her car and put her bag on the seat next to her. The new key started the engine perfectly, and the brakes screeched slightly as she reversed out of her space too fast. She turned and headed for the exit. It wasn't until she saw John—in the rearview mirror—staring after her that she realized how rude she'd just been.

He was smiling slightly, as if he found the situation funny.

Which made her speed away even faster.

Safely ensconced at the desk in her new room at the Holiday Inn, Constance called her boss's office to let her know why she'd had to move, and ended up speaking to her friend Lynn, the office receptionist.

"It's a bummer that you live with your parents. I wonder if you can claim the loss on their homeowner's insurance."

"I doubt they have any. Their insurance is faith in God. Even if they did, filing a claim would raise the premium."

"If the motel doesn't offer compensation you could sue."

"I'd never do that."

"You're too much like your parents. Living in the wrong century."

"I happen to like this century."

Lynn laughed. "Okay, okay. So how is it going with John Fairweather? Is he as gorgeous as he looks on the internet?"

Constance shifted in her chair. "I don't know what you're talking about."

"I know you like to pretend you're a nun, but I'm sure you can tell whether a man is good-looking or not."

"He's okay looking, I guess." That stupid smile inched across her lips again. Thank goodness no one was here to see it.

"So, how old is he?"

"Early thirties, maybe?"

"That's not too old for you."

"Lynn! What on earth would make you think he and I have anything in common?" They didn't. Nothing. She'd thought about it on the drive over here.

"You're both human. Both single. And you're very pretty, Constance, though you do your best to hide it."

"Would you stop?" She pushed her glasses up her nose. Was she really pretty enough to attract the interest of John Fairweather? It didn't seem possible.

"I'm just excited that you're away from your parents'

overly watchful and critical gaze. You need to make the most of it."

"I've been quite busy getting burned out of my motel room and trying to go through the New Dawn's paperwork."

"All work and no play makes—"

"I'm already dull, and quite happy that way." At least she had been until last night. Suddenly her mind kept churning with odd ideas. That kiss had started something. She kept thinking about it. Feeling his lips on hers. Feeling his arms around her.

Obviously she had to make sure that didn't happen again, but she could kiss someone else, couldn't she? "Maybe I should join one of those dating services when I get back."

"What!" Lynn's stunned response showed that she'd revealed way too much. Now she couldn't even remember how she'd led up to that. "You're finally coming to your senses? It's him, isn't it? Those smoldering dark eyes. Those powerful broad shoulders. I know you're far too principled to be attracted to his money, so it must be his looks."

"Nonsense. He's very intelligent. Nice, too." She froze, realizing that she'd just proved that she liked him.

Silence greeted her on the other end. "Really?" said Lynn slowly.

"Well, I don't know. I only met him yesterday. He's probably just being polite so I won't delve too far into his books."

"I wouldn't blame him. I shouldn't be kidding around like this, though. He does have a reputation as a lothario. I want you to spread your wings, but don't fly right into a fox's den."

"One minute you're encouraging me and the next you're

telling me to back off. It's lucky I have no interest in anything except the books here."

"I can't believe I suddenly feel like I have to warn you off having an affair with John Fairweather."

"I can't believe it, either." *And I also can't believe how much I need warning off!* "Obviously you've forgotten that I'm the same Constance Allen who's only ever dated one man."

"Well, as soon as you get home I'm going to make sure you start dating someone new. When do you get back here, anyway?"

"It'll probably take a week or so. The BIA said I can request more time if I need it. It all depends on what I find."

"I hope you find something. That's always good for business."

"You're actually hoping that a crime is in progress?" Constance's gut clenched at the possibility. "I'm hoping that everything checks out fine. Then I can get out of here as soon as possible." And preserve what was left of her dignity.

Four

She picked up a couple of suits and blouses and a pair of shoes at a local Macy's. It was nearly four by the time she made it back to New Dawn to go over the books. Her eyes darted about, on high alert for any signs of John Fairweather. But she didn't see his imposing form anywhere. He wasn't in the lobby or the elevator. Or leaning over someone's cubicle on the office floor.

He also wasn't in his office, where she sat at the round table, which was inconveniently at coffee table height, and resumed her journey through the files. Where was he? He might be angry that she'd blown him off at lunch. Still, he needed to realize that she was here to do a job, and they'd already spent way too much time together. It would probably be more appropriate to the situation if they weren't interacting at all. On the other hand, her BIA contact had said that often the best information came during an inadvertent slip in casual conversation, so she should spend as much time as possible with the tribal members.

She shook her head. This whole situation was far too confusing for her. Just the fact that Lynn could encourage her one minute and warn her off the next proved that nothing about it made sense. She'd rather be surrounded by quiet and predictable columns of figures.

Which, supposedly, she was right now. Unfortunately

the atmosphere vibrated with the absence of John Fairweather.

Constance stayed until seven-thirty and pored over the files he'd shown her and plenty he hadn't. Nothing aroused her suspicion. If anything, John's accounting methods were somewhat redundant and labor-intensive, and could benefit from some streamlining and a software upgrade.

Relief mingled with disappointment as she descended to the lobby without encountering him. Apparently he'd already forgotten about her and moved on to new pastures. He was probably out on the town right now with some willowy model.

She strode through the lobby, challenging herself not to look around for him. Why did she want to see him? All he did was get her flustered. As Lynn had pointed out, he was a notorious playboy and Constance was peering behind the curtains of his successful operation.

Still, it had been nice of him to personally bring her to the hotel last night, and to pick up her car this morning. On the other hand, if he had her car moved, why hadn't they brought it right to the hotel instead of to some expensive restaurant, where he had apparently intended to continue his inappropriate seduction?

She made her way through the parking lot to her car, brain spinning. Was she upset that he wasn't here to flirt with her and harass her? She should be appalled and disgusted—and suspicious—of his attempts to seduce her. Red flags stuck out of this mess in every direction. Her career at Creighton Waterman would be ruined, and she could lose her accounting credentials, if anyone learned about that kiss. Yet she'd as much as told Lynn that she was attracted to John.

Now she was thinking about him as John?

What was happening to her?

* * *

The next morning she arrived early enough to be the first person in the offices. She'd just settled into browsing through some figures, when John's deep, melodious "Good morning" made her jump. Which was ridiculous since she sat in his office.

"Hello, Mr. Fairweather." She said it as primly as possible. She didn't want him to have any idea of what he'd been doing to her in her dreams last night.

"Mr. Fairweather? Don't you think we're a little beyond that? In fact, I was thinking I should call you Connie."

She blinked rapidly. "No one calls me Connie."

"All the more reason." He sat down on the opposite side of the round table. "What's your nickname?"

"I don't have one."

"I don't believe you." He leaned back. "What do your folks call you?"

"Constance. It's what they named me, so I guess they like it. What do yours call you?"

"John." His eyes twinkled. "So you do have a point. You look great this morning. Did you finally get some sleep?"

Constance felt heat rising to her cheeks. "I did, thank you. The Holiday Inn is very nice."

"I'm sure it is." He cocked his head. "Shame about the twenty-minute drive."

"I don't mind." Why was she getting flustered?

"I'll try not to take it personally."

Of course she was getting flustered. He was staring right at her and flirting.

She watched as he rose from the chair, bowed slightly and left the room. She stared after him, through the open door. Part of her wanted to slam the door and sag against it; another much less reliable part of her wanted to run after him and call, "But wait!"

She closed the door quietly, but resisted turning the lock. As soon as she sat down again, her phone rang and she jumped as if she'd been stung. It was Nicola Moore from the BIA, according to the display. She answered it with as much professional dignity as she could manage.

"Hello, Constance. How are things?"

"Fine. Everything's fine."

"I heard about the fire. I hope that hasn't shaken you up too much."

"It was a shock, but luckily there was no loss of life." She kept quiet about John's role in helping at the fire. There was no need for Nicola to know how much time they'd spent together.

"Have you had a chance to get to know some of the key players yet?"

She hesitated. She wanted to say, *I'm an accountant. I'm better with numbers than people,* but she knew that would be unprofessional. "Sure, I've spoken with several."

"Don't be afraid to get a feel for their personal business. That can often be the most revealing information."

"Uh, sure." Her response wasn't too professional. Still, the request seemed odd. Maybe she just wasn't familiar enough with this kind of work. She knew the BIA regularly conducted audits of various Indian ventures, so they must know what they were doing. "I'll do my best."

She frowned as she hung up. John had done a pretty good job keeping her safely sequestered in his office and away from people. Maybe it was a good idea to move around and take a look at the numbers from the casino floor. There was no reason she couldn't observe the tellers in action, taking people's hard-earned money. It might help stir up her righteous indignation, which seemed to have cooled a bit. She needed to remind herself what this whole enterprise was all about. From an early age, she'd been taught that gambling was wrong, and she still didn't like it much.

She shoved the cap on her pen and put away the latest files she'd looked at. All predictably clean and tidy and all columns adding up to the right amounts. Maybe she was taking John's operation too much at face value. Time to get out there and look under the hood. Feeling like an intrepid reporter, she lifted her bag and headed for the door. She scanned the floor quickly to make sure John wasn't around. Nope. Just two employees sitting quietly at their computers, so she headed downstairs.

She approached the area where the cashiers sat with some trepidation. They were behind a barrier, like at a train station, but it was decorated to look more like an elegant bar than a check-cashing joint. To gain entrance she'd have to go in through the back, and she wasn't sure if they'd let her.

She opened a door marked "staff only," rather surprised that it wasn't locked.

"Can I help you?" A pretty girl with long, curly black hair stood in the hallway behind the door.

"My name's Constance Allen, I'm—"

The girl thrust her hand out. "I know exactly who you are. John told us you might want to see back here. I'm Cecily Dawson. Come in." She smiled, though Constance saw a hint of suspicion in her eyes. Hardly surprising under the circumstances.

"Is it okay if I watch the cashiers for a while?"

"Sure, follow me." She led Constance into the large room, where all the cashiers sat along one wall facing out. Cecily beckoned to a dark-skinned man standing behind the row of cashiers, tapping something into his phone. "Darius, this is Constance Allen."

He pocketed his phone and walked toward her. "A plea-

sure to meet you, Constance. John told us all about you."
His handshake was firm and authoritative. He held her
gaze, and her hand, with confidence. He was almost as
dangerously handsome as John.

"Is there somewhere I can sit down, out of the way?"

"No need to be out of the way." He touched her arm,
and she stifled the urge to flinch. "Come stand with me
and watch the whole operation."

"Darius manages the cashiers. He's always on the look-
out for trouble."

"In whatever form it may arrive." He shot her a dark
gaze filled with mischief.

Constance blinked. "I don't want to get in your way."

"If you're in my way, I'll move." His half smile contained a hint of suggestion. He was flirting with her, too?
Maybe this was part of their shtick at the casino. Constance
was beginning to regret coming down here. "Each cash
register records a sale in our central system and all the
records are checked four times a day against the takings.
I watch the customers to see if anyone's acting suspicious.
It's my job to look for cracks in the system, too, so let me
know if you think we could improve upon anything."

"Do you get a lot of suspicious activity?"

"Not so far. We have a lot of controls in place to prevent employees from getting tempted to put their hand in
the till. That's more of a problem than the customers at
some casinos."

"Are you all members of the Nissequot tribe?"

"Cecily and I are, and Brianna at the end." He pointed
to a blonde girl counting out cash at high speed. "Frank,
Tessa and Marie are just hoping to marry into the tribe one
day." He grinned when Marie, a middle-aged woman in a
conservative suit, turned to blow him a kiss. "But we're
one big happy family."

His phone beeped and he checked the screen. "Our fear-less leader is heading this way," he said to the cashiers. "Look like you're working." He winked at her.

Constance pretended she hadn't seen it. And now John was coming? She braced herself. The cashiers dispensed money with warm customer service and brisk efficiency. They joked and seemed to be enjoying themselves. It wasn't like this at Creighton Waterman. Joviality was frowned upon. In fact, one junior accountant, Daniel Bono, had recently been let go for smiling too much in meetings, or at least that was the rumor.

Customers were streaming into the casino, which struck Constance as a little odd since it was a Wednesday morning. "Why are so many people here at this time of day?"

"We have tour buses pick them up in Boston, Worcester, Springfield. We're adding more routes all the time. A lot of our customers are retirees. We run a brisk trade at the nursing homes."

"Should the elderly be gambling with their life savings?" She felt her brow rise.

Darius's wicked smile reappeared. "Maybe their heirs don't think so, but it's their money, right?"

She shook her head. "I don't get why people want to do this."

"It's fun. Like buying a lottery ticket."

"Do you gamble?"

He shook his head. "John discourages us from gambling. He thinks it's better to put your money in the bank. As far as I know, Don Fairweather is the only gambler in the family. Have you met him?"

"I have. He seems like quite a character."

"I heartily agree."

John burst into the room at that moment. His piercing gaze zeroed in on her. "I was looking for you."

"Now you've found me." She tilted her chin up, proud that she managed to sound so calm. "I was just observing how the cashiers work."

"I see you've met my cousin Darius. He only graduated from college two years ago and he's turning into my right-hand man."

Darius smiled. "I've learned everything from the best."

John put his arm around Darius. "He moved here all the way from L.A. to join the tribe. We're working on the rest of his branch of the family."

"They're not quite ready to move into the backwoods." Darius shrugged. "But the way things are going, this won't be the backwoods for long."

John looked at Constance for a moment. "I'd like to show you around some more."

"I think I've seen everything there is to see. I came through the gaming rooms and passed the slot machines on my way over here."

"Not just the casino and hotel. The whole reservation."

She felt herself frown. Was he trying to shunt her away from here for some reason? She'd barely had time to observe anything. Suspicion crept over her.

On the other hand, she had a feeling Nicola Moore would want her to see as much of the place as possible. "Okay."

"Excellent. We'll start with the museum. Darius can tell you what a passion of mine that has become."

Darius nodded. "It's a labor of love, all right. And thousands of hours of expert research."

"It's not easy to uncover history that's been deliberately buried. Let's go." John gestured toward the door, and she went ahead of him, nodding and smiling to the other employees, and grateful that John hadn't tried to take her hand or put his arm around her.

They walked back through the gaming rooms to the lobby. Retirees were busy wasting their savings in the slot machines, and a surprisingly large number of other people were hunched over the tables as well.

"I didn't know you had a museum."

"There's a lot you don't know." He smiled mysteriously. "All of it good, of course."

"If you're covering up a fraud, you're doing it very well."

"I take pride in everything I do." He lifted a brow slightly, taunting her.

"Are you trying to make me suspicious?" She was conscious of matching his stride as they strolled out of the gaming room and across the lobby.

"Nothing could be further from my mind." Then he touched her. Her stomach drew in and her pulse quickened as he rested his hand at the base of her spine and ushered her though a doorway she'd never noticed before, marked "Hall of Heritage."

It led into a large, gallery-like room with polished wood floors and high walls. Glass cases held artifacts and sleek, printed text and pictures decorated the walls. "It looks like a real museum." She walked ahead of him, curious. One of the first exhibits was a glass case containing a sheaf of age-tinted pages and a quill pen. There was a blown-up photograph of the front page on the wall next to it.

"That's the original treaty between the Nissequot and the governor of Massachusetts in 1648. Two thousand acres of land was given to us then."

"Two thousand? I thought the reservation was less than two hundred."

"They chipped away at it bit by bit over the years."

"The state?"

He shook his head. "Mostly private individuals, farmers, businessmen, greedy people."

"Your ancestors must have sold it to them."

"I could say that greedy people come in all creeds and colors, but research has taught me to give my ancestors the benefit of the doubt and respect that they were just trying to survive."

"You can't really fault them for that. Apparently they managed." She smiled at him. The museum didn't have that many items, but they were carefully arranged and displayed with a good deal of written information accompanying them. A long green cloak in one case caught her eye. It didn't have feathers or beading, but an embroidered trim in black brocade.

"Not what you'd expect, is it?" He looked at her curiously.

"I don't know what I'd expect."

"People seem to want baskets and moccasins and old pots. Precontact stuff. They forget that the history of the Nissequot continues after the settlers arrived. That cloak was worn by Sachem John Fairweather, the man I was named after, when he opened the doors to the first free school in this part of Massachusetts. It remained open until 1933, when the last pupil dropped out to look for work during the Depression."

"Is the building still there?" She could see a grainy photograph of six people in Victorian-era clothing standing outside a neat white building.

"It is indeed. I'm restoring it along with my grandparents' old farmhouse."

"That's very cool. I have no idea of my own family's history before my grandparents' generation."

"Why not?"

She shrugged. "I don't suppose any of us thought it was that interesting."

"Where is your family from, originally?"

"I don't know. All over, I suppose. Maybe that's the problem. It's easy to get excited about ancestry when it's all from one place with a distinct culture. If one person's from Poland and another from Scotland and another from Italy or Norway, no one really cares."

"Well, the truth is that the Nissequot are from all over the place, at this point. I don't even know who my own father was. The Fairweathers are my mother's family. Sometimes you just have to pick a common thread and go with it, and that's what we're doing here. We did find an eighteenth-century Bible with the New Testament written out phonetically in the Nissequot language, though. That's our biggest coup so far. A scholar at Harvard is putting together a Nissequot dictionary by comparing it with a contemporary English version."

She looked up at an enlarged line drawing of a man and woman in more traditional-looking dress. "Is that how you imagine your ancestors looked?"

"Nope. That's a real drawing done by the daughter of one of the first governors of Massachusetts in her personal journal. It was found by relentless digging through old records and hoping for the best. It's time-consuming and way outside my realm of expertise, but it's all coming together piece by piece."

"Impressive."

He led her through the gallery, then disarmed the emergency exit with a key code and pushed through an exterior door out into the bright sunlight. A large black truck was parked right behind the building. "My unofficial vehicle. Get in."

"Where are we going?"

"To meet my grandparents." Curious, she climbed in. His truck wasn't quite as pristine as his sedan. He lifted a pile of papers off the passenger seat so she could sit down. There was an unopened can of soda in the cup holder, and music—the Doors—started as soon as he turned on the engine. There was also a Native American–looking thing with feathers on it hanging from the rearview mirror. "They're going to like you. I can tell."

"Why?" They were hardly likely to appreciate someone who was there for the express purpose of digging up dirt on their reservation.

"You're nice."

"Nice? I'm not nice at all."

His loud laugh echoed through the cab. "True, it was cold of you to blow me off at lunch yesterday. But they'll think you're nice."

She glanced at her reflection in the wing mirror nearest to her. She wasn't sure anyone had accused her of being nice before. Organized, efficient, polite, helpful, exacting, prim, persnickety…a range of flattering and not so flattering words sprang to mind, but nice was not among them. "I'm not sure that nice is good in my line of work."

"Maybe you're in the wrong line of work?" He shot her a challenging glance.

"Look who's talking."

"I'm nice." He glanced in the rearview mirror, then over at her. She jerked her eyes from his gaze and stared out the window, taking in how they were traveling along another featureless wooded road to nowhere. "Ask anyone."

"I'm not sure that's the first word that would spring to mind if I asked someone to describe you. I'd think *bullheaded, relentless* and *determined* would be right up there. And that's just going from the newspaper articles I read about you."

"Don't believe everything you read in the papers."

"I don't, but where there's smoke, there's usually fire." That was one of the first tenets of forensic accounting. The tricky part was finding a live ember after someone had carefully tried to put the fire out.

"They do say I'm an arrogant SOB. I'm guessing you'd agree with that." She saw the corner of his mouth lift in a smile.

"For sure." She felt her own treacherous mouth smile along. "And they say you cooked up the entire Nissequot tribe just so you could open a casino and rake in billions."

"That's pretty much true." He turned and stared right at her. "At least that's how it started, but it's snowballed into a lot more than that."

"Don't you think it's wrong to exploit your heritage for profit?"

"Nope." He looked straight ahead as they turned off one winding road onto another. "My ancestors survived war, smallpox, racism and more than four hundred years of being treated like second-class citizens. Hell, they weren't even American citizens until 1924. The powers that be did everything they could to grind us out of existence and they very nearly succeeded. I don't feel at all bad about taking advantage of the system that tried to destroy us." His voice was cool as usual, but she could hear the passion beneath his calm demeanor. "If I can do something to lift up the people who've survived, then I feel pretty damn good about it."

Constance had no idea what to say as they pulled up in front of a neat yellow neocolonial house with a front porch and a three-car garage.

John had jumped out of the car and opened her door before she managed to gather her thoughts. "What're you waiting for?"

"Uh, I don't know." She'd never felt more lost for words around anyone. "Is this the original farmhouse?" she asked, taking advantage of his offered hand as she climbed down from the cab.

"Oh, no. We just built this three years ago. The old place was kind of a wreck. No insulation, no real heat and A/C. My grandparents were ready to move into someplace shiny and new."

The front door opened and a white-haired man appeared on the front porch. "Hey, Big John."

"His name is John as well?"

"Yes." They walked up the slate front path.

"Does that make you Little John?"

He smiled. "I suppose it does. But if you call me that I won't be responsible for my actions."

She wanted to laugh. As they climbed the steps she could see that the younger John towered over his grandfather by at least eight inches and was fifty-plus pounds heavier, all of it solid muscle.

"This is Constance. She's come here all the way from Ohio to be a thorn in my side."

Big John stuck out a gnarled hand. "Pleased to meet you, Constance." He shook her hand with warmth, using both hands to embrace it. "It's not easy to be a thorn in this man's side. His hide is too tough. Come in."

She followed him into a sunlit foyer, where they were greeted by a tall, rather beautiful woman of about seventy. "This is my mom, Phyllis. She's actually my grandmother, but she raised me so I've always called her Mom."

"Hello, Constance." She also had a firm handshake. Constance could see where John got his inquisitive gaze. She thought it was cute that he called her Mom. "It's not often that John brings a young lady to visit us." Her bright eyes scanned Constance from head to toe.

"Oh, I'm actually not…" Not what? A young lady? She glanced nervously at John.

"Not what?" he said unhelpfully.

"I'm here on business." She glanced from his grandmother to his grandfather. "For the Bureau of Indian Affairs."

"Is that so," said Big John. His expression hardened. She was beginning to get the impression that the BIA was not a much-loved organization.

"I was just showing her our museum. Since she's interested in Indian affairs and all." Constance saw a smile tugging at the corner of John's mouth. "Then I thought she should meet the real reasons we're all here. My mother died when I was young," he told her, "and my grandparents brought me up to be aware of our Nissequot roots. I have to admit that when my friends played cowboys and Indians I wanted to be a cowboy so I could have the gun." He smiled mischievously. "And I wasn't all that interested in hearing stories about how the world was created on the back of a turtle."

His grandfather laughed. "He just wanted to know if the Nissequot liked to fight."

"But they stubbornly persisted in teaching me everything they knew, and it must have taken root somewhere under my thick hide, because I remembered it all."

"How did you know the legends yourselves? Are they all written down somewhere?" Constance couldn't help her curiosity.

"Some stories are. Others are recited or sung," replied Phyllis. "As long as there's one person in each generation left to pass the stories along, they don't die out. Even the family members who've come back to us from places like Chicago and L.A. knew something about their heritage—a song their grandmother used to sing, or just that they were from the Nissequot tribe, even though no one else had ever heard of it. We're so blessed to have John. He's the kind of leader needed to bring the tribe back from near extinction and make it flourish again."

"And there I thought I was just trying to make a buck." He winked at Constance.

"The spirit moves in mysterious ways," said his grandfather. "Sometimes none of us are sure what we're doing until we can look back later. We thought we were trying to run a dairy operation, but we were really keeping our claim on the land going until John was ready to take over."

"John bought us eight cows last Christmas as a present." Phyllis smiled at him.

"Beef cattle," John cut in. "Aberdeen Angus. No more milking." He shrugged. "The place didn't feel right with no cattle on it."

"He missed the sound they make."

"They're an investment. Good breeding stock."

Phyllis smiled at Constance. "He's a lot more sentimental than he'd have you believe."

John huffed. "Nonsense. We'd better get going. I wanted Constance to see that we're not just numbers on a balance sheet or names on a census."

"It was nice to meet you." Constance smiled and waved goodbye, then followed John, who was already halfway out the door. His grandparents stood looking after them, amusement glowing on their faces. He bounded down the front steps and jumped back into the car. The engine was already running by the time she maneuvered herself into her seat.

"They seem very nice."

"Like me." He winked.

"I have to admit that you do seem nicer than all the media stories make you out to be."

"I told you not to believe everything you read. Don't start thinking I'm a pushover, though. I'm as ruthless as I need to be." He tilted his stony jaw as if to prove it.

"Ruthless, huh?"

He focused his dark eyes on her as they paused at the end of the driveway. A shiver of arousal jolted her and she remembered the alarming power he had over her. "Merciless."

John Fairweather knew exactly what he was doing at every moment. Including when he'd kissed her. And she'd better not forget that.

Five

That afternoon, back in John's office, Constance focused on expenses and other outgoings. Expenses were large, as would be expected, and there were definitely some extravagances, but nothing she hadn't seen at other booming corporations.

Around six o'clock she emerged from John's office, ready to head for her hotel. She was relieved that she could be done here in a day or two. Everything was checking out and she and John would no doubt both be relieved to see the back of each other.

Speaking of John's back, there it was, barring the hallway to the elevators. Her heart rate rose just at the sight of him, which was ridiculous. He stood in conversation with a young payroll employee named Tricia.

"Good night," she muttered as she skirted carefully around them.

"Constance!" His voice boomed through her consciousness. "Come down and watch the action on the floor with me. It really picks up in the evenings. You should see the place when it's busy."

"No, thanks. I need to get back to the hotel." She kept her eyes focused on the far end of the hallway. But he moved past her and pressed the button for the elevator before she reached it.

"You're knocking off work to relax when you should be examining the details of our operations? I'm shocked, Constance."

Her gaze darted to him as an urge to defend herself rushed over her. "It's really just the paperwork that interests me."

He lifted a dark brow. "I think you're being remiss in your duties. I'd think the BIA would want to know all the gory details of how we operate. I wouldn't be surprised if they wanted a full report on everyone who works here."

"They'll need to hire a private investigator for that. I'm an accountant." The elevator opened and she dived in. Of course he came right after her.

His proximity did something really annoying to her body temperature. Suddenly she was sweating inside her conservative suit. Maybe her new blouse had too much synthetic fabric in it. She felt a frown form on her brow and attempted to smooth it away. She didn't want him to know that his presence rattled her so much.

"You've only observed the casino during the day so far. We're virtually empty then. You should really take a look at the place during the evenings, when most of our customers are here. It's the best way to see how we do business."

He did have a point. If she were her boss, she'd tell her to stay. Should she really let her inappropriate attraction to John Fairweather prevent her from doing her job properly? "I suppose you're right. There's no need for you to accompany me, though. I don't want to bother you."

Constance saw that familiar sparkle of mischief in his dark eyes. "On the contrary. It would be my pleasure."

When the elevator doors opened, she prepared for him to try to slide his arm through hers, or take her hand, but he simply gestured for her to go first. She walked ahead of him toward the game rooms. Was he looking at her behind? She felt her hips swing a little more than usual, and immediately tried to prevent it. She was probably letting her imagination run away with her, which she confirmed when she turned to find him texting on his phone.

He's not attracted to you, Constance. Why would he be? He just kissed you because he could. He's that kind of man.

"Let's get you a drink."

"No!" The protest flew from her mouth so loudly it made her glance around.

He smiled. "We have fresh-squeezed fruit juice at the bars. Leon does an amazing concoction of fresh pineapple juice with fresh coconut milk and a dash of his secret spices. Totally nonalcoholic."

"That does sound good." Coconut milk was supposed to be healthy and she'd never tried it.

He ordered two of the drinks, which arrived in large glass goblets with the casino's sunrise logo on them. He lifted his glass. "Here's to you discovering everything there is to know about us, and liking what you see."

She merely nodded. She wasn't supposed to hope that she'd like everything she saw. That would discourage her from looking for problems. She sipped her drink, though, and found it creamy and delicious. "I admit this is really good. I usually just drink soda when I'm out. I guess I'll have to branch out."

"I'm always asking them to invent new beverages. There's no reason why us nondrinkers should be left out in the cold."

"You don't drink alcohol?"

"Nope. I steer well clear of it. It killed my mom."

"What? I thought she was really young when she died."

"She was twenty. She died in a car wreck. Drove off an overpass. It would never have happened if she'd been sober."

"I'm so sorry."

"Me, too. I don't remember her at all. I was only six months old when she died. Luckily for me, she'd left me with a friend for the night. My grandparents made me swear never to touch the stuff and I've never seen a reason to defy them."

"Very sensible." Her prim reply embarrassed her. John had endured a devastating loss. It must be so odd to grow up not knowing the woman who gave birth to you. "Do you get mad at her for not being there for you?"

He paused, and looked right at her with a curious expression in his eyes. "Yes. When I was younger I was angry with her for not being more careful. Seems crazy, really. It does make me keep a close eye on the younger kids here, though. Especially the ones who've moved away from family to join us. I'm a big fan of stern lectures."

She smiled. "You sound like my parents. I grew up on a steady diet of stern lectures."

"And look how well you turned out."

"Some would say I'm far too conservative for my own good."

"And I'd be one of them." He winked. "Still, that's better than some of the alternatives. Let's go watch the roulette tables."

"You're not going to make me play, are you?"

He laughed. "I'm not going to make you do anything you don't want to."

What was it about Constance that got under his skin? John stood next to her as the wheel spun and the ball danced between black and red. She was so unlike the usual stream of glamorous women who hung around him, sniffing the scent of money or promising a steamy affair.

Constance stood with her arms crossed over her prim

suit, eyes fixed firmly on the table and not a hint of flirtation in her gestures.

But he knew she was as attracted to him as he was to her. The shine in her eyes when she looked at him, the glow in her cheeks, the way she angled her body toward him unconsciously—it all spoke of the desire that crackled between them so forcefully you could almost hear it snap in the air.

She didn't want to like him. Or to want him. But somehow that only heightened the tension building as they stood next to each other, pretending to focus on the white ball.

It dropped into a slot and the wheel slowed to a halt. One woman squealed with delight and smiled as the croupier slid a pile of chips toward her. John glanced at Constance and saw the tiny hint of a smile that hovered about her pretty mouth. "That's why they keep coming back," he said softly.

"I can see how it would be fun." She leaned into him so he could hear her but no one else could. Her scent tugged at his sense. "But I'd still rather make money the old-fashioned way."

"Me, too. I'll take hard work over chance any day of the week." He leaned still closer until he could almost feel the heat of her skin. "But everyone's different."

Did he like her because she was different? It didn't really make sense. There was no good reason to flirt with and tempt this woman. She was here on professional business and it was inappropriate for him to even have sensual thoughts about her.

Yet he couldn't seem to stop.

As he'd promised, he had no intention of making her do anything she didn't want to. But making her want to? That was a whole different story.

* * *

One time at a college mixer someone had given Constance a glass of orange juice mixed with vodka—without mentioning the vodka. She still remembered the way the world around her had grown blurry, and she'd found herself laughing at things that weren't even funny. She felt like that right now, though she was sure she'd had nothing but fruit juice all evening.

"...and then after we won every game that season, they wouldn't let me go." John leaned into her again, brushing her arm with his. Her skin sizzled inside her suit. "It was a pain in the ass. All I wanted to do was study statistics, and I had to get all this tiresome fresh air and sunshine."

She laughed. He'd been telling her about how he'd joined the college football team entirely for the scholarship money and then accidentally became their star player. Of course he had. He was one of those people who effortlessly succeeded at everything they tried. Or maybe not effortlessly. He just made it look that way.

"It must get annoying being so good at everything."

"You think I'm bragging?"

"I'm pretty sure of it." She narrowed her eyes, trying to hide her smile. He hadn't really volunteered any information she hadn't asked for. She wanted to know more about him. At first she told herself she was doing "research." Now she was too darn curious to stop. "What did your team members think of you?"

"Oh, at first they made fun of me. Teased me for being from the backwoods of Massachusetts. They stopped laughing when they saw how fast I could run, though."

"Can you still run fast?" Her hand accidentally brushed his as she raised her drink to her lips. They'd moved to a sofa near the blackjack tables, where they had a good view of the whole room. Her thigh jostled against his, too. The sofa was soft and they kept sinking into it. The crowds milled about the gaming tables, ignoring them completely.

"I don't know. I haven't tried lately. I'm still pretty quick on the squash court, though. Do you play any sports?"

"No." Maybe she should start. All this energy building up inside her needed some place to go. Right now she felt like jumping up and running around the room. "My parents thought sports were a waste of time."

"And you never did anything they didn't want you to?"

"Nothing major. I read some books they didn't approve of, and they never knew I had a boyfriend."

"You kept your lover a secret from them?" He bumped against her, teasing.

"It wasn't like that."

"No? It certainly sounds like it."

"He was at college with me in a different town, so they never met him."

"And you didn't mention him. Was he someone they wouldn't have approved of?" He raised a brow.

She chuckled. "No. That's the funny part. He was so dull they'd probably have liked him." Was she really talking about Phil? She'd tried to shove him out of her mind. Which was hard, because six years later he was still the only boyfriend she'd ever had.

At least now she could admit he wasn't exactly the man of her dreams.

"Why were you dating him if he was dull?"

"I like dull."

John peered into her eyes. The effect of his dark gaze was anything but dull. Sensations she'd never felt before trickled through every part of her. "Why?"

"Predictable. Reassuring. I don't enjoy surprises."

"Or at least you think you don't." One brow lifted slightly. "Come with me."

He took her hand gently and helped her up from the squishy sofa. "Where are we going?"

"It's a surprise."

"I already told you I don't like them." Anticipation rippled in her tummy.

"I don't believe you." He led her across the busy game room to the bank of shiny elevators. Her hand pulsed inside his. They were walking along like a couple, and while it horrified her, the realization gave her a strange thrill. She should pull her hand from his, but she didn't.

He pressed the button for the highest floor and shot her a mysterious look.

"I'm not even going to ask," she murmured, trying to keep her eyes on the door. Even while she knew he was flirting with her and leading her on, she trusted John not to pull any fast moves. They'd been talking for a while and he was clearly a man who took the concept of personal honor seriously. He saw himself as a role model for the younger members of the tribe and he'd said more than once that he never did anything he wouldn't want them to know about.

Of course, maybe he was just trying to undermine her defenses by appearing principled and thoughtful.

What a shame it was working.

The elevator opened at the top floor and she was surprised when the doors parted to reveal the night sky. "Wow, a roof terrace." A broad expanse of marble, ringed with potted plants, glowed under the stars. "How come there's no one up here?"

"It's not open to the public unless it's booked for an event and, as you can see, there's nothing happening here tonight except us."

Us. What did he mean by that? Nothing, probably. "That's a lot of stars." She felt as though she could see forever, bright galaxies twinkling all the way to infinity.

"It's nice being up here above all the lights. You can see clearly. I come up here when I need to get perspective."

"Feeling like a tiny speck in the vast universe certainly puts everything in perspective."

"Doesn't it, though? All the worries that keep us little humans awake at night are nothing in the grand scheme of things."

He still held her hand, which had grown quite hot. They walked across the terrace to a seating area and he guided her onto a large sofa and sat down next to her.

What am I doing? Up here there was no pretense that they were still working. Or that she was researching anything. She was simply sitting with John, her right thigh fully pressed against his left one as they both sank into the soft cushions. The cool night air emphasized the warmth of his body.

"What do you worry about, Constance?" His hand squeezed hers very gently.

"Sometimes I worry that I'll never move out of my parents' house." She laughed, trying to lighten the moment.

"Why haven't you? You must earn enough to rent your own place."

"I don't know, really. I keep thinking that I will, then another month or year passes and I'm still there."

"Maybe you've been waiting to meet the right man."

"Probably." The confession surprised her. "After all, I've always been told a nice girl is supposed to live at home until she gets married." She shrugged.

"Why haven't you met the right person yet?"

"I work at an accounting firm. It's not exactly a hotbed of romance." She smiled.

"Don't accountants need love, too?"

"Apparently so." Was he trying to suggest that she go back and date one of her coworkers? That would be a strange suggestion from a man still holding her hand in his. "Why haven't *you* married?" Curiosity pricked at her, even though she was pretty sure she knew the answer. Why would a man in John's position want to settle down with one woman when he could have a different one every week if he wanted?

"I have been."

His answer shocked her so much she tried to pull her hand from his. "You're divorced?" Her hand flew free, and the chill night air assaulted her hot palm.

He nodded. "A long time ago. You're shocked."

"I didn't read that when I was researching you."

"It's not common knowledge. I was married in high school, right before I went away to college. I thought it would help keep us together despite the physical distance."

"Which was only a hundred miles or so."

"Less than fifty, actually." He grinned. "Young and stupid."

"Why did you split up?"

"I was so busy with school that I didn't make enough time for her and she met someone else. It proved to me that a marriage isn't something that just happens. It takes a lot of work to keep it alive."

"And that scared you off trying it again?" She attempted to pull her thigh away from his but once again the sofa was too deep and she kept falling against him.

"Pretty much." His eyes twinkled in the darkness. "I know I've got my hands full with my business, and now with running the tribe, so I don't want to disappoint someone else."

"Oh." She felt a surprising sting of disappointment, which annoyed her. Had she really imagined somewhere in the darkest recesses of her mind that John might have real feelings for her? She was getting carried away! "So you probably won't get married again."

"I damn sure will." His conviction startled her. "Don't count me out yet."

"I can see you feel strongly about it." Her smile matched his. How did he keep doing that to her? Any sensible woman would leap to her feet and go admire the view on the far side of the patio, away from this man who freely admitted he didn't have time for a relationship.

"Oh, I do feel strongly about it. In addition to any personal considerations, I have a responsibility to the Nissequot tribe to help produce the next generation." He winked.

She couldn't help laughing. "That's a weighty responsibility. Does it mean you have to marry another Nissequot?"

"Nope." His gaze grew more serious. "We made sure there were no requirements for any particular amount of Indian blood in tribal members. I hate the idea that people have to choose who they marry carefully or abandon their heritage."

"I'd imagine those kinds of rules are in place to keep the benefits—government funds, casino profits and that kind of thing—to a limited number of people."

"And what good does that do anyone? Except the people trying to keep us small in the hope that we'll fade away eventually. I'd prefer to expand to include everyone. Growth and change are the core facts of life. If you try to keep something static, it will just die. I'm here to make sure the opposite happens." He took her hand again, and she didn't pull it back. He lifted it to his lips and kissed her palm, which sizzled with awareness under his lips.

Why did she let him do that? He wasn't serious about her. He was playing with her.

Or was he?

His dark eyes had narrowed and fixed on hers with an

expression so intense that she couldn't breathe. Heat radiated through her and her body inched closer to his without any effort on her part. She should be trying to back away, or standing up and walking back to the elevator. But her entire body seemed to be in thrall to his.

His lips touched hers very softly, just brushing them. It wasn't even a kiss. She closed her eyes as she drank in the subtle male scent of him. Her tongue itched to meet his, which it did as their mouths opened slightly and welcomed each other into a real kiss.

Her fingers crept under the jacket of his suit and into the folds of his shirt. His large hands settled one on either side of her waist, gathering her to him. She was aware of the roughness of his chin as he shifted and deepened the kiss. She leaned into him, pulling at his shirt until her fingers slid underneath it and she touched the warm skin of his back.

Heat unfurled in her core, spreading through her like smoke. John lifted her onto his lap, still kissing her, and she welcomed the closeness. Her nipples were so sensitive she could feel the fabric of his lapels even through her blouse and bra, and she pressed herself against him, unable to resist the pull of sensation.

She had no idea how long they kissed. All she knew was that she didn't want to stop. The pleasure of holding him, of touching him and kissing him, was so intense she couldn't remember anything like it. When their lips finally separated slightly, she could barely pull herself together enough to open her eyes.

"There's something very powerful between us," John murmured, his voice a rumble in her consciousness.

"Yes," she whispered. Words seemed too literal in the heady sensual atmosphere of the dark night. It was easier to say what she wanted with her body, with her mouth. She licked his lips gently, savoring the taste of him. When his hand moved higher, she guided it over her breast, enjoying the weight of his palm on her desire-thickened nipple.

When he pulled back she uttered a groan of protest. She didn't want him to stop.

"Come with me." He lifted her carefully to her feet, supporting her with his arm. She was so intoxicated with arousal that she could barely walk.

"Where are we going?" It was hard forming words.

"Somewhere more private."

"This is private." No one was watching them. Only the twinkling gaze of a hundred million stars. She didn't want to leave. She didn't want anything to break the spell binding them together.

"More comfortable, too." He squeezed her. "Don't worry. It's close." They walked slowly back to the elevator, with his arm around her waist. The effort of putting one foot in front of the other tugged her out of the sensual haze she'd slipped into. What was she doing? She'd kissed John again. Kissing him one time could be seen as an accident. Kissing him twice? That was deliberate.

She wanted to kiss him again, too. What had come over her? She must be in the grip of some kind of madness. Still, she wasn't going to pull away from the warm embrace of his arm. Instead she rested her hand on his, enjoying the closeness.

At the elevator he pressed the button. "Are we going down to the lobby?"

He looked rather disheveled from her running her hands all over him. She probably did, too. "No need to. The elevator also leads directly into my suite."

"Oh, good." Her own words made her blink. She was glad about him taking her to his private apartment?

Yes. She was. Which didn't make any sense at all. She

should insist on going straight to her car and back to her hotel for a cold shower.

They stepped into the unpleasantly bright space of the elevator and she shielded her eyes from the shining mirrors by leaning against his chest as he pressed the button. His suite was on the highest floor, right beneath the roof terrace, so in a few seconds the doors opened and they stepped out, right into his suite.

"Do strangers from the hotel ever press the wrong button and end up in your room?"

He smiled and shook his head. "You have to enter a code to go to this floor or the terrace. Don't worry. No one will disturb us."

They stepped out into his suite. A wide foyer led into a spacious living room with a wall of windows. Comfortable sofas faced what must have been an impressive view in daylight. Shelves held a collection of photographs and objects. She was curious about the things he had gathered in his home, but he led her past them and through another door into his bedroom. Decorated in a simple, masculine style, the room held nothing but a low platform bed and a dresser. Three wooden masks hung on the wall opposite. She stared at them for a moment. "Don't you feel weird with these faces watching you?"

He laughed. "They're hundreds of years old. I'm sure they've seen it all before."

No doubt they'd seen a lot right here in John's bedroom. She glanced warily at the bed. How many women had writhed in his arms there? Was she really going to be the next in a long procession of girls who succumbed to his seemingly irresistible charms? What was she doing? She knew she shouldn't be here, but she didn't want to be anywhere else.

John turned to her, slid his arms around her waist and

held her close. He was several inches taller, so he had to incline his head to kiss her. Her mouth rose effortlessly to meet his and the kiss drew her back into that private realm where nothing else really mattered.

Six

John sensed her doubts even as he kissed her. Constance could hardly believe she was here in his bedroom. He could hardly believe it either. Still, his disbelief mingled with a sense of wonder as he held her close and kissed her with feeling.

She didn't have much experience. He could tell that by her sense of surprise and her awkward reaction to his simple advances. Somehow that only stoked his passion. This beautiful woman had been quietly living her life, free from desire and its complications, peering into corporate records and keeping her heart safe.

Constance was like a safe with a long and complicated combination, and his fingers itched to turn the dial until she clicked open for him. The image appealed to him. He wanted to unlock the door to her heart and let himself in.

He helped her carefully out of her suit jacket and laid it on the chair. Her blouse had a silky texture and he could feel the warmth of her body through it, so he let himself enjoy the sensation of her skin through the fabric while he kissed her.

Then he started to unbutton it. First just one button. Then another kiss. Then the second button. More kissing. Her eyes opened slightly as he went for the third button, and the sparkle of excitement in them fired his arousal.

Her hands roamed under his shirt, feeling the muscle along his back. When they dipped into the waistband of his pants, the sudden rush of sensation made him gasp. He was so hard it was difficult to be patient and careful with her, but that was the only way to unlock her closely guarded safe and enjoy the intimacy he craved. He knew he'd blow everything if he tried to rush. He wanted this to be as enjoyable for her as he knew it would be for him.

He guided her to the edge of the bed and sat her gently down, then knelt in front of her and pulled her shirt back to reveal her bra. She watched him curiously, eyes shining, as he lowered his mouth over her breast and dampened the fabric of her bra with his tongue. Already firm, her nipple thickened under his caress, and she let out a small murmur of pleasure.

She ran her fingers through his hair, encouraging him as he licked and sucked first one breast and then the other. Then he lowered his head to trace a line down toward her belly button. She inhaled sharply as he reached the waistband of her skirt.

"Lie back," he murmured, stroking her cheek with his thumb.

She blinked, not questioning anything, then eased herself down onto the soft bedcover. Her thighs clenched together as he unbuttoned the top of her skirt—which opened at the side—and started to slide it down her shapely legs.

He wanted to tell her to relax, but had a feeling that words might have the opposite effect. Sometimes it was better to touch than talk.

The removal of her skirt revealed pretty lace-trimmed panties that rather surprised him. He'd expected utilitarian cotton. And she must have bought them since the fire. Had she known he'd see and enjoy them? Had she bought them for him? It was hard to imagine, but the thought made him smile.

He didn't part her legs, which she still pressed together tightly, although he longed to taste her through the lacy fabric. Instead he kissed her thighs, her knees and her legs right down to her toes. She softened and relaxed as he traveled along her smooth skin.

He ventured tentatively toward her female center, wanting to explore every delicious inch of her. The soft silk of her panties didn't conceal the heat radiating from her core. She flinched slightly as he flicked his tongue over her, then whimpered softly as he sucked her through the delicate fabric.

Once she was thoroughly relaxed and pulsing with heat and pleasure, all resistance kneaded away, he slid off her shirt. She eagerly reached for his shirt buttons, tugging at them, as a smile spread across her face. Her hungry energy surprised him. She wanted to see him naked almost as much as he wanted to be naked with her. Together they undid his belt and shed his pants, and pulled off his shirt. Then she hesitated, frowning slightly, staring at his briefs.

He was aroused almost to the point of madness, and it showed. He wondered for a second if she'd freeze up and try to backtrack—something that just might kill him at this moment. Instead he almost died anyway when she slid her fingers inside the waistband of his underwear and took hold of him.

Constance couldn't remember being this aroused *ever*. Part of her couldn't believe she had her fingers wrapped gently but firmly around John's impressive erection. The rest of her really wanted to feel him inside her right now.

She heard his sharp intake of breath as she stroked him. It gave her a thrill that he was so excited, too.

"Hold on," he rasped. "Before we get carried away and forget."

He reached into a nearby dresser and brought out a condom packet. She hadn't even thought about contraception. She wasn't on the pill, either. Why would she be? Obviously common sense had deserted her.

Sheathed, he came close and she wrapped her hand around him again. Her body was almost trembling with anticipation as she guided him into her, not that he needed any help, and he lowered his chest over hers. He kissed her very softly right as he entered her—so slow and careful—and she felt her hips lift to greet his.

The powerful sensation of him inside her quickened her breath. She could feel her fingers clawing at his back, traveling into his hair, but she didn't seem to have any control over them. Luckily that didn't matter because he took control, moving with gentle intensity, driving her further and further into an intense world of pleasure and passion.

"I'm crazy about you," he whispered in her ear, as her breath quickened to the point of gasping. The sensation of his hot breath on her ear only heightened her pleasure.

"Me, too." Did that even make any sense? Nothing made sense, except kissing him more and reveling in the sensation of him deep inside her. His big body moved over hers with ease, shifting position to send her closer yet to the brink of…something.

Sensation was building inside her and she became more aware of it as John sucked her earlobe gently while filling her over and over again. Something was creeping through her, a wave of pleasure, or a whole tide of it, starting in the clenched tips of her toes and rising up her legs and sweeping over her belly until she felt as though she was drowning in it. Distant moaning and shrieking sounds might have come from her mouth, but she couldn't be sure. John uttered a low groan and gathered her so tightly in his arms she thought she might disappear into him completely. She wanted to say something but she couldn't make a sound, just little gasps that burst from her lips onto the hot skin of his shoulder as he clung to her.

"Am I crushing you?" John eased himself off her slightly by propping himself on his elbows.

"No." His powerful physique felt no heavier than a down comforter, enveloping her in its warmth. "You feel fantastic."

"You, too." He kissed her so softly she almost wanted to cry.

Cry? Strange emotions suddenly welled up inside her. She didn't even really know what had happened. Was that an orgasm? She'd read about them but had never come close to experiencing one before. Her body still pulsed and tingled with the aftereffects. Her heart squeezed and she held John close. She felt incredibly intimate with him right now. Which wasn't surprising, considering that they were both naked in his bed.

On his bed. With the lights on.

Her eyes cracked open as she managed to regain some grip on her consciousness. They hadn't even taken the time to climb under the covers. In fact, they weren't even at the right end of the bed.

She swallowed, trying to make sense of what had just happened. John stroked a tendril of damp hair from her forehead. "You're very passionate, Constance."

Coming from his mouth, her dull and prim name seemed sensual and evocative. "So are you, John." His name was even duller than hers, and he was the most exciting and intriguing man she'd ever met. Apparently names didn't have too much to do with anything.

"Let's get under the covers." A smile shone in his eyes.

"Okay." She let him lift her, her body feeling almost weightless in his strong embrace, and slide her under the soft white covers. Then he settled next to her and wrapped his arms around her. A soft kiss on her cheek felt so romantic she thought for a second that she must be dreaming.

She wasn't, though. There was no way she could conjure the intoxicating scent of his skin in a dream. Or the slightly rough feel of his cheek against hers, or the sparkle of amusement—and passion—in his eyes. This was real, and it was happening to her, Constance Allen, right here, right now.

"I really don't know how I ended up here." She felt like being honest.

"It's the most natural thing in the world. Two people being attracted to each other and wanting to be together."

"I don't get why you're attracted to me, though." No doubt any dating manual would issue stern warnings against such a blatant display of insecurity. But she couldn't help wondering what John Fairweather saw in her.

He wanted her, there was no doubt about that. She could feel it in the way he looked at her, in the way he made love to her, in the way he held her close, his breath on her cheek.

"I don't know where you've gotten the idea that you're not desirable. You're a beautiful woman." He stroked her cheek with his thumb.

"I am not! I'm quite ordinary looking."

"Who told you that? You have the prettiest hazel eyes I've ever seen. So curious and a little wary. When you look at me I get a jolt of something I can't explain."

Her eyes? "But I wear glasses. Where are they, anyway?"

"On the chest over there. I made sure to put them somewhere safe."

"I don't even remember taking them off." She reached

automatically for her nose, where she usually pushed them up.

"You didn't. I did." His smile made her smile—as usual. "Apparently you can see pretty well without them."

"I just need them for reading. They're a mild prescription." She could see John clearly enough right now, his dark eyes peering into hers.

"So how come you wear them all the time?"

She shrugged, or attempted to, in his arms. "I feel more comfortable with them on. Then I don't have to worry about taking them on and off to read. I do spend a lot of time reading, even if it's mostly numbers."

"Something to hide behind. I don't think you're comfortable with your own beauty."

She laughed. "I don't think I'm comfortable with much of anything, except doing my job to the best of my ability. And right now I'm not doing so well with that, either."

"Because you're sleeping with the subject of your investigation?"

"Who's sleeping?"

He chuckled. "Do you feel guilty?"

"Of course. Don't you?"

"For seducing you? No, I don't feel at all guilty. Like I said, it's the most natural thing in the world for two people who are drawn to each other to enjoy each other's company."

Of course it was, to him. That's why he had so many girlfriends. He probably never said no when he saw something, or someone, he wanted. "My boss would kill me if she knew I was in bed with you right now."

"She won't find out." He lowered his lips to hers in a soft kiss.

No. She wouldn't. This little…affair—because there

was no better word for it—had to be kept under wraps. Which meant it was wrong.

If Constance had any sense she'd push John off her right now and run screaming back to her hotel.

But she didn't want to. She wanted to lie here in his arms, to feel his rough cheek against hers. To enjoy the warm, protective embrace of his strong arms and his satisfied sigh in her ear. In fact she couldn't remember the last time she felt so completely relaxed and content.

She'd spent too many lonely nights in her bedroom. Too many solitary hours dreaming of moments like this. Everyone, including her own parents, thought she had no feelings at all. That she lived to work. That her brain was filled with numbers and spreadsheets and she spent all her spare time doing elaborate computations. But she was just like everyone else, though she hid it well. She craved companionship, romance, love.

Love? Well, she wasn't going to find that with John Fairweather. A tiny stab of regret poked at her heart. She could probably fall in love with him quite easily on the briefest acquaintance. Despite his reputation as a callous, money-orientated playboy, she'd learned he was a man of principle who put those principles into practice every day. The media was so wrong about him. Or maybe they were jealous. She could now grow quite angry thinking about the callous things she'd read about him and the tribe.

"Your heart's beating faster." His gruff voice tickled something deep inside her.

"I was just thinking about how wrong everyone is about you."

He laughed. "Are they, though? I don't lose a single moment of sleep worrying what other people think. I don't care about them at all. Maybe that's what they hate the most."

"I admire your independent spirit."

"Do you?" He sounded surprised. "I thought you were convinced that everything I stand for is wrong."

"That's when I thought you stood for gambling and drinking and cheating people out of their hard-earned money. Now I know those things are means to an end. You wouldn't be in the gambling business at all if it weren't for you trying to build the tribe, would you?"

He watched her for a moment. "I admit, the software business was a lot less complicated." A smile tugged at his mouth. "In fact, I'm planning to get back into it. We've been working on some database software to improve our business operations here and I plan to release a beta version in the next three months or so."

"Maybe it will be more successful than the casino."

"That's hard to imagine, but you never know."

"Most people would be resting on their laurels and enjoying the fruits of their hard work, but you're always trying something new."

"Maybe I'm just restless." He shifted, bumping against her and stirring desire.

"I'm not like that at all." She let out a sigh. "I'm very dull, really. I don't have any desire to set the world on fire. I'm just trying to save enough to buy my own house and move out."

"The world would be a crazy place if everyone was like me. Can you imagine? A blend of different types of people is much more peaceful and productive." He kissed her cheek.

Her skin stirred under his lips. "I suppose you're right." Was that why he liked her—she provided a pleasantly dull contrast to his high-octane self?

"Opposites attract." He squeezed her, and she reveled in the sensation of his big body pressed against hers.

"Apparently so." She caressed the thick muscle of his back. It was hard to believe she lay here in his arms, completely naked. It felt oddly natural. As had their lovemaking. Much more so than the hurried fumblings with the college boyfriend she'd planned to spend the rest of her life with.

Right now she could easily imagine herself and John having an actual relationship. Surely they were already, to a certain extent? Except that she was here to investigate his company for improprieties and she'd probably be fired if anyone found out about this.

"What's the matter?" He must have heard her breathing quicken.

"I can't believe we're in bed together."

He paused, and stroked her shoulder. "Nothing happens by accident."

"No? I didn't plan this and I don't think you did, either."

His chest rumbled with a chuckle. "You're right. But we can both be discreet."

She wasn't sure if it was a question or a command. Either way it hurt. Which it shouldn't have, because she certainly didn't want him telling anyone. "Of course."

No promises. No expectations.

No future.

She'd fallen into his arms knowing this was crazy, but she hadn't been able to help herself. Too many nights in her lonely bedroom, wondering if a man would ever hold her again. Too many dreams that hadn't come true. The last few years of loneliness had apparently left her in a desperate and dangerous condition and brought her here into John Fairweather's bed.

"We're not entirely opposites, you know." John kissed her cheek softly.

"No? How are we similar?"

"We're both stubborn and determined."

"I think I'm going to take that as an insult. I was raised to be obedient and compliant." She raised a brow.

"Well, something went wrong." He winked, and the sparkle of humor in his eyes did something strange to her belly. "Because I can tell you make up your own mind about everything."

"What makes you say that?"

"You're here, aren't you? In my arms." He squeezed her gently, and her heart tripped a little.

"I'm not sure my mind was involved in this at all. I suspect other, less intellectual parts of my body were involved."

His chest rocked with laughter. "To a certain extent, yes, but you're here and thinking right now and I don't notice you running for the door."

"Trust me, I'm thinking about running for the door." She glanced at it, as if to make sure the way was clear.

"Guess I'll have to keep a tight hold on you, then." His arms circled her completely, which felt fabulous. She didn't want to move from their embrace. "Because I don't want you to go."

"I'm sure you'd have no trouble finding someone to take my place here." She regretted the jealous-sounding words the moment they came out.

"I'm not at all interested in anyone else. I bet you'd be surprised by how long it's been since I slept with a woman."

"Really?" Her own curiosity embarrassed her.

"I won't lie. I sowed some wild oats when I was younger, especially after my marriage fell apart. I'd been a true romantic up until then and I couldn't believe that the forever she'd promised me had turned out to be less than a year. I probably got revenge on myself more than anyone else. I was mad at myself for trusting her."

"I was mad at myself for trusting in my ex. And he didn't even cheat on me. At least not that I know of."

"It's hard to put your faith in other people once you've been let down. Is that why you haven't been serious with anyone else?"

She paused, not wanting to tell the truth. But she wasn't really cut out for fibbing. "No one's even asked me out since then."

"In five or six years?" His incredulity made her bite her lip.

"Nope. Not once." Maybe that explained why she'd leaped so willingly into John's entirely unsuitable arms.

"That's insane. You are kind of intimidating, though. It probably takes someone as obnoxious as me to be arrogant enough to try."

"Intimidating? I think of myself as being humble and unassuming."

His deep belly laugh rocked her. "You can think of yourself that way all you want. The truth is you're a demanding and rather judgmental woman who probably scares the pants off most men."

"Oh." She frowned. "That doesn't sound good."

"I like it." His grin warmed her. "If you have high expectations of yourself, you should have them of others, too. I know I do."

"Hmm. Now that you put it like that, it doesn't seem so bad." Her head rested on his bicep, which was more comfortable than the softest pillow. "I suppose you're right that a lot of people find me unapproachable. I turn down so many lunch invitations and weekend plans from co-workers that people rarely invite me anywhere anymore."

"Why do you turn them down?"

"I think they're silly. I go to the office to work, not socialize."

"See? You are unapproachable." His grin revealed those even white teeth. "They're right to be afraid. What about your church? You said your family is religious. Didn't you meet anyone there?"

"Not anyone I was interested in."

"So you're also picky." He stroked a tendril of hair off her cheek.

"Shouldn't I be? What's the point of pretending you like someone when you don't?"

"None whatsoever." He grinned. "I guess that means you like me."

"I wouldn't say that," she teased. Why was he so easy to talk to? "But apparently I am attracted to you."

"And I'm attracted to you." His gentle kiss made her lips tingle. "There's some serious chemistry between us."

There was. It snapped in the air and sensitized her skin where their bodies touched. Pheromones. Mysterious substances that science barely understood, which coaxed humans into situations any sane person would avoid. Like lying cheek to cheek with the man whose business you were investigating.

"It's a shame chemistry doesn't last and that after a while you have to actually be compatible and get along." She wanted to let him know she didn't expect this crazy fling to go anywhere. Or maybe she just wanted to reject him before he could reject her.

"You have to start somewhere." He kissed her again. She wished he'd stop doing that! It stirred all kinds of sensations deep in her belly. Sensations that made her wish he were inside her again. What kind of woman had he turned her into? "How do you know we're not perfectly compatible?"

"Us? That's funny." She didn't want him to think his words had any effect on her, but they did. They were both good with numbers. Both hardworking and determined. She would have once said that he was a notorious playboy and she was the exact opposite, but her current position here in his arms proved that she wasn't so entirely different from him when the opportunity for romance presented itself.

Romance? Where had that word come from? There wasn't anything terribly romantic about their relationship so far. Romance was flirtation and candlelit dinners and hopeful conversations. They'd gone straight from zero to sixty with very little preamble.

She'd better not let herself start thinking that this was a romance, or she was likely to end up with a broken heart.

"I don't think it's so funny at all. My grandparents are very different and they've been together for almost fifty years. He was wild and considered himself a beatnik. He wrote terrible poetry and played the trumpet, and he was getting ready to run away to New York and become a jazz musician when he met my grandmother while delivering milk to a local depot. She'd just moved here with her family from Minnesota and had never dated or kissed a boy in her life. She was training to become a schoolteacher and spent her evenings reading and knitting. He charmed her and she tamed him and they've been together ever since."

"Oh." A dangerous charmer and a good girl. Sounded familiar.

"He was very good-looking. She always said that she never stood a chance against him."

"Have they been happy?" She was genuinely curious. People always talked about those opposites-attract relationships, but she didn't know how often they really worked out.

"Very. They've had their ups and downs, of course. My mom—the one who gave birth to me—was even wilder than my grandfather when he was young, and it ended up killing her. Her death put a strain on their relationship, as a child's death often does. My grandmother blamed my grandfather for not being stricter with her, and he blamed her for not being more accepting. He felt that if my mom had still lived at home maybe she wouldn't have gone out drinking and driving on the night she died."

"If things were different, maybe you wouldn't have been born." She stroked the wrinkle that had formed between his brows. "So much of life depends on chance."

She'd never had that thought before. She was a planner, and unapologetic about it. She'd had her whole life mapped out from about age eleven: she'd intended to meet and marry a nice, appropriate spouse during college, then work for several years to build their finances and buy a house before they started a family. She'd planned her career in accounting and made sure to keep abreast of all developments in the field so she'd always have in-demand skills. When her marriage plans had derailed, she'd continued full speed ahead with the other elements of her life blueprint, assuming that everything would slot into place eventually, even if not on her anticipated schedule. She hadn't spent a single moment thinking about the rather scary mechanics of chance.

"You're right. All the hard work in the world won't get you anywhere without at least a dash of luck, too. I can't tell you how many times the fate of this casino, even the whole tribe, rested on a decision made by strangers who didn't have any real stake in the outcome. There were certainly enough people hoping that it wouldn't happen. And plenty that would like to shut us down right now."

"Do you think that's what they would do if I found

that you were actually cooking your books?" Her stomach clenched. She could probably wreak havoc on John's entire existence.

"I don't doubt that they'd try. Believe me, it makes it easy to stay honest."

"Why are so many people opposed to the casino?"

"Well, there are the people who are against it for the same reasons as you." He touched her lips with a finger. "You know, gambling, drinking, people wasting time having fun. But I suspect even more of them are just jealous. They think we're getting away with something. Enjoying some benefit that they can't have because they're not Indian. No one likes to feel excluded."

"I suppose you're right, but isn't it supposed to be a reparation of sorts for past injustices?"

"I think some people see it that way, especially people who are trying to justify their gambling losses as a charitable donation." He winked. "But really it's just a recognition of past treaties, allowing us sovereignty over our own lands and people. So many of these agreements were ignored or broken over the centuries, and now things are changing. There's no element of payback in it. If anything you'd think Americans would be glad that we're finally getting with the program and embracing the complicated laws and unbridled capitalism that have made this country so powerful and influential."

John was so charming it was hard to imagine anyone disagreeing with him once they'd talked to him face-to-face. "So basically, you're just trying to fit in."

"Exactly." His wicked grin made her smile in response. And kiss him. She couldn't help herself. Something about him had totally undermined her defenses. He kissed her back. It was warm and invigorating, and soon he had to reach for another condom.

Bliss filled her as John entered her again, banishing the years of loneliness and wanting. Her body blossomed under his affectionate caresses, and her inhibitions faded away as their intimacy deepened. Was it really this easy to find happiness with another person?

She drifted off to sleep in his calm embrace, feeling utterly at peace with the world. Right now she could easily imagine herself and John as a couple, sharing their days and nights, their thoughts, their dreams.

Could this taste of paradise turn into her real life?

Seven

Constance awoke with a jolt. Sunlight streamed through a crack in the curtains, announcing that the day was well under way.

John was gone, his side of the bed rumpled and empty.

She blinked, trying to read her watch. Ten-fifteen? She'd slept half the morning away. Why hadn't John woken her? She clutched the covers around her, trying to cover her nakedness, even though she seemed to be alone in here. Where were her clothes? She barely remembered taking them off. They were probably on the floor somewhere.

She spotted them neatly draped over a chair on the far side of the room. John must have picked them up this morning. How embarrassing! She lay here sleeping while he was up and about. Right now he was probably in a meeting or doing his daily perusal of the previous night's takings, and she was just waking up from a sensual dream.

She sprang out of bed and hurried across the room, then tried to tug her clothes on so fast it was more difficult than if she'd taken her time. She kept glancing about the room as if someone was watching. She checked her phone and saw several messages, mostly from work. There was no way she could even listen to them, never mind return the calls, while standing in John Fairweather's bedroom!

Her suit was wrinkled, probably from lying in a heap

all night. She couldn't manage to get her hair to cooperate either. She certainly hoped she could get out of here without running into anyone. And she had to drive all the way to her hotel and back before she could even get to work.

She tried to use the elevator that opened right into the suite, but she couldn't get the door to open. It required some kind of code she didn't know. Cringing with embarrassment, she cracked open the door that led into a hotel hallway. A cleaner's cart sat two doors down. She'd better get out of here before they wandered in with the vacuum. Glancing around and scurrying like a cartoon character, she darted for the public elevators at the far end of the hall.

Constance pressed the button and gritted her teeth with impatience. She couldn't remember a single occasion in her life before now that she'd needed to skulk about and conceal her shockingly inappropriate activities.

Naturally the elevator opened right into the elegant main lobby, which was unusually well populated for a weekday morning. Worse yet, she could see John giving a television interview in front of the decorative mural on the far side of the room. The cameraman with his bulky mike and the aggressively tanned male reporter almost blocked her way to the main exit, and she hesitated for a minute to plan her escape.

John hadn't seen her yet and she wanted to make sure he didn't. She didn't want him to smile and wave or otherwise draw attention to her.

"…investigated by the Bureau of Indian Affairs on suspicion of fraud…" The reporter's words assaulted her ears as she got closer. Little did they know the BIA's official investigator was trying to sneak past them wearing yesterday's underwear, with John Fairweather's DNA licked into its fabric.

John was talking now, looking directly at the reporter.

She seized her chance to break for the door, avoiding his gaze as she strode across the lobby, heels clicking. Luckily the camera was facing the other way so she wouldn't be caught on tape making her escape.

She burst out into blinding sunlight with her adrenaline pounding and fumbled for her car keys, desperate to escape before anyone saw her or tried to talk to her.

Back in her hotel room, after showering and washing away John's passionate touch, Constance called the office. "Nicola Moore of the BIA called about six times for you," Lynn whispered into the phone. "She's getting hysterical. Where have you been? There's been some kind of exposé article published about the New Dawn casino and she wants to know if it's true."

That would explain the TV reporter in the lobby. "What does it say?"

"The usual stuff, how they've grown too big too fast and it can't be legit."

"That's hardly a news story."

"There's some stuff about his uncle. I forget the guy's name but apparently he has a colorful past. Money laundering or something similar."

Constance frowned. John's uncle Don? She didn't like the guy much. He gave off a sleazebag vibe. "Everything's still checking out fine. They're very profitable because there are people here throwing their money away twenty-four hours a day."

"Are you sure you're not blinded to iniquity by John Fairweather's dazzling smile?"

"Of course I'm sure," she retorted. "Sorry. Didn't mean to sound so snappy." What a shame she couldn't explain why she hadn't gotten too much sleep last night. "I'm starting to get annoyed with all the negative opinions that keep cropping up, when I can't find any justification for them. I can't help but think people are just jealous and resent the tribe's success. Why shouldn't they have some prosperity for a change? They've been kicked around since the 1600s. It's about time they got to enjoy life a bit. I don't know why people get so upset that they're making money."

"Maybe because they don't pay taxes on it?"

"Actually, they do pay some taxes. It was built into their agreements with the state. And they provide employment in an otherwise depressed area. I've totally revised my opinion of the place and I wish everyone else would do the same."

"You sound very passionate."

Passionate? What an odd choice of word. She'd certainly experienced passion last night. It dwarfed her most ambitious daydreams. "Nonsense. I'm entirely practical. I can't see why it's okay for corporations to make money hand over fist and interpret laws to meet their needs, but not tribes. This is America. We love money and profits. You and I wouldn't have a job without them!"

Lynn laughed. "So true. Anyway, you'd better call Ms. Moore. She's getting on my nerves."

"Will do. Hopefully I'll be home in a day or two." A twinge of sadness shot through her. Once she left she probably wouldn't ever see John again. Which would make last night's tryst a one-night stand. Shame swept over her in a hot tide. She'd fallen so easily into his arms. Worse yet, she craved the feel of his arms around her right now. Of his hot kisses claiming her mouth, the powerful sensation of him moving inside her.

"Are you still there?" Lynn asked.

"Yes. Yes. Just going over some notes." Now she was lying. What next? If anyone found out that she'd had an affair with the man whose business she was supposed to be investigating, she'd be fired. She'd probably lose her accreditation and would never be able to find another job in the field.

"They must be pretty interesting notes. And you're missing some exciting happenings here at Creighton Waterman. Someone walked in on Lacey, the new trainee, getting up close and personal with Aaron Whitlow."

"What?" Mr. Whitlow was the straitlaced senior executive who gave them their annual reviews. "He must be twice her age. Maybe even three times!"

"I know. Everyone is freaking out. Worse yet, the person who saw them was Leah, the head of personnel."

"Did Lacey get fired?"

"She did. It makes me mad. Why does she have to leave? Why not him?"

"He's in a position of power."

"That's hardly fair. She should file a sexual harassment lawsuit. But she didn't want to. She said it was consensual. She was so upset, crying and red faced. I think she really cared about him."

Constance swallowed. "It is odd that relationships at work are so taboo. That is where most of us spend our time, after all."

"It's because we're supposed to behave like robots who only care about doing our jobs. Not actual people with feelings. Whitlow's acting more robotic than ever, of course. Muttering orders under his breath, looking down his snooty nose at people. It does make me laugh to picture him fooling around with a much younger woman. Apparently she was sitting on his desk with her skirt up around her waist!"

"Yikes." Constance wanted to cringe. Desire. The same thing that had lured her irresistibly into John's encouraging arms. When examined in the cold light of day, it was embarrassing and inappropriate. What would Lynn—or anyone—say if they could have seen her last night, writhing with pleasure in John's bed?

"The scandal has certainly livened things up around here, let me tell you. You're missing all the fun."

"You know I hate gossip." She tried to stay out of the petty squabbles around the watercooler.

"I'll certainly never see Whitlow in the same light again, that's for sure."

"Isn't he a widower? Maybe he was lonely." Great. Now she was defending a man who'd fooled around with a much younger employee. Of course as a transgressor herself, she could sympathize with him in a way she'd never have been able to imagine even a week ago.

Maybe this whole experience was part of her journey toward greater compassion and understanding. It was pretty humbling, all right. "I have another call coming in."

"All right. Call Nicola Moore at the BIA before she comes down there looking for you."

"Will do." She hung up and grabbed the other call, adrenaline firing because she could see it was John.

"Good morning, gorgeous."

Heat rose up from her chest. "Good morning yourself. I can't believe you let me sleep in like that. I'm so embarrassed."

"You looked so peaceful that I didn't want to disturb you. I had to get up for a media interview."

"I saw you doing it." She didn't want to say what she'd heard about the accusations against his uncle. It didn't seem appropriate given their professional relationship. Still, she wanted to hear how he'd describe it. "What were they asking you about?"

He paused for a moment. "Nothing very interesting. The usual stuff."

So he was going to hide it from her. Surely he'd know she could see it on the news or read it on the internet? "I suppose they're often hoping to stir up a story. Speaking of which, there's a sex scandal going on at my office right now. If they had any idea what I was up to I'd be out on my ear."

"I won't tell them. It's none of their business."

"I suppose not. You're not sleeping with me to cloud my judgment, are you?" She said it in jest, but once the words were out she realized she wasn't entirely kidding.

He laughed. "If I was, would it be working?"

"Of course not. I have tremendous integrity." She was trying to convince herself as much as him.

"Tremendous, huh? That is impressive. And I'd expect nothing less of you. Seriously, though, you should probably know that the media has got a wild hair about my uncle Don. I'm sure it will blow over soon, but they're trying to find him guilty of something, so you may as well hear it from me and not from the BIA."

"What do they think he's done?"

"I don't know. I don't think they care. Anything they can cook up will do. Want to get together for lunch? It's almost noon."

"Noon?" She gulped. "I can't. I'm not even at the casino. I'm still at my hotel getting changed. I need to focus completely on work for the rest of the day."

"And the night?"

"And the night." She blinked. No sense giving him a chance to make plans that were going to rope her even deeper into this impossible affair. One night with him had been intoxicating enough. Another and she might never regain her sanity. "I really need to concentrate on my work. Last night was…"

"Wonderful."

"Yes, it was." She had to admit it. "But I'm here to do a job." *And we both know this is going nowhere.*

"That's true, but I want to make sure you don't work too fast. I don't want to lose you any sooner than I have to."

So he could easily admit that their affair had a built-in end. The little pang of sorrow surprised her. "I do have other projects I need to get back to."

"It's a shame your office isn't local. Why would they hire someone from Ohio to investigate a casino in Massachusetts?"

"I think they do that to encourage impartiality. Since I'm not local, I have no stake in building or maintaining a relationship with the New Dawn casino."

"Just with its owner." His voice was silky and seductive.

"That was an accident."

"A very happy one."

"As long as no one finds out about it." And really, how happy could it be when she'd be home alone in a few days, lonely as ever?

"Concealment does not come naturally to me." She heard frustration in his voice. "In fact, I'm hating this need for secrecy. I much prefer to be frank and up front in my dealings with everyone."

"But you do understand that my job and my reputation depend on keeping this secret?" Panic gripped her quietly.

"Believe me. I do. And I hold myself entirely responsible for the delicate predicament we find ourselves in." He paused, and the silence hummed for a moment. "Can I come over to your hotel?"

She sucked in a breath as visions of John's large form in her tiny hotel room crowded her imagination. "No. I really have to work."

"Bummer." He sounded so disappointed that she had to smile.

"I have more calls to return. I'll see you at the office."

"I'll make sure of it." She could hear the smile in his voice, and it made her chest ache a little. She was really going to miss John. Which was ridiculous. She'd only known him a few days and in many ways he was the most infuriating man she'd ever met.

Yet she still liked him so much. And she liked that he'd told her about the suspicions regarding his uncle. As she dialed the number for Nicola Moore at the BIA, she was pretty sure she'd be hearing Don's name again.

She was right. Nicola immediately launched into a tirade against him.

"Don Fairweather has been previously investigated for money laundering."

"Was he convicted?" Constance glanced around her room to see if there was anything else she needed to bring to the office. It crossed her mind that she could bring a change of underwear. She told her mind to get back to business.

"No. It went to trial but the jury apparently didn't find the prosecutor's evidence convincing enough."

"Oh. So he was found innocent."

"Or they just didn't look hard enough. I want you to make sure to look in places where no one would expect. There was a case recently at another casino where three of the workers managed to pocket hundreds of thousands of dollars by creating fraudulent receipts from the slot machines to bring to the cashiers. One of them created the receipts, one was the runner between the slot machines and the tills, and the other was the cashier. As you can imagine, it was a neat little racket for a while."

"How did the casino figure out what was going on?"

"Keen observation."

"You do realize that I'm a forensic accountant and not

a private detective?" She had been told she was doing a routine audit of their books. Now that she was here, it appeared that her contact had definite suspicions, or at least was trying to plant some in her mind. That didn't sit too well with Constance when she needed to stay objective.

"Indeed, Ms. Allen, we're well aware of that. We simply expect you to find whether the paperwork is truly reflective of the casino's activities."

"I understand. I'll look into every avenue I can think of."

She hung up and found herself glancing at her underwear drawer again. What if she packed a bag with extra panties and a whole new outfit so she didn't have to come back to the hotel at all?

The blunt thought shocked her. What would her parents think if they knew what she was doing? They'd issued stern warnings about stepping foot inside such a den of iniquity, and now she was having a sexual affair with a man she wasn't even in a relationship with.

She'd never have slept with her ex-boyfriend if she hadn't been utterly convinced that one day—soon—they'd be man and wife. But Phil did not have the looks or the charm of John Fairweather.

No. She couldn't bring a change of clothes. That would be admitting that she planned to do something inappropriate. If something happened spontaneously, that was different. Going into the New Dawn casino with a deliberate intention to have sex with the man she was investigating seemed far more dangerous and inappropriate. Premeditation, after all, was often the difference between manslaughter and murder.

An unplanned crime—or night—of passion was a little different.

She jumped when the phone rang, as if the person calling could read her thoughts.

And maybe they could. "Hi, Mom."

"Hello, sweetheart, are you busy?"

"Yes, very, I'm afraid." She didn't want to get into a conversation that might involve little white lies.

"How long are they going to keep you out there in Massachusetts? It's the church picnic this weekend and I promised you'd run the till. Sally is baking two hundred cupcakes to raise money for the mission in Kenya."

It was Thursday. The thought that in two days she could be back in Ohio, miles away from John, chilled her. "I don't know if I'll be back. I thought I would be, but it keeps getting more complicated. I'm sure you can run the till." She felt a bit guilty. She usually enjoyed helping out at these events. It was fun to see people coming together for a good cause. Now all she could seem to think about was herself and the affair she shouldn't be having.

"I already promised to run the lemonade stand. I suppose Sally's daughter can manage, though. I do wish you were back home. I worry about you being so far away and with the wrong sort of people."

"There's nothing to worry about. They're all quite normal, really. It's a business like any other." She glanced at her face in the mirror, wondering if her nose was getting longer. There was nothing normal about John Fairweather. He was larger than life in every possible way.

"I know people visit casinos of their own free will, but profits from gambling just seem like the wages of sin."

"They're wages like any others when you look at the account books, and that's all I'm here to do. How's Dad doing? Is he taking that new medication the doctor gave him?" Her father's cholesterol had tested high recently. She was so used to taking care of them. If anything, they'd grown even more dependent on her since she moved back home from college, and she wondered how they'd manage without her if she did move out. Especially if she moved away to a different state.

Not that she should even be thinking along those lines since it was very unlikely to happen.

"Your dad is taking his medicine, but he won't stop putting mayonnaise on everything. You'll have to talk some sense into him when you come home. It's odd here without you. The house feels empty and there's no one to do the dishes after dinner."

She had to smile. "I miss you, too. I'm still not sure when I'll be home, but hopefully by next week."

They wished each other goodbye and Constance hung up, then sighed, thinking about the endless nights of putting dishes into the machine and watching alarmist news shows that stretched ahead of her like a lonely highway. Then she shoved her phone in her pocket and headed out the door.

Without a change of underwear.

Constance spent the afternoon stalking the cashiers and wandering around the game rooms. Luckily for her, the New Dawn did not have any kind of middlemen between the customers and the cashiers. Everyone had to bring their own chips to the cashier to turn them into money.

Nothing untoward seemed to be happening at the tables, either. John had told her that the dealers were all experienced professionals, mostly from Atlantic City or Vegas, though he was hoping to train some local people soon.

She walked among the tables watching the customers gamble. People won money. Others lost money. Some won it then lost it. There was nothing that looked fishy. She paused at a roulette table, and watched the croupier spin the wheel.

"Hello, gorgeous." That deep, rich voice in her ear sent a shiver of warm lust to her core.

She resisted the urge to spin around and instead turned very slowly to face John. A smile was already creeping across her face and she worked hard not to let it get too goofy. "Good afternoon, Mr. Fairweather."

"I see you're examining our operations again with that eagle eye of yours. Do you like what you see?"

"Like it? Not so much. I'm still not a fan of gambling." She smiled primly. His own easy expression didn't budge. "And I really should keep my findings confidential at this point, don't you think?"

Now she did see a flicker of surprise in his eyes. "What findings?"

"Any findings I should happen to make." She attempted an air of sphinxlike calm. "I'm not saying I've found anything unusual."

"But you're not saying you haven't." He frowned. "You will tell me if you find anything, won't you? I'd be damn surprised, but I'd want to know right up front."

She hesitated. "My first responsibility is to my client."

"The BIA."

"I'd consider it a personal favor if you'd tell me about anything you find first." His face was now deadly serious.

"I don't think I'm in a position to offer personal favors. I'm here to do a job." This was getting awkward. He obviously thought she'd found something unexpected in the books that she didn't want him to know about it. Still, if she did, she should keep it secret while she investigated, so the casino wouldn't have a chance to cover it all up before she reported back to her client.

She glanced up and saw his uncle Don throw down some chips at a distant roulette table.

"I have no desire to interfere with your performance on the job you've been hired to do. You know that. But honestly, if you find anything amiss, I'd be as keen to know about it as anyone else." His earnest expression preyed on her emotions.

"I'll tell you if I find anything," she whispered. "I really do believe you want everything to be aboveboard. But so far, so good." She smiled. "Though I shouldn't be telling you that."

In the distance, Don swiped up a fistful of chips from the table with a smile and shoved them in his pocket. Darius, who managed the cashiers, had told her that Don gambled. She supposed there was nothing illegal in it. Or was there? This was a perfect instance of where she needed to do her own research rather than asking John about it.

Don Fairweather was now heading toward them, a confident smile on his rather wrinkled face. Constance braced herself. She'd better be on alert to see if she could pick up any information to substantiate or debunk the rumors about him.

"Consorting with the enemy, eh, John?" Don turned to her and winked. "You know I'm just kidding. We welcome the scrutiny of the BIA and all their friends in the media. Life would be dull if everyone just let us go about our business."

"My contact mentioned money-laundering charges against you." She looked at Don and came right out with it. She wanted to hear if his answer would be any less evasive and uninformative than John's. And something about Don's nonchalant attitude pushed her buttons and she wanted to see how he reacted under pressure.

"Load of bull. I used to own a chain of dry cleaners.

We were laundering shirts, not money." His grin challenged her to argue. "As you probably know, they didn't find enough evidence to convict me of anything."

"Don was found not guilty," John cut in. "By a jury of his peers."

"Not that I have any true peers, of course."

"Don is by far the most arrogant of the Fairweathers." John shot a wry glance at Constance.

"Which is saying quite a bit with you around," Don retorted with a crinkly smile. "We keep each other on our toes."

"That we do. One of my favorite things about the New Dawn is that I get to work with family every day." John wrapped his arm around Don. "Sometimes it's a challenge, but maybe that's why I enjoy it so much."

"You'd be bored if life was too easy. And neither of us knew there were so many of us. Some of them barely even knew they had Indian ancestry until John got them excited about this place. Now the kids are begging him to dig up some old songs and dances so they can compete in the big powwows."

John shook his head. "Easier said than done. I vote that they just make up their own. Why does our culture have to be old and historic? Why can't it be fresh and new?"

"Won't win any prizes with that. The judges are traditional. We already have strikes against us because we don't look like most people's idea of an Indian."

"Then people need to change their perceptions, don't they, Constance."

"I suppose they do." How did he always charm her into agreeing with him? She really didn't have an opinion of any kind on the matter. She did think it was sweet how John obviously worked hard to create a sense of community, and was paying a fortune to academics to dig up the

Nissequot tribe's shared history. "And if anyone can do that, it's you."

She blushed, realizing that she'd just praised him in front of his uncle. Don's eyebrows rose a tad. Did he suspect anything between her and John? That would be disastrous. Don Fairweather was something of a loose cannon, aside from his dubious reputation. "I really must get back to the offices."

"I'll ride up with you." John's low voice gave the innocent offer a suggestive tone.

"Actually, I need to get something from my car first." She didn't want Don to see them disappearing together.

John wouldn't tell Don about their liaison, would he? She really didn't know. Don was his uncle and they were obviously close. She reminded herself that she barely knew John at all. She nodded to them primly and hustled toward the lobby. She didn't actually need anything from her car but she'd fiddle around in there for a minute or so. Anything to get away from John's dark, seductive gaze.

She futzed around with her bag on the passenger seat for a moment, then pulled it out and closed the car door. She turned toward the casino and gasped when she found John right in front of her.

"I'm not letting you sneak off."

"I wasn't trying to sneak off." She lifted her chin. "I was getting my phone charger."

"Oh." His smile suggested that he knew it was a ruse. "You looked like you were running away from something."

"Your uncle Don doesn't know about…us, does he?"

John shrugged. "I haven't told him anything. Even if he figured it out, he'd be discreet. He's got enough skeletons in his own closet that he's not going to throw open the door to anyone else's."

Why was that not at all reassuring? "I don't think we should walk back in together."

"Why not?" He looked a little put out. "I'm the CEO of the place. I hardly think it's inappropriate of me to escort the forensic accountant up to the offices." He leaned in and whispered in her ear, "Even if I do know how she looks without her clothes on."

Constance sucked in a breath. Heat flushed her entire body and she wasn't sure if it was embarrassment or lust. It didn't really matter. Neither was at all helpful right now.

"You're incorrigible." Luckily there was no one else around.

"I know. It's an affliction. Do you think you can cure me?"

"I doubt it. I also have no intention of trying." She shifted her bag higher on her shoulder. "And I have work to do."

"Let's go." He led the way, then waited for her to catch up so they could enter the lobby together. She held her chin high, self-conscious as she walked with him through the public space. The staff all knew who she was by now. Did they suspect anything? She felt so different than she had even yesterday, it was hard to imagine that she could still look the same from the outside.

When they reached the office, John ushered her in, then followed her and closed the door. She heard the lock click and felt his arm reach around her waist and her backside crushed up against his hard form.

"Constance, you're making me crazy."

She tried to hide her smile. "Maybe you were crazy already."

"I don't know what you've done to me."

"I can't imagine that I've done anything." His big

hand splayed over her belly, where all kinds of sensations churned. "I'm just trying to do my job."

"And I keep distracting you." His lips brushed her neck and heat flickered low inside her.

"Yes. Very much so."

"I think you needed some distraction." His low voice sent a rumble of desire to her toes.

"So I'll be unable to properly investigate your books? You'll make me think you're trying to hide something."

"Maybe there is something I'm trying to hide." His voice contained more than a hint of suggestion, and she felt his erection jostle against her. She was slightly appalled by how arousing that was. What had happened to her since she met John Fairweather? It was as though a switch had turned on inside her. Now energy coursed through her veins whenever she was around him. Her mind strayed in previously forbidden directions and her body ached to do all kinds of things that she knew were wrong.

"What are we doing?" she asked in a half whisper.

His mouth played below her ear, heating her skin. "I think I'm kissing your neck."

"This is foolish."

"I won't argue with you." He went back to kissing her neck. Her nipples were starting to tingle.

"So shouldn't we stop?"

His mouth worked its way up to her ear and he nibbled softly on her earlobe, which sent a surprising surge of sensation to her core. "Definitely not."

He spun her around and kissed her full on the mouth. Her lips parted to welcome him and she felt her arms wrap enthusiastically around him without her permission. They kissed for a solid ten minutes, until she was in a thoroughly befuddled state. Then he excused himself with a polite nod and left her all alone, in a state of agonizing arousal, with nothing but ledger books for company.

She stared at the door. What a nerve! Now he had her all worked up and he'd waltzed off? He hadn't even said where he was going or when he'd be back. How could she work now that he'd left her with blood pounding in every part of her body other than her brain?

She glanced at her watch and saw that it was nearly seven o'clock. She'd wasted most of the afternoon seeing nothing downstairs. Except for Don Fairweather swiping those chips off the table.

Of course she'd seen him put chips down to bet, so nothing truly suspicious had happened, but wasn't it rather a conflict of interest for him to gamble in the tribe's own casino? He wasn't involved in the day-to-day operations on the floor. He did publicity and booked the bands, but he was obviously fairly intimate with all the other workers. She'd noticed his jovial exchanges with at least half a dozen employees on the floor. Which was hardly proof of wrongdoing.

She heaved a sigh of relief to find that thinking about Don helped dissipate the fog of passion that John had left her in. She turned to the computer and had a look through the entries from a year ago. There was no point in looking at new data, since everyone knew she was here so any would-be crooks would be on their best behavior. As usual everything seemed to add up.

Often with forensic accounting she wasn't looking for overt proof of wrongdoing. White-collar criminals were usually smart and knew how to cover their tracks. She had to look closely to find tiny holes or data that was just a little different from the norm. Then she at least had a clue for somewhere to stick in her shovel and start digging. So far she'd had no luck. Every time she'd thought she found an interesting anomaly, it had turned out to be a dead end.

On instinct she decided to look for internal records of tribal members gambling. They were easy enough to find in the casino databases, which were very well organized and clearly labeled, probably by John himself. Don wasn't the only member who gambled, but he was by far the heaviest gambler. Someone called Mona Lester had some losses, and an Anna Martin had some small winnings, but Don had won more than fifty thousand dollars last year. Could he be up to something, or was he just lucky?

The door clicked open and John appeared again. She closed the spreadsheet window with a flash of guilt. Which was ridiculous. He knew she was here to dig into the files, so she was hardly going behind his back. Still, it felt wrong to kiss a man then go looking for fraud in his own computer system.

One more reason why this whole affair was a big mistake.

He closed the door behind him and leaned against it. His sleek dark suit did nothing to conceal the raw masculinity of his body. Especially not now that she'd seen it naked. "You're coming to my house for dinner."

"You mean your suite." Her response seemed easier than choosing to accept or decline his invitation. Not an invitation, really. More of a command.

"No, I mean my house. I'm just living in the suite while I renovate the old farmhouse. The kitchen's finished, so I have everything I need to make dinner for you."

"You can cook?"

"Absolutely."

She blinked, not sure what to believe. Was there anything he couldn't do? "I can't really say no, then, can I?"

"Of course not." He offered a hand to help her from her seat behind the desk.

She must be out of her mind. But, he could cook? That was pretty irresistible. And she could go back to her hotel right after dinner. "I'll drive in my car." Then she could take off any time she wanted.

"Sure. You can follow me."

The road to his house was long and winding, an old farm road that led past his grandparents' new house and through fields dotted with grazing cattle. Gnarled apple trees lined the drive and framed the austere form of John's white farmhouse. A new cedar-shake roof gleamed gold in the lowering sun and stickers still ornamented the shiny new windows. A Dumpster filled with construction debris and a cement mixer were among the signs that a major renovation was still in progress.

"We stripped it right back to the old post-and-beam framing, and added stud walls and insulation. There's almost nothing left of the original house, but it's starting to look like it used to in its heyday. All the major work is done. Now they're reinstalling the original woodwork. I should be back living here in a month or so."

"It looks lovely." She was surprised that a notorious bachelor like John would even want a big old house when he could be catered to by staff at his own luxury hotel.

"It's coming together really well. I can't wait to move in. I'm going to get a dog."

"What kind?"

"I don't know yet. Something big. And cute. I'll adopt it from a shelter."

"That's a great idea. I've always wanted a dog."

"Why don't you get one?"

"I need to move out of my parents' house first. My mom doesn't like them."

He nodded. He must think it pathetic that she still lived at home with her parents at age twenty-seven. She needed to put moving out at the top of her goals for the coming year.

They walked up solid stone steps to the front door, which was still stripped bare of paint. John opened it and ushered her in. She glanced around his inner sanctum, taking in all the authentic details he'd had lovingly preserved.

"This house was built in 1837 by one of my ancestors. He and his sons handcrafted a lot of the woodwork themselves."

She stroked a turned cherry bannister. "This must have been quite a labor of love before power tools became common."

"All the more reason to restore it to its original beauty." He led her into a bright kitchen with ivory cabinets and big center island. "Do you like shrimp?"

"Love it."

"Good, because I've had it marinating since this morning."

"You knew you were going to ask me over?"

"Of course."

His arrogance should have been annoying. "What if I said I didn't like shrimp? Or I was allergic."

He shot her a cheeky smile. "I've got some chicken prepared as well."

"You're ready for anything, aren't you?"

"I try to be."

He grilled the shrimp and some corn on the cob outdoors, and they ate it with an elaborate salad they made together of feta cheese and pear tossed with spring greens. The million-dollar view from his bluestone patio looked over pastures and rolling wooded hills. Constance couldn't remember a time she'd been anywhere so beautiful. Her own drab environs in an unprepossessing part of Cleveland were depressing by comparison. Yet soon she'd be back there, looking off the back porch over the weedy garden, remembering this delicious dinner and her dangerously charming host.

Dark clouds were gathering along the horizon as the sun disappeared behind the trees. Raindrops spotted the patio as they brought the plates back inside, and by the time they loaded them in the dishwasher, rain was pounding on the darkened windows.

While John brewed the fresh-ground coffee, thunderclaps boomed overhead. "You'd better wait until this stops." Anticipation shimmered in his gaze.

She reached into her bag. "Let me check the satellite images on my phone to see how big the storm looks."

"I already did. It's going to continue all night."

Eight

Had John somehow planned this storm along with everything else about this evening? He seemed so vastly in control of his life and nearly everyone else's that it might just be possible. She wasn't a pawn here. She had free will. "I'm sure I can drive in it."

"I won't allow it." He towered over her in the dimly lit kitchen.

"What makes you think you can allow it or not allow it? You're not my boss."

"But I am concerned about your safety. These back roads can wash out in this kind of storm. Some of the worst messes I see as a volunteer firefighter are one-car accidents where someone tried to drive at night in the wrong weather. It's too hard to see the road when you're out in the woods in rainy darkness."

"I suppose you do have a point," she muttered. "But I can't sleep with you."

"I believe we've passed that milestone already."

"I know, but that was a one-time, spur-of-the-moment thing. If I stay over again…"

"It'll mean you actually like me." His teeth flashed in a wicked grin.

She had no idea how to respond to that. Especially since

it was true. "I don't know why I like you. You're insufferably arrogant."

"You find that refreshing because you're used to dealing with wimps."

"That's not true at all." *I'm not used to dealing with anyone.* She couldn't believe she'd actually admitted to John that she hadn't even been on a single date since she broke up with her college boyfriend.

"Then maybe I'm just likable." He crossed the kitchen in two strides and placed his hands on her hips. Heat flared between them. His gentle but insistent kiss left her speechless, and she noticed how her treacherous fingers were already sliding lower to the curve of his backside. How did he do this to her?

She didn't want to tell him she liked him. He might take it the wrong way and think she wanted some kind of real relationship with him. That was impossible, of course.

She knew that. Which was why she shouldn't be here kissing a man who had no honorable intentions toward her.

Nevertheless, she found herself kissing him back with passion that that flowed from somewhere deep inside her. This was the kind of thing they'd warned her about in Sunday school. That her parents tut-tutted over when other girls from her neighborhood had affairs that quickly fizzled out, sometimes leaving them pregnant. They thought you shouldn't even kiss someone until there was a ring or a promise in the picture.

Constance had neither, and yet her fingers now tugged at John's tie and the buttons on his shirt.

"Let's go upstairs." He didn't wait for an answer but swept her along with his powerful arm around her waist. He kissed her neck with each step, caressed her backside as she walked ahead of him. Under his admiring gaze and tender touch she felt unbelievably desirable. She even had a swing in her step she'd never felt before. Being with John Fairweather was doing something very strange to her mind and body.

"This is my room." She walked into an impressive chamber with a beamed cathedral ceiling. A big hand-hewn bed gave the room a masculine air. Framed maps decorated the walls, and she peered at one as they went past. "Those are the historical survey maps of our land and the town around it." They were all different. She could see the territory marked out for the Nissequot shrinking as the maps leaped over the decades. By the early part of the twentieth century, the word *Nissequot* wasn't even there and it was marked as Fairweather Farm.

"They were trying to squeeze you out of existence."

"Almost worked, too."

He wrapped his arms around her from behind as she stood in front of the most recent map. It was from the previous year and showed the Nissequot territory proudly marked in green, expanded and with the casino buildings at its center.

"What's the blue area?"

"That's what we're planning to buy next. Even that won't take us all the way back to our colonial-era hunting grounds, but it'll give us room to grow."

Her heart filled with pride at all he'd accomplished. Which didn't really make sense, since she had nothing to do with it and he wasn't hers to begin with.

"Now, where were we?" He spun her slowly around, sliding his hands along the curve of her waist. The thunder still rumbled outside and rain hammered against the glass of the windows, but it all faded to nothing when his lips touched hers. Her eyes slid closed and she leaned into him, enjoying the closeness she hadn't even known she craved. Lost deep in the kiss, it wasn't until she opened her eyes to undo his belt buckle that she realized all the lights had gone out.

"Have we lost power?"

"Looks that way." He kissed her forehead. "We're generating plenty of our own electricity, so I don't think we need it."

She laughed. "Shouldn't we at least call the electric company?"

"Nah. They can tell when we lose power. The casino and hotel have backup generators, so they won't miss a beat."

He'd taken off her jacket and undone her blouse, and now he unzipped her skirt so it fell to the floor. The black velvet darkness felt very intimate. She managed to get his belt unhooked and his pants and shirt off, which involved some giggling and fumbling. Then they made their way to the soft surface of the bed.

He held her tight as they rolled together, pressing their bodies into the mattress and each other. She loved the heaviness of him, how big he was. When she was on top she kissed his face all over, then eased down to his shoulders and neck, leaving a trail of kisses. She wanted to explore his body, and the total darkness made her bold.

She liked the roughness of the hair on his chest. There wasn't much of it, just enough to create an interesting and masculine texture. She traced it lower, to where she could feel his hardness waiting for her. She let her tongue explore his erection, turning off any whispers in her mind of how this was indulgent and sinful. She loved the way he moved in response to everything she did, aroused to the point where he couldn't keep still. John groaned softly as she took him into her mouth and sucked, then let her tongue play about the tip of his penis.

She'd never done this before. Never even thought about

it! She enjoyed the control she had over him. She could feel the desire, the passion that racked his strong body.

"Oh, Constance. We need to find a condom."

She laughed, so aroused she could hardly think. Thank goodness he was more sensible than she. "I love how you're so responsible."

"It goes with being a leader of the tribe. I don't want to create any new members except on purpose." He chuckled and she heard him groping around in the darkness, opening a door in the nightstand. It reminded her that she was not the first woman to come to his bed. She wouldn't be the last, either.

But as he rolled the condom on in the dark, she didn't seem to care. Constance was so aroused that she took him inside her effortlessly, welcoming him into her body. Still on top, she moved slowly, experimenting with the sensations she created in herself and in him. As pressure built inside her she moved faster, letting the feelings wash over her and surprise her as her body did what it wanted.

John pulled her toward him and rolled them over again so he was on top, then he kissed her softly and started a different rhythm that soon had her gasping aloud and moaning his name.

She'd never done that before, either.

He took her almost to the brink, then pulled back, slowing down and kissing and caressing her until she felt she might burst. She tried to urge him with her hips, but he was too heavy, and only chuckled at her attempts to drive the motion. "Impatient!" he scolded her. "Everything in due time." He moved very slowly and quietly, layering kisses over her ears and neck, heightening the already intense reactions taking place inside her.

She was so aroused that she could barely breathe by the time he finally brought them both to a blistering climax that lit up the darkness with an explosion of inner electricity she'd never even dreamed was possible.

"I saw fireworks," she gasped when she could finally speak again.

"Good," was all he replied, so obnoxiously confident that she wanted to slap him—or hug him. She chose the latter.

John buried his face in her hair. They lay side by side, wrapped in each other. This seduction had taken him by surprise and it just kept gathering steam.

He hadn't realized that looking past her glasses into those hazel eyes would put him under her quiet spell. Now he didn't want Constance to leave at all. The power was back on and a soft light illuminated the room.

"Did you put your glasses somewhere safe?"

"They're on the bedside table." Her soft voice was a balm to his spirit.

"Good. I didn't remember you taking them off and I don't want them to get broken."

"That's sweet of you."

Yeah. She was bringing out the sweet in him. He wanted to cherish her and take care of her. He loved to feel her relaxing in his arms. Letting go of the prickly armor she'd used to hold him at bay. It was magic to feel her opening up and exploring her own sensuality—and driving him half-insane in the bargain.

He kissed her cheek. "You're something else, Constance Allen."

"I'm certainly something else from who I thought I was. There have been a lot of surprises for me here in Massachusetts."

"You're surprised that I'm not the greedy crook the media make me out to be."

"I had no preconceptions about you. I strive to be entirely open-minded. It's essential in my work. If you go in with opinions, it will skew how you perceive the data."

"You had no idea you'd succumb to my famous charms."

"Now that is true." Her eyes sparkled with humor. "I'm still not sure what the heck I'm doing in your arms."

"Relaxing."

"It's not very relaxing knowing that if my boss—or anyone else—found out I'd be fired and probably lose my accounting credentials."

"That's why you're not thinking about that part." He didn't want her to go back to her job and Ohio. He wanted her to stay here.

The thought struck him like a bolt of lightning. The thunder rolling outside echoed a storm that raged quietly in his heart. He was falling for Constance Allen. "Where are you hoping to go next in your career?"

"I'd like to achieve partner eventually. At least, I suppose I would. That's the logical peak of my career. If I manage not to destroy it between now and then."

"Have you ever wanted to do anything else?" Possibilities blossomed in his imagination. She could manage the casino's accounts. After a reasonable cooling-off period from her assignment, of course. Their personal relationship would seem to develop naturally out of her employment at the casino.

Uh-oh. His feelings for Constance were making him creative.

"Not really. When I was younger I wanted to be a teacher, but I grew out of that. I'm better with numbers than people."

He cocked his head. "I can see you being a teacher. And I think you're just fine with people."

"I don't know. What if the kids didn't listen to me?"

Every now and then, when she was bored out of her mind with a particular project, she wondered if she'd made the wrong choice.

"Numbers don't talk back."

"Not often, anyway." Soft and warm, she lay still against his chest. She no longer seemed ready to run away. "Though I'm always hoping that they'll yell at me. Especially in a forensic investigation."

"Like the one you're doing now." He stroked her hair.

"Exactly. I can't believe I'm lying in your arms when I'm going to be combing through your books looking for fraud tomorrow."

"Surely you've seen all you need to see by now. It's hard to prove there's absolutely no wrongdoing, but at what point do you call it quits?"

She stiffened slightly. "When the BIA tells me to."

"They still aren't satisfied?"

"They just want me to be thorough. I'm sure they're as anxious as you are to have everything check out so they can forget about the whole thing."

"I hope so. They could put us right out of business if they had a mind to. Believe me, I have no interest in doing anything that isn't entirely aboveboard. I know we're under scrutiny and that our work can stand up to it."

"Then you have nothing to worry about. I'm sure they'll get bored with paying my hourly rate soon."

"I hope not." He held her tight. "Or I might have to convince you to quit and move here." There, he'd said it. He was clearly losing his sanity, but it was a relief to get it off his chest.

She stilled. "Very funny."

"You think I'm kidding?"

"I know you're kidding."

"Don't be so sure. I like you." He kissed her on the nose. "And you like me, too."

She laughed. "I do. But not enough to throw away my life and career to prolong a steamy affair with you." He heard an odd note in her voice. Sadness. She was already mourning the end of their relationship, even as they lay nestled in each other's arms.

"It doesn't have to end." His voice emerged a little gruffer than he'd intended.

"I suppose you could always move to Ohio." She raised one of her slim brows.

"That wouldn't be ideal."

"See? It's impossible. We have our separate lives already planned out and this is just a big mistake that we couldn't seem to avoid." She said it so seriously that he laughed.

"Speak for yourself. I don't consider this to be a mistake at all. This is the best evening I can remember having. Followed closely by last night."

"You must have a short memory, that's all." She closed her eyes for a second, as if enjoying a thought, then opened them. "You'll have forgotten all about me in a month. In six months you won't even remember my name."

"How could I forget a name like Constance? I can't believe you won't let me call you Connie."

"Knowing you, I can't believe you haven't started doing it anyway, regardless of what I think."

"I'm more sensitive than you take me for." He caressed her soft cheek. "In fact, I can be quite soft hearted."

It was the honest truth. Which he usually kept to himself. He'd prided himself on keeping his emotions in check for a long time. Something about Constance made him want to let his guard down. He knew she wasn't interested in his money, or his notoriety, or even his dashing good looks. To appeal to her he'd have to be honest and prove to her that he wasn't the hard-hearted lothario she believed him to be.

Was he really trying to convince her to stay here? His logical mind argued against it but something deep in his gut told him that if he let her go he'd regret it, possibly for the rest of his life.

"I didn't bring a change of underwear."

"We sell some nice panties in the shop." He grinned. "I can pick some up for you."

"No! That'll just get the staff wondering who they're for. I'll go back to my hotel first thing in the morning. Don't let me sleep in, okay?"

"I'll wake you. Though it will cause me pain to tug you from your dreams." He sounded pretty sappy. For some reason around Constance that felt okay. He could tell she liked it. She had a tiny smile across her mouth and her eyes were closed. She looked utterly relaxed and at peace. Which, considering the circumstances and her personality, was quite something.

He could easily imagine her lying here in his bed, in his arms, for a long time to come. Getting to that point, however, was going to take some careful management of what could be a very explosive situation. He regretted joking around with Don about flirting with her. Though maybe that would help throw him off the scent. He didn't want Don to know about any of this until the time was right, which would likely be months from now, as his uncle could have a big mouth.

Constance Fairweather. The name had an old-fashioned sound that was strangely appealing to him.

Her breathing slowed as she slipped into sleep. All her resistance had evaporated and she was totally comfortable and relaxed here, with him. Of course her family probably wouldn't be too thrilled about him taking her several states away, but they could easily move here and he could build them a nice house like the one his grandparents lived in. He'd learned from experience that all obstacles could be overcome with the right planning and some patience. She liked him, he could tell. There was no way she would be here if she didn't. And he liked her.

So what could go wrong?

Constance was awakened by John's gentle kiss on her cheek. She blinked and took in the sight of his handsome face, wondering if she was still dreaming.

"Good morning, gorgeous. I made us breakfast. You've got plenty of time to eat before hitting the road to your hotel."

"Okay." She must be dreaming. And why wake up?

They ate a feast of fresh fruit and scrambled eggs with toast, drank freshly brewed coffee and juice and chatted about their childhoods, which had both been somewhat outside the mainstream in their own way. As the hands on the vintage wall clock headed toward eight o'clock, she found herself reluctant to leave.

Sitting here chatting with him felt utterly natural. He was just so easy to talk to, and so warm and such a good host. He was spoiling her for all other men. Not that any other men were knocking on her door, but it was going to be hard to find someone whose company she enjoyed as much as John's.

Of course, there was plenty wrong with him. He was far too good-looking. She didn't value looks at all. In fact, they tended to make her assume someone was arrogant and conceited—which in John's case was entirely correct. Yet since his cocky attitude was justified by his impressive competence, somehow it seemed appropriate.

She knew he was a notorious playboy. She was just another notch on his hand-hewn bedpost. One in a long line of women, and probably less enticing than most. Once she went back to Ohio, she'd never see him again and very soon there would be another woman in his bed and sitting here at his kitchen table.

The thoughts made her gut clench with sadness. Which was exactly why she shouldn't have let herself fall into this…liaison in the first place. He could easily add it to his list of pleasurable experiences and move on. She didn't have a list of pleasurable experiences and this was going to stand out as one of the most amazing, unexpected and wonderful events of her life.

Fantastic.

John's phone kept making noises, and eventually he picked it up and looked at his messages. "Sounds like the media's still making noise about Don today."

"Do you think he's done anything wrong?" she couldn't help asking.

"No." He answered quickly. "He's made some…ill-advised choices in the past, but I know he wouldn't do anything to jeopardize what we've built here. He likes people to think he's a bad boy. He thinks it's a cool image. Doesn't bother me. All publicity is good publicity to a certain extent. We're still new enough that a lot of people haven't been here yet and you never know what will get them off the couch."

"Don sounds like quite a character."

"Oh, he is. Sometimes he drives me nuts, but he was the first person to jump on board when I came up with the idea for this place. My grandparents thought it was impossible."

"Why?"

"Too big. Too bold. How can you take a tired dairy farm in the middle of nowhere and turn it into a thriving attraction? But we're not the first, and we won't be the last. Don had faith in my ability to pull it off and he's worked hard to make it happen."

"I can tell you have a lot of affection for him."

"I do. He's my uncle. And under his flashy exterior he's a big softy." John smiled.

Oh, dear. He was being adorable again. Couldn't he be a jerk just to make it easier for her to go back home? "I'd better get going."

"I'll lead the way."

John watched Constance head for the highway to her hotel, then returned to the offices. Don was in the lobby, chatting with one of the desk clerks. He brightened at the sight of John. "Ready for breakfast?"

"I grabbed something at home."

"What'd you do that for?"

"No reason." Don would die laughing if he knew. "Just hungry, that's all." The truth. His night had been rather more athletic than usual. And he still had a distinct spring in his step. Constance was full of intriguing surprises.

"Come have coffee with me then. We can glare at any reporters and scare them off."

"It's usually better to just answer their questions with a smile." Why were reporters still sniffing around? Nothing had happened lately to arouse their suspicion. "Have you seen any today?"

"I had a phone call this morning asking questions about your lady friend."

John stiffened. "Constance?" He realized he might have revealed too much. "Ms. Allen from the BIA?"

Don nodded. "Somehow word got out that they're looking into our books. I suppose they're going on the theory that where there's smoke there's probably a fire."

"But there isn't."

"You know that, and I know that, and we just have to wait for them to realize that."

"Hmm." The press couldn't possibly suspect anything between him and Constance, could they? That would be bad, for her and for him and for the casino. Don didn't seem to suspect anything.

"She good in bed?"

John froze. "Who?"

Don nudged him. "You can't fool me. I've known you since you were two feet high. I can see the way you look at her."

"I have no idea what you're talking about." John maintained a calm demeanor but inside he was starting to sweat. Was his newfound passion for Constance really so obvious? It was essential to keep it a secret until her investigation was over and the results had been announced—for her sake, if not his own.

"Miss Constance Allen, forensic accountant. I bet she's a freak under that conservative suit."

"You're disgusting. Who do we have booked to perform in September?"

"I just booked Jimmy Cliff. I'm working on Celine Dion."

"You keep working. I'm heading up to the office." John headed toward the elevators, blood pumping.

Right now he was ready for Constance to leave.

Not because he didn't want to see her again. Because he wanted to be done with all the secrecy and subterfuge, and that couldn't end until she was no longer investigating him. He needed her to go back to Ohio, wrap up her assignment, and then they could start over again.

And that couldn't happen soon enough.

* * *

Back at her hotel, Constance showered and returned some phone calls. It was Friday and the perfect day to pack up and leave, but for some reason she had a feeling she'd no longer be irritated by a request to stay for a few more days. She wasn't ready to say goodbye to John. In fact she was secretly hoping they'd get to spend at least one more night together.

She knew such thoughts were possibly signs of appalling moral degeneration, but she couldn't remember ever having this much fun with anyone before, and she wasn't ready to go back to her humdrum existence yet.

She called the BIA with considerable trepidation. She was starting to feel like a total fraud as far as they were concerned. If they knew what she was up to with John, they'd fire her firm on the spot and probably sue her for damaging their reputation. She decided to mention the closest thing to a discovery that she'd come across. "Don Fairweather gambles in the casino. He had substantial winnings last year. More than fifty thousand."

"Did he pay taxes on his winnings?"

"I'm not sure. I haven't looked at the individual tribal members' tax returns."

"Request them, and take a look."

"Which members?" Was she going to have to look into the returns of every low-level staffer? She felt like rubbing her hands together. That would take several days.

She didn't want to look into John's, though. That seemed far too personal.

"Anyone who's been gambling," Nicola replied. "You'll quickly find out who's honest. And request returns for the key players, including John Fairweather. Take a look at income, expenses, deductions. Poke around a bit. Look into at least five people in total."

"Aren't tax returns confidential? What if they won't allow me access?"

"Then I'll secure a subpoena."

Constance felt jumpy and anxious as she pulled back into the casino parking lot. Personal income tax records? Many people didn't even like sharing the information with their spouse. She took the elevator up to the offices, hoping John wasn't there. It was awkward seeing him in the professional context of the office after what had gone on between them. She always felt her blood heat at the first glimpse of him, then that embarrassing slow smile wanting to creep across her face. And she'd rather request his tax records in a polite text or email than have to look into his eyes while she asked to pry into his personal business.

Of course he was there. Larger than life and twice as handsome. He was talking to a man she recognized from the cashier's office as she approached, but he dismissed him with a nod. The twinkle in his eyes warred with his cool and professional demeanor.

"Hi, Constance."

She straightened her shoulders and tried to affect a disinterested expression. "Good morning." As if she was saying it for the first time.

"Good morning. I trust you slept well." His low voice caused awareness to ripple through her. They walked toward his office together.

"Very well, thank you." He should know. He'd had to wake her up from her blissful slumber. She kept her voice clipped. "Can I speak to you in private?"

"Of course." They took the elevator up to his office. She could feel his curiosity heating the atmosphere as they rode up in silence. She did her best to avoid his glance, afraid of the effect it might have on her.

She took a deep breath. "My contact at the BIA has

requested that I look into the personal tax returns of several key people."

His expression darkened. "Who?"

"You." She spat it right out. She'd chosen people from different departments and in different stages of life so there would be some variety, and she'd included the three gamblers. "Your uncle Don, Paul McGee, Mona Lester, Susan Cummings, Anna Martin and Darius Carter."

"Darius? He's just a kid. He barely even pays taxes."

She shrugged. She'd picked him because he held a key role in the day-to-day running of the casino. "Shall I speak to each person individually?"

"Why these people?"

"They were chosen more or less at random." She didn't want to go into detail. It really wasn't his business. He must have read her reluctance because he paused for a moment, but didn't ask more questions.

"I'll talk to them." His brow had furrowed.

"Do you think any of them will object?"

"I'll make sure they don't. Besides, we all filed the taxes already, so what is there to hide?"

"Exactly."

"I'll have them all for you by the end of the day."

"Much appreciated." Phew. That was easy. As long as none of the individuals objected, of course.

"I want to kiss you." His voice was ripe with suggestion.

"I don't think that's a good idea." Her own voice was barely a whisper. Her lips twitched to do exactly what he'd suggested. "I have work to do."

"So do I. But that doesn't stop me wanting you."

"You're trouble."

"I can't argue with you. I certainly seem to be trouble where you're concerned." They'd reached his office. "Though I don't have any regrets."

He closed the door. They kissed for a solid five minutes, tongues tangling and biting each other's lips until their breath came in ragged gasps.

"I used to be a dignified professional, I'll have you know," she stammered when their lips finally parted.

"I used to be a sane man. Since you showed up here everything has gone out the window." Cool and calm as always, in his dark gray suit and pale blue shirt he looked the picture of sanity. Of course he was probably just pretending to be besotted with her. Or maybe even allowing himself to be as a temporary condition. He'd be over her before she even drove across the Ohio state line. "I hope it will take a while to go through all our returns."

"I hope not. It's embarrassing and totally unprofessional, but I really don't want to find anything wrong here." She couldn't believe she'd confessed that to him.

"Uh-oh. I hope I'm not compromising your professional integrity." His wicked grin warmed her as his big hands squeezed her hips gently.

"Nothing could compromise my professional integrity. Believe me, if I found something, I'd report it."

"I love that about you, Constance. I bet everyone always knows where they stand with you."

"I used to think so. I'm sure my employer would be rather surprised if they knew you were squeezing my butt right now."

He slid his hand back up to her waist with a rueful expression. "True. But since our intimacy doesn't affect your professional integrity, they really shouldn't mind at all."

"Perhaps not, but I'm sure they would." She straightened his pale yellow tie, which had gotten crooked. "Now you and I should at least pretend to do some work. Preferably in separate rooms, as we don't seem to be too professional anymore when we're in the same space."

"All right, Constance. I'll see you later, and I'll have everyone go home at lunch and pick up their tax returns."

"Perfect." Could it really be that easy? "And I might need to speak to each of them individually after I've had a chance to look over the paperwork. I might even need to look at their personal banking records to make sure everything adds up." She held her breath. No one wanted a total stranger looking into their personal finances. On the other hand, it was one of her favorite things to request, since the person's reaction told you a lot about how honest they were.

"I'll warn them. And I consider myself warned." He winked. He didn't look at all worried, which was quite a relief.

She had one more question for him. One she already knew the answer to. "Do any of the tribal members gamble in the casino?"

"I don't do it myself and I prefer that other employees don't. Besides, they know better than anyone that over time the house always wins. Don likes to play a little, but no one else gambles regularly. Believe me, I keep close tabs on all our employees, especially the younger ones."

"Does Don win?"

"He says he does." John winked. "Whether he's telling the truth is a whole different story. We do keep files on employee gambling, though."

"Could I take a look at those?" No need to mention that she'd already seen them and knew Don had big winnings. It would be interesting to see from Don's tax return whether he was claiming them. She felt a little guilty pretending to be totally in the dark, but at least now she felt as though she was actually doing her job.

"Of course." He leaned over the laptop on the desk and tapped a few keys. The file she'd found by herself popped up. "You won't find my name in there."

"I'm glad that you don't gamble."

"Me, too. It's much safer being the house than trying to beat it."

He didn't even glance at the file, so confident that the records were all aboveboard and would speak for themselves. She loved how honorable John was. Another kiss on the lips and a warm hug left her dizzy. Her heart ached as the door closed behind him. If parting from him now hurt her even a little, how was she going to feel when he was gone for good?

Nine

John didn't invite her over that night. She didn't know whether to be relieved or disappointed as she drove back to her hotel, the employees' tax returns sitting on her passenger seat. He probably had some kind of meeting. Or something important to do. Or bigger plans. It was Friday night, after all.

If she had a life she'd drive back to Ohio for the weekend. But it made more sense to stay here, save the gas money and bill more hours.

For dinner, she ate a Chinese chicken salad and drank a Diet Coke at her hotel room desk while she watched the news. The pile of tax returns now stared at her from the end of her bed. She was literally afraid to look at them. Normally the prospect of delving into freshly unearthed personal papers filled her with unreasonable glee. Now it just made her nervous about confronting her own principles.

What if she found something in John's tax return? Excessive write-offs or under-reporting of taxes owed, maybe. She'd be duty bound to report her findings, or even any suspicions. Should she tell him first, so he'd have a chance to explain? She'd told him she would, but that would go in the face of everything she'd learned about forensic accounting. Never give people a chance to cover their tracks.

He hadn't said anything at all about whether it was easy or hard to convince the employees to hand over their returns. Maybe they respected him so much they'd do anything he asked. She'd expected at least someone to put up a fight. So far it was all going too smoothly. For reasons she couldn't put her finger on, that made her nervous.

She picked his tax return off the pile first with trembling fingers. His income was exorbitant, of course, but most of it was from personal investments that had nothing whatsoever to do with New Dawn. He'd only paid himself a salary of one hundred thousand from the casino and hotel. That impressed her. He'd taken plenty of personal deductions and travel expenses, but nothing out of the ordinary. His return looked similar to many she'd seen belonging to successful company owners and high-level executives. He'd paid a great deal in taxes, mostly capital-gains tax, so the government should be quite happy to have John Fairweather as a taxpayer. After several hours combing through the schedules, she heaved a sigh of relief and moved on.

Darius's and Anna's returns reflected their modest incomes and were totally uncomplicated, and they'd both received a small amount of money back when they filed. Anna had reported her small gambling winnings, so there was no problem there. Mona had gotten divorced in the middle of the year, so her return was more elaborate, but still nothing to arouse suspicion.

She left Don's for last. It was almost as thick as John's and she soon discovered that he actually earned more than John from New Dawn. No doubt it was John's way of keeping a senior family member happy. Still, the salary was far from outrageous for a senior executive at such a profitable enterprise, and Don had paid taxes at a high rate and taken fairly reasonable deductions.

But as she combed through the schedules, she saw nothing at all about proceeds from personal gambling. Her Spidey-sense tingled with alarm. Normally this was a good feeling that she was about to earn her keep and justify her employment at a top accounting firm. But right now it came with an uncomfortable sense of foreboding. She went through the return again. Still no sign of any winnings or losses. Since the casino workers openly admitted to him gambling, and she'd seen him do it with her own eyes, it was clearly an omission. Even though table games like roulette and blackjack didn't require that the casino submit Form W2-G to the IRS, the gambler was certainly required to declare winnings and she'd seen the records detailing Don's fifty thousand dollars in profits.

Her phone rang and she almost jumped out of her skin. It was Lynn from work. What was she doing calling on a Friday night? "Hi." Constance hoped she could get her off the phone quickly.

"I hope you're back in Cleveland because you're the only person I know who will go see the new Disney movie with me."

Constance couldn't help laughing. "I would love to see it, but I'm still in Massachusetts."

"Why didn't you drive home for the weekend? I guess you can't bring yourself to leave the sexy casino boss."

"What? You're crazy. I barely even see him." She realized she'd spoken too fast and too loud.

"Oh, boy. I did hit a nerve. I always knew you'd be interested if the right man came along."

"You're talking nonsense. I could care less about John Fairweather."

Lynn laughed. "Don't you mean *couldn't* care less? If you could care less then it means you care quite a bit."

"You know what I mean." Constance leaped to her feet and paced in her small hotel room. "I'm only interested in his financial data." Now she was lying to her closest friend. "Which is checking out fine."

"What a bummer. I was hoping for a dramatic exposé and scandal that would lead to a big bonus for you next spring."

"I'm just doing my job. I have no expectations of any kind when I look into a company's books."

"I know, I know. It's just so much more interesting when you find information that someone was trying to hide."

Now would be the perfect time to mention the telling absence of gambling data on Don Fairweather's tax return. Yet she kept quiet. She'd promised to tell John about anything she found. It chilled her to realize that she felt more loyalty to John than to her own firm. Still, she wouldn't lie or cover anything up. As soon as she'd told John, she'd report back to her firm, and to the BIA.

Hopefully since it was just a personal matter, and not to do with the casino itself, it would be a storm in a teacup and blow over quickly.

"You're very quiet. Are you okay?" She'd almost forgotten Lynn was still on the phone.

"I'm fine. Just a bit preoccupied. These last few days have been a blur of numbers and figures. Casino books make corporate records look refreshingly dreary by comparison. I can't wait to settle back into my peacefully dull routine."

"Nothing's dull around here. Whitlow gave his resignation. It turned out Lacey wasn't the first young employee who's been under his desk. There's a class action suit in the works. It's all anyone's talking about."

"Wow." That could mean a partnership spot opening up. Not that she'd be eligible. She'd likely be considered too young. Still…

"Old goat. It's amazing what men will risk for a little nooky. Makes you glad to be a woman."

She laughed. "Hardly. The men who get themselves into trouble are usually doing something with a woman." Someone like her, for example, who would apparently risk her career for a few brief moments of bliss.

It didn't make any sense at all, yet she'd done it.

"True. Humans are irrational creatures. That's what makes us so interesting."

"Yes, indeed." She'd turned out to be far more dangerously human than she'd ever expected.

"Do you need anything?" Lynn's question took her by surprise.

"Not that I can think of. I'm sure I'll be back next week."

"And you've found nothing at all?"

She hesitated. "I'll tell you everything when I get back."

"So you did find something?" Lynn's voice was a breathy whisper.

"Don't twist my words. I'm still investigating." The last thing she needed was the office administrator sparking rumors.

"My lips are sealed."

"Good. Keep them that way and have a good weekend. I've got to go."

Constance hung up the phone, breathing a little faster than usual. She really wished she hadn't given Lynn the idea that something was up. On the other hand, it would have been weird to say she'd found nothing, then reveal in a day or two that in fact she had uncovered tax fraud. This whole situation was getting far too complicated.

And now she had to tell John. She wanted to email him

or text him, but somehow putting words in print felt wrong. They could be saved and used in some kind of legal situation. She didn't want to call him in case the phones were monitored. He might even record incoming and outgoing calls himself as some kind of protection. And she knew it was inappropriate to tell him before reporting back to the people who had hired her.

There was nothing for it but to hunt him down in person and figure out what to do from there.

When Constance arrived at the casino the next morning, John was in the lobby talking to Don. Since it was the weekend they had on more casual clothing: John wore a fitted shirt and faded jeans that hugged his powerful thighs and Don was dressed all in black like a movie mobster. She tugged her gaze away and headed for the bank of elevators. She didn't want to have to make polite conversation with a man she was about to report for tax fraud. Who knew how many years he'd been doing it? He could be in for a hefty fine or even a prison term.

She had no choice but to pass quite close to the two men, but she skirted around an electronic display that showed a list of the day's events so they couldn't see her.

"It's a good thing she's sweet on you." As she passed by, Don's words made her ears prick. "I don't like her snooping through our tax records. Make sure you wine and dine her tonight. We don't want her getting creative." Constance froze, despite knowing she was in a crowded lobby where others could see her, even if John and his uncle couldn't. Did Don know they were having an affair?

"My tax records are entirely accurate and I assume yours are, too." John's voice sounded dismissive. And why didn't he say something about her not being bribable? She was offended that he didn't defend her honor. On the other hand, maybe that would have been too much. He was being subtle.

Don laughed. Which sounded very false under the circumstances. "Don't you worry about me. She won't find anything in my taxes. And I'm the one who told you seducing her was a good idea. You should listen to me more often."

Constance's mouth dropped open and her heart hammered. She glanced at the bank of elevators, which now seemed about a mile away across the shiny marble floor. Had they planned this together? Was she a victim of a plot between them?

She blinked, hardly able to believe it.

"Don't be too smart for your own good, Don." John's voice made her jump. Wasn't he going to deny that they had planned her seduction? Her breathing became audible and she looked around, hoping no one was watching. She couldn't believe they were having this conversation right in the lobby where anyone could hear it.

John was now asking about a band due to perform that night. He'd simply changed the subject without contradicting Don? A sense of betrayal crept over her and chilled her blood. Suddenly she was glad she'd found the discrepancy in Don's taxes. John deserved the media's ugly attention and anything that came from it if he was the kind of person who'd deliberately set out to charm and cajole her into bed for his own purposes.

She lifted her chin and marched for the elevators as fast as she could, praying that no one would talk to her. She counted the seconds while she waited for an elevator to take her up to the office floor. What a disaster.

"Hey, Constance, where are you going?" John's voice boomed across the marble space. "It's Saturday."

She spun around.

"Up to the office floors. They are open on the weekends, I hope." She responded as primly as she could. How could he talk to her so casually in full view of the other employees and guests? Did he want them all to know they'd been intimate? Probably he did. Maybe he thought it was funny.

"Weren't you even going to say hello?"

"I could see you were in conference."

"In conference?" He laughed. "Don was just telling me about the new Maserati he ordered. Crazy. I told him I hope I won't get to practice using the Jaws of Life on it."

No mention of Don's thanking him for seducing her. And his own complicit silence. "Can we meet in your office?" She needed to talk to him. They'd gone too far for her to just go back home, report her findings and pretend they'd never slept together. The situation could blow up in her face if he decided to retaliate. Her hands were shaking and she hoped she wouldn't cry.

"But of course." His voice contained more than a hint of suggestion. "I'd be delighted to get you behind closed doors."

She glanced up at the security cameras. She hadn't even noticed them before. Hopefully no one ever listened to the tapes. "It's something serious."

All humor vanished from his expression. "About the returns?" And his voice was hushed.

"Let me tell you upstairs."

John closed the door behind them, and for once this did not lead to a passionate kiss. Which was good, because she would have had to slap him. "Is there something wrong?"

Her heart beat so fast she could barely think. "It's Don's return. He didn't declare any gambling winnings."

He frowned. "He certainly should have."

She swallowed. "The company records detail substantial winnings. You can see them for yourself in your own files."

"I'm sure there's some explanation."

She drew in an unsteady breath. "I'm telling you first because I promised I would." Though now she was having second thoughts about it. Did he really deserve it if he'd only flirted with her for his own protection? "But I have to tell my boss at Creighton Waterman, and I have to tell the BIA."

"Give me some time to figure out what's going on. I'll talk to Don."

"I can't. I'm paid to do a job here. I have to report what I found and I've already done something wrong by telling you first." *On top of all the other things I've done wrong in your bed.*

"He must have forgotten to report the winnings. Don has more money than he knows what to do with. I told you about the Maserati."

"There may well be a reasonable explanation, but I'm here to look for discrepancies and I found one. You admitted yourself that he gambles, and I've heard the same from other employees." She lifted her chin and defied him to argue with her.

"He makes no secret of it."

"Yet he didn't mention it on his tax return."

John drew in a long breath, swelling his broad chest. For a split second she ached to hug him, but instead she held herself stiffly at bay. He frowned. "Don's a key employee here. Something like this could really damage the casino's reputation. You know the kind of scrutiny we're under. I can't afford the bad publicity."

"If you don't want bad publicity perhaps you should be more careful about how you conduct yourself. Seducing the accountant who's sent to inspect your accounts probably isn't too smart, for a start." She braced for his response, glad she'd been bold enough to say it.

"That took me by surprise as much as you."

"Oh, really. That's not what I overheard downstairs."

He frowned. "You overheard Don? He was just kidding around."

"And you didn't contradict him."

His expression softened. "I didn't want to dignify his innuendo with a response. He really has no idea what happened between us."

She swallowed. "Good. As you can imagine I would appreciate it if you didn't discuss our indiscretions with anyone."

"Of course not. I never would." He held out his hand, but she stayed rigid.

"Everything that happened between us was a mistake and I regret it. Now I have a responsibility to report my findings to the people who hired me."

He took in a long slow breath, his expression grim. "The BIA is going to come down on us all like a ton of bricks."

"I have to do my job."

"I can see that." His jaw was set. She wondered for a tense moment if he'd attempt to flirt and cajole her out of making her report. He didn't. He watched her silently for what felt like an eternity.

She realized at last how utterly vulnerable she was. Her future, her career lay in this man's hands. He could end it, and ruin her reputation, in a single phone call if he chose.

"I understand." His words were cool, controlled. His eyes didn't plead with her, but the emotion she saw in them reminded her of the tender moments they'd shared.

At least she'd thought at the time they were tender moments.

"I'm going to call my contact now." She picked up her bag, burning with the desire to get out of here as fast as possible and never come back. He opened the door and stepped aside. Heat and tension flashed between them as she passed him.

Or maybe that was only in her imagination.

She heard the door click shut behind her after she passed through it, and her heart almost broke as she realized this would be the very last time she'd ever see John.

John pressed his body against the door, partly to stop himself from jerking it back open and striding after Constance. It was no use trying to argue with her. Her mind was made up and she was going to report what she found.

Could Don really have been stupid enough to fail to report his gambling activities?

He already knew the answer in his gut. He also knew how enthusiastically the circling media vultures would eat up the story.

And he couldn't even call Don, or a lawyer, because in doing so he'd have to reveal that Constance gave him privileged information. He wouldn't betray her confidence. She'd done him a big favor by telling him what she'd found. More so when she now suspected that he'd seduced her as a means to an end. He'd wanted to argue with her and try to convince her that his feelings for her came from the heart but there was no way she'd believe him now. She'd assume he was trying to butter her up and convince her to conceal her findings, which would only make her more suspicious and angry.

He cursed and banged his fist on the door. Why did life have to get so complicated? Everything was going smoothly until Constance Allen came along. His once-wild uncle had seemed to be settling into the life of a prosperous and trustworthy executive. Everyone in the tribe was getting along well, which was no easy feat when you brought people from all over the country to a small town in the sticks. And business was booming.

Now the harsh spotlight would fall on them once again. John knew as well as anyone that if someone was looking for a reason to make the Nissequot disappear, they could try to use this as a starting point and keep the tribe tied up in legal wrangling until the moon turned blue. That was much the same strategy that had been used by the powers that be to whittle away the tribe's land and population in the first place.

His number-one priority was to make sure that didn't happen. His second priority would be to forget all about Constance Allen. Her findings threatened to tear the fabric of the tribe. If anyone found out he'd been intimate with her while she was looking for dirt on them, it would undermine their trust in him. Don already suspected that they'd had an affair. John certainly hadn't confirmed his uncle's suspicions, but maybe by simply ignoring Don's snide comments, he'd tacitly admitted something. He'd have to manage Don carefully—never an easy feat—to make sure he didn't decide to throw hints to the press and make this ugly situation into a hot scandalous mess that could bring them all down.

He growled in frustration. Just this morning life had looked so rosy and promising. He'd missed having Constance in his bed last night due to preexisting plans with an old friend, but he'd consoled himself with the prospect of having her there for many years to come.

Not anymore. It had literally never crossed his mind that she would find something amiss. He knew the books of this casino way better than he knew the backs of his hands, and he'd vouch for them with his life. The financial affairs of the tribal members were also his concern, and he'd been pretty confident about them, too.

But Don? Apparently the smoke the media was fanning had come from a fire somewhere, and who knew what else that slippery old devil might be up to. His hand itched to pick up his phone and call his uncle, but he held the urge in check. He owed Constance that much.

But no more.

Tears blurred Constance's eyes by the time she hurried across the parking lot to her car. She climbed in and slammed the door, started the ignition with trembling fingers, and pulled out of the parking lot as fast as she could. She felt like a traitor here, which was ridiculous since she had no personal allegiance to the New Dawn casino. She shouldn't have any personal feelings for its founder, either.

The problem was that she did. Hearing that he'd discussed seducing her with his uncle should kill them stone dead. Was she a fool to believe John's denial? She wanted to believe him. And she remembered only too well how wonderful she'd felt with John's arms around her. How she'd come alive in his bed, letting herself explore a sensual and passionate side she'd never dared admit to before.

It would be very hard to just bury all those feelings again, even if the relationship had been in the wrong place, at the wrong time, with the wrong man.

She needed to call the BIA as soon as possible, just in case John did succumb to the temptation to warn his uncle. She couldn't afford to have word get out that she'd spoken to him about her findings. Nicola Moore had told her to get in touch at any time of the day or night if she had something important to report. She pulled into the parking lot of a fast-food restaurant and dialed Nicola Moore's cell number.

When Nicola answered, Constance got right to the point. "I'm sorry to call you on the weekend, but I've found a discrepancy." She kept her voice as calm as she could. "It might be nothing—" she swallowed "—but I've done all the research I can reasonably do into the situation from my end."

She told Moore about Don's reported gambling and its absence from his tax return. She'd only looked at one year, but she knew that this probably wasn't an isolated issue. From here on out it would be a matter for the IRS to investigate further. Her work was done, and she should feel a sense of pride and accomplishment in it, yet somehow she felt just the opposite.

"Good work. This will give us a foothold for further investigation."

"I didn't find any irregularities in the financials for the casino itself, just for this one executive." She wanted to limit the damage she'd cause to the New Dawn's reputation. Not that it should be any of her business.

"We've had our eye on Don Fairweather for some time. It's hard to understand why John Fairweather lets him play a substantial role in the company when he has a shady past."

"He's not directly involved in the financial operations at all. He books the bands and handles PR." Constance heard herself speaking quickly, defending John's choice to employ his uncle, and cursed herself for standing up for him. Obviously, she still cared about him. She'd let herself believe that he had real feelings for her, and now she felt foolish for being so gullible. She couldn't get away fast enough. She knew that John felt strongly about including all members of the family—and by extension the Nissequot tribe—and managing them appropriately. She also knew he couldn't control their personal choices.

"So I'm done here, right? It would be really awkward for me to hang around after making these accusations." She realized that didn't sound professional. In reality it had been awkward all along to have people know she was there looking for trouble. But she truly couldn't stand it if she had to see John again now that she knew the truth about his involvement with her.

"Yes, we'll have our legal team take it from here. Just forward all the relevant paperwork to me and I'll be in touch if I need anything further. Good work."

Heart heavy, Constance gathered her belongings from her hotel room and immediately began the long, lonely drive back to Ohio. Back to her former life of quiet work in her gray office and quiet evenings at home with her parents.

No kisses waited for her. No strong arms. No fiery passion to bring her body to life.

The worst part was that somehow her mind—or her body—couldn't accept that it was all over. She kept waiting for the phone to ring. For John to say that he'd known all along she was there for a reason, that it didn't make any difference that she'd done her job, even if it meant his family member would get in trouble.

Part of her still believed that what they'd shared was real. They'd had such great conversations, and experienced so much intimacy. Surely even if he'd started out to soften her up for business reasons, it had developed into something more. Or was it all in her head?

They hadn't even said goodbye. The last thing he'd said to her was, "I understand." But did he?

Would he have preferred for her to lie to her boss? To lie to the BIA? Then his little plan would have really paid off. She would have proved that she'd really loved him. Lucky thing she was not the kind of person who would ever do that. If she had nothing else left, at least she had her integrity, and of that she was fiercely proud.

At the office that Monday, her boss, Lucinda Waldron, was all smiles. "Well done, Constance. This was a tough assignment and once again you've proven yourself to be one of our rising stars. And it's a real bonus that you don't have a family to worry about. It's hard to find an employee who doesn't mind spending some time away from home. I have an interesting assignment coming up in Omaha that I think you'd be perfect for. I should know more details in a day or two."

"Great." She managed a smile. Omaha? And why not? As her boss pointed out, she had no life and no obligations. Not even a pet to worry about. They could ship her all over the country to ferret through companies' books and no one would even care except her parents, who would have to do their own dishes after dinner.

In her office she looked through her in-box with a heavy heart. All the employee expense reports for the last three months were in there. She was chosen to go through them, as she was considered the most trustworthy and least indulgent employee. Lynn had told her that just the idea that Constance Allen would be checking their expenses kept people from putting frivolous items on there.

Great.

"I've found the perfect man for you." Lynn peeped around her door.

"Shh! Someone will hear you." She didn't want to chat about men and dating. The whole thing seemed like a really bad idea. Obviously her judgment was questionable at best and who knew what might happen if she started putting herself in the way of available men so soon after John.

"It's not a crime to date, you know. Do you remember Lance from corporate?"

"I'd never date a coworker." And mostly she remembered Lance's receding chin. Which wasn't fair, really, as he had always been perfectly nice to her.

"You won't have to. He offered his resignation. He's going to KPMG."

"Which likely means he'll be moving to a different city. Long distance would never work."

"Why not? Better than not dating at all. Besides, you could always move."

"Leave Cleveland? What would my parents do?"

"I'm sure they'd survive."

"I'm not attracted to him."

"You barely know him. You have to give someone a chance. You might have amazing chemistry."

She looked right at Lynn. "Are you attracted to him?"

Lynn bit her lip and thought for a moment. "No. But I figured you'd want someone stable and quiet and…"

"Boring? What if I want someone wild and dangerous and exciting?" She leaned back in her chair. "What if I want someone totally different from me, who can help shake me out of my dull and rigid existence and make me look at the world with fresh eyes?"

Lynn stared at her. "Do you?"

She adjusted her glasses. "I don't want to date anyone." There was no way she could even consider looking at another man while John's handsome face hovered in her consciousness. And while his betrayal echoed in her heart. She still could hardly believe their whole affair had been planned from the start. "I have too many other things going on."

"Like reorganizing your bookshelf?"

"There's a church fund-raiser to plan."

"There's always a church fund-raiser to plan. I'm not going to let you waste your life anymore. It's time you burst out of your shell." Lynn winked and walked away.

Constance sank back in her chair. If only Lynn knew that she'd already left her shell and would never be happy in it again.

Ten

John walked into Don's rather lavish office and threw the newspapers down on his desk. "See what you've done?" Stories about the tax evasion had leaked to the press—or been planted.

"It's a load of bull."

"So you didn't gamble and win that money?" He crossed his arms and waited for a response.

"I don't remember."

"That won't cut it."

"It's worked for some American presidents I could name."

"Well, you aren't one, and you aren't senile either, so you'd better hire a lawyer and figure out what the two of you are going to say. The New Dawn is not going under the bus with you, Don. You know how I feel about following the rules. We're under way more scrutiny than the average business and I don't condone any activity that could even be seen as bending the rules."

"Sometimes you need to redefine a rule."

"Now is not one of those times. Since you aren't denying that you've gambled and failed to declare it, I have no choice but to terminate your position."

Don rose to his feet, frowning. "Are you kicking me out of the tribe, too?"

"This is business, Don, purely business. You'll always be family, but I can't have you working at the New Dawn while you're under investigation for breaking the law."

"Is it a paid leave of absence?"

John clenched his hand into a fist. "Is this my hand or is it a deadly weapon?"

"All right, all right. I can't believe you're just kicking me out. Whatever happened to innocent until proven guilty?"

"If you were declaring your innocence, I might feel differently, but you're not. I trusted you, Don. You've been my confidant and right-hand man at almost every phase of this project. I can't believe you'd risk it all to save yourself a few pennies you can well afford to part with."

"I'll pay whatever I owe."

"You know it won't be as easy as that. They're going to dig into your papers going back years."

His uncle's face darkened. "That won't be good. I told you I didn't want you to give her my returns."

"You didn't tell me it's because they were fraudulent."

"I didn't write any lies on them. I may have just not told the whole truth."

John suppressed a curse. "All this could have been easily avoided if you just did what you were supposed to do." Despite his anger, John felt a twinge of sorrow for Don. Why were some people constitutionally unable to play by the rules? "If you think a law is wrong then you can work to change it. You can't just ignore it."

Don shoved some items from his drawer—expensive Cross pens, technological gadgets—into his leather briefcase. "Everything's easy for you. You've always been the golden boy."

"I've worked my ass off for everything I've achieved and I'm not going to let you throw it all away." John wanted to take Don by the scruff of the neck and hurl him down the hallway, but he restrained himself. He also wanted to cuss his uncle out for ruining all his elaborate plans to keep Constance in his life, but he knew better than to clue Don in to that secret.

Don looked up from his desk and peered at him. "Shame you didn't use your charm to run Constance Allen off the property as I suggested."

"Charm usually has the opposite effect."

"Not on a sexless automaton like that one. A calculator in a suit."

John's hands were forming fists again without his permission. "You keep your thoughts on Ms. Allen to yourself."

"Oh, did I touch a nerve? I suppose you've seen more of what's under that suit than I gave you credit for. What if I tell the press about that, huh?"

"You wouldn't."

"Wouldn't I?"

"There's nothing to tell," he growled. "Just get out of here before I throw you out." Fury churned in his gut. Now that Constance had overturned Don's applecart, there was basically no way he could invite her into the family without it causing a major rift. Not that she'd want to come, anyway. He'd promised her all would be aboveboard, only to be proved wrong by his own flesh and blood. And now she thought he'd seduced her in a deliberate ploy to interfere with her investigation.

"I can see you have feelings for her." Don hoisted his bag onto his shoulder.

"I don't. Except that I'm mad she wouldn't let me deal with this myself. I could have made you declare all your back taxes without dragging the law into this."

A knock on the door made them both turn. "Mr. Fairweather." Angie, one of the desk clerks, appeared. "The police are here."

"I knew they'd turn up sooner or later." John shoved a hand through his hair. "Why not just send them up?"

"I'm so glad you're back home, dear." Constance peeled carrots while her mom chopped chicken breast for a pie. She'd been home for three days and they'd all settled back into their dull, familiar routine as if she'd never left. "Maybe you can talk some sense into your father about eating better. His cholesterol still isn't down where it should be and he keeps insisting on eggs and sausage for breakfast in the morning. He's even making it himself when I refuse."

"I'll bake some healthy muffins tomorrow morning. I think the best strategy is to tempt him away from the bad things he loves rather than just making him eat stuff he hates."

"You're so right, dear. I hadn't really thought of that. I've been trying to convince him to eat oatmeal and he won't even touch it. I knew you'd come up with something. I hope your job isn't going to send you away again."

"Actually my boss was talking about an assignment in Omaha. They seem to like the fact that I'm single and have no obligations."

"But you have an obligation to me and your father. You should tell them that."

"You should get used to me being gone, Mom. What if I get married?"

Her mom laughed. "You? You're married to your job. I can't even imagine you with a man. And honestly, sometimes I think they're more trouble than they're worth."

Constance's grip tightened on the peeler. Did her own mother seriously not think that she'd want to get married and have a family? Then again, why should she? Constance hadn't dated anyone at all the entire time she'd been living at home and she'd rebuffed several efforts to set her up with people she had no interest in or attraction to.

The truth was, she hadn't been interested in anyone until she met John. Why did she have to finally fall for someone so unsuitable and impossible? It could never have worked out, even if their affair hadn't been a shocking breach of professional conduct. He was a seasoned playboy who had apparently seduced her for his own purposes—at least initially—and if they hadn't been torn apart by circumstance he would have grown bored with her and cast her aside eventually.

"Why are your hands shaking?" Constance saw her mom's penetrating gray gaze fall on her fingers and she tried to peel faster. "I knew you never should have gone to that den of vice. You've looked like a ghost ever since you got back. Sally told me she read on the internet there's a big investigation going on there now. Tax evasion. I told her it was you that found out about it." She clucked her tongue. "Hardly a surprise, of course. It's always the people with the most money who are least willing to part with it. Still, I'm sure it was exhausting having to interact with people like that."

"I'm just tired." No need to mention all the stray emotion racking her and keeping her awake at night. "It was a challenging job. A lot of papers and computer files to go through. I worked really long hours." *And then played even longer hours.*

The memory of John's strong arms around her haunted her in the dead of night. Her body still tingled with awareness whenever she thought of him. Which was unfair, because she knew that right now he must hate her.

She'd seen the stories online. Don had been arrested

and charged with tax evasion and John had bailed him out with five hundred thousand dollars of his own money. He certainly wouldn't be lying around in bed thinking about how much he missed the woman who'd given the IRS probable cause for a full investigation of New Dawn. There was even talk of the casino being closed down while it was under investigation, and she knew from her examination of the books that would mean millions in losses for John and the tribe.

When he thought of her it must be with resentment and anger. Still, if she had to do it over, she wouldn't do anything differently. She'd bent her rules by leaking the information about John's uncle to him, but in the end, she'd stuck to her principles and done the job she was paid to do.

The affair with John was a whole different story. Would she let that happen again? She wasn't entirely sure she'd let it happen in the first place. It had just happened. What evolved between them had crept over her like a thunderstorm and she suspected there was nothing she could have done to control or stop the thunder and lightning flashing in her body—and her heart—when John was around.

Lucky thing she wouldn't see him again. The IRS had taken over the investigation and her firm had sent their final bill to the BIA. She could wash her hands of the whole sticky mess.

Except that she couldn't get John Fairweather out of her mind.

She'd just scraped the carrot peelings into the bin and was removing the full bag when the door to the kitchen flung open and her dad peered in. "Son of a gun, Constance, you're not going to believe what that fellow on the news just said."

"What, Dad?" Probably something to do with the upcoming local election he was up in arms about.

"That Native American from the casino who was arrested for tax evasion just claimed that the leader of the tribe engaged in personal relations with the accountant who came to investigate them. Isn't that you?"

Constance fumbled and the bin liner and its contents spilled onto the floor. "What?" Her voice was a shaky whisper. Blood roared in her ears. Or maybe it was the sound of her whole world crashing down around her.

"Said he wasn't the only one bending a few rules and he thought people should know the truth about the BIA's investigator who pointed the finger at him." Her dad's voice trailed off as he surveyed the mess on the floor. "It's not true, is it, sweet?"

She scrambled to pick up the slimy carrot peelings, plastic cheese wrappers and crumpled damp paper towels from the tile floor and shove them back in the bag. Could she really lie to her own parents?

"Constance Allen." Her mother's voice rang out. "You heard your father. Tell us this minute that these evil accusations are entirely false."

She rose shakily to her feet and held her hands under the tap, trying to rinse off the garbage. "They're not false." She couldn't even look at them as she said it. She picked up the sponge and knelt back down to try to wipe up the mess.

"You had an affair with the man you were sent to dig up dirt on?" Her mother moved closer.

"I was sent to look at the company's books. I did my job." She rinsed the sponge and wrung it out. Then she looked up at her parents standing there, so close to her, in the small kitchen where she'd made dinner with her mother for so many years. "I didn't mean to do anything else, but…" How did she explain what happened? "He was very handsome and kind, and I was very foolish."

"I have no doubt that man deliberately set out to seduce

you in order to pervert the course of your investigation."
Her mother's mouth pinched into a tight knot.

"Maybe he did." She put the sponge down, hands still
trembling. "But I never altered anything about the way I
conducted my work. As you've already heard, I uncovered
tax evasion by one of his relatives."

"Did you sleep with this man?" Her mother's hissed
question made her shrink inside her clothes.

"Sarah! How can you ask such a question?" Her dad's
shocked expression only deepened Constance's sense of
humiliation and sadness.

"I did, Mom. I'm sorry, Dad. It's just the truth. I'm not
proud of it. To this day I really don't know what came over
me. He was quite a man." She let out a sigh and wished
she could release the tension that heated the air in the
kitchen almost to the boiling point. "Apparently I'm only
human after all."

"I knew you should never have gone to that gambling es-
tablishment. A place like that isn't safe for a nice young girl."

"It's not the place, Mom. It's me. I've been living under
a rock too long. I didn't realize how lonely I was. How
much intimacy and affection could appeal to me."

"This man must have no sense of honor at all if he'd
tell the media about your…interaction with him." Her father's usually placid brow had furrowed. "Then again, it
was the other man on the news. The one you accused of
tax evasion." He cleared his throat. "I suppose the dust
will settle sooner or later."

"Oh, dear." Her mother's hand was now pressed to her
mouth. "You'll be fired, won't you?"

"Probably." Her voice was hollow. She had no appetite
whatsoever for carrots and chicken potpie. "In fact, I suppose I should offer my resignation."

"There's always a spot for you behind our counter. Our customers do love you," her dad tried to reassure her.

Constance cringed at the thought of serving people who'd heard about her transgressions.

"Are you trying to set our daughter up as a carnival sideshow, Brian? She can't be seen in public with scandal like this flying around. Though I suppose she could reorganize the shelves in the stockroom. Goodness, what will the pastor think?"

Constance hit breaking point and watched herself throw the sponge down in the sink and run from the room, leaving them staring after her. She'd known it was wrong to sleep with John and she'd done it anyway. He had been too much for her to resist. Now she'd lose her career over him and she probably deserved it. At least stupidity wasn't a crime and she wouldn't end up with a criminal record for her mistake.

She hurled herself down on the bed, tears hovering just behind her eyes. How was John coping with all of this? Was he embarrassed by the news of their liaison becoming public, or did he think it was funny? She'd loved the way that nothing rattled him and he went about his business with such good humor.

Maybe she could learn to do the same. She'd need all the sense of humor she could muster to get through the coming days and weeks.

John pounded along the trail, past the grazing cows and towards the shady woods. It wasn't his style to run away from problems, but right now he needed to let off steam. A twig snapped behind him and he spun around, expecting to see another nosy reporter.

Worse, he saw Don, sweating and panting, trying to catch up with him.

"Get lost."

"Wait! I want to apologize."

"It's way, way too late for that." Anger rushed him—again—and he turned and kept running, faster. At least his uncle Don was one problem he really could outrun.

But the footsteps got closer. "You forgot I was a sprinter in high school," rasped Don.

"Sprinting will only get you but so far. Like cheating, and lying." John kept running, though the urge to turn around and knock Don to the ground tightened his biceps.

"I promise I'll never lie or cheat again." Don gasped the words as he ran. "I'll never gamble again."

"How about if you never speak again?" John yelled. Don kept getting closer, his wiry frame must be fitter than it looked.

"That I can't promise. See? I'm not lying." Don was almost level with him.

John spun around and shoved out his hand, which caught Don in the chest with the satisfying force of a punch. Don doubled over as the air rushed out of his lungs. "I should knock you senseless."

"But that would be a crime and you're well above that."

"Exactly." John looked down on Don, who panted, hands on his knees. "And I'm trying to build the Nissequot tribe, not kill off its members with my bare hands."

"I really am sorry."

"For what? There's so much for you to regret that I can't keep track. You're being investigated for fraud along with the business I've staked everything on. You could go to prison. And on top of that you decided to announce to the local news that I had an affair with the BIA's investigator."

"I was mad at you. I didn't think they they'd really believe me. I didn't even believe it myself. You should have told me it was true and I would have kept my mouth shut. It is true, isn't it?"

"As if I would ever confide in you. I wouldn't trust

you with my grocery list at this point." He should have rebuffed Don's innuendo, instead of ignoring it. Denied his suspicions.

Except that they were true.

Even now he couldn't get Constance out of his mind for a solid minute. He'd hoped that the vision of her soft hazel eyes would fade. It had been three days and now he was seeing her face everywhere he looked.

"I know you think I'm stupid, and in all honesty, sometimes I am," Don panted, sweat dripping from his tanned forehead. His black T-shirt was soaked through. "But I know there was something between you and Miss Constance Allen. And not just sex, either. If you ask me, you're going to pieces without her."

John jerked to his feet. "Going to pieces? You're the one losing your mind. I've never been calmer. I'm just trying to think of how to prevent the enterprise we spent years building, and the tribe we've poured our lifeblood into, from being destroyed by a few strokes of a pen. I'm not even thinking about…her."

Don rose to his feet and wiped sweat from his brow. "You can't fool me, boy. I've known you too long. You need to go after her and win her back."

He certainly wasn't going to tell Don that he'd been thinking about it. "I'm sure the media would just love that."

"I'm serious. It's not a crime to fall in love. She still did her job and ratted me out."

"She has principles, unlike a certain scumbag relative of mine."

Don crossed his arms. "I'm serious. I don't want you blaming me for you losing the love of your life as well as creating an embarrassing mess in the press."

John blew out hard. "I don't need your advice to run my life, thanks. I think I can do a much better job of that by myself."

Don persisted. "So go get her."

John drew in a breath. The breeze cooled his face and a bird chirped in a nearby tree. "Although right now I hate you more than any man alive, for once you might be right about something."

John ordered a ring from Tiffany's in Manhattan and arranged to have it couriered to meet him at the airport in Cleveland. He chose a simple ring, since he knew Constance wouldn't like anything ostentatious. He had to guess the size, but they assured him it would be easy to fix if necessary. He chartered a plane at the local airport and boarded it with anticipation snapping through his muscles.

Was he jumping the gun by planning a proposal rather than simply inviting her back into his life? Possibly. But getting her to move from Ohio to Massachusetts would take a huge leap of faith on her part and he wanted her to know that he meant to offer her everything—including marriage.

The word echoed in his brain. Marriage was permanent. For life. Usually that would scare him right out the door, but now it had a reassuring, solid ring to it that steadied his hand on the wheel. His grandmother always said that when you met the right person, you just knew. You didn't have to date the woman for years or know every single thing about her to know that you were meant for each other. And his grandparents had been together long enough to test his grandmother's theory.

John trusted his gut. It had steered him right many times in the past, even when everyone else and basic common sense suggested otherwise. His gut told him that Constance was the woman he'd been waiting for all these years. He needed her in his life, in his arms, in his bed.

Now all he had to do was convince her. And that meant

convincing her that his intentions had been honorable from the start of their affair.

He arrived at the Cleveland airport and met the courier with the ring in the arrivals terminal. The diamond solitaire was as simple and lovely as he'd hoped, and his nerves sizzled as he tucked it into his pants pocket. Then he rented a car and programmed the GPS to take him to the address he'd found on the internet.

Blood thundered in his veins as he pulled into the driveway of her parents' modest house in a sleepy Cleveland neighborhood. She'd probably be freaked out that he'd stalked her online to find her address. If she wasn't sufficiently alarmed just to see him here at all. Her car was already in the driveway, so she was here. And the large white van with a hardware store decal on the side must belong to her parents, who were probably home, too. He parked behind it.

He never got nervous going into all-or-nothing business meetings or negotiating million-dollar deals. Climbing the Allen family's scuffed doorstep, however, he felt his nerves tingling. He pushed the bell and heard a chime sound on the other side of the door.

"Oh, goodness. Who can that be?" He could hear a woman's stressed-sounding voice in the distance and could make out a person's fast-approaching silhouette through the patterned glass oval in the door. He steadied himself as the door swung open and plastered on an encouraging smile. A small woman with a neat brown bob appeared in the doorway.

"Hello, you must be Mrs. Allen." He extended his hand.

"Leave us alone," the woman said, and then slammed the door in his face. Maybe she thought he was a reporter.

He rang the doorbell again. "I'm not a journalist," he called. "Or a salesman." He saw her blurry silhouette halt. "I'm a friend of Constance's."

He watched the woman turn and walk back through the glass. The door cracked open and a pair of very suspicious gray eyes peered at him. "Constance has been taken ill."

"What?" He stepped forward, one hand on the door. "What's wrong with her?"

"Who are you?" Constance's mom was a little shorter than her daughter, and dressed in a plaid blouse and navy slacks.

"My name is John Fairweather." He extended his hand again. "I'm pleased to meet you." He quietly put one knee in front of the door in case she tried to slam it again. Not a moment too soon, because he soon felt the force of the door against his arm and leg.

"Get out of my doorway, you…you scum!"

John drew in a deep breath. "I think there's a misunderstanding. Constance investigated my company, but it was my uncle's records that she found wanting, not mine."

The small woman stopped pushing on the door and came alarmingly close, her face crinkling with rage. "You seduced an innocent young girl," she hissed. "You should be ashamed of yourself."

He decided not to protest that Constance wasn't that young or that innocent. "Your daughter is a very unique and special person, and I'm sure that much of the credit for that goes to you, Mrs. Allen. I admire her integrity and am proud to know her."

"Well, she doesn't want anything to do with you, that's for sure. She'll probably get fired now that ugly rumors are flying around." At least she wasn't trying to slam the door on him anymore. "What have you got to say for yourself about that?"

"Constance has nothing to hide. She did her job with thoroughness and even ruthlessness. I'm sure her employer will find no fault with her. May I see her, please?"

Was she really sick? She must be under a lot of stress.

As John mulled it over, a timid-looking man with a receding hairline appeared at the end of the hallway. "What's going on, dear?"

"This is John Fairweather, Brian." She spoke very deliberately, without taking her eyes off him. John watched her husband put two and two together.

"You're not welcome here, I'm afraid." He glanced nervously at his wife. "You'd best go back to where you came from."

"I'm in love with your daughter." Desperation made him cut right to the point. He knew Constance must be in there somewhere. "Please, let me see her."

He smiled, to hopefully seem less threatening, but he was serious about what he said next. "I'm not going to leave until I talk to her. I'll camp out on your front lawn if necessary." Since their front lawn was about as big as a king-size bed and had a fake fountain on it, he hoped it wouldn't come to that.

Mrs. Allen glanced up and down the street. The sun was setting and so far the only people watching them were two kids on bikes. She narrowed her eyes and shot him a chilling look. "Perhaps you'd better come in."

He tried not to beam with too much excitement as he stepped over the threshold into their narrow hallway.

"Constance, dear," her father called up the stairs. "Could you come down, sweetheart?"

All eyes turned anxiously to the gloomy stairs. But no door opened. Listening hard, John could hear music playing up there. Impatience and excitement fired through him. "I think she's got the radio on and can't hear you. Would it be okay with you if I go knock on her door?"

Normally he'd have marched straight up, but since he intended for these people to be his future mother- and father-in-law, more delicate handling was called for.

The Allens looked at each other. Sarah had closed the

door behind John to block out the prying eyes of neigh-bors. "I suppose so," she muttered. "You can hardly make things worse than they already are."

He bounded up the stairs, feeling his pants pocket on the way to check the ring was still there, and knocked on the door. A song by Adele was playing.

"I need some time alone, Mom."

"It's me. John."

The music snapped off.

"What?"

The sweet sound of her voice made his heart swell, and his fingers reached for the door handle. But he hesitated. What if she wasn't decent? He didn't want to blow it.

"John Fairweather. I drove here to see you."

The door flung open so fast he felt his hair shift in the breeze. She was dressed in striped pajama pants and a white T-shirt and looked as though she'd been crying. She also looked unbearably beautiful and fragile, and he wanted to take her in his arms.

"You've got quite a nerve." She said it softly, as if she wasn't really listening to herself. She studied his face, then he felt her take in the rest of his body before looking back into his eyes with a confused expression.

"That's hardly news." He felt a grin spreading across his face. "I missed you."

"Did you tell Don about our affair?" Her gaze hardened. Pain hovered in her eyes.

"Never. He made it all up, in fact. I never told him any-thing about us. He was just mad—mostly at me because I fired him from his position."

"But you didn't deny it."

"I can't deny it. It's the truth." A smile tugged at the corner of his mouth, but he struggled to suppress it.

She frowned. "It's a shame you didn't get what you wanted, isn't it?"

"What do you mean?"

"It's a pity your plot to seduce me didn't throw me off the course and make me leave. Or convince me to cover up the truth. I overheard your conversation with Don in the lobby."

"There was never any kind of plot. Don suggested it, but I never had the slightest intention of following through."

"You just kissed me on the first night you met me because I'm so unbelievably irresistible?" She cocked her head.

"Exactly." The smile struggled over his mouth again.

"I'm not that dumb, John."

"You're not dumb at all. You're sharp as a tack and that's one of the many reasons I'm crazy about you."

She frowned and looked confused. "Why are you here? I'm not going to deny the affair if that's what you're hoping. I'd rather lose my career than tell a lie that big."

"I feel the same way." He reached for the ring in his pocket. No use beating about the bush. When she saw it she'd know he was serious. "I realize we've only known each other a short time." He pulled out the box and watched her brow furrow. "But there's something between us, something different." For once, he struggled for words. "I love you, Constance. I love you and I need you in my life. I've never met anyone like you before and I want to spend the rest of my days with you. Will you marry me?"

Eleven

Constance stared at John. It was hard enough to comprehend that he was here in her bedroom. She certainly didn't believe that he'd just asked her to marry him.

"Aren't you mad at me?" She'd pictured him cursing her and wishing she'd never been born. She knew the kind of scrutiny his casino and his whole tribe were under right now.

"For being honest and trustworthy? No way. I love you all the more for it."

She blinked. He looked ridiculously handsome, with that wary expression on his face and the pale blue box open in his hand. And that sure was a beautiful ring.

"You can't be serious. About marrying me, I mean."

"Constance, you know me well enough to know that I wouldn't joke about something like this. I love you, and I want you to be my wife." Humor twinkled in his eyes, as usual. He was always so confident. He was sure she'd say yes.

Constance stared from his face to the ring and back. This was beyond anything she could imagine. She'd never thought for a minute that John would want to turn their affair into something permanent. She hadn't allowed herself a dream that crazy. "You can't be serious."

"Are you okay in there, Constance?" She heard her father's voice on the other side of the door, which John had closed behind him.

"Yes, Dad. I'm fine." *At least I think I am. I'm not sure. I might be dreaming.*

"You're killing me, Constance. I'm in love with you." John sank to one knee on the pale green carpet. "Please say you'll marry me."

Tears sprang to her eyes. She could hear the sincerity in his voice, feel it in the air between them. "Yes." The word sounded so strange coming from her mouth. The whole situation was so surreal. But it was the only answer she could give.

He rose to his feet, dark eyes shining. "May I kiss you?"

She bit her lip, and glanced at the door. Both of her parents were probably standing outside. She looked back at John and his loving gaze melted her. "Okay."

His lips covered hers and she lost herself in the kiss, holding him tight. Kissing him again was such a sweet relief after the lonely nights and anxious days since she'd left him. He wrapped his strong arms around her, holding her up as her already shaky knees threatened to give way.

"God, I missed you so much," he breathed, pressing her against him when they finally broke for air. "I hate being without you. Will you come back with me right now?"

She bit her lip. "What about my job? They're being really supportive. They don't believe the allegations that I had an affair with you and I couldn't bring myself to admit it. Now they'll have good cause to fire me when they find out it's true and I didn't confess."

He ran his thumb over her lip as his face creased into a grin. "I do like the way you take your responsibilities so seriously. It's one of the many sexy things about you. They're going to know for sure that we had an affair when you tell them you're marrying me."

"Yes, but I need to reassure them that it didn't interfere with me fulfilling my professional responsibilities. What if they think you're back here to curry favor in the hope that I can get the IRS off your back?" She was only half kidding.

"I don't live my life worrying about what other people think." Undeterred, he kissed her mouth softly. "I know that if I choose to do what's right, I can hold my head high in front of anyone. Including your parents." He glanced in the direction of the door with a wink. "Do you think we should go tell them?"

She nodded, apprehension zinging inside her. "I suppose there's no way around that."

He opened the door to find both of them standing in the hallway outside her bedroom.

"We overheard," said her mother, with a dazed expression.

"Mom!"

"And we appreciate this young man having the honor and decency to make an honest woman of you." Her mother looked right at John.

"You do?" John looked astonished.

Her father cleared his throat. "Under the circumstances I'm truly convinced that you love our daughter. I won't say we approve of the business you're in, but we have no intention but to wish you both the best."

"You do?" It was Constance's turn to express her shock and disbelief. "I'll have to move to Massachusetts." She figured she might as well lay it all out.

"And we hope that you'll both move to Massachusetts with us," John cut in. "You'll find it's a lovely place to live."

"We do have a business to run here," Sarah explained. "But I'm sure we'd be happy to come visit."

Constance stared from one of her parents to the other,

then back to John. Did he have magical powers of persuasion? The media had as much as accused him of that when he'd created a tribe out of a few family members and a multimillion-dollar company on a few weedy acres in the backwoods.

"I look forward to getting to know you both." John shook their hands heartily. "Will you allow me to take you all out to dinner to celebrate?"

Her father still looked a bit stunned, but in a happy way. "We'd be delighted."

After a congenial dinner at her parents' favorite Italian restaurant, John and Constance drove to a nearby hotel. Once inside the room, with the door closed, they stopped and stared at each other. "Am I dreaming?" She stood about one foot from him, beside the bed, in the dimly lit room. "Because I have had strange and vivid dreams lately."

"If you're dreaming then I guess it means I'm in your dream." He held her gaze. "Which is fine with me. As long as neither of us wakes up." His lips curved into a mischievous half smile.

She felt her own now-familiar smile creep to her mouth in response. "I don't think either of us is the type to sleepwalk through life, so I suspect we're wide awake right now."

He lifted a brow. "I think you'll have to pinch me to find out."

She inhaled slowly, then reached around for his backside. It wasn't easy to pinch that much hard muscle, but she managed, at the cost of heating her blood a few more degrees.

"Yep. I'm awake." His eyes had darkened with desire. "Now for you." He slid his hands around her hips until he was cupping her rear. Then he squeezed and lifted her up so fast that she gasped as adrenaline rushed through her. "Uh-huh. You are, too." Still holding her off the ground, he let her rest against his big body and slowly slide down. She felt the hard jut of his erection through his dark pants, and it made her breath catch. "Awake, and if I'm not mistaken, every bit as aroused as I am."

She bit her lip and nodded. Heat pooled deep inside her and clouded her thinking. When her toes touched the floor, her fingers reached for the buttons on his shirt. She could hear her breathing quicken as she pulled each button from its hole and exposed his broad, muscled chest. His big fingers struggled with the tiny buttons on her blouse, and his expression of intense concentration made her chuckle.

She kissed his chest and inhaled the rich, masculine scent of him, then let her mouth trail down to where his pants sat low on his hips. It excited her to see how aroused he was. She heard his breath hitch and saw his stomach contract as she kissed his hard flesh through the expensive fabric of his pants. Then she undid the catch and the zipper with trembling fingers and slid the pants down over his powerful thighs.

It drove her crazy that this man was so intensely excited by her, ordinary little Constance Allen, who spent her days surrounded by file cabinets and calculators. But his passion-filled gaze and fierce erection left no doubt.

He slid her skirt and stockings off and pulled her onto the bed. For a moment they lay side by side, enjoying the vision of each other naked.

Seeing their surroundings made her remember that they were in a busy hotel with paper-thin walls and middle managers making phone calls in the rooms around them. "Maybe we should put the radio on."

He winked. "You're so practical. I love that about you.

And you're right. We don't need everyone in the Inn and Suites to hear your cries of passion." He reached for the radio next to the bed and turned the dial until he found a slow song. "And speaking of practical, I still have enough sense left to remember to use a condom." He fished in his bag and pulled out the packet, then opened it and settled back on the bed with her.

The soft sounds of sexy music filled the room as he rested his broad hand on her hip and slid it slowly up her waist to her breast. She watched his chest rise as he ran his fingers over her breast, stimulating her nipple. She was already so aroused that she let out a gasp. "I want you inside me," she pleaded, hardly able to believe it was her talking. She'd had no idea until she met John that she was capable of this kind of desire.

"With no foreplay?" He looked surprised.

"I don't need foreplay right now." She pressed her mouth to his for one breathless instant. "And I can see you don't either."

"True." He groaned as she wrapped her hand around him, then took the condom from him and rolled it on. With confidence and conviction that surprised her, she slid underneath him and guided him inside her. Her hips rose as he entered her and the sense of relief and exhilaration took her breath away. It felt so right. She lifted her hips to meet his and they moved together, both already on the brink of explosion, so much pent-up need and desire ready to burst over them.

"I love you." Her confession sprang from her lips— she couldn't hold back the words. Her feelings for him had been growing inside her from the first moment they kissed—maybe even the first moment they met—and she could now acknowledge what they meant. As she came to this realization, she felt the first waves of her orgasm spread through her like a tornado unwinding.

"I love you, too, sweetheart." He moved over her with a slow intensity that unraveled her completely. "I love you so, so…" His words were lost as he climaxed and she gripped him as hard as she could, fingers pressing into the hard muscle of his back.

She felt him pulsing inside her, and her heart filled until she thought it would burst. She didn't care if everyone at work knew she'd had an affair with the man she was sent to investigate. She didn't care if they fired her from her job. She didn't care if she never worked in accounting again. She didn't care about anything except being here, with John, right now.

And for the rest of her life.

His big body rested so comfortably on hers. "…So much."

She wanted to laugh, but couldn't find the energy. All the anxiety and worry and tension of the last few days had been wrung out of her by their lovemaking. The aftershocks of her orgasm trickled through her, sending a silly giggle to her chest. "What have you done to me? I feel like a completely different person when I'm with you."

"With me you're exactly the person you're supposed to be. Me, too. I was so caught up in trying to make money and avoid any romantic entanglements that I was running every minute. You were so caught up in trying to be Little Miss Perfect that you needed someone to trip you right up and stop you in your tracks."

"And catch me as I fell."

She felt his chuckle vibrate through both of them. Then he rolled gently off her until they were side by side, hugging each other. "To catch you and hold you tight so you couldn't slip away." His soft kiss sent yet another smile spreading across her lips.

She remembered the ring on her finger and pulled her hand up to stare at it. One stunning diamond in a minimalist platinum setting.

"I wanted something classic and perfect, with no unnecessary embellishment. Like you."

"It's so gorgeous. It must have cost a fortune." The diamond itself was set so that it didn't stick out or look ostentatious, but on close inspection she could see it was very large.

"What's the point of having a fortune if you can't spend it on the really important things? And you're the most important thing that has ever happened to me." His voice had a raw, honest edge to it that made tears spring to her eyes.

"I feel like I should give you something, too." What did you give the man who had everything? And if he didn't have it yet, he could buy it tomorrow.

"You are. You." He pulled her fingers gently to his lips and kissed them.

The truth of his words shocked her little. In agreeing to marry him she had given herself to him, which, she knew, meant giving up her life in Ohio and moving to Massachusetts, away from all her friends and family. She'd have to quit her job even if they didn't fire her.

"What's the matter?" He stroked her cheek.

"I'm thinking about all the changes ahead. Where will I work?"

"Well, the New Dawn has been accused of nepotism, and with good reason." He winked. "We do like to employ family members."

She frowned. "What would I do there?"

He pulled back and looked at her with a serious expression. "Whatever you think is important and interesting.

Your financial expertise could certainly be put to good use. You could even take over that part of the daily operations from me so I can focus on booking celebrities and hustling some good PR. I suspect I'll be better at that than Uncle Don was."

She inhaled sharply. "I still can't believe that he went to the press about us."

"He can be a real ass sometimes. Especially since he didn't even know we actually were involved." He ran his thumb over her lips. "I'm providing him with the best legal counsel so hopefully he won't spend the next few decades in jail, but he might wish he was safely behind bars by the time I'm done letting him know what I think about his behavior."

"You'd be surprised by how many people don't pay taxes." She ran her fingers through his hair. "They think that they earned the money, and it should be theirs to keep. Even people who have millions just think they can keep silent about it on their returns and nothing will happen. Yet they're still driving on roads and sending their kids to schools paid for by our taxes."

"Human nature. It's a constant battle for some of us to pretend to be civilized." He winked. "And trust me, I don't pay any more taxes than I have to myself. It'd probably be part of your job to finesse that, as well."

"I've been doing that for much bigger corporations for years. Maybe I'd like to do something else."

"Like what?"

She bit her lip and thought for a minute. The idea was outrageous, but then so was everything else about being here. "I always wanted to teach. My parents told me that the schools are full of unteachable, rowdy hoodlums and that I'd be miserable, which is why I pursued a career with numbers, but sometimes I wonder if I made the wrong choice."

"Interesting." He peered at her. "Now that we are gathering tribal members from far and wide, we have a lot to teach them about the business. Maybe you could start there, then get your teaching credentials and branch out to teaching in the schools."

"I like that idea." Her mind was racing, which was funny since her body still hummed with the aftereffects of their lovemaking. "It would be nice to work with people instead of numbers for a change."

"I think you'll be great at it." He kissed her softly on her mouth.

"I'll resign tomorrow. I wonder if they'll make me work for a final two weeks, or if they'll escort me out the door with my possessions in a cardboard box."

His eyes twinkled. "Once they know you're marrying me, probably the latter."

She felt a grin spread across her face. "I guess that's a good thing, under the circumstances."

"It most certainly is."

Epilogue

Thanksgiving

"Some people say that Native Americans shouldn't celebrate Thanksgiving." John stood at the head of the crowded table in the dining room of their meticulously renovated farmhouse. The fine cherry table was laden with fresh local turkey, roasted corn, chestnuts, maple-glazed squash with walnuts and glistening cranberry sauce. "They say that it was a foolish mistake of our ancestors to show the Pilgrims how to eat and survive in our land. They think it would have been better to let them starve to death."

He paused and looked around at the gathered guests. His grandparents beamed proudly and Constance wondered if they'd heard this speech before. "I disagree. Every choice we make in life shapes who we become and I'm proud to be a descendant of those who chose to offer the hand of friendship. I prefer to hope for the best and that's how I live my life. Our people have certainly been through many trials and tribulations since then, but we're still here and we're looking forward to a vibrant future."

He raised his champagne flute, and Constance lifted hers. She still couldn't believe this tall, handsome man was her husband. "And that future has just grown a little bit brighter…" He glanced at her and she smiled back. They'd talked about when to make their announcement and decided this was the perfect time. She felt butterflies in her stomach, fluttering around the tiny baby growing there.

"Because we're expecting a new member of the Nissequot tribe, who should be joining us sometime in June."

His grandmother gasped and turned to her husband. "A baby? Oh, John, did you hear that?"

"I heard it." He beamed and patted her hand. "That's wonderful."

The round of congratulations made Constance blush, and a sudden rush of emotion propelled her to her feet. A hush fell over the room as she looked around, feeling such a strong connection to the people gathered there. "These last few months have been a whirlwind. In May I was still living quietly in my childhood bedroom in Ohio, in June I got the assignment that would bring me here for the first time and now, in November, I'm an expectant mother, married to an amazing man, living in a lovely farmhouse in Massachusetts and pursuing a teaching license. I'm still a bit shell-shocked by it all, but I'm so grateful for the way you've all welcomed me into your midst and made my transition to my new life so easy and enjoyable."

Even her parents were smiling. They'd driven up here for the wedding, and now for Thanksgiving, and John's relentlessly charming grandfather had taken over the task of winning their hearts for the Nissequot tribe and casino. Although he still had a way to go, he'd made impressive progress.

John raised his glass. "I already find it hard to remember what life was like before you came here. Every day I'm grateful for the BIA investigation that brought you into our lives." A chuckle rumbled around the room. "Even Don says he's glad Constance caught up with him before he dug himself into an even deeper hole. He's lucky to have got off with only a six-week sentence."

The casino had shrugged off the scandal and the publicity from it brought in more people than ever, so New

Dawn was growing from strength to strength. "Next year we should be able to complete the purchase of seven hundred acres along our eastern border and break ground on the water park." Amusement twinkled in his eyes as he looked at Constance. The water park had been her idea. She liked the idea of expanding in a family-friendly direction and offering summer camps there for kids from all over the region. "Every day around here is a new adventure and I'm glad to be sharing them with my soul mate."

"I love you," she said softly.

"I love you, too, sweetheart." He spoke the words just to her, and emotion flowed directly between them despite all the people gathered around them. "And I'm thankful that I get to spend the rest of my life with you."

She felt tears well in her eyes and was about to blame the pregnancy hormones when she noticed that she wasn't the only one having that reaction. "Sometimes there's so much to be thankful for that it's hard to know where to start, so I suggest we all enjoy this delicious meal before it gets cold," she said.

John's grandfather chimed in. "I like the way you think. We give thanks to the Creator for this fine meal and the pleasure of sharing it together. Let's eat!"

* * * * *

"I saw the way you were looking at me just now. It isn't too late to re-negotiate, Jules."

The heat of his gaze instantly warmed the blood pumping through her veins. He very quickly made her aware of every inch of her body and how she responded to him.

"Yes it is," she said. "Way, way too late."

"Well then, I guess I'm just trying to be nice."

He made her reluctance to accept his offer seem childish. "Of course," she said, but a part of her still wondered. There were too many undercurrents running between their every interaction.

They had been apart for so long, most days it was easy to ignore what had happened between them. But now they were looking at months together. In close quarters.

Julianne had the feeling that the pressure cooker they'd kept sealed all this time was about to blow.

* * *

Her Secret Husband
is a Secrets of Eden story:
Keeping their past buried isn't so easy
when love is on the line.

HER SECRET
HUSBAND

BY
ANDREA LAURENCE

All rights reserved including the right of reproduction in whole or in part in any form. This edition is published by arrangement with Harlequin Books S.A.

This is a work of fiction. Names, characters, places, locations and incidents are purely fictional and bear no relationship to any real life individuals, living or dead, or to any actual places, business establishments, locations, events or incidents. Any resemblance is entirely coincidental.

This book is sold subject to the condition that it shall not, by way of trade or otherwise, be lent, resold, hired out or otherwise circulated without the prior consent of the publisher in any form of binding or cover other than that in which it is published and without a similar condition including this condition being imposed on the subsequent purchaser.

® and ™ are trademarks owned and used by the trademark owner and/or its licensee. Trademarks marked with ® are registered with the United Kingdom Patent Office and/or the Office for Harmonisation in the Internal Market and in other countries.

Published in Great Britain 2014
by Mills & Boon, an imprint of Harlequin (UK) Limited,
Eton House, 18-24 Paradise Road, Richmond, Surrey, TW9 1SR

© 2014 Andrea Laurence

ISBN: 978-0-263-91481-8

51-1014

Harlequin (UK) Limited's policy is to use papers that are natural, renewable and recyclable products and made from wood grown in sustainable forests. The logging and manufacturing processes conform to the legal environmental regulations of the country of origin.

Printed and bound in Spain
by Blackprint CPI, Barcelona

Andrea Laurence is an award-winning contemporary romance author who has loved books and has been writing stories since she learned to read and write. She always dreamed of seeing her work in print and is thrilled to be able to share her books with the world. A dedicated West Coast girl transplanted into the Deep South, she's working on her own "happily ever after" with her boyfriend and five fur-babies. You can contact Andrea at her website, www.andrealaurence.com.

To My Fellow Desire Divas
Jules Bennett & Sarah M. Anderson—

The day my editor announced my first sale to
Harlequin Desire on Twitter, I was greeted with
congratulations from a hundred people I've never
met. You were two of the first to welcome me
as fellow Harlequin Desire Authors and you've
had my back ever since that day. I never felt like
the new kid in class. Thanks for the support,
the laughs and the Lego movie trailers.

One

"Your dad's heart attack was pretty serious this time."

The doctor's words did little to make Heath Langston feel better about his foster father's condition. He stood outside Ken Eden's hospital room, listening to the doctor's prognosis. He felt helpless, which was not the way he liked it. He might be the youngest of the "Eden boys," but he owned his own advertising firm on Madison Avenue. He'd single-handedly developed one of the most successful ad campaigns of the last year. He was used to everyone, from his secretary to his business partner, looking to him to make decisions.

But this was serious stuff. Life and death. Not exactly his forte. Ken and Molly Eden's only biological child, Julianne, hadn't stopped crying since she arrived. Heath preferred to keep things light and he'd much rather see Julianne smile, but even he couldn't find anything to make a joke about right now.

The Edens' five children had rushed to their family farm in Cornwall, Connecticut, the moment they'd gotten the call about Ken's heart attack. Heath had gotten into his car and bolted from New York City, not knowing if his foster father would be alive by the time he got to the hospital. His biological parents had died in a car accident when he was only nine years old. He was a grown man now, the CEO of his own company, but he wasn't ready to face losing another parent.

Heath and Julianne were the last to arrive and were receiving the report the others had already heard.

"He's stable now, but we were lucky," the doctor continued. "That aspirin Molly gave him may have made all the difference."

Julianne's tiny figure stood in front of him. Despite the doctor's serious words, Heath couldn't keep his eyes from going to her. She took after Molly, being petite but powerful. Today, she looked even smaller than normal, with her shoulders hunched over and her head dipped down to focus her eyes on the floor. Her blond hair had been long and loose when she'd first arrived, but after sitting forever in the waiting room, she'd clipped it up into a messy twist. She shivered at the doctor's words and tried to snuggle deeper into her green cashmere sweater.

Heath put a reassuring hand on her shoulder. His brothers each had their fiancées to hold for support, but he and Julianne were both alone. His heart went out to her. He hated seeing his feisty, confident artist looking so broken. Although they'd grown up in the same house, she had never been a sister in his mind. She had been his best friend, his partner in crime, and for a short time, the love of his life.

Knowing they had each other in this dark moment made him feel better. Tonight, he hoped they could put their tumultuous past behind them and focus on what was more important. Since Julianne didn't pull away, she had to feel the same. Normally, she would give him a playful shove and artfully dodge the physical contact, but not today.

Instead, her body slumped against him for support, her back pressing into his chest. He rested his cheek against the gold strands of her hair and deeply breathed in the scent that was imprinted on his brain. She sighed, sending a tingle of awareness traveling along his spine. The sensation turned the doctor's voice into a muffled mutter in the distance. For a moment, there was only him and her. It wasn't the most appropriate of times, but he would revel in the contact.

Touching Julianne was a rare and precious experience. She had never been a very physically demonstrative person, unlike Molly, who hugged everyone she met, but she kept an even greater distance from Heath. No matter what had happened between them all those years ago and who was to blame, in a moment like this he regretted the loss of his best friend the most acutely.

"He's going to need open-heart surgery. After that, he'll have to stay in ICU a few days until we can move him to a regular room."

"How long until he'll be able to come home?" Julianne asked, making Heath feel guilty for where his mind had strayed. Even as they touched, she was focused on something more important than the two of them and their history together. It was enough for him to straighten up and put some distance between their bodies once again. He opted to focus on the doctor's answer instead.

The doctor frowned. "I don't like to set expectations on this kind of thing, but as I told the others, he's going to be with us a week at least. He might need to go into a rehab center for a while. Maybe he could be at home if there's a bed downstairs and a nurse could be brought in. After that, he's going to have to take it easy for a few months. No lifting, no climbing stairs. He won't be cutting down pine trees this Christmas, that's for sure."

That decided it. With everything else that was going on, Heath had already been thinking of taking a few months off to return to his foster parents' Christmas-tree farm. A body had been discovered on former family property last Christmas and it had recently been identified as Tommy Wilder, a foster child who had stayed briefly on the farm. Heath and the other Eden children knew that Tommy had been dead nearly sixteen years, but the police investigation was just now heating up.

Heath had been torn between wanting to keep up with every news story on television about Tommy and wishing he could just pretend the bully had never existed. Unfortunately, he knew well that ignoring issues wouldn't make them go away.

As much as he hated to admit it, it was time for Heath to come home and answer for what he'd done. It was just Ken and Molly on the farm now, and although they knew nothing about the truth behind Tommy's disappearance, they were having to deal with the police investigation on their own. According to his only biological brother, Xander, the stress of Sheriff Duke threatening to arrest Ken had put him into the hospital today.

It was bad enough that one person was dead because of Heath's mistakes. He couldn't bear it if someone else, especially someone innocent like Ken, also fell victim.

The doctor disappeared and he and Julianne made their way back to the waiting room area, where the rest of the family was assembled. His three brothers and their fiancées were scattered around the room. Some were reading magazines, others were focused on their phones. All looked tired and anxious. "I'll be coming to stay at the farm until Dad is better," he announced to the group. "I can handle things."

"I know it's only the beginning of October, but Christmas will be here before you know it," his oldest foster brother, Wade, pointed out with a frown furrowing his brow. "The last quarter of the year is always a nightmare. You can't take all that on by yourself."

"What choice do we have? All of you are busy. My business partner can run Langston Hamilton for a few months without me. And I've got Owen," Heath added, referring to the Garden of Eden Christmas Tree Farm's oldest and most faithful employee. "He can help me with the details. When Christmas comes, I'll hire some of the high school and college boys to bag and haul trees."

"I'm coming home, too," Julianne announced.

The whole family turned to look at her. She'd been fairly quiet since she had arrived from the Hamptons, but only Heath seemed to realize the significance of her decision. She was volunteering to come home, even knowing that Heath would be there. While she visited the farm from time to time, it was very rare that the boys were there aside from Christmas celebrations. Volunteering to spend months with Heath was out of character for her, but she wasn't exactly in a good headspace.

Despite how small and fragile she looked, there was a sternness in her eyes. Unfortunately, Heath knew that look well. The hard glint of determination, like emeralds, had set into her gaze, and he knew she wouldn't be dissuaded from her decision. Once Julianne's mind was made up about something, there was no changing it.

Even without Heath there, her coming to the farm was a big deal. Julianne was a sculptor. Both her studio and her boutique gallery were in the Hamptons. It wasn't the kind of job where you could just pick up your twelve-hundred-pound kiln and work wherever you like.

"What about your big gallery show next year?" Heath said. "You can't afford to lose two or three months of work to come down here."

"I'm looking to set up a new studio anyway," she said.

Heath frowned. Julianne had a studio in her home. The home she shared with her boyfriend of the last year and a half. It was a personal record for her and everyone thought Danny might be a keeper. Looking for a new studio meant looking for a new place to live. And possibly a new relationship.

"Has something happened with you and Danny?" their brother Brody asked, saving Heath the trouble of nosing into her love life.

Julianne frowned at Brody, and then glanced around at her protective older brothers with dismay. She obviously didn't want to talk about this now, or ever. "Danny and I are no longer 'Danny and I.' He moved out about a month ago. I needed a change of scenery, so I've sold the house and I'm looking for something new. There's no reason why I can't move back for a few months while Dad recuperates. I can help around the farm and work on my art pieces when we're closed. When Dad's feeling better, I'll look for a new place."

Heath and the other boys looked at her dubiously, which only made the color of irritation flush her pale, heart-shaped face. "What?" she said, her hands going to her hips.

"Why didn't you say anything about your breakup with Danny? And selling your house? You two were together a long time. That's a pretty big deal," Xander noted.

"Because," Julianne explained, "three of you guys have gotten engaged recently. It's bad enough that I'll be going stag to all of your weddings. I wasn't exactly looking forward to telling all of you that I've got yet another failed relationship under my belt. Apparently I'm doomed to be the old maid in the family."

"That's hardly possible, Jules," Heath said.

Julianne's cool, green gaze met his. "Point is," she continued, deliberately ignoring his words, "I'm able to come home and help, so I will."

Heath could tell by her tone that the discussion was over for now. Taking her cue, he turned to the rest of his siblings. "Visiting hours are about over, although you'll pay hell to get Mom from Dad's bedside. The rest of us probably need to say good-night and head back to the farm. It's been a long, stressful day."

They shuffled into Ken's hospital room, the dark, peaceful space ruined by the beep of Ken's heart monitor and the low rumble of the voices on his television. There was one light on over the bed, illuminating Ken's shape beneath the off-white blanket. He was nearly as pale as the sheets, but it was a big improvement over the blue-tinged hue his skin had taken on earlier. His light blond, nearly white hair was disheveled from constantly pulling out his oxygen tube and putting it over the top of his head like a pair of sunglasses. Molly had obviously forced it back into his nose recently.

She was sitting in a reclining chair beside him. It was the kind that extended into a bed and that was a good thing. Molly wasn't going anywhere tonight. Her normally cheery expression was still pasted onto her face, but that was more for Ken's benefit than anything. Heath could tell there wasn't much enthusiasm behind it. They were all struggling just to keep it together for Dad's sake.

Ken shifted his gaze from his favorite evening game show to the group of children huddled at his bedside. Heath realized they must look ridiculous standing there. Five rich, successful, powerful people moping at their father's hospital bed, unable to do anything to help. All their money combined couldn't buy Ken a new heart.

At least, not *legally*. Since they'd already done their fair share of dancing on the wrong side of the law and had enough police lurking around their property to prove it, they'd stick with the doctor's recommendations for now.

"There's not much happening here tonight," Ken said. He tried to cover the fact that speaking nearly winded him, but he had to bring his hand to his chest and take a deep breath before saying anything else. "You kids get on home and get some rest. I'll be here. I'm not going anywhere, anytime soon."

Julianne stepped to his side and scooped up his hand. She patted it gently, careful not to disturb his IV, and leaned in to put a kiss on his cheek. "Good night, Daddy. I love you."

"I love you too, June-bug."

She quickly turned on her heel and moved to the back of the group so others could take their turns. She'd let the tears on her cheeks dry, but Heath could see more threatening. She was trying to hold them in and not upset Ken.

One by one, the rest of them said good-night and made their way out to the parking lot. The hospital was a good distance from Cornwall, so they merged onto the highway and made the long, dark drive back to their parents' farm.

Wade and Tori returned to their nearby home, but the rest of the family continued on to the farm. The boys each parked at the bunkhouse, leaving an impressive display of luxury vehicles out front. Heath was last, pulling his Porsche 911 Carrera in between Xander's Lexus SUV and Brody's Mercedes sedan.

Twenty-five years ago, the old barn had been converted into a guest house of sorts, where the foster children who came to live at the Garden of Eden would stay. It had two large bedrooms and baths upstairs and a large common room with a small kitchenette downstairs. It was filled with old, but sturdy furniture and all the comforts teenage boys needed. Heath was the youngest of the four boys who had come to the farm and stayed until adulthood. These days they spent their time in multimillion-dollar mansions and apartments, but this farm was their home and when they returned, the boys always stayed in the bunkhouse.

Heath watched Julianne pull her red Camaro convertible up closer to the main house. The old Federal-style home was beautiful and historic, but it didn't have enough space for a large crew of children. Ken and Molly had a bedroom, their daughter, Julianne, had a room and there was one guest room.

She stood on the porch, fumbling with her keys and looking lost. Heath didn't like that at all. Normally, Julianne was a woman who knew exactly what she wanted from life and how to get it. But tonight she looked anything but her normally spunky self. Nearly losing Ken right after things went south with Danny must have been more than she could take.

Heath grabbed his overnight bag from the trunk of his Porsche and followed the group into the bunkhouse. He set his duffel bag on the old, worn dining room table and looked around. The downstairs common room hadn't changed much since he'd moved in, aside from the new flat-screen television Xander had purchased during his recent stay.

There was a sense of comfort in being back home with his family. He imagined that wouldn't be the same for Julianne, who would be returning to an empty house. Heath might not be the person she'd choose to stay with her tonight, but he wasn't going to argue with her about it. He wasn't leaving her alone.

"Hey, guys," he said to his brothers and their fiancées as they settled in. "I think I'm going to sleep in the big house tonight. I don't like the idea of Jules being alone. Not after the day we've had."

Xander nodded and patted him on the shoulder. "That's a good idea. We'll see you in the morning."

Heath picked up his bag, stepped out and then jogged across the grass and gravel to the back door.

Julianne knew she should go to bed; it had been a very long day with unexpected twists and turns, but she wasn't sleepy. She'd woken up worried about her work and the fallout of her latest failed relationship. Then the phone rang and her world turned upside down. Her previous worries were suddenly insignificant. She'd dropped everything, thrown some clothes in a bag and hit the road.

Even now, hours later, she was still filled with nervous energy. There was a restless anxiety in her muscles, the kind that urged her to go to her workshop and lose herself in the clay. Usually, immersing herself in her work helped clear her mind and solve her problems, but all the pottery in the world wouldn't fix this.

She settled for a cup of chamomile tea at the kitchen table. That might bring her brain down a few notches so she could sleep. She was sitting at the table, sipping the hot tea, when she heard a soft tap at the door. The door almost immediately opened and before she could get up, Heath was standing in the kitchen.

"What is it?" she said, leaping to her feet. "Did the hospital call? Is there a problem?"

Heath frantically shook his head, making one curl of his light brown hair dip down into his eyes. He held up his hands in surrender and she noticed the duffel bag on his shoulder. "No, no problem. Dad's fine," he insisted. "I just didn't want you to be alone in the house tonight."

The air rushed out of her lungs in a loud burst. Thank goodness Dad was okay. Her heart was still racing in her chest from her sudden panic as she slipped back down into her chair. She took a large sip of the scalding tea and winced. After the day she'd had, she didn't need Heath hovering nearby and the distracting hum of his presence in her veins. An hour after they had left the hospital, she could still recall the weight of his hand on her shoulder and the comforting warmth of his chest pressed against her. The contact had been innocent, but her eyes had fluttered closed for a moment to soak in the forbidden contact. She'd immediately snapped herself out of it and tried to focus on her father's health.

"I'll be okay alone," she said.

Heath dropped his bag onto the wooden floor and flopped in the chair across from her. "No, you won't."

She sighed and pinched the bridge of her nose between her thumb and middle finger. She could feel a headache coming on and that was the last thing she needed. Of course, she could take one of her migraine pills and knock herself out. That was one sure way to get to sleep tonight, but what if something happened to Dad?

When she looked up at her guest, she found herself getting lost in the light hazel depths of his eyes. Heath was always happy, always ready with a joke or a smile. But tonight, his expression was different. There was a softness, a weariness, that lined his eyes. He looked concerned. Worried. But not for Ken. At least not entirely. He was concerned about her.

As always.

Julianne wouldn't make light, even in her own mind,

of Heath's protectiveness of her. He had gone to extraordinary lengths to keep her safe. She knew that anytime, day or night, she could call him and he would be there. But not just because they were family and he cared about her. There was a great deal more to it than that and tonight was not the night she was willing to deal with it.

"Thank you," she said at last. She wasn't going to put up a fight and force him into the bunkhouse. She didn't have the energy to argue and frankly, it would be nice to have someone in the big, creaky house with her. No matter what had happened between them over the years, she always knew she could count on him to respect her boundaries.

"It feels weird to be in the house without Mom and Dad," he said, looking around at the large, empty kitchen. "Mom should be fussing at the sink. Dad should be tinkering with farm equipment outside."

He was right, but she didn't want to think about things like that. Those thoughts would require her to face the mortality of her aging parents. Dad would come home this time, but eventually, he wouldn't. She'd rather pretend they were immortal, like she had believed as a child. "Would you like some tea?" she asked, ignoring his words.

"No, I'm fine, thanks."

She wished he would have accepted the tea. That would have given her something to do for a couple of minutes. Instead, she had to sit idly and wait for the questions she knew were coming. They hadn't been alone together and able to really talk since before she had left for college eleven years ago. That had been by design on her part. There were so many thoughts, so many feelings she didn't want to deal with. Looking into Heath's eyes brought everything back to the surface. The burning attraction, the anxiety, the overwhelming feeling of fear...

"So, what happened with you and Danny? That seemed kind of sudden."

Julianne sighed. "We decided we wanted different things, that's all. I wanted to focus on my art and building my career. Things have really taken off and I want to strike while the iron is hot. Danny wanted to take our relationship to the next level."

A spark of interest flickered in Heath's light eyes, his full lips pursing with suppressed amusement. "He proposed?"

"Yes," she said, trying not to let the memories of the uncomfortable moment flood into her mind. She'd told him repeatedly that she wasn't interested in marriage right now, and kids were far, far on the horizon. And yet he'd asked anyway. He seemed to mistake her hesitation as her playing hard to get or using reverse psychology with him. She wished she knew why. She'd given him no signals otherwise. "I refused, as politely as I could, but he didn't take the rejection very well. After that, we decided if we weren't moving forward, we were stagnating. So he moved out."

Danny had been a great guy. He was fun and exciting and sexy. At first, he hadn't seemed interested in settling down. Given her situation, he was the perfect choice. She didn't want to get too serious, either. They wouldn't have even moved in together if he hadn't needed a new place on short notice. He must have seen that as a positive relationship step, when in fact it was simply practicality and economics. In time, it was just easier to stay together than to break things off and cause an upheaval.

"You didn't want to marry him?" Heath asked.

Julianne looked up at him again and shook her head in exasperation. That was a ridiculous question. He knew full well why she'd turned him down. "No, I didn't. But even if I *did*, what was I going to say to him, Heath?"

There was a long, awkward silence before Heath spoke again. "Jules?"

"Listen, I know I brought it up, but I really don't want to talk about it tonight." Julianne sipped the last of her tea and got up from the table. "With Dad and the stuff with Tommy, I can't take any more drama."

"That's fine," he said as he leaned back into the wooden chair and watched her walk into the kitchen. "But considering we're going to be spending the next few months together, you need to come to terms with the fact that we need to talk about it. We've swept the issue under the rug for far too long."

She knew when she made the decision to come home that this would happen. No matter how uncomfortable it might be, she knew they needed her help on the farm, so that was where she would be. There wasn't anywhere else for her anyway. She had sold her house. Closing was next week, and then she was officially homeless. She had to come back here. And she had to deal with her past once and for all.

Julianne looked over at the funny, charming man that had stolen her heart when she was too young and messed up to know what to do about it. Even now, the soft curve of his lips was enough to make a heat surge through her veins and a longing ache in her belly. It took almost no effort at all to remember how it felt when he'd kissed her the first time in Paris. The whisper of his lips along her neck as they admired the Sagrada Família in Barcelona…

Her parents thought they were sending their two youngest children on an exciting graduation trip through Europe. Little did they know what freedom and romantic settings would ignite between their daughter and their youngest foster child. Heath wasn't her brother. She'd known him before his parents died and had never thought of him like a brother. He was her best friend. But if she ever wanted him to be something more, she had to deal with the past.

"Agreed," she said. "Once Dad is stable and we have some time alone to talk, I'm ready to deal with it."

Heath narrowed his gaze at her and she knew instantly what he was thinking. He didn't believe her. She'd been feeding him excuses and dragging her feet for years. He probably thought she got some sort of sick pleasure from drawing all this out, but that was anything but true. She was stuck between not wanting to lose him and not knowing what do with Heath if she had him.

A lifetime ago, when they were eighteen and far, far from home, he'd wanted her. And she'd wanted him. At least, she thought she had. She was young and naive. Despite the attraction that burned at her cheeks when he touched her, she'd found she couldn't fully give herself to him in the heat of the moment.

"It's been easy to ignore while both of us were in school and building our careers," Heath said. "But it's time. Your recent breakup is one of several signs we can't disregard any longer. Whether you like it or not, eventually you and I are going to have to face the fact that we're still married."

Two

He'd laid his cards out on the table. This would end, and soon. After several minutes spent in silence, waiting for her to respond to his declaration, Heath finally gave up. "Good night, Jules," he said, pushing up from his seat.

With Ken's attack, he understood if she couldn't deal with this tonight, but he wasn't waiting forever for her. He'd already wasted too much time on Julianne. He picked his bag up off the floor, and carried it down the hall and up the stairs to the guest bedroom.

The guest room was directly across the hall from Julianne's room and next to the bathroom they would share. He could count on one hand how many times he'd slept in the big house over the years. It just wasn't where he was drawn to. The big house was beautiful and historic, filled with antiques and cherished knickknacks. Most anyone would be happy to stay here, but Heath always felt like a bull in a china shop when he was in the house.

As kids, the bunkhouse was the ideal boy zone. They could be rowdy because the furniture was sturdy but old, there were no breakable antiques and downstairs was all wood flooring, so they could spill and not stain the carpet. There was a big television, video games, a foosball table and an inexhaustible supply of soda and other snacks to fuel growing boys. Things had changed over the years, but being there with his brothers again would make it feel just the same.

Tonight, he made an exception and would stay in the big house for Julianne's sake, but it would be a mistake for her to confuse his gesture as weakness where she was concerned. Any love he had for her had fizzled away when she'd slammed her dorm room door in his face.

For years, he'd been as patient as he could stand to be. He knew now that he had been too nice. He'd given her too much space and let her get too contented. There was no incentive for her to act. That was going to change. He had no intention of being easy on her while they were here. Whatever it took, no matter how hard he had to push her out of her comfort zone, he would leave this farm a happily divorced man. Heath knew he shouldn't enjoy watching Julianne squirm, especially tonight, but he did.

Eleven years of marriage without his wife in his bed could do that to a guy.

He opened the door to the guest room and put his bag down on the white eyelet bedspread. The room was intricately decorated, like the rest of the house, with antique furniture, busy floral wallpaper, lacy curtains and shelves filled with books and framed pictures. As he kicked out of his Prada loafers, he noticed a portrait on the wall in a carved, wooden frame.

It was of Julianne. One of her elementary school pictures, although he couldn't be sure what year. Her golden hair was pulled up into a ponytail, a sprinkle of freckles across her nose. She was wearing a pink plaid romper with a white turtleneck underneath it. She looked just as he remembered her.

He had fallen in love with Julianne Eden the first time he'd seen her. They were in Mrs. Henderson's fourth-grade class together. The cheerful blonde with the curly pigtails and the bright smile had sat right next to him. Whenever he forgot his pencil, she would loan him one of hers. They were pink and smelled like strawberries, but he didn't care. He left his pencil at home on purpose just so he could talk to her.

He'd fabricated childish plans to marry Julianne one day. It seemed like a pipe dream at the time, but one day on the playground, she kissed him—his very first kiss— and he *knew* that she was meant to be his. He'd even made her a Valentine's Day card to tell her how he felt.

He never gave her the card. The weekend before their class party, his parents were killed in a car accident. Heath had been in the car at the time, but his injuries, while serious, had not been fatal. When he was finally discharged from the hospital, both he and his brother, Xander, had found themselves in the care of Family Services. The next thing he knew, they were living at the Christmas-tree farm on the edge of town and the beautiful golden-haired girl of his dreams was supposed to be his "sister."

He had outright rejected that idea right away. They might live in the same home, but not once in twenty years had he ever referred to her as "sis" or "my sister." She was Jules, usually; Julianne when he was speaking about her to the uninitiated.

He'd given up the dream of ever marrying his childhood love soon after coming to the Garden of Eden. Julianne never kissed him on the playground again. They were friends, but that was all. It wasn't until they were seniors in high school and the only kids left on the farm that things started to change between them. The trip to Europe had been the tipping point. Unfortunately, it hadn't tipped in his favor for long.

That seemed to be Julianne's M.O. Since they'd broken up, she had dated, but from what he could tell, never seriously and never for long. None of the brothers had ever met a boyfriend. She never brought one home to the farm. Danny had come the furthest, moving in with Julianne. She didn't really let any man get close, but Heath wasn't certain what was the cause and what was the effect. Did their marriage fail because she didn't do relationships, or did her relationships fail because she was married?

He had unpacked a few things and was halfway undressed when he heard a soft tap at his door. "Come in," he called out.

Julianne opened the door and stuck her head in. She started to speak, and then stopped, her gaze dropping from his face to his bare chest. He tried not to move, fighting the urge to puff up his chest and suck in his stomach. He liked to think he looked pretty good without all that, but it was such a reflex. He jogged the High Line every morning and lifted weights. As a child, he was always the smaller, scrappier of the boys, but no longer. He might be the shortest, at six feet, but he could take any of his brothers and look good doing it.

The dumbstruck Julianne seemed to agree. A crimson flush rose to her delicate, porcelain cheeks. Her full bottom lip hung, useless, until her tongue shot across it and her mouth slammed shut.

If Heath had known strutting around shirtless would get this kind of reaction from her, he would have done it a long time ago. Nothing made her more uncomfortable than the topic of sex. If he'd pushed the issue, perhaps he'd be happily single or happily married right now. Watching her reaction, he thrust his hands in his pockets. His Dolce & Gabbana slacks rode lower with the movement, exposing the trail of hair beneath his navel and the cut of his muscles across his hips.

Julianne swallowed hard and then shook her head and shifted her gaze away to the nearby armoire. "I'm s-sorry," she stuttered. "I didn't realize you were…"

"It's okay," Heath said with a sly smile, enjoying her discomfort. "I'm not bashful and it's nothing you haven't seen before."

She shook her head, sending a wave of the luxurious golden strands over her shoulders. "I don't remember you looking like *that*," she said, quickly bringing her hand up to cover her mouth. She looked embarrassed to share her observation aloud.

Heath glanced down at the display of his own body and shrugged. "I'm not eighteen anymore."

He supposed he would be struck just as hard to see her topless after all this time. Hell, he'd barely seen her naked back then. Sometimes when he was feeling particularly masochistic, he would allow himself to imagine what she looked like now beneath her sweaters and her jeans. The teenage girl he loved had become a very sexy and gifted woman. Any gangliness had been replaced with lush curves and soft, graceful movements. Beautiful and aggravating.

She stood awkwardly in the doorway, nodding, not looking at him, not saying anything for a few moments.

"Did you need something?" Heath prompted at last.

Her green gaze shifted back to his, her purpose suddenly regained. "Yes. Well, I mean, no. I don't *need* anything. I, uh, just wanted to say thank you."

"Thank you? For what?"

"For staying here with me tonight. I know you'd rather be laughing and chatting with Xander and Brody. You guys never get to see one another."

"I see them more than I get to see you," Heath said before he could stop himself. It was true. As children, they had been inseparable. She was his best friend. The marriage that should have brought them even closer together had driven them apart and he still didn't understand why. "I miss you, Jules."

A sadness crept into her eyes, a frown pulling down the corners of her mouth. "I miss you, too, Heath."

"Be honest. You avoid me. Why?" he asked. "Even if we divorced, I get the feeling that you'd still be uncomfortable around me."

"I'm not uncomfortable," she said, but not convincingly.

"Am I being punished for what happened between us?"

Julianne sighed and slumped against the door frame. "It's not about punishing you. And no, it's not about what happened in Europe, either. There are just things in our past that I don't like thinking about. It's easier to forget when I don't see or talk to you."

"Things in our past? Wait…" he said. "Are you blaming me for what happened with Tommy Wilder?"

"No!" she spoke emphatically, raising her palm up to halt him. "You are my savior. The one who protected me when no one else could."

"But you think of that horrible night when you look at me?" Heath was almost nauseated at the thought.

"No," she insisted again, but less forcefully. "If that were true, I never could've fallen for you. It's just easier for me to focus on the future instead of dwelling in the past. Our relationship is in my past."

"Not according to the public records office. It is very

much current and relevant. Ignoring things won't change them. It just makes it worse."

Julianne chuckled and crossed her arms over her chest. "Believe me, I know. I just don't know what else to do about it."

"We get divorced. We can't just stay married forever."

"It's worked okay so far."

Now it was Heath's turn to laugh. "Says the woman that just broke up with her boyfriend when he proposed."

"I didn't…" she began to argue, and then stopped. "This conversation has strayed from what I'd intended when I knocked. Thank you, again," she repeated. "And good night."

Heath watched her slip through the doorway. "Good night," he replied just as the door shut. Once he was certain she was settled in her room, he cast off the rest of his clothes and crawled into bed in his boxer shorts. The bed was soft and inviting, the sheets smelling like the lavender soap Molly used for linens and towels. The bed very nearly forced him to relax, luring him to the edge of sleep faster than he ever thought possible.

Things hadn't worked out between him and Julianne, but he wasn't stupid. He had long ago set aside any idea that their farce of a marriage might become something real. They'd never even consummated it. He'd thought she would come around eventually. It was her first time, perhaps she was just nervous. But then she left for her art program in Chicago without even saying goodbye. He chased after her, driving all night to figure out what was going on. He'd imagined a romantic moment, but instead, she'd told him their marriage was a mistake, he needed to forget it ever happened and practically shut her dorm room door in his face.

He'd been devastated. Then the devastation morphed

into anger. Then indifference. After that, he'd decided that
if she wanted a divorce so badly, she could be the one to
file. So he'd waited.

Eleven years.

As she'd mentioned, it hadn't been a problem. At least,
logistically. He hadn't met a single woman that made him
want to walk down the aisle again, but it was the principle of the thing. She didn't want him, and yet she was re-
sistant to let him go. Julianne always seemed to have an
excuse. They were broke. They moved around too much
after school to establish residency. They were busy starting their businesses. Her appointment with her divorce
attorney was rescheduled, and then rescheduled again.

After a while, he began to wonder if she would rather
stay married and keep it a secret than file for divorce and
risk people finding out she'd married *him*. Her big mistake.

He'd known her since they were nine years old and
he still didn't understand what went on in that beautiful
blond head of hers.

Julianne sat in a rocking chair on the back porch clutching a big mug of steaming coffee. She had barely slept last
night and she desperately needed the infusion of caffeine
to make it through today. She'd lain in bed most of the
night thinking about Heath and how he was so close by.
Her mind had wandered to their first trip together and how
wonderful it had been. Even as young as they were, he'd
known just how to touch her. With the backdrop of Europe, so romantic and inspiring, behind them, she thought
she might be able to overcome the fear. She'd been wrong.

The familiar ache of need had curled in her belly, but
she'd smothered her face in the pillows until it faded. It
didn't matter how much she'd loved him back then. How
much she wanted him. It didn't stop the fear from nearly

strangling her with irrational panic. If she couldn't give herself to Heath, the one who protected her, the one she was closer to than anyone else... When it came down to it, she had been too messed up back then to be with anyone.

Heath was right, though. They needed to move on. She'd dragged her feet. Hoping the words would come easier after all this time, she made excuses. If the years had taught her anything, it was that the truth could be more painful than a lie. She lied for everyone's sake, including her own. To have a real, honest relationship with Heath, she would have to tell him the truth about their wedding night. And she just couldn't do it.

That meant that all there was left to do now was clean up the tattered remains of their relationship.

And there would be time for that soon. Other more pressing issues had to be addressed first, like arranging her move and seeing her father through his heart surgery, but even those could wait until after she'd had her coffee and settled into her day. It was early. The sun had just come up. Heath was still asleep and there was no sign of life from the bunkhouse. For now, it was just her, the cool air and the pine forest that spread out in front of her.

At one time in her life, those trees had been her sanctuary. Whenever something was troubling her, she could walk through row after row, losing herself in them. And then Tommy Wilder came to the farm. She never imagined someone could hurt her so badly and not kill her. The physical scars healed, but the emotional ones lingered. The trees had turned their backs on her that day, and she'd refused to go out there any longer. The boys had gladly picked up her share of chores in the field and she took on more responsibility in Molly's Christmas store. Her mother thought that it was Julianne's budding artistic spirit that drove her out of the trees and into the shop.

That was so far from the truth. It was actually the other way around. Her refuge in the shop had fueled an artistic creativity in her she didn't know she had. She started helping Molly decorate and make wreaths, but soon she was painting the windows and molding Nativity scenes out of clay. She was keeping so many painful, confusing things inside; it was easy to give her mind over to the intricacies of her art. It was only her good fortune that she was talented at what she did and was able to turn her therapy into a career.

The rumble of car tires across the gravel caught her attention. A moment later, Molly's Buick rounded the house and parked beside her Camaro.

Julianne got up and walked to the stairs to meet her. "Morning, Mama. Is Daddy doing okay?"

Molly nodded. "He's fine. Feeling well enough to shoo me home for a while. His surgery is tomorrow morning, so he wants me to take a break now, while I can."

That sounded like Daddy. He hated to be fussed over, just like she did. "I've made some coffee."

"Thank goodness," Molly said, slowly climbing up the stairs. "That sludge at the hospital hardly qualified."

They went inside and Julianne poured her a large mug with a splash of cream and one spoon of sugar. She joined her mother at the kitchen table, where she and Heath had had their uncomfortable conversation the night before. Looking at the weary, worn-out woman across from her, Julianne knew she just couldn't let her parents find out she'd eloped with Heath right out of high school.

It wasn't because of *whom* had she married, or even *how*. If Julianne hadn't been such a mess and things worked out, Molly wouldn't have been happy about them eloping, but she would have come around. The problem was explaining what went wrong between them and why she wasn't willing to work things out. Everyone would want to know how they could marry and break up in an instant. She couldn't even tell *Heath* that. How could she tell her parents, who had no clue that Tommy had ever laid a hand on her, much less ruined their daughter?

Julianne refused to be anything other than the cool and confident daughter of Ken and Molly. She supposed it was growing up as the only child of parents who desperately wanted more children. They loved her without question, but at the same time, they were always vocal about their disappointment in having only one. When they started taking in foster children, it made it even harder to get attention. At first, she tried to excel in school to prove to them that she was good enough to make up for being the only one. She was well-behaved, polite and never caused the tiniest problem for her parents.

It had worked. To a point. They were always quick to praise her, but her parents continued to bring in foster children. Perfection became her way to stand out and get noticed. It wasn't until after the incident with Tommy that she threw an uncharacteristic fit and demanded her parents stop bringing in other children and pay attention to her for once. It was selfish. And she felt horrible doing it. But she couldn't risk another boy coming to the Garden of Eden who might look at her the way Tommy did.

"Are you doing okay this morning?" Molly asked her.

"Yeah. Heath stayed in the guest room so I wouldn't be alone. We talked last night and a couple of us are going to come stay here for a few months. Through the New Year, at least, to help with Christmas and such."

Molly's chin shot up—her mother was ready to argue—but she stopped herself and nodded. They both knew she couldn't run the farm alone. Her petite frame and increasingly stiff fingers couldn't haul Christmas trees twice her size. Having the kids here would take the pressure off of her and keep Ken resting the way he should. "Which of you are coming up?"

"Heath and I. He's taking a few months away from the advertising agency. I've sold my house in Sag Harbor and I'm moving here until Dad is better, then I'll find someplace new."

"What about you and, uh…" Molly's voice trailed off.

Her mother couldn't remember the name of her boyfriend. That said volumes about her ill-fated relationship history. "Danny," Julianne offered. "We've broken it off."

"Oh," Molly said. "I'm sorry to hear that."

"Liar," Julianne said, smiling into her coffee mug as she took a sip.

Molly shrugged, but didn't argue with her on that point. "I've been speaking with a private medical care company about bringing your father home to recuperate instead of putting him in a nursing home. They recommended moving a bed downstairs, and they could provide a live-in nurse for a few weeks."

"That sounds perfect." She wanted her father to have the best possible care, but she hated the idea of him in a nursing home, even if temporarily.

"Well, except that you'd have to stay in the bunkhouse. We'd need to move one bed downstairs and have the other for the nurse. Is that okay?"

"Absolutely," Julianne responded, although the idea of close quarters with Heath didn't thrill her. Last night was bad enough. "It will give me some room to store my equipment, too."

"Speaking of which, what about your studio? And your gallery showing? You have to keep working, don't you?"

"The store is fine without me. My place in the Hamptons does too well to move and my staff there run it beautifully. As for my studio, I'm thinking I can work here and it wouldn't impact the show. Since I'm staying out there, maybe I can use part of the bunkhouse."

"You know," Molly said, "the storage room there hasn't been used in ages. We could clean that out and you could use it."

"Storage room?"

"Yes. You know what I'm talking about. In the bunkhouse, under the staircase. It's about twelve by twelve, I'd say, with a window and its own door to the outside. That's where we used to hide your Christmas presents when you all were small. Right now, I think it might just have some boxes of the boys' old toys and sporting equipment."

Honestly, she hadn't given much thought to the nook under the stairs. Her time in the bunkhouse was usually spent watching television or messing around with the boys, not surveying the property. "Now I remember. If it's as big as you say, that would be perfect."

"If Heath is staying," Molly continued, "perhaps he can help you get the space ready. There should be some time before the holiday rush begins."

"What am I helping out with?" Heath stumbled sleepily into the kitchen in jeans, a casual T-shirt and bare feet. His light brown hair was tousled. It was a far cry from his expensive tailored suits and perfectly styled hair, but it impacted Julianne even more powerfully. This morning, he looked more like the Heath she'd fallen in love with. The successful, powerful advertising executive was a stranger to her.

"We need you to help clean out the old storage room in the bunkhouse," Molly answered.

He located a mug and made his own cup of coffee. "The one where you hid our Christmas presents?"

A light flush of irritation rose to Molly's cheeks. Julianne had her mother's same pale, flawless complexion. It was always quick to betray their feelings. They blushed bright red at the slightest provocation.

"You knew about that?" Molly asked.

Heath smiled and took a step farther from his mother under the guise of looking in the cabinet for something to eat. "We've always known, Mom. We just didn't have the heart to tell you."

"Well, hell," Molly said, smacking her palm against the table. "Just as well we turn it into a studio, then."

"Mom says that Dad's surgery is tomorrow," Julianne added, steering the conversation in another direction.

Heath pulled down a box of cereal and nodded. "Once we're certain that he's doing okay after surgery, I'll probably head back to New York for a few days and get my things. I need to make arrangements with work and such, but I can probably be back up here in two or three days."

Julianne nodded. She had plenty of things to take care of, too. "Same here. I've got to close on the house. Most of my things are already boxed up. I'll put what I can in storage somewhere and bring the rest."

"How are you going to get all your stuff into that little bitty sports car?" Heath asked.

"The Camaro is bigger than your Porsche," she countered.

"Yeah, but I'm not hauling all your sculpting supplies and tools. What about your kiln?"

"I'm selling it locally," Julianne said, although she didn't know why he was so concerned. "I wanted a new one anyway, so I'll get it delivered here."

Heath frowned at her and crossed his arms over his chest in irritation. She tried not to focus on the way the tight fabric stretched across his hard muscles when he moved, but her eyes were instantly drawn to it. She followed the line of his collar to the lean cords of his neck and the rough stubble along his jaw. Her gaze stopped short when she noticed his amused smirk and arched eyebrow. He'd caught her. At that, she turned her attention back to her coffee and silently cursed herself.

"You need movers," he persisted. "And a truck. I can get you one."

Julianne scoffed at the suggestion. This was so typical of the way the last few years had gone. They avoided the big issues in their relationship and ended up quibbling about stupid things like moving trucks. She supposed to others, they seemed like bickering siblings, when in fact they were a grumpy, married couple. "I might need a truck, but I don't need you to pay for it. I'm capable of handling all that myself."

"Why won't you—"

"We'll discuss it later," she interrupted. She wasn't going to argue with him in front of Molly. She eyed her mother, who was casually sipping her coffee and sorting through her mail.

As if she could feel the tension in the room, Molly set down her stack of bills and stood up. "I'm going to go take a shower," she announced. She took the last sip of her coffee and went upstairs, leaving the two of them alone.

Heath took Molly's seat with a bowl of cereal in one hand and a mug of coffee in the other. "It's later."

"You paying for my movers looks suspicious," she complained. And it did. She made decent money. She didn't need someone to handle it for her, especially Heath playing knight in shining armor.

"I wasn't planning on paying for it. My agency handles the Movers Express account. The CEO owes me a favor. I just have to make a call. Any why is it suspicious? If Wade or Xander offered the same thing, you'd take them up on it without question."

"Because I understand their motives," Julianne said.

Heath's brows went up in surprise. "And what are my motives, Jules? Do you think I'll demand my rights as a husband in exchange for it? Sex for a moving truck? That's certainly a new one on me. Shoot. I should have made that part of the deal up front." His light hazel eyes raked over her, a devious smile curling his lips. He leaned across the table and spoke in a low, seductive tone. "I saw the way you were looking at me just now. It isn't too late to renegotiate, Jules."

The heat of his gaze instantly warmed the blood pumping through her veins. He very quickly made her aware of every inch of her body and how she responded to him. She wished he didn't have that power over her, but the moment she'd looked at him as something more than a friend, it was like a switch had flipped and she hadn't been able to reverse it. She also hadn't been able to do anything about the attraction.

"Yes, it is," she said, dropping her gaze to her coffee mug in the hopes she could suppress her stirring libido. "Way, way too late."

"Well then, I guess I'm just trying to be nice."

He made her reluctance to accept his offer seem childish. "Of course," she said, but a part of her still wondered. There were too many undercurrents running between their every interaction. Whenever Heath was nice to her, whenever he did something for her, she couldn't help but wonder why. He had every reason to be angry with her. She'd treated him terribly, practically throwing his love back in his face.

On their trip to Europe, they had lain on the grass at the base of the Eiffel Tower and watched the lights twinkling on the hour. There, he'd confessed to her that he had been in love with her since the fourth grade. Swept up in the moment, she told him that she loved him, too. Their relationship had begun in Paris. The marriage started and ended in Gibraltar just three days later. She'd pushed him away for his own good, but he'd never understand that. All he saw was that she turned her back on him and wouldn't tell him why.

For a while he was angry with her. He didn't talk to her for their entire freshman year of college. Then he avoided her, doing internships instead of coming home for the summer. Their interactions were short, but polite. It took years, but eventually, he went back to the funny, easygoing Heath she'd always loved.

The light banter and humor covered up their issues, however. They had both been apart for so long, most days it was easy to ignore what happened between them on the graduation trip. But now they were looking at months together. In close quarters.

Julianne had the feeling that the pressure cooker they'd kept sealed all this time was about to blow.

Three

Ken's surgery went perfectly the next day. He spent twenty-four hours in ICU, and then he was moved to a regular room. Once he was off the ventilator and able to talk, Ken demanded everyone go home and stop hovering over him like it was his deathbed.

As instructed, Brody and his fiancée, Samantha, drove back to Boston. When Ken had his attack, Xander had been in Cornwall to move his ten-year-old son and new fiancée, Rose, to D.C. to live with him. He'd sent them along without him, so he gathered up the last of their things and met up with them back in D.C. Wade and Tori lived nearby and agreed to watch the farm while Heath and Julianne went home to make arrangements and make the transition to their new, temporary home.

Heath had offered to drive with Julianne and help with her move, but of course, she'd declined. He didn't know if she just didn't trust him, or if she felt too guilty to accept things from him after she'd broken up with him. He liked to think it was guilt.

The drive to Manhattan was quick, about two and a half hours. He called his business partner as he reached Chelsea and asked Nolan to meet him at his place to go over details while he packed. He found a metered spot on the street as he got off the phone. It was a great spot, considering how much he needed to load into the car. Some days he wasn't so lucky and wished he'd gotten a place with parking.

He hadn't been looking for a condo in this area when he first started shopping, but he'd fallen in love with the modern feel and large rooftop terrace that was bigger than his first New York apartment. Everything else, including parking, fell to the wayside. It was close enough to the office, near a subway stop and one of his favorite restaurants was a block up the street. He couldn't pass it up.

Heath had cleaned all the perishables out of his refrigerator and had his largest suitcase packed when he heard the buzzer for the outer door of the building. He hit the release to let Nolan in and waited there for him to come out of the elevator. "Hey, man. Thanks for coming by."

Nolan smiled and straightened his tie as he walked down the hallway. It was the middle of the week, so he was dressed more for work than Heath, who was in his jeans and NYU alumni sweatshirt.

"How's your dad doing?" Nolan asked.

Heath urged him inside and shut the door. "He's stable. I think he's going to pull through fine, but as I mentioned earlier, I'm going to be gone a few months while he recovers."

"Totally understandable. I think everything will go smoothly at the office. The only account I worry about with you gone is J'Adore."

Heath went to the refrigerator and pulled out two bottles of sparkling water. He opened them both and handed one over to Nolan. "The cosmetics account? Why do they worry you?"

"Well—" Nolan shrugged "—it has more to do with the owner's preference for *Monsieur Langston*."

"Oh," Heath replied. Now he understood. The French cosmetics company was a great account. They'd helped J'Adore break into the high-end American cosmetics market in the last year. Thanks to his company's marketing campaign, J'Adore was the trendiest new product line for the wealthy elite. The only issue was the owner, Madame Cecilia Badeau. She was in her late fifties, wealthy and eccentric, and she had Heath in her sights. For a while he was concerned they would lose the account if he didn't make himself…*available* to her.

"Thank goodness you're married, man," Nolan said, flopping down onto the sleek, white leather couch.

There was that. It was the first time he was thankful to have that stupid piece of paper legally binding him to Julianne. In order not to offend Madame Badeau, Heath had to tell her he was married. It came as quite a shock to her, as well as Nolan, who was also in the room at the time. They were the only other people who knew he and Julianne were married. He explained that Julianne traveled for her work and was always out of town when he was asked about her. Madame Badeau had immediately backed off, but she still insisted the account be personally handled by Heath.

"I think she'll understand that I've taken a leave of absence."

Nolan looked at him, his dark brows pointedly drawn together with incredulity. "I sincerely hope so, but don't be surprised if you get a call."

"After a month on the farm, I might be happy to answer." Heath hadn't spent more than a few days back at the Garden of Eden Christmas Tree Farm since he'd graduated from college. Avoiding Julianne had meant avoiding his family, although he was beginning to think that was the wrong tactic. He was out of sight, out of mind with her. From now on, he was going to be up close and personal.

"Are you going to be running that huge place all by yourself?" Nolan asked.

"No," Heath said, sliding onto the other end of the couch. "Julianne is going back for a while, too."

Nolan sputtered, obviously trying not to choke on his sip of water. "Julianne? Your *wife*, Julianne?"

Heath sighed. "Technically, yes, but I assure you it means nothing. I mean, I told you we never even slept together, right?"

"I still don't know what you could've done to ruin a marriage within hours of your vows."

Heath had wondered that same thing a million times. One moment, he had achieved his life's dream and married his glorious Julianne. The next, she was hysterically crying and screaming for him to stop touching her. The moment he let her go, she ran into the bathroom of their hotel room and didn't come out for two hours.

"I don't know. She never would tell me what changed. She was happy. The perfect, beautiful blushing bride. She responded to me, physically. Things were going fine until they weren't. All she would ever say was that she was sorry. She thought she could be with me, but she just couldn't do it."

"Was she a virgin? My high-school girlfriend was a nervous wreck our first time."

"That's what I thought. I never asked her directly, that felt weird, but that was my assumption. I kept thinking she'd warm up to the idea. She didn't." When he'd first told his partner about his crazy marriage, Heath hadn't elaborated and Nolan had been kind enough not to press him for details. Now, facing months with Julianne, he was glad he had someone to talk to about it.

Nolan scoffed. "What about when you got home?"

"I was trying not to push her. She asked not to tell anyone about the marriage right away and I agreed. I thought she needed time, and we had a few weeks before we both went to school. One morning, I came in from the fields and her car was gone. She'd left early to go to Chicago and didn't tell me or say goodbye."

"What did you do?"

"I followed her up there. She wouldn't even let me into her room. I'd never seen such a hard, cold expression on her face before that day. She told me getting married was a mistake. She was so embarrassed, she couldn't bear to tell anyone about it. Then she told me to go home and forget it ever happened."

"Do you think there's more to it than what she told you?"

"Some days, yes, some days, no. I do think she was ashamed to tell people that she married me. Especially our parents. She's always been too concerned with what people think. Jules had to have Molly and Ken's approval for everything. Maybe she didn't think she would get it for our marriage."

"Or?"

That was the big question. Something just didn't add up. If she had been so concerned about their parents finding out what happened, she either wouldn't have married him at all or she would have panicked when they returned home and had to face telling them. But she had panicked on their wedding night without any warning that his eighteen-year-old self could pick up on. They had kissed and indulged in some fondling in the days before the wedding and again that night. It wasn't until all the clothes came off that the mood shifted.

Then there was fear in her eyes. Sudden terror. And he'd barely touched her, much less hurt her. He'd had eleven years to live that night over and over in his mind and still didn't know what he did wrong.

"I have no idea. I just know that whatever the issue is, she doesn't want to talk about it."

"Why are you two still married, then? You're not still in love with her, are you, Heath?"

"I'm not," Heath assured him. "That boyhood crush died a long time ago, but it's more complicated than that."

"Enlighten me."

"At first, I thought she would change her mind. We had broken up, but I was certain she would realize she was overreacting about the sex and after being apart for a while she would miss me and decide she really did love me and want to be with me." He sighed, remembering how many nights he'd lain in bed naively fantasizing about her revelation. "But she didn't. She just pretended it never happened and expected me to do the same. She wouldn't talk about it."

"Then divorce her," Nolan suggested. "Be done with it."

Heath shook his head. "I know that I should, but there's no way I'm letting her off the hook that easily. I definitely think it's time to wrap the whole thing up between us, but she left me. I'm going to make her finish the job."

Nolan didn't look convinced. "That hasn't worked so well for you so far."

"I just think she needs a little incentive. Something to push her to make a move."

"What have you got in mind?" Nolan asked, his eyes

lighting up with his wicked imagination. He was the perfect business partner for Heath. They were both devious to a fault, but Heath had the creativity and Nolan had the business smarts.

He could still picture her flushed cheeks and stuttering speech when she was faced with his half-naked body. That really was the key. "I'm going to go back to the house and help Jules set up her new studio there. I'll do everything I need to around the farm. But I'm not going to pretend like nothing ever happened between us. I'm not going to sit on my hands and ignore that we're still attracted to one another."

"You're still into her? After everything that has happened? That's kinda twisted, man."

Heath shrugged. "I can't help it. She's even more beautiful than she was back then. I've always been attracted to her, and if she was honest with herself, she'd have to admit she's still got a thing for me, too. I'm going to try to use it to my advantage. Sex was always our problem, so I intend to push the issue and make her so uncomfortable, she will be all too happy to file for divorce and put this behind her. By the time I come back to New York, I expect to be a free man."

Nolan nodded slowly and put his bottle of water onto the coffee table. "And that's what you want, right?"

Heath wasn't sure what his business partner meant by that. Of course he wanted this to be over. And it would be. There was no way that Julianne would take him up on his sexual advances. She'd run, just like she always did, and he could finally move on. Just because he was still attracted to Julianne didn't mean that anything would come of it.

"Absolutely." Heath smiled wide, thinking of all the ways he could torture his bride over the next few weeks.

When it was all said and done, he would get his divorce and they would finally be able to move on.

But he sure as hell wasn't going to make it easy on her.

No one was around when Julianne arrived in her small moving truck. She wouldn't admit it, but Heath had been right. She needed help moving. There was more than she could fit in the car, so she decided to skip the storage rental and just bring it all with her. By the time she had that realization, she was already in Sag Harbor staring down the piles of stuff she didn't remember accumulating, so she ended up renting a truck one-way and towing her Camaro behind it the whole way.

She pulled the truck up behind the bunkhouse, where it would be out of the way until she could unload everything. Her clothes and personal things could go into her bedroom, but all the supplies for her studio would have to wait. She'd scoped out the storage room before she left and knew it would take time to clean it out. She'd considered doing it then, but Heath had insisted she wait until he was back from New York and could help her.

She opened the door to the storage room to give it a second look. The room was dim, with only the light coming in from one window, so she felt around until she found a light switch. A couple of fluorescent bulbs kicked on, highlighting the dusty shelves and cardboard boxes that filled the space. Molly was right—with a little elbow grease it would be the perfect place for her to work.

The hardwood floors continued into the storage room. There were several sturdy shelving units and open spaces for her to put her equipment. The brand-new, top-of-the-line kiln she ordered would fit nicely into the corner. She couldn't wait to get settled in.

Julianne grabbed her large rolling suitcase and threw

a duffel bag over her shoulder. She hauled them slowly up the stairs and paused at the landing between the two bedrooms. She wasn't sure which one to use. She'd never slept in the bunkhouse before. Whenever she came home, she used her old room, but that was going to be unavailable for a few weeks at least until Dad was able to climb the stairs again. She reached for the doorknob on the left, pushing the door open with a loud creak.

It was a nice, big space. When she was younger the rooms had been equipped with bunk beds that would allow the Edens to take in up to eight foster children at a time. Wade, Brody, Xander and Heath had stayed at the Garden of Eden until they were grown, but there were a dozen other boys who came and went for short periods of time while their home situations straightened out.

She was relieved to see the old bunks had been replaced with two queen-sized beds. They had matching comforters and a nightstand between them. A large dresser flanked the opposite wall. She took a step in and noticed the closet door was ajar and a suitcase was lying open inside it. And a light was coming from under the bathroom door. Heath was back. She hadn't noticed his car.

Before she could turn around, the bathroom door opened and Heath stepped out. He was fresh from the shower. His hair was damp and combed back, his face pink and smooth from a hot shave. The broad, muscular chest she caught a glimpse of a few days before was just as impressive now, with its etched muscles and dark hair, only this time his skin was slick. He had a towel wrapped around his waist, thank goodness, but that was the only thing between her and a fully naked Heath.

Once upon a time, the sight of her naked husband had launched her into a complete panic attack. The cloud of confused emotions and fear had doused any arousal she might have felt. Eleven years and a lot of therapy later, only the dull ache of need was left when she looked at him.

Heath wasn't startled by her appearance. In fact, her appraising glance seemed to embolden him. He arched an eyebrow at her and then smiled the way he always seemed to when she was uncomfortable. "We've really got to stop meeting like this."

A flush rushed to her cheeks from a mix of embarrassment and instant arousal. She knew Heath could see it, so that just made the deep red color even worse. "I'm sorry. I've done it again." Julianne backed toward the door, averting her eyes to look at anything but his hard, wet body and mocking grin. "I parked the moving truck out back and didn't realize you were here. I was trying to figure out which room I should use."

"You're welcome to use this one," Heath said. He sat down on the edge of one of the beds and gave it a good test bounce. "That would prove interesting."

"Uh, no," she said, slipping back through the doorway. "The other room will be just fine."

Her hands were shaking as she gripped the handle of her luggage and rolled it to the opposite bedroom. When she opened the door, she found it to be exactly the same as the other one, only better, because it didn't have her cocky, naked husband in it.

She busied herself hanging up clothes in the closet and storing underthings in the dresser. Putting things away was a good distraction from the sexual thoughts and raging desire pumping through her veins.

Julianne was setting out the last of her toiletries in the bathroom when she turned and found Heath in her doorway, fully clothed.

"Do you need help bringing more things in?"

"Not tonight. Tomorrow, maybe we can work on clearing out the storage room and then I can unload the rest of my supplies there. There's no sense piling up things in the living room. I don't have to return the truck for a few days."

"Okay, good," he said, but he didn't leave.

Julianne stood, waiting for him to speak or do something, but he just leaned against her door frame. His hazel gaze studied her, his eyes narrowing in thought. A smile curled his lips. She had no idea what he was actually thinking, but it was unnerving to be scrutinized so closely.

Finally, she returned to putting her things away and tried to pretend he wasn't inspecting her every move. There was something about the way he watched her that made her very aware of her own body. It happened every time. He didn't have to say a word, yet she would feel the prickle of awareness start up the back of her neck. Her heart would begin pounding harder in her chest. The sound of her breath moving rapidly in and out of her lungs would become deafening.

Then came the heat. What would start as a warmness in her cheeks would spread through her whole body. Beads of perspiration would start to form at the nape of her neck and the valley between her breasts. Deep in her belly, a churning heat would grow warmer and warmer.

All with just a look. She tried desperately to ignore him because she knew how quickly these symptoms would devolve to blatant wanting, especially if he touched her. Eleven years ago, she was too frightened to do anything about her feelings, but she'd come a long way. There was nothing holding her back now. Whether or not Heath still wanted her, he seemed happy to push the issue. How the hell would she make it through the next few months with him so close by? With no brothers or other family here to distract them?

"I'm surprised you're staying in the bunkhouse," Heath said at last.

"Why is that?" Julianne didn't turn to look at him. Instead, she stuffed her empty duffel bag into her luggage and zipped it closed.

"I would've thought you'd want to stay as far away from me as possible. Then again," he added, "this might be your chance to indulge your secret desires without anyone finding out. Maybe you're finally ready to finish what we started."

Julianne turned to look at him with her hands planted on her hips. Hopefully her indignant attitude would mask how close to the truth he actually was. "Indulge my secret desires? Really, Heath?"

He shoved his hands into the pockets of his gray trousers and took a few slow, casual steps into the room. "Why else would you stay out here? I'm sure things in the big house are much nicer."

"They are," she replied matter-of-factly. "But Daddy will be coming home soon and there won't be a room for me there. Besides, being out here makes me feel more independent. My studio will be downstairs, so it's convenient and I'll be less likely to disturb Mom and Dad."

"Yes," he agreed. "You can stay up late and make all the noise you want. You could scream the walls down if you felt inclined."

Julianne clenched her hands into fists at her sides. "Stop making everything I say into a sexual innuendo. Yes, I will be staying out here with you, but that's only because it's the only place to go. If there were an alternative, I'd gladly take it."

Heath chuckled, but she could tell by the look on his face that he didn't believe a word she said. "You're an awfully arrogant bastard," she noted. "I do not want to sleep with you, Heath."

"You say that," he said, moving a few feet closer. "But I know you better than you'd like to think, Jules. I recognize that look in your eye. The color rushing to your cheeks. The rapid rise and fall of your breasts as you breathe harder. You're trying to convince yourself that you don't want me, but we both know that you hate leaving things unfinished. And you and I are most certainly unfinished."

He was right. Julianne was normally focused on every detail, be it in art or life. She was an overachiever. The only thing she'd found she couldn't manage was being a wife. Just another reason to keep their past relationship under the covers.

A tingle of desire ran down her spine and she closed her eyes tightly to block it out. Wrong choice of words.

"Were you this arrogant when we eloped?" she asked. "I can't fathom that I would've fallen for you with an ego this large."

Heath looked at her, the smile curling his lips fading until a hard, straight line appeared across his face. "No, I wasn't this arrogant. I was young and naive and hopelessly in love with a girl that I thought cared about me."

"Heath, I—"

"Don't," he interrupted. He took another step forward, forcing Julianne to move back until the knobs of the dresser pressed into her rear end. "Don't say what you were going to say because you and I both know it's a waste of breath. Don't tell me that you were confused and scared about your feelings for me, because you knew exactly what you were doing. Don't bother to tell me it was just a youthful mistake, because it's a mistake that you refuse to correct. Why is that, I wonder?"

Julianne stood, trapped between her dresser and Heath's

looming body. He leaned into her and was so close that if she let out the breath she was holding and her muscles relaxed, they might touch. Unable to escape, her eyes went to the sensual curve of his mouth. She didn't care for what he was saying, but she would enjoy watching him say it. He had a beautiful mouth, one that she'd secretly fantasized about kissing long before they'd gone to Europe and long after they came back.

"Maybe," he added, "it's because you aren't ready to let go of me just yet."

It was just complicated. She'd wrestled with this for years. She wanted Heath, but the price of having him was too high for both of them to pay. And yet giving up would mean letting go of the best thing that ever happened to her. "Heath, I—"

"You can lie to everyone else," he interrupted. "You can even lie to yourself. But you can't lie to me, Jules. For whatever reason, the time wasn't right back then. Maybe we were just too young, but that's no longer the case. You want me. I want you. It's not right or wrong, black or white. It's just a fact."

His lips were a whisper away from hers. Her own mouth was suddenly dry as he spoke such blunt words with such a seductive voice. She couldn't answer him. She could barely think with him this close to her. Every breath was thick with the warm scent of his cologne and the soap from his shower.

Heath brought his hand up to caress her cheek. "It's time for you to figure out what you're going to do about it."

Julianne's brow drew down into a frown. "What I'm going to do about it?"

"Yes. It's pretty simple, Jules. You either admit that you want me and give yourself freely and enthusiastically to your husband at last. Or…you get off your hind end and file for divorce."

Julianne's mind went to the last discussion she'd had with her attorney. He could draw up the paperwork anytime. It was a pretty cut-and-dried arrangement with no comingled assets. She just had to tell him to pull the trigger. It was that simple and yet the thought made her nearly sick to her stomach. But what was her alternative? Staying married wouldn't solve their problems. And if marriage meant sleeping with Heath, there would just be sex clouding their issues.

"Why can't this wait until we're both back in New York and can work through the paperwork privately? Don't we have enough going on right now? I'm not really interested in either of your options."

A wicked grin curled Heath's full lips, making her heart stutter in her chest. "Oh, you will be. There's no more stalling, Jules. We've both lived in New York long enough to have addressed it privately, if that was what you really wanted. If you don't choose, I'll make the decision for you. And if *I* file for divorce, I'll go to Frank Hartman."

Frank Hartman was the family attorney and the only one in Cornwall. Even if Heath didn't spread the news she had no doubt that their parents would find out about their marriage if he filed with him. That would raise too many questions.

"Your dirty little secret will be out in the open for sure. I'll see to it that every single person in town finds out about our divorce." His lips barely grazed hers as he spoke, and then he started to laugh. He took a large step back, finally allowing her a supply of her very own oxygen.

"You think on that," he said, turning and walking out of her bedroom.

Four

Heath stumbled downstairs the next morning after pulling on some clothes. He could smell coffee and although still half-asleep, he was on a mission for caffeine. He'd slept late that morning after lying in bed for hours thinking about Julianne. After he'd walked out of her room, he'd shut his door, hoping to keep thoughts of her on the other side. He'd failed.

It would take a hell of a lot more than a panel of wood to do that. Not after being so close to her after all this time apart. Not after seeing her react to him. She was stubborn, he knew that, but she'd gotten under his skin just as he'd gotten under hers.

Part of him had enjoyed torturing her a little bit. He wasn't a vindictive person, but she did owe him a little after what she'd done. He wasn't going to get a wife or an apology out of all this. He'd just be a lonely divorced guy who couldn't tell the people he was closest to that he was a lonely divorced guy. His brothers, whom he typically turned to for advice or commiseration, couldn't know the truth. Poor Nolan would end up with the burden of his drama. He could at least watch her squirm a little bit and get some satisfaction from that. The whole point was to make her so uncomfortable that she would contact her lawyer.

But what had bothered him the most, what had kept him up until two in the morning, had been the look in her eyes when he'd nearly kissed her. He'd been close enough. Just the slightest move and their mouths would have touched. And she wanted him to kiss her. She'd licked her lips, her gaze focused on his mouth with an intensity like never before. It made him wonder what she would have done if he had.

He hadn't kissed Julianne since their wedding night. Heath never imagined that would be the last time he would kiss his wife. They'd been married literally a few hours. Certainly things wouldn't go bad that quickly. Right?

With a groan, he crossed the room, his gaze zeroing in on the coffeepot, half the carafe still full. He poured himself a cup and turned just in time to see Julianne shuffle into the kitchen with a giant cardboard box in her arms.

Despite the chilly October weather outside, she had already worked up a sweat moving boxes. She was wearing a thin tank top and a pair of cutoff jean shorts. Her long blond hair was pulled up into a messy bun on the top of her head with damp strands plastered to the back of her neck.

Heath forced down a large sip of hot coffee to keep from sputtering it everywhere. Man, she had an amazing figure. The girl he'd married had been just that—a girl. She'd been a tomboy and a bit of a late bloomer. She had still been fairly thin, a tiny pixie of a thing that he sometimes worried he might snap when he finally made love to her.

Things had certainly changed since the last time he'd run his hands over that body. He'd heard her complain to Molly about how she'd gained weight over the years, but he didn't mind. The tight little shorts she was wearing were filled out nicely and her top left little to his imagination. His brain might not be fully awake yet, but the rest of his body was up and at 'em.

"What?"

Julianne's voice jerked him out of his detailed assessment. He was staring and she'd caught him. Only fair after her heavy appraisal of him over the last few days. "You're going to hurt yourself," Heath quickly noted. He tried leaning casually against the kitchen counter to cover the tension in his body.

Her cool green gaze regarded him a moment before she dropped the box by the staircase with a loud thud and a cloud of dust. It joined a pile of four or five other equally dusty boxes. "I'm supposed to be helping you with that," he added when she didn't respond.

She turned back to him, rubbing her dirty palms on her round, denim-clad rear end. "I couldn't sleep," she said, disappearing into the storage room. A moment later she came back out with another box. "You weren't awake."

"I'm awake now."

She dropped the box to the floor with the others. "Good. You can start helping anytime then." Julianne returned to her chores.

"Good morning to you, too," he grumbled, drinking the last of his coffee in one large sip. Heath put his mug in the sink and walked across the room to join her in the storage room.

He looked around the space, surveying the work ahead of them. Clearing out the room would be less work than figuring out what to do with all the stuff. He plucked an old, flattened basketball out of one box and smashed it between his hands. Just one of a hundred unwanted things left behind over the years. They'd probably need to run a couple loads to the dump in Ken's truck.

"Is there a plan?" he asked.

Julianne rubbed her forearm across her brow to wipe away perspiration. "I'd like to clear the room out first. Then clean it so we can move my things in and I can return the truck. Then we can deal with the stuff we've taken out."

"Fair enough." Heath tossed the ball back into the box and picked it up.

They worked together quietly for the next hour or so. After the previous night's declarations, he expected her to say something, but he'd underestimated Julianne's ability to compartmentalize things. Today's task was cleaning the storeroom, so that was her focus. She'd used the same trick to ignore their relationship for other pursuits over the years. He didn't push the issue. They'd get a lot less cleaning done if they were arguing.

When the room was finally empty, they attacked the space with brooms and old rags, dusting away the cobwebs and sweeping up years of dust and grime. Despite their dirty chores, he couldn't help but stop and watch Julianne every now and then. She would occasionally bend over for something, giving him a prime view of her firm thighs and round behind. The sweat dampened her shirt and he would periodically catch a glimpse as a bead of perspiration traveled down into the valley between her breasts.

He wasn't sure if it was the hard work or the view, but it didn't take long for Heath to get overheated. As they were cleaning the empty room, he had to whip his shirt off and toss it onto the kitchen table. He returned to working, paying no attention to what was going on until he noticed Julianne was watching him and not moving any longer.

Heath paused and looked up at her. She had her arms crossed over her chest, suggestively pressing her small, firm breasts together. He might enjoy the view if not for the irritated expression puckering her delicate brow. "Is something wrong, Jules?"

"Do you normally run around half-naked or is all this just a show for my benefit?"

"What?" Heath looked down at his bare chest and tried to determine what was so offensive about it. "No, of course I don't run around naked. But I'm also not usually doing hard, dirty labor. Advertising doesn't work up much of a sweat."

Julianne was frowning, but he could see the slight twist of amusement in her lips. He could tell she liked what she saw, even if she wouldn't admit that to herself.

"It seems like every time I turn around, you're not wearing a shirt."

Heath smiled. "Is that a complaint or a pleasant observation?"

Julianne planted her hands on her hips, answering him without speaking.

"Well, to be fair, *you've* barged into my bedroom twice and caught me in various states of undress. That's not my fault. That's like complaining because I don't wear clothes into the shower. You make it sound like I've paraded around like a Chippendales dancer or something." Heath held out his arms, flexing his muscles and gyrating his hips for effect.

Julianne brought her hand to her mouth to stifle a giggle as he danced. "Stop that!" she finally yelled, throwing her dust rag at him.

Heath caught it and ended his performance. "You're just lucky I left my tear-away pants in Manhattan."

She shook her head with a reluctant smile and turned

back to what she'd been cleaning. They finished not too long after that, then piled their brooms and mops in the kitchen and went back in to look around.

"This isn't a bad space at all," Julianne said as they surveyed the empty, clean room. "I think it will make the perfect studio."

Heath watched her walk around the space, thinking aloud. "Is it big enough for all of your things?"

"I think so. If I put the new kiln over here," she said, "my big table will fit here. I can use this shelf to put my pieces on that are in progress. My pottery wheel can go here." She gestured to a space below the window. "And this old dresser will be good to store tools and supplies."

She seemed to have it all laid out in her mind. They just had to bring everything in. "Are you ready to unload the truck?"

Julianne shook her head and smoothed her palm over the wild strands of her hair. "Maybe later this afternoon. I'm exhausted. Right now, all I want to do is take a shower and get some lunch."

Heath couldn't agree more. "I'll probably do the same. But proceed with caution," he said.

"Caution?" Julianne looked at him with wide, concerned eyes.

"Yes. I *will* be naked up there. And wet," he added with a sly grin. "You've been forewarned."

Julianne was certain this was going to be the longest few months in history.

She'd quickly taken her shower and sat down on the edge of the bed to dry her hair. She could hear the water running in his bathroom when she was finished, making her think of his warning. He was wet and naked in the next room. She was determined to miss out on that event this time. Running into him once was an accident. Twice could be considered a fluke. A third time was stalking. Julianne wasn't about to give Heath the satisfaction of knowing she enjoyed looking at him. She did; he had a beautiful body. But she'd already gotten her daily eyeful of his hot, sweaty muscles as they worked downstairs.

That was more than enough to fire up her suppressed libido and set her mind to thinking about anything but cleaning. She shouldn't feel this way. It had been over a month since Danny moved out. Not a tragic dry spell by any means and she was more than capable of managing her urges. But somehow, the combination of Heath's friendly eyes, charming smile and hard body made her forget about all that.

It had been like that back in high school. She had gone years having Heath live with her family, trying to keep her attraction to him in check. Heath had been the first boy she'd ever kissed. She liked him. But somehow, once he came to the farm, it seemed inappropriate. So she tried to ignore it as he got older and grew more handsome. She tried to tell herself they were just friends when they would talk for hours.

By their senior year, they were the only kids left on the farm and it was getting harder for her to ignore the sizzle of tension between them. After what had happened to her five years earlier, she hadn't really dated. She'd kissed a boy or two, but nothing serious and nothing remotely close enough to hit her panic button. It was easy. Heath was the only one who got her blood pumping. The one who made her whole body tingle and ache to be touched. So she avoided him.

But it wasn't until they were alone in Paris that she let herself indulge her attraction. There, with the romantic twinkling lights and soft music serenading them, he'd told her he loved her. That he'd always loved her. This had to be the right thing to do. She loved him. He was her best friend. Heath would never hurt her. It was perfect.

Until her nerves got the best of her. Kissing was great. Roaming hands were very nice. But anything more serious made her heart race unpleasantly. Heath thought maybe she was saving herself for marriage and that would remove the last of her doubts. So they got married. And it only got worse.

Julianne sighed and carried the blow-dryer back into the bathroom. Funny how the thing that was supposed to bring them together forever—the ultimate relationship step—was what ended up dooming them.

It was easy to forget about her problems when her brushes with Heath were few and far between. They were both busy, and usually he didn't want to talk about their issues any more than she did. That did not seem to be the case any longer. She could tell that something had gotten into him, but she didn't know what. Perhaps Ken's second heart attack made him realize life was too short to waste it married to someone who didn't love him like she should. Or maybe he'd found someone else but hadn't told anyone about it yet.

That thought was enough to propel her out of the room and downstairs for some lunch. She didn't like thinking about Heath with someone else. That called for an edible distraction. It was a terrible habit to have, but she was an emotional eater. It had started after Tommy attacked her and it became a constant battle for her after that. Her therapist had helped her recognize the issue and to stop before she started, but when things weren't going well, it was nothing a cheeseburger and a Diet Coke wouldn't fix. At least for an hour or so.

At the top of the staircase, Julianne paused. She could

hear Heath's voice carrying from the kitchen. At first, Julianne thought he might be talking to her. She started down the stairs but stopped when she heard him speak again. He was on the phone.

"Hey, sweetheart."

Sweetheart? Julianne held her breath and took a step backward so he wouldn't see her on the stairs listening in. Who was he talking to? A dull ache in her stomach that had nothing to do with hunger told her she'd been right before. He hadn't mentioned dating anyone recently, but that must be what all the sudden divorce talk was about. Why would he tell her if he were seeing someone special? She was a slip of paper away from being his ex-wife, all things considered.

"Aww, I miss you, too." Heath listened for a moment before laughing. "I know it's hard, but I'll be back before you know it."

There was a tone to his voice that she wasn't used to hearing—an intimacy and softness she remembered from the time they spent together in Europe. This woman obviously had a special place in Heath's life. Julianne was immediately struck with a pang of jealousy as she listened in. It was stupid. They'd agreed that if they weren't together, they were both free to see other people. She'd been living with Danny for a year and a half, so she couldn't complain.

"You know I have to take care of some things here. But look on the bright side. When all this is handled and I come home, we can make that Caribbean vacation you've been dreaming about a reality. But you've got to be patient."

"Hang on, baby," Julianne muttered to herself with a mocking tone. "I gotta ditch the wife, then we can go frolic on the beach." And to think he'd been acting like he had been interested in something more between them. When he'd pressed against her, she was certain he still wanted her—at least short-term. He apparently had longer-term plans with someone else.

"Okay. I'll call again soon. 'Bye, darling."

Julianne choked down her irritation and descended the stairs with loud, stomping feet. When she turned toward the kitchen, Heath was leaning casually against the counter, holding his cell phone and looking pointedly at her. He had changed into a snug pair of designer jeans that hugged the thick muscles of his thighs and a button-down shirt in a mossy green that matched the color of his eyes. This was a middle-of-the-road look, a comfortable median between his sleepy casual style and his corporate shark suits. He looked handsome, put together and, judging by the light in his eyes, amused by her irritation.

"Something the matter?" he asked.

"No," she said quickly. There wasn't anything wrong. He could do whatever and whomever he wanted. That wasn't any concern of hers, no matter how spun up she seemed to be at the moment.

It was just because she'd never been faced with it before. That was it. Neither she nor Heath had ever brought anyone home to meet the family. They both dated, but it was an abstract concept that wasn't waved in her face like a red cape in front of a bull.

"I know you were listening in on my conversation."

She took a deep breath and shrugged. "Not really, but it was hard to ignore with all that mushy sweetheart nonsense."

The corners of Heath's mouth curled in amusement. "What's the matter, Jules? Are you jealous?"

"Why on earth would I be jealous?" she scoffed. "We're married, but it doesn't really mean anything. You're free to do what you want. I mean, if I wanted you, I could've had you, so obviously, I wouldn't be jealous."

"I don't know," Heath said, his brow furrowing. "Maybe you're starting to regret your decision."

"Not at all."

She said the words too quickly, too forcefully, and saw a flash of pain in Heath's light hazel eyes. It disappeared quickly, a smile covering his emotions the way it always did. Humor was his go-to defense mechanism. It could be maddening sometimes.

"You seem very confident in your decision considering you still haven't filed for divorce after all this time. Are you sure you want rid of me? Actions speak louder than words, Jules."

"Absolutely certain. I've just been too busy building my career to worry about something that seems so trivial after all this time."

Heath's jaw flexed as he considered her statement for a moment. He obviously didn't care for her choice of words. "We've never really talked about it. At least not without yelling. Since it's so *trivial*, care to finally tell me what went wrong? I've waited a long time to find out."

Julianne closed her eyes and sighed. She'd almost prefer his heated pursuit to the questions she couldn't answer. "I'd really rather not, Heath. What does it matter now?"

"You left me confused and embarrassed on my wedding night. Do you know how messed up it was to take my clothes off in front of a girl for the first time and have you react like that? It's ego-crushing, Jules. It may have been more than a decade ago, but it still matters."

Julianne planted her hands on her hips and looked down at the floor. This was no time for her to come clean. She couldn't. "I don't have anything more to tell you than I did before. I realized it was a mistake. I'm sorry I didn't correct it until that inopportune time."

Heath flinched and frowned at her direct words. "You seemed happy enough about it until then."

"We were in Europe. Everything was romantic and exciting and we were so far from home I could forget all the reasons why it was a bad idea. When faced with…" Her voice trailed off as she remembered the moment her panic hit her like a tidal wave. He was obviously self-conscious enough about her reaction. How could she ever explain to him that it wasn't the sight of his naked body per se, but the idea of what was to come that threw her into a flashback of the worst day of her life? She couldn't. It would only hurt him more to know the truth. "When faced with the point of no return, I knew I couldn't go through with it. I know you want some big, drawn-out explanation as though I'm holding something back, but I'm not. That's all there is to it."

"You are so full of crap. I've known you since we were nine years old. You're lying. I know you're lying. I just don't know what you're lying about." Heath stuck his hands in his pockets and took a few leisurely steps toward her. "But maybe I'm overthinking it. Maybe the truth of the matter is that you're just selfish."

He might as well have slapped her. "Selfish? I'm selfish?" That was great. She was lying to protect him. She'd left him so he could find someone who deserved his love, but somehow she was selfish.

"I think so. You want your cake and you want to eat it, too." Heath held out his arms. "It doesn't have to be that way. If you want me, I'm right here. Take a bite. Please," he added with emphasis, his gaze pinning her on the spot and daring her to reach out for him.

Julianne froze, not certain what to do or say. Part of her brain was urging her to leap into his arms and take what he had to give. She wasn't a scared teenager anymore. She could indulge and enjoy everything she couldn't have before. The other part worried about what it would lead to. Her divorce attorney's number was programmed into her phone. Why start something that they were on the verge of finishing for good?

"Maybe this will help you decide." Heath's hands went to her waist, pulling her body tight against him. Julianne stumbled a bit, colliding with his chest and placing her hands on his shoulders to catch herself. Her palms made contact with the hard wall of muscle she had seen so many times the last few days but didn't dare touch. The scent of his shower-fresh skin filled her nose. The assault on her senses made her head swim and her skin tingle with longing to keep exploring her newfound discovery.

She looked up at him in surprise, not quite sure what to do. His lips found hers before she could decide. At first, she was taken aback by the forceful claim of her mouth. This was no timid teenager kissing her. The hard, masculine wall pressed against her was all grown up.

In their youth, he had never handled her with less care than he would a fragile piece of pottery. Now, he had lost what control he had. And she liked it. They had more than a decade of pent-up sexual tension, frustration and downright anger between them. It poured out of his fingertips, and pressed into her soft flesh, drawing cries of pleasure mingled with pain in the back of her throat.

Matching his ferocity, she clung to his neck, pulling him closer until his body was awkwardly arched over hers. Every place he touched seemed to light on fire until her whole body burned for him. She was getting lost in him, just as she had back then.

And then he pulled away. She had to clutch at the countertop to stay upright once his hard body withdrew its support.

His hazel eyes raked over her body, noting her undeniable response to his kiss. "So what's it going to be, Jules? Are the two of us over and done? Decide."

There were no words. Her brain was still trying to process everything that just happened. Her body ached for him to touch her again. Her indecisiveness drew a disappointed frown across his face.

"Or," he continued, dropping his arms to his side, "do like you've always done. A big nothing. You say you don't want me, but you don't want anyone else to have me, either. You can't have it both ways. You've got to make up your mind, Jules. It's been eleven years. Either you want me or you don't."

"I don't think the two of us are a good idea," she admitted at last. That was true. They weren't a good idea. Her body just didn't care.

"Then what are you waiting for? End it before you sink your next relationship." Heath paused, his brow furrowing in thought. "Unless that's how you like it."

"How I like what?"

"Our marriage is your little barrier to the world. You've dated at least seven or eight guys that I know of, none of them ever getting serious. But that's the way you want it. As long as you're married, you don't have to take it to the next level."

"You think I like failing? You think I want to spend every Christmas here watching everyone snuggled up into happy little couples while I'm still alone?"

"I think a part of you does. It might suck to be alone, but it's better than making yourself vulnerable and getting hurt. Trust me, I know what it's like to get your heart ripped out and stomped on. Being lonely doesn't come close to that kind of pain. I'm tired of you using me, Jules. Make a decision."

"Fine!" Julianne pushed past him, her vision going red as she stomped upstairs into her room. He'd kissed her and insulted her in less than a minute's time. If he thought she secretly wanted to be with him, he was very, very wrong. She snatched her cell phone off the bed and went back to the kitchen.

By the time she returned, the phone was ringing at her attorney's office. "Hello? This is Julianne Eden." Her gaze burrowed into Heath's as she spoke. "Would you please let Mr. Winters know that I'm ready to go forward with the divorce paperwork? Yes. Please overnight it to my secondary address in Connecticut. Thank you."

She slammed her phone onto the kitchen table with a loud smack that echoed through the room. "If you want a divorce so damn bad, fine. Consider it done!"

Five

The rest of the afternoon and most of the next day were spent working. They focused on their chores, neither willing to broach the subject of their argument and set off another battle. The divorce papers would arrive at any time. They had things to get done. There was no sense rehashing it.

They were unloading the last of her equipment from the rental truck when Heath spied Sheriff Duke's patrol car coming up the driveway.

Julianne was beside him, frozen like a deer in the oncoming lights of a car. He handed her the box he'd been carrying. "Take this and go inside. Don't come out unless I come get you."

She didn't argue. She took the box and disappeared through the back door of the storage room. He shut the door behind her and walked around the bunkhouse to where Duke's Crown Victoria was parked beside his Porsche.

Duke climbed out, eyeballing the sports car as he rounded it to where Heath was standing. "Afternoon, Heath."

Heath shook his hand politely and then crossed his arms over his chest. This wasn't a social call and he wouldn't let his guard down for even a second thinking that it was. "Evening, Sheriff. What can I do for you?"

Duke slipped off his hat, gripping it in his left hand. "I just came from the hospital. I spoke with your folks."

Heath tried to keep the anger from leaching into his voice, but the tight clench of his jaw made his emotions obvious as he spoke. "You interviewed my father in the hospital after open-heart surgery? After he had a heart attack the last time you spoke? Did you try to arrest him this time, too?"

"He's not in critical condition," Duke said. "Relax. He's fine. Was when I got there and was when I left. The doctors say he's doing better than expected."

Heath took a deep breath and tried to uncoil his tense muscles. He still wasn't happy, but at least Ken was okay. "I assume you're not here to give me an update on Dad as a public service to the hospital."

A faint smile curled Duke's lips. "No, I'm not. Would you care to sit down somewhere?"

"Do I need a lawyer?" Heath asked.

"No. Just wanting to ask a few questions. You're not a suspect at this time."

"Then no, I'm fine standing." Heath wasn't interested in getting comfortable and drawing out this conversation. He could outstand the older officer by a long shot. "What can I help you with?"

Duke nodded softly, obviously realizing he wasn't going to be offered a seat and some tea like he would if Molly were home. "First, I wanted to let you know that Ken and

Molly are no longer suspects. I was finally able to verify their story with accounts of others in town."

"Like what?" Heath asked.

"Well, Ken had always maintained he was sick in bed all that day with the flu. I spoke to the family physician and had him pull old records from the archives. Ken did come in the day before to see the doctor. Doc said it was a particularly bad strain of flu that year. Most people were in bed for at least two days. I don't figure Ken was out in the woods burying a body in the shape he was in."

"He was sick," Heath added. "Very sick. Just as we've told you before."

"People tell me a lot of things, Heath. Doesn't make it true. I've got to corroborate it with other statements. We've established Ken was sick that day. So, how did that work on the farm? If Ken wasn't working, did the whole group take the day off?"

"No," Heath answered with a bit of a chuckle. Sheriff Duke obviously hadn't grown up on a farm. "Life doesn't just stop when the boss is feeling poorly. We went on with our chores as usual. Wade picked up a few of the things that Ken normally did. Nothing particularly special about it. That's what we did whenever anyone was sick."

"And what about Tommy?"

"What about him?" Heath wasn't going to volunteer anything without being asked directly.

"What was he doing that day?"

Heath sighed and tried to think back. "It's been a long time, Sheriff, but if I had to guess, I'd figure he was doing a lot of nothing. That's what he did most days. He tended to go out into the trees and mess around. I never saw him put in an honest afternoon's work."

"I heard he got into some fights with the other boys."

Heath wasn't going to let Duke zero in on his brothers

as suspects. "That's because he was lazy and violent. He had a quick temper and, on more than one occasion, took it out on one of us."

Sheriff Duke's dark gaze flicked over Heath's face for a moment as he considered his answers. "I bet you didn't care much for Tommy."

"No one did. You know what kind of stuff he was into."

"I can't comment on that. You know his juvenile files are sealed."

"I don't need to see his files to know what he'd done. I lived with him. I've got a scar from where he shoved me into a bookcase and split my eyebrow open. I remember Wade's black eye. I know about the stealing and the drugs and the fights at school. You can't seal my memories, Sheriff." Some days he wished he could.

Duke shuffled uncomfortably on his feet. "When was the last time you saw Tommy?"

"The last time I saw him…" Heath tried to remember back to that day. He spent most of his time trying not to think about it. The image of Tommy's blank, dead stare and the pool of blood soaking into the dirt was the first thing to come to mind. He quickly put that thought away and backed up to before that moment. Before he heard the screams and found Tommy and Julianne together on the ground. "It was just after school. We all came home, Molly brought us some snacks to the bunkhouse and told us Ken was sick in bed. We finished up and each headed out to do our chores. I went into the eastern fields."

"Did you see Tommy go into the woods that day?"

"No." And he hadn't. "Tommy was still sitting at the kitchen table when I left. But that's where he should've been going."

"Was he acting strangely that day?"

He had been. "He was a little quieter than usual. More

withdrawn. I figured he'd had a bad day at school." Tommy had also been silently eyeing Julianne with an interest he didn't care for. But he wasn't going to tell Duke that. No matter what happened between the two of them and their marriage, that wouldn't change. He'd sworn to keep that secret, to protect her above all else, and he would. Even if he grew to despise her one day, he would keep his promise.

"Had he ever mentioned leaving?"

"Every day," Heath said, and that was true. "He was always talking big about how he couldn't wait to get away. He said we were like some stupid television sitcom family and he couldn't stand any of us. He said that when he was eighteen, he was getting the hell out of this place. Tommy didn't even care about finishing school. I suppose a diploma didn't factor much into the lines of work he was drawn to. When he disappeared that day, I always figured he decided not to wait. His birthday was coming up."

Duke had finally taken out a notepad and was writing a few things down. "What made you think he ran away?"

This was the point at which he had to very carefully dance around the truth. "Well, Wade found a note on his bed. And his stuff wasn't in his room when we looked the next morning." The note and the missing belongings were well-documented from the original missing-persons report. The fact that they never compared the handwriting to any of the other children on the farm wasn't Heath's fault. "It all added up for me. With Ken sick, it might have seemed like the right day to make his move." Unfortunately, he'd made his move on Julianne when she was alone in the trees.

"Did he ever talk to you about anything? His friends or his plans?"

At that, a nervous bit of laughter escaped Heath's lips. "I was a scrawny, thirteen-year-old twerp that did nothing but get in his way. Tommy didn't confide in anyone, but especially not in me."

"He didn't talk to your brothers?"

Heath shrugged. "Tommy shared a room with Wade. Maybe he talked to him there. But he was never much for chatting with the rest of us. More than anything he talked *at* us, not *to* us. He said nothing but ugly things to Brody, so he avoided Tommy. Xander always liked to keep friendly with everyone, but even he kept his distance."

"And what about Julianne?"

Heath swallowed hard. It was the first time her name had been spoken aloud in the conversation and he didn't like it. "What about her?"

"Did she have much to do with Tommy?"

"No," Heath said a touch too forcefully. Sheriff Duke looked up at him curiously. "I mean, there was no reason to. She lived in the big house and still went to junior high with me. If they spoke, it was only in passing or out of politeness on her part."

Duke wrote down a few things. Heath wished what he'd said had been true. That Tommy hadn't given the slightest notice to the tiny blonde. But as much as Julianne tried to avoid him, Tommy always found a way to intersect her path. She knew he was dangerous. They all did. They just didn't know what to do about it.

"Were they ever alone together?"

At that, Heath slowly shook his head. He hoped the sheriff didn't see the regret in his eyes or hear it in his voice as he spoke. "Only a fool would have left a little girl alone with a predator like Tommy."

Heath had been quiet and withdrawn that night. Julianne expected him to say *something*. About what happened with Sheriff Duke, about their kiss, about their argument or the divorce papers…but nothing happened. After Duke left, Heath had returned to unloading the truck. When that was done, he volunteered to drive into town and pick up a pizza.

While he was gone, the courier arrived with the package from her attorney. She flipped through it, giving it a cursory examination, and then dropped it onto the kitchen table. She wasn't in the mood to deal with that today.

Heath's mood hadn't improved by the time he got back. He was seated on the couch, balancing his plate in his lap and eating almost mechanically. Julianne had opted to eat at the table, which gave her a decent view of both Heath and the television without crowding in his space.

There was one cold slice of pizza remaining when Julianne finally got the nerve to speak. "Heath?"

He looked startled, as though she'd yanked him from the deep thoughts he was lost in. "Yes?"

"Are you going to tell me what happened?"

"You mean with Sheriff Duke?"

"I guess. Is that what's bothering you?"

"Yes and no," he replied, giving her an answer and not at the same time.

Julianne got up and walked over to the couch. She flopped down onto the opposite end. "It's been a long week, Heath. I'm too tired to play games. What's wrong?"

"Aside from the divorce papers sitting on the kitchen table?" Heath watched her for a moment before sighing heavily and shaking his head. "Sheriff Duke just asked some questions. Nothing to worry about. In fact, he told me Ken and Molly are no longer suspects."

Julianne's brow went up in surprise. "And that's good, right?"

"Absolutely. The conversation was fine. It just made me think." He paused. "It reminded me how big of a failure I am."

It didn't matter what happened between them recently. The minute he needed her support she would give it. "You? A failure? What are you talking about?" Every one of her brothers was at the top of their field with millions in their accounts. None were failures by a long shot. "You're the CEO of your own successful advertising agency. You have a great apartment in Manhattan. You drive a Porsche! How is that a failure?"

A snort of derision passed his lips and he turned away to look at the television. "I'm good at convincing people to buy things they don't need. Something to be proud of, right? But I fail at the important stuff. When it matters, it seems like nothing I say or do makes any difference."

She didn't like the tone of his voice. It was almost defeated. Broken. Very much unlike him and yet she knew somehow she was responsible. "Like what?"

"Protecting you. Protecting my parents. Ken. Saving our marriage…"

Julianne frowned and held her hands up. "Wait a minute. First, how is a nine-year-old boy supposed to save his parents in a car crash that he almost died in, too? Or keep Dad from having another heart attack?"

"It was my fault we were on that road. I pestered my father until he agreed to take us for ice cream."

"Christ, Heath, that doesn't make it your fault."

"Maybe, but Dad's heart attack *was* my fault. The second one at least. If I'd come clean to the cops about what happened with Tommy, they wouldn't have come here questioning him."

He was being completely irrational about this. Heath had been internalizing more things than she realized. "And what about me? How have you failed to protect me? I'm sitting right here, perfectly fine."

"Talking with Sheriff Duke made me realize I should've

seen it coming. With Tommy. I should've known he was going to come for you. And I left you alone. When I think about how bad it could've been…" His voice trailed off. "I never should've left you alone with him."

"You didn't leave me alone *with* him. I was doing my chores just like you were, and he found me. And you can't see the future. I certainly don't expect you to be able to anticipate the moves of a monster like he was. There's no reason why you should have thought I would be anything but safe."

He looked up at her at last, his brow furrowed with concern for things he couldn't change now. "But I *did* know. I saw the way he was looking at you. I knew what he was thinking. My mistake was not realizing he was bold enough to make a move. What if you hadn't been able to fight him off? What if he had raped you?" He shook his head, his thoughts too heavy with the possibilities to see Julianne stiffen in her seat. "I wish he had just run away. That would've been better for everyone."

The pained expression was etched deeply into his forehead. He was so upset thinking Tommy had attacked her. She could never ever tell Heath how successful Tommy had been in getting what he'd wanted from her. He already carried too much of the blame on his own shoulders and without cause. Nothing that happened that day was his fault. "Not for the people he would have hurt later."

Heath shrugged away what might have been. "You give me credit for protecting you, but I didn't. If I had been smart, you wouldn't have needed protecting."

Julianne scooted closer to him on the couch and placed a comforting hand on his shoulder. "Heath, stop it. No one could have stopped Tommy. What's important is everything you did for me once it was done. You didn't have to do what you did. You've kept the truth from everyone all this time."

"Don't even say it out loud," he said with a warning tone. "I did what I had to do and no matter what happens with Sheriff Duke, I don't regret it. It was bad enough that you would always have memories of that day. I wasn't about to let you get in front of the whole town and have to relive it. That would be like letting him attack you over and over every time you had to tell the story."

It would have been awful, no question. No woman wants to stand up and describe being assaulted, much less a thirteen-year-old girl who barely understood what was happening to her. But she was strong. She liked to think that she could handle it. The boys had other ideas. They—Heath especially—thought the best thing to do was keep quiet. Unlike her, they had to live with the fear of being taken away. They made huge sacrifices for her, more than they even knew, and she was grateful. She just worried the price would end up being far higher than they intended to pay.

"But has it been worth the anxiety? The years of waiting for the other shoe to drop? We've been on pins and needles since Dad sold that property. If you had let me go to the police, it would be long over by now."

"See…" Heath said. "My attempt to protect you from the consequences of my previous failures failed as well. It made things worse in the long run. And you knew it, too. That's why you couldn't love me. You were embarrassed to be in love with me."

"What?" Julianne jerked her hand away in surprise. Where the hell had this come from?

Heath shifted in his seat to face her head-on. "Tell the truth, Jules. You might have been intimidated by having sex with me or what our future together might be, but the nail in the coffin was coming home and having to tell your parents that you'd married *me*. You were embarrassed."

"I was embarrassed, but not because of you. It was never about you. I was ashamed of how I'd let myself get so wrapped up in it that I didn't think things through. And then, what? How could we tell our parents that we eloped and broke up practically the same day?"

"You're always so worried about what other people think. Then and now. You'd put a stranger ahead of your own desires every time. Here you'd rather throw away everything we had together than disappoint Molly."

"We didn't have much to throw away, Heath. A week together is hardly a blip in the relationship radar." How many women had he dated for ten times as long and didn't even bother to mention it to the family? Like the woman on the phone packing her bags for the Caribbean?

"It makes a bigger impact when you're married, I assure you. What you threw away was the potential. The future and what we could have had. That's what keeps me up at night, Jules."

It had kept her up nights, too. "And what if it hadn't worked out? If we'd divorced a couple years later? Maybe remarried and brought our new spouses home. How would those family holidays go after that? Unbelievably awkward."

"More awkward than stealing glances of your secret, estranged wife across the dinner table?"

"Heath…"

"I don't think you understand, Jules. You never did. Somehow in your mind, it was just a mistake that had to be covered up so no one would find out. It was an infatuation run awry for you, but it was more than that for me. I loved you. More than anything. I wish I hadn't. I spent years trying to convince myself it was just a crush.

It would have been a hell of a lot easier to deal with your rejection if it were."

"Rejection? Heath, I didn't reject you."

"Oh, really? How does it read in your mind, Jules? In mine, the girl I loved agreed to marry me and then bolted the moment I touched her. Whether you were embarrassed of me or the situation or how it might look…in the end, my wife rejected me and left me in her dust. You went off to art school without saying goodbye and just pretended like our marriage and our feelings for each other didn't matter anymore. That sounds like a textbook definition for rejection."

Julianne sat back in her seat, trying to absorb everything he'd said. He was right. It would have been kinder if she'd just told him she didn't have feelings for him. It would have been a lie, but it would have been gentler on him than what she did.

"Heath, I never meant for you to feel that way. I'm sorry if my actions made you feel unwanted or unloved. I was young and confused. I didn't know what to do or how to handle everything. I do love you and I would never deliberately hurt you."

He snickered and turned away. "You love me, but you're not *in love* with me, right?"

She was about to respond but realized that confirming what he said would be just as hurtful as telling him she didn't love him at all. In truth, neither was entirely accurate. Her feelings were all twisted where Heath was concerned. They always had been and she'd never successfully straightened them out.

"Go ahead and say it."

Julianne sighed. "It's more complicated than that, Heath. I do love you. But not in the same way I love Xander or Brody or Wade, so no, I can't say that. There are other feelings. There always have been. Things that I don't know how to…"

"You want me."

It was a statement, not a question. She raised her gaze to meet his light hazel eyes. The golden starbursts in the center blended into a beautiful mix of greens and browns. Heath's eyes were always so expressive. Even when he tried to hide his feelings with a joke or a smile, Julianne could look him in the eye and know the truth.

The expression now was a difficult one. There was an awkward pain there, but something else. An intensity that demanded an honest answer from her. He knew she wanted him. To tell him otherwise would be to lie to them both. She tore her eyes away, hiding beneath the fringe of her lashes as she stared down at her hands. "I shouldn't."

"Why not? I thought you weren't embarrassed of me," he challenged.

"I'm not. But we're getting a divorce. What good would giving in to our attraction do?"

She looked up in time to see the pain and worry vanish from his expression, replaced by a wicked grin. "It would do a helluva lot of good for me."

Julianne was hard-pressed not to fall for his charming smile and naughty tone. "I'm sure you'd be pleased at the time. So would I. But then what? Is that all it is? Just sex? Is it worth it for just sex? If not, are we dating?"

"Running off with me was very much out of character for you," he noted. "You can't just do something because it feels good and you want to. You have to rationalize everything to the point that the fun is stripped right out."

"I'm trying to be smart about this! Fun or not, you want us to get divorced. Why would I leap back into your bed with both feet?"

"I didn't say I wanted us to get divorced."

That wasn't true. He'd had her pressed against the dresser when he'd made his ultimatum. He'd demanded it yesterday. The papers were three feet away. "I distinctly recall you—"

"Saying you needed to make a choice. Be with me or don't. No more straddling the fence. If you don't want me, then fine. But if you do…by all means, have me. I'm happy to put off the divorce while we indulge in our marital rights."

Julianne frowned. "Do you even hear yourself? Put off our divorce so we can sleep together?"

"Why not? I think I deserve a belated wedding night. We've had all of the drama of marriage with none of the perks."

"You just want to catch up on eleven years of sex."

"Maybe." He leaned in closer, the gold fire in his eyes alight with mischief. "Do you blame me?"

The low, suggestive rumble of his voice so close made her heart stutter in her chest. "S-stop acting like you've lived as a monk this whole time. Even if you did, eleven years is a lot to catch up on. We do still have a farm to run and I have a gallery show to work on."

"I'm all for making the most of our time together here. Give it the old college try."

Julianne shook her head. "And again, Heath, what does that leave us with? I want you, you want me. I'm not about to leap into all this again without thinking it through."

"Then don't leap, Jules. Test the waters. Slip your toe in and see how it feels." He smiled, slinking even closer to her. "I hear the water is warm and inviting." His palm flattened on her denim-covered thigh.

The heat was instantaneous, spreading quickly through her veins until a flush rushed to her cheeks. She knew that all she had to do was say the word and he would do all the things to her she'd fantasized about for years. But she wasn't ready to cross the line. He was right. She did strip the spontaneity out of everything, but she very rarely made decisions that haunted her the way she had with him. She didn't want to misstep this time. She had too many regrets where Heath was concerned. If and when she gave herself to him, she wanted to be fully content with making the right choice.

"I'm sure it is." She reached down and picked up his hand, placing it back in his own lap. "But the water will be just as warm tomorrow."

Six

Julianne rolled over and looked at the clock on the dresser. It was just after two in the morning. That was her usual middle-of-the-night wake-up time. She'd gone to sleep without issue, as always, but bad dreams had jerked her awake about thirty minutes ago and she'd yet to fall back asleep.

She used to be a fairly sound sleeper, but she woke up nearly every night now. Pretty much since Tommy's body was unearthed last Christmas. As much as they had all tried to put that day out of their heads, there was no escaping it. Even if her day-to-day life was too busy to dwell on it, her subconscious had seven to eight hours a night to focus on the worries and fears in the back of her mind.

As much as he wanted to, Heath couldn't protect her forever. Julianne was fairly certain that before she left this farm, the full story would be out in the open. Whether she would be moving out of the bunkhouse and into the jailhouse remained to be seen. Sheriff Duke smelled a rat and he wouldn't rest until he uncovered the truth. The question was whether the truth would be enough for him. A self-defense or justifiable homicide verdict wouldn't give him the moment of glory he sought.

With a sigh, Julianne sat up in bed and brushed the messy strands of her hair out of her face. Tonight's dream had been a doozy, waking her in a cold sweat. She had several different variations of the dream, but this was the one that bothered her the most. She was running through the Christmas-tree fields. Row after row of pine trees flew past her, but she didn't dare turn around. She knew that if she did, Tommy would catch her. The moment his large, meaty hand clamped onto her shoulder, Julianne would shoot up in bed, a scream dying in the back of her throat as she woke and realized that Tommy was long dead.

You would think after having the same nightmares over and over, they wouldn't bother her anymore, but it wasn't true. It seemed to get worse every time. Most nights, she climbed out of bed and crept into her workshop. Something about the movement of the clay in her hands was soothing. She would create beauty and by the time she cleaned up, she could return to sleep without hesitation or nightmares.

For the last week, she'd had no therapeutic outlet to help her fall back asleep. Instead she'd had to tough it out, and she would eventually drift off again around dawn. But now she had a functioning workshop downstairs and could return to the hypnotizing whirl of her pottery wheel.

She slipped silently from the bed and stepped out into the hallway. The house was quiet and dark. She moved quickly down the stairs, using her cell phone for light until she reached the ground floor. There, she turned on the kitchen light. She poured herself a glass of water, plucked an oatmeal raisin cookie from the jar on the counter and headed toward her new studio.

The fluorescent lights flickered for a moment before turning on, flooding the room with an odd yellow-white glow. Heath had worked very hard to help her get everything in place. A few boxes remained to be put away, and her kiln wouldn't be delivered for another day or two, but the majority of her new workshop was ready to start work.

Julianne finished her cookie and set her drink on the dresser, out of the way. One of the boxes on the floor near her feet had bricks of ready-to-use clay. She reached in to grab a one-pound cube and carried it over to her wheel. A plate went down on the wheel, then the ball of soft, moist gray clay on top of it. She filled a bucket with water and put her smoothing sponge in it to soak.

Pulling up to the wheel, she turned it on and it started to spin. She plunged her hands into the bucket to wet them and then closed her slick palms over the ball of clay. Her gallery showing would be mostly sculpted figurines and other art pieces, but the bread and butter of her shop in the Hamptons was stoneware pieces for the home. Her glazed bowls, mugs, salt dishes and flower vases could be found in almost any home in the area.

When she woke up in the night, vases were her go-to item. Her sculptures required a great deal of concentration and a focused eye. At three in the morning, the creation of a vase or bowl on her spinning wheel was a soothing, automatic process. It was by no means a simple task, but she'd created so many over the years that it came to her as second nature.

Her fingers slipped and glided in the wet clay, molding it into a small doughnut shape, then slowly coaxing it taller. She added more water and reached inside. The press of her fingertips distorted the shape, making the base wider.

Cupping the outside again, she tapered in the top, creating the traditional curved flower-vase shape. She flared the top, forming the lip.

With the sponge, she ran along the various edges and surfaces, smoothing out the rough and distorted areas. Last, she used a metal tool to trim away the excess clay at the base and turned off the wheel.

She sat back with a happy sigh and admired her handiwork. When she first started sculpting, a piece like that would have taken her five tries. It would have collapsed on itself or been lopsided. She would press too hard and her thumb would puncture the side. Now, a perfect piece could be created in minutes. She wished everything in her life was that easy.

"I've never gotten to watch you work before."

Julianne leapt at the sound of Heath's voice. She turned around in her rolling chair, her heart pounding a thousand beats a minute in her chest. She brought a hand to her throat, stopping just short of coating herself in wet clay. "You shouldn't sneak up on a girl like that."

He smiled sheepishly from the doorway. "Sorry. At least I waited until you were done."

Heath was leaning against the door frame in an old NYU T-shirt and a pair of flannel plaid boxer shorts, and for that, she was thankful. She would lose her resolve to resist him if he came down in nothing but a pair of pajama pants. As it was, the lean muscles of his legs were pulling her gaze down the length of his body.

"Did I wake you?" she asked.

"I don't recall hearing you get up, but I woke up for some reason and realized I forgot to plug my phone into the charger. I left it in the kitchen accidentally." He took a few steps into the workshop. "I can't believe how quickly you did that. You're amazing."

Julianne stood up from her stool and took her metal spatula out of the drawer beside her. Uncomfortable with his praise, she lifted the metal plate and moved the wet vase over onto the shelf to dry. "It's nothing."

"Don't be modest," he argued. "You're very talented."

Julianne started the wheel spinning again and turned away to hide her blush. "Would you like to learn to make something?"

"Really?"

"Sure. Come here," she said. She eyed his large frame for a moment, trying to figure out the best way to do this. "Since I'm so short, it's probably easiest if you stand behind me and reach over. I can guide your hands better that way."

Heath rolled the stool out of the way and moved to her back. "Like this?"

"Yes." She glanced back at the position she had deliberately put them in and realized how stupid it was. Perhaps she would be smarter to talk him out of this. "You're going to get dirty. Is that okay?"

He chuckled softly at her ear, making a sizzle of awareness run along the sensitive line of her neck. "Oh, no, I'd better change. These are my good flannel boxers."

Julianne smiled at his sharp, sarcastic tone and turned back to the wheel. No getting out of this now. "Okay, first, dip your hands in the water. You have to keep them good and wet."

They both dipped their hands in the bucket of water, then she cupped his hands over the clay and covered them with her own. "Feel the pressure I apply to you and match it with your fingers to the clay."

They moved back and forth between the water and the clay. All the while, Julianne forced herself to focus on the vase and not the heat of Heath's body at her back.

The warm breath along her neck was so distracting. Her mind kept straying to how it would feel if he kissed her there. She wanted him to. And then she would realize their sculpture was starting to sag and she would return her attention to their project.

"This feels weird," Heath laughed, gliding over the gray mound. The slippery form began to take shape, their fingers sliding around together, slick and smooth. "And a little dirty, frankly."

"It does," she admitted. On more than one occasion, she'd lost herself in the erotic slip and slide of the material in her hands and the rhythmic purr of the wheel. That experience was amplified by having him so close. "But try to control yourself," she said with a nervous giggle to hide her own building arousal. "I don't want you having dirty thoughts every time you see my artwork."

Heath's hands suddenly slipped out from beneath hers and glided up her bare arms to clutch her elbows. The cool slide of his clay-covered hands along her skin was in stark contrast to the firm press of heat at her back. It was obvious that she was not the only one turned on by the situation.

"Actually, the artwork isn't what inspires me…."

A ragged breath escaped her lips, but she didn't dare move. She continued working the vase on her own now, her shaky hands creating a subpar product. But she didn't care. If she let go, she would touch Heath and she wasn't sure she would be able to stop.

Easing back, Heath brushed her hair over the other shoulder and, as though he could read her mind, pressed a searing kiss just below her ear. She tipped her neck to the side, giving better access to his hungry mouth. He kissed, nibbled and teased, sending one bolt of pleasure after the other down her spine.

She arched her back, pressing the curve of her rear

into the hard ridge of his desire. That elicited a growl that vibrated low against her throat. One hand moved to her waist, tugging her hips back even harder against him.

"Jules…" he whispered, sending a shudder of desire through her body and a wave of goose bumps across her bare flesh.

She finally abandoned the clay, letting it collapse on itself, and switched off the wheel before she covered his hands with her own. Their fingers slipped in and out between each other, his hands moving over her body. "Yes?" she panted.

"You said the waters would be just as warm tomorrow. It's tomorrow," he said, punctuating his point with a gentle bite at her earlobe.

That it was.

Julianne had been wearing a flimsy little pajama set when he walked in, but Heath was pretty sure it was ruined. The thin cotton camisole and matching shorts were sweet and sexy at the same time. The clothes reminded him of the girl he'd fantasized about in high school, and the curves beneath it reminded him of the ripe, juicy peach of a woman she was now.

He couldn't stop touching her, even though he knew his hands were covered in clay. Gray smears were drying up on her arms and her bare shoulders. The shape of his hand was printed on the cotton daisy pattern of her pajamas. A streak of gray ran along the edge of her cheek.

And he didn't care.

It was sexy as hell. Julianne was always so put together and mature. He loved seeing her dirty. He was so turned on watching her skilled hands shape and mold the clay. He wanted those hands on himself so badly, he had to bite his own lip to keep from interrupting her before she was finished. Even now he could taste the faint metallic flavor of his own blood on his tongue.

When Julianne finally turned in his arms to face him, he had to stop himself from telling her she was the most beautiful thing he'd ever seen in his life. Messy hair, dirty face and all. He'd already made the mistake of telling her too much before. It was a far cry from a declaration of love, but he intended to play this second chance much closer to the vest.

Julianne looked up at him, her light green eyes grazing over every inch of his face before she put her hands on each side of his head and tugged his mouth down to hers. The instant their lips met, colored starbursts lit under his eyelids. A rush of adrenaline surged through his veins, making him feel powerful, invincible and desperate to have her once and for all.

Their kiss yesterday hadn't been nearly enough to quench his thirst for her. It had only made his mouth even drier and more desperate to drink her in again. She was sweet on his tongue, her lips soft and open to him. The small palms of her hands clung to him. The moist, sticky clay felt odd against his skin as it started to dry and tighten, but nothing could ruin the feel of kissing her again.

It was like a dream. He'd stumbled downstairs, half-asleep, to charge his phone. He never expected to find her there at her wheel, looking so serene and focused, so beautiful and determined. Having her in his arms only moments later made him want to pinch himself and ensure he really was awake. It wouldn't be the first dream he'd had about Julianne, although it might be the most realistic.

Julianne bit on his lip, then. The sharp pain made him jerk, the area still sensitive from his previous self-inflicted injury. He pulled away from her, studying her face and coming to terms with the fact that she was real. After all these years she was in his arms again.

"I'm sorry," she said, brushing a gentle fingertip over his lip. "Was that too hard?"

Heath would never admit to that. "You just startled me, that's all."

Julianne nodded, her gaze running over the line of his jaw with a smile curling her lips. Her fingertip scraped over the mix of stubble and clay, making the muscles in his neck tighten and flex with anticipation. "I think we need a shower," she said. "You're a very, very dirty boy."

A shower was an awesome idea. "You make me this way," he replied. With a grin, Heath lifted Julianne up. As tiny as she was, it was nothing to lift her into the air. She wrapped her legs and arms around him, holding him close as he stumbled out of the workshop and headed for the stairs.

When they reached the top of the staircase, her mouth found his again. With one eye on his bedroom up ahead, he stumbled across the landing and through the door. He prayed there weren't any clothes or shoes strewn across the floor to trip him and he was successful. They reached into the bathroom and he pulled one hand away from a firm thigh to switch on the lights.

He expected Julianne to climb down, but she clearly had no intention of letting go of him. Not even to take off their clothes. She refused to take her mouth off of his long enough to see what she was doing.

She reached into the shower, pawing blindly at the knobs until a stream of warm, then hot, water shot from the nozzle. Julianne put her feet down onto the tiles and then stepped backward into the stall, tugging Heath forward until he stumbled and they both slammed against the tile, fully dressed. Their clothes were instantly soaked, and were now transparent and clung to their skin.

Her whole body was on display for him now. Her rosy nipples were hard and thrusting through the damp cotton top. His hands sought them out, crushing them against his palms until her moans echoed off the walls. His mouth dipped down, tugging at her tank top until the peaks of her breasts spilled out over the neckline. He captured one in his mouth, sucking hard.

The hot water ran over their bodies as they touched and tasted each other. Most of the clay was gone now, the faint gray stream of water no longer circling the drain. Their hair was soaking wet, with fat drops of water falling into his eyes as he hovered over her chest. It was getting hard to breathe between the water in his face and the steam in his lungs, but he refused to let go of Julianne long enough to change anything.

A rush of cold air suddenly hit his back as Julianne tugged at his wet shirt. She pulled it over his head and flung it onto the bathroom floor with a wet *thwump*.

"I thought you were tired of me running around without my shirt on," he said with a grin.

"You said it was okay in the shower, remember?"

"That I did." Leaning down, he did the same with her top and her shorts. She was completely exposed to him now, her body a delight for his eyes that had gone so long without gazing upon it. He wanted to take his time, to explore every inch and curve of her, but Julianne wasn't having it. She tugged him back against her, hooking her leg around his hip.

Lifting her into his arms once again, he pressed her back into the corner of the shower, one arm around her waist to support her, the other hand planted firmly on her outer thigh. The hot spray was now running over his back and was no longer on the verge of drowning them.

Julianne's hands reached between them, her fingers finding the waistband of his boxers and pushing them down. He wasn't wearing anything beneath. Without much effort, she'd pushed the shorts low on his hips and exposed him. He expected her to touch him then, but instead, she stiffened slightly in his arms.

"Heath?"

Julianne's voice was small, competing with the loud rush of the shower and the heavy panting of their breaths, but he heard her. He stopped, his hands mere inches from the moist heat between her thighs.

She wasn't changing her mind again, was she? He wasn't sure he could take that a second time. "Yes?"

"Before we…" Her voice trailed off. Her golden brown lashes were dark and damp, but still full enough to hide her eyes from him. "I don't want to tell anyone about us. *This*. Not yet."

Heath tried not to let the hard bite of her words affect him. She kept insisting she wasn't embarrassed of him and yet she repeatedly went out of her way to prove otherwise. He wanted to ask why. To push her for more information, but this wasn't exactly the right moment to have an in-depth relationship discussion. What was he going to say? He was wedged between her thighs, his pants shoved low on his hips. Now was not the time to disagree with her. At least not if he ever wanted to sleep with his wife.

"Okay," he agreed and her body relaxed. He waited only a moment before sliding his hand the rest of the way up her thigh. His fingers found her slick and warm, her loud cry more evidence that she wanted him and was ready to have him at last. He grazed over her flesh, moving in sure, firm strokes, effectively ending the conversation.

Julianne arched her back, pressing her hips hard into his hand and crying out. Her worries of a moment ago vanished and he intended to plow full steam ahead before she changed her mind, this time for good.

Heath braced her hips in his hands, lifting her up, and then stopping just as he pushed against the entrance to her body. He didn't want to move at this snail's pace; he wanted to dive hard and fast into her, but a part of him kept waiting for her to stop him. He clenched his jaw, praying for self-control and the ability to pull away when she asked.

"Yes, Heath," she whispered. "Please. We've waited this long, don't make me wait any longer."

Heath eased his hips forward and before he knew it, he was buried deep inside her. That realization forced his eyes closed and his body stiff as a shudder of pleasure moved through him. Pressing his face into her shoulder, he reveled in the long-awaited sensation of Julianne's welcoming heat wrapped around him.

How many years, nights, days, had he fantasized about the moment that had been stolen away from him? And now he had her at last. He almost couldn't believe it. It was the middle of the night. Maybe this was all just some wild dream. There was only one way to test it.

Withdrawing slowly, he thrust hard and quick, drawing a sharp cry from her and a low growl of satisfaction from his own throat. He could feel Julianne's fingers pressing insistently into his back, the muscles of her sex tightening around him. He was most certainly awake. And there was no more reason to hold back.

Heath gripped her tightly, leaning in to pin her securely to the wall. And then he moved in her. What started as a slow savoring of her body quickly morphed into a fierce claiming. Julianne clung to him, taking everything he had to give and answering his every thrust with a roll of her hips and a gasp of pleasure.

Everything about this moment felt so incredibly right. It wasn't romantic or sweet. It was fierce and raw, but that was what it needed to be. After eleven years of waiting… eleven years of other lovers who never quite met the standard Julianne had set. He was like a starving man at a buffet. He couldn't get enough of her fast enough to satiate the need that had built in him all these years.

Yet even as he pumped into her, his mind drifted to that night—the night they should have shared together in Gibraltar. They should have been each other's first. It would have been special and important and everything he'd built up in his mind. Instead, he'd given it up to some sorority girl whose name he barely remembered anymore. He didn't know who Julianne finally chose to be her first lover, but even all these years later, he was fiercely jealous of that man for taking what he felt was his.

He was going to make himself crazy with thoughts like that. To purge his brain, he sought out her mouth. He focused on the taste of her, instead. The slide of her tongue along his own. The sharp edge of her teeth nipping at him. The hollow echo of her cries inside his head.

His fingers pressed harder into the plump flesh of her backside, holding her as he surged forward, pounding relentlessly into her body. Julianne tore her mouth from his. The faster he moved, the louder Julianne's gasps of "yes, yes" were in his ear. He lost himself in pleasure, feeling her body tense and tighten around him as she neared her release.

When she started to shudder in his arms, he eased back and opened his eyes. He wanted to see this moment and remember it forever. Her head was thrown back and her eyes closed. Her mouth fell open, her groans and gasps escalating into loud screams. "Heath, yes, Heath!" she shouted.

It was the most erotic sound he'd ever heard. The sound went straight to his brain, the surge of his own pleasure shooting down his spine and exploding into his own release. He poured into her, his groans mixing with hers and the roar of the pounding water.

At last, he thought as he reached out to turn off the water. He'd waited years for this moment and it was greater than he ever could have anticipated.

Seven

He signed them.

Well, if that wasn't the cherry on top, Julianne didn't know what was. She didn't know exactly when it happened, but as she sat down at the kitchen table the next morning, she noticed the divorce papers were out of the envelope. She flipped through the bound pages to the one tabbed by her attorney. There she found Heath's signature, large and sharply scrawled across the page beside yesterday's date.

Well, at least he had signed it *before* they had sex.

That didn't make her feel much better, though. She had already woken up feeling awkward about what happened between them. She'd crept out of his bed as quietly as she could and escaped to the safety of downstairs.

Their frantic lovemaking in the middle of the night certainly wasn't planned. Or well-thought-out. It also wasn't anything she intended to repeat. He'd caught her in a vulnerable moment. Somehow, at 3:00 a.m., all the reasons it seemed like a bad idea faded away. Well, they were all back now. Eleven years' worth of reasons, starting with why they'd never had sex in the first place and ending with that phone call to his "sweetheart" the other night. They weren't going to be together. Last night was a one-time thing.

But even then, coming downstairs and finding their signed divorce papers on the table felt like a slap across the face somehow.

This was why she'd asked him to keep this all a secret. There was no sense in drawing anyone else into the drama of their relationship when the odds were that it would all be over before long. No matter what happened between them last night, they were heading for a divorce. He'd said that he didn't want a divorce, he wanted her to choose. Apparently that wasn't entirely true. For all his sharp accusations, he seemed to want to have his cake and eat it as well.

With a sigh, she sipped her coffee and considered her options. She could get upset, but that wouldn't do much good. She was the one who had the papers drawn up, albeit as a result of his goading. She couldn't very well hold a grudge against him for signing them after she'd had them overnighted to the house.

As she did when she got stuck on one of her sculptures, she decided it was best to sit back and try to look at this situation from a different angle. She and Heath were getting a divorce. It was a long time coming and nothing was going to change that now. With that in mind, what did sleeping with Heath hurt? She'd always wanted him. He'd always wanted her. Their unfinished wedding night had been like a dark cloud hovering overhead for the last eleven years.

When she thought about it that way, perhaps it was just something they needed to do. Things might be a little awkward between them, but they hadn't exactly been hunky-dory before.

Now that they'd gotten it out of their system, they could move forward with clear heads. But move forward into what? The divorce seemed to be a hot-button issue. Once that was official and they stopped fighting, what would happen? There was a chemistry between them that was impossible to deny. Now that they'd crossed the line, she imagined that it would be hard not to do it again.

What if they did?

Julianne wasn't sure. It didn't seem like the best idea. And yet, she wasn't quite ready to give it up. Last night had been…amazing. Eleven years in the making and worth the wait. It made her angry. It was bad enough that Tommy had attacked her and she had the shadow of his death on her conscience. But the impact had been so long-lasting. What if her wedding night with Heath had gone the way it should have? What if they'd been able to come home and tell their parents and be together? She felt like even long after he was dead, Tommy had taken not only her innocence, but also her future and happiness with Heath.

Back in college when her mind went down into this dark spiral, her therapist would tell her she couldn't change the past. All she could do was guide her future. There was no sense dwelling on what had happened. "Accept, acknowledge and grow" was her therapist's motto.

Applied to this instance, she had to accept that she'd had sex with Heath. She acknowledged that it was amazing. To grow, she needed to decide if she wanted to do it again and what the consequences would be. Why did there have to be negative consequences? It was just sex, right? They could do it twice or twenty times, but if she kept that in perspective, things would be fine. It didn't mean anything, at least not to her. Since he had signed the divorce papers first, she'd have to assume he felt the same way.

In fact… Julianne reached for the divorce decree and the pen lying there. She turned back to the flagged page and the blank line for her signature. With only a moment's hesitation, she put her pen to the paper and scrawled her signature beside his.

"See?" she said aloud to the empty room. "It didn't mean anything."

There. It was done. All she had to do was drop it back in the mail to her lawyer. She shoved the paperwork back in the envelope and set it aside. For a moment, there was the euphoria of having the weight of their marriage lifted from her shoulders. It didn't last long, however. It was quickly followed by the sinking feeling of failure in her stomach.

With a groan, she pushed away her coffee. She needed to get out of the bunkhouse. Running a few errands would help clear her mind. She could stop by the post office and mail the paperwork, pick up a few things at the store and go by the hospital to see Dad. Her kiln wouldn't be delivered until later in the afternoon, so why not? Sitting around waiting for Heath to wake up felt odd. There was no reason to make last night seem more important than it was. She would treat it like any other hookup.

She found it was a surprisingly sunny and warm day for early October. That wouldn't last. The autumn leaves on the trees were past their prime and would drop to the ground dead before long. They'd have their first snow within a few weeks, she was certain.

She took advantage of the weather, putting the top down on her convertible. There would still be a cold sting to her cheeks, but she didn't mind. She wanted the wind in her hair. Pulling out of the drive, she headed west for the hospital. With all the work on her studio, she hadn't been to see her father for a couple days. Now was a good time. Molly's car was at the house, so Dad was alone and they could chat without other people around. Even though her father didn't—and couldn't—know the details of what was bothering her, he had a calming effect on her that would help.

She checked in at the desk to see what room he was in now that he was out of intensive care, and then headed up to the fourth floor. Ken was sitting up when she arrived, watching television and poking at his food tray with dismay.

"Morning, Dad."

A smile immediately lit his face. He was a little thinner and he looked tired, but his color was better and they'd taken him off most of the monitors. "Morning, June-bug. You didn't happen to bring me a sausage biscuit, did you?"

Julianne gave him a gentle hug and sat down at the foot of his bed. "Dad, you just had open-heart surgery. A sausage biscuit? Really?"

"Well…" He shrugged, poking at his food again. "It's better than this stuff. I don't even know what this is."

Julianne leaned over his tray. "It looks like scrambled egg whites, oatmeal, cantaloupe and dry toast."

"It all tastes like wallpaper paste to me. No salt, no sugar, no fat, no flavor. Why did they bother saving me, really?"

Julianne frowned. "You may not like it, but you've got to eat healthier. You promised me you'd live to at least ninety and I expect you to hold up your end of the bargain."

Ken sighed and put a bite of oatmeal in his mouth with a grimace. "I'm only doing this for your sake."

"When do you get to come home? I'm sure Mom's version of healthy food will be better tasting."

"Tomorrow, thank goodness. I'm so relieved to skip the rehab facility. You and I both know it's really a nursing home. I might be near death, but I'm not ready for that, yet."

"I'm glad. I didn't want you there, either."

"Your mother says that you and Heath are both staying in the bunkhouse."

"Yes," she said with a curt nod. She didn't dare elaborate. The only person who could read her better than Heath was her dad. He would pick up on something pretty easily.

"How's that going? You two haven't spent that much time together in a long while. You were inseparable as kids."

Julianne shrugged. "It's been fine." She picked up the plastic pitcher of ice water and poured herself a glass. Driving with the top down always made her thirsty. "I think we're both getting a feel for one another again."

"You know," he said, putting his spoon back down on his tray, "I always thought you two might end up together."

The water in her mouth shot into different directions as she sputtered, some going into her lungs, some threatening to shoot out her nose. She set the cup down, coughing furiously for a few moments until her eyes were teary and her face was red.

"You okay?" he asked.

"Went down the wrong way," she whispered between coughs. "I'm fine. Sorry. What, uh…what makes you say something like that?"

"I don't know. You two always seemed to complement each other nicely. Neither of you seem to be able to find the right person. I've always wondered if you weren't looking in the wrong places."

This was an unexpected conversation. She wasn't entirely sure how to respond to it. "Looking in the family is frowned on, Dad."

"Oh, come on," he muttered irritably. "You're not related. You never even lived in the same house, really. It's more like falling for the boy next door."

"You don't think it would be weird?"

"Your mother and I want to see you and Heath happy. If it turns out you're happy together, then that's the way it is."

"What if it didn't work out? It's not like I can just change my number and pretend Heath doesn't exist after we break up."

Ken frowned and narrowed his eyes at her. "Do you always go into your relationships figuring out how you'll handle it when they end? That's not very optimistic."

"No, but it's practical. You've seen my track record."

"I have. Your mother told me the last one didn't end well."

He didn't know the half of it. "Why would dating Heath be any different? I mean, if he were even remotely interested, and I'm certain he's not."

Her father's blue-gray eyes searched her face for a moment, then he leaned back against the pillows. "I remember when you were little and you came home from school one day all breathless with excitement. You climbed into my lap and whispered in my ear that you'd kissed a boy on the playground. You had Heath's name doodled all over the inside of your unicorn notebook."

"Dad, I was nine."

"I know that. And I was twelve when I first kissed your mother at the junior high dance. I knew then that I was going to be with her for the rest of my life. I just had to convince her."

"She wasn't as keen on the idea?"

Ken shrugged. "She just needed a little persuading. Molly was beautiful, just like you are. She had her choice of boys in school. I just had to make sure she knew I was the best one. By our senior year in high school, I had won her over. I proposed that summer after we graduated and the rest is history."

Julianne felt a touch of shame for not knowing that much about her parents' early relationship. She had no idea they'd met so young and got engaged right out of school. They were married nearly ten years before they finally had her, so somehow, it hadn't registered in her mind. "You were so young. How did you know you were making the right choice?"

"I loved your mother. It might not have been the easy choice to get married so young, but we made the most of it. On our wedding day, I promised your mother a fairy tale. Making good on that promise keeps me working at our marriage every day. There were hard times and times when we fought and times when we both thought it was a colossal mistake. But that's when you've got to fight harder to keep what you want."

Julianne's mind went to the package of paperwork in her bag and she immediately felt guilty. The one thing she never did was fight for her relationship with Heath. She had wanted it, but at the same time, she didn't think she could have it. Tommy had left her in shreds. It took a lot of years and a lot of counseling to get where she was now and, admittedly, that wasn't even the healthiest of places. She was a relationship failure who had just slept with her husband for the first time in their eleven-year marriage.

Maybe if things had been different. Maybe if Heath's parents hadn't died. Or if Tommy hadn't come to the farm. Maybe then they could have been happy together, the way her father envisioned.

"I'll keep that in mind when I'm ready to get back in the saddle," she said, trying not to sound too dismissive.

Ken smiled and patted her hand. "I'm an old man who's only loved one woman his whole life. What do I know about relationships? Speaking of which—" he turned toward the door and grinned widely "—it's time for my sponge bath."

Julianne turned to look at the door and was relieved to find her mother there instead of a young nurse. "Well, you two have fun," she laughed. "I'll see you tomorrow at the house."

She gave her mom a quick hug and made her way out of the hospital. Putting the top up on the convertible, she drove faster than usual, trying to put some miles between her and her father's words.

He couldn't be right about her relationship with Heath. If he knew everything that had happened, her father would realize that it just wasn't meant to be. They would never be happy together and she had the divorce papers to prove it.

Julianne cruised back into town, rolling past Daisy's Diner and the local bar, the Wet Hen. Just beyond them were the market and the tiny post office. No one was in line in front of her, so she was able to fill out the forms and get the paperwork overnighted back to her lawyer's office.

It wasn't until she handed over the envelope and the clerk tossed it into the back room that her father's words echoed in her head and she felt a pang of regret. She hadn't fought. She'd just ended it. A large part of her life had been spent with Heath as her husband. It wasn't a traditional marriage by any stretch, but it had been a constant throughout the hectic ups and downs of her life.

"Ma'am?" the clerk asked. "Are you okay? Did you need something else?"

Julianne looked up at him. For a brief second, the words *I changed my mind* were on the tip of her tongue. He would fetch it back for her. She could wait. She wasn't entirely certain that she wanted this.

But Heath did. He wanted his freedom, she could tell.

She'd left him hanging for far, far too long. He deserved to find a woman who would love him and give him the life and family he desired. Maybe Miss Caribbean could give him that. That was what she'd intended when she broke it off with him originally. To give him that chance. She just hadn't had the strength to cut the last tie and give up on them.

It was time, no matter what her dad said. "No," she said with a smile and a shake of her head. "I'm fine. I was just trying to remember if I needed stamps, but I don't. Thank you."

Turning on her heel, she rushed out of the post office and back out onto the street.

Heath was not surprised to wake up alone, but it still irritated him. He wandered through the quiet house and realized at last that her car was not in the driveway. It wasn't hard to figure out that last night's tryst had not sat well with her. As with most things, it seemed like a good idea at the time.

They had been on the same page in the moment. It had been hot. More erotic than he ever dared imagine. They fell back to sleep in each other's arms. He'd dozed off cautiously optimistic that he might get some morning lovin' as well. That, obviously, had not panned out, but again, he was not surprised.

Frankly, he was more surprised they'd had sex to begin with. He dangled the bait but never expected her to bite. His plan had always been to push their hot-button issue, make her uncomfortable and get her to finally file for divorce. He never anticipated rubbing clay all over her body and having steamy shower sex in the middle of the night. That was the stuff of his hottest fantasies.

Of course, he'd also never thought she would cave so

quickly to the pressure and order the divorce paperwork the same day he demanded it. He expected spending weeks, even months wearing her down. She had already held out eleven years. Then the papers arrived with such speed that he almost didn't believe it. He'd wanted movement, one way or another, so he figured he should sign them before she changed her mind again.

Sleeping with her a few hours later was an unanticipated complication.

Heath glanced over at the table where he'd left the papers. They were gone. He frowned. Maybe she wanted this divorce more than he'd thought. He'd obviously given her the push she needed to make it happen, and she'd run straight to the post office with her prize.

He opted not to dwell on any of it. He signed, so he couldn't complain if she did the same. What was done was done. Besides, that's not why he was here anyway. Heath had come to the farm, first and foremost, to take care of things while Ken recovered. Dealing with Julianne and their divorce was a secondary task.

Returning to his room, he got dressed in some old jeans, a long-sleeved flannel shirt and his work boots. When he was ready he opted to head out to the fields in search of Owen, the farm's only full-time employee. It didn't take long. He just had to hop on one of the four-wheelers and follow the sound of the chain saw. They were in the final stretch leading up to Christmas-tree season, so it was prep time.

He found Owen in the west fields. The northern part of the property was too heavily sloped for people to pick and cut their own trees. The trees on that side were harvested and provided to the local tree lots and hardware stores for sale. Not everyone enjoyed a trek through the cold to find the perfect tree, although Heath couldn't fathom why. The tree lots didn't have Molly's hot chocolate or sleigh rides with carols and Christmas lights. No atmosphere at all.

Most of the pick-and-cut trees were on the west side of the property. The western fields were on flat, easy terrain and they were closest to the shop and the bagging station. He found Owen cutting low branches off the trees and tying bright red ribbons on the branches.

At any one time on the farm there were trees in half a dozen states of growth, from foot-tall saplings to fifteen-year-old giants that would be put in local shopping centers and town squares. At around eight years with proper trimming, a tree was perfect for the average home; full, about six to seven feet tall and sturdy enough to hold heavier ornaments. The red ribbons signified to their customers that the tree was ready for harvest.

"Morning, Owen."

The older man looked up from his work and gave a wave. He put down the chain saw and slipped off one glove to shake Heath's hand. "Morning there, Heath. Are you joining me today?"

"I am. It looks like we're prepping trees."

"That we are." Owen lifted his Patriots ball cap and smoothed his thinning gray hair beneath it before fitting it back on his head. "I've got another chain saw for you on the back of my ATV. Did you bring your work gloves and some protective gear?"

Heath whipped a pair of gloves out of his back pocket and smiled. He had his goggles and ear protection in the tool chest bolted to the back of the four-wheeler. "It hasn't been so long that I'd forget the essentials."

"I don't know," Owen laughed. "Not a lot of need for work gloves in fancy Manhattan offices."

"Some days, I could use the ear protection."

Owen smiled and handed over the chain saw to Heath. "I'm working my way west. Most of this field to the right will be ready for Christmas. Back toward the house still needs a year or two more to grow. You still know how to tell which ones are ready for cutting?"

He did. When he was too young to use the chainsaw, he was out in the fields tying ribbons and shaping trees with hedge clippers. "I've got it, Owen."

Heath went off into the opposite direction Owen was working so they covered more territory. With his headset and goggles in place, he cranked up the chain saw and started making his way through the trees. It was therapeutic to do some physical work. He didn't really get the chance to get dirty anymore. He'd long ago lost the calluses on his hands. His clothes never smelled of pine or had stains from tree sap. It was nice to get back to the work he knew.

There was nothing but the buzz of the saw, the cold sting of the air, the sharp scent of pine and the crunch of dirt and twigs under his boots. He lost himself in the rhythm of his work. It gave him a much-needed outlet as well. He was able to channel some of his aggression and irritation at Julianne through the power tool.

His mind kept going back to their encounter and the look on her face when she'd asked him to keep their relationship a secret. Like it had ever been anything but a secret. Did she think that once they had sex he would dash out of the house and run screaming through the trees that he'd slept with her at last? Part of him had felt like that after finally achieving such an important milestone in their marriage, but given he'd signed the divorce papers only a few hours before that, it didn't seem appropriate.

It irritated him that she wouldn't just admit the truth.

She would go through the whole song and dance of excuses for her behavior but refused to just say out loud that she was embarrassed to be with him. She wanted him, but she didn't want anyone to know it.

Up until that moment in the shower, he'd thought perhaps that wasn't an issue for them anymore. She might not want people to know they eloped as teenagers, but now? Julianne had been quick to point out earlier in the night just how "successful" he was. He had his regrets in life, but she was right. He wasn't exactly a bad catch. He was a slippery one, as some women had discovered, but not a bad one.

And yet, it still wasn't enough for her. What did she want from him? And why did he even care?

He was over her. Over. And he had been for quite some time. He'd told Nolan he didn't love her anymore and that was true. There was an attraction there, but it was a biological impulse he couldn't rid himself of. The sex didn't change anything. They were simply settling a long overdue score between them.

That just left him with a big "now what?" He had no clue. If she were off mailing their divorce papers, the clock was ticking. There were only thirty or so days left in their illustrious marriage. That was what he wanted, right? He started this because he wanted his freedom.

Heath set down the chain saw and pulled a bundle of red ribbons out of his back pocket. He doubled back over the trees he'd trimmed, tying ribbons on the branches with clumsy fingers that were numb from the vibration of the saw.

He didn't really know what he wanted or what he was doing with his life anymore. All he knew was that he wasn't going to let Julianne run away from him this time.

They were going to talk about this whether she liked it or not. It probably wouldn't change things. It might not even get her back in his bed again. But somehow, some way, he just knew that their marriage needed to end with a big bang.

Eight

Julianne returned to an empty bunkhouse. The Porsche wasn't in the driveway. She breathed a sigh of relief and went inside, stopping short when she saw the yellow piece of paper on the kitchen table. Picking it up, she read over the hard block letters of Heath's penmanship.

There's a sushi restaurant in Danbury on the square called Lotus. I have reservations there tonight at seven.

With a sigh, she dropped the note back to the table. Heath didn't ask her to join him. He wasn't concerned about whether or not she might have plans or even if she didn't *want* to have dinner with him. It didn't matter. This was a summons and she would be found in contempt if she didn't show up.

Julianne knew immediately that she should not have run

out on him this morning. They should have talked about it, about what it meant and what was going to happen going forward. Instead, she bailed. He was irritated with her and she didn't blame him. That didn't mean she appreciated having her evening dictated to her, but the idea of some good sushi was a lure. She hadn't had any in a while. Daisy's Diner wasn't exactly known for their fresh sashimi.

She checked the time on her phone. It was four-thirty now and it took about forty-five minutes to drive to Danbury. She'd never been to Lotus, but she'd heard of it before. It was upscale. She would have just enough time to get ready. She hadn't exactly gone all-out this morning to run some errands around town, so she was starting from scratch.

Julianne quickly showered and washed her hair. She blew it dry and put it up in hot rollers to set while she did her makeup and searched her closet for something to wear. For some reason, this felt like a date. Given they'd filed for divorce today, it also felt a little absurd, but she couldn't stop herself from adding those extra special touches to her makeup. After a week surrounded by nothing but trees and dirt, the prospect of dressing up and going out was intriguing.

Except she had nothing to wear. She didn't exactly have a lot of fancy clothes. She spent most of her time covered in mud with a ponytail. Reaching into the back of the closet, she found her all-purpose black dress. It was the simple, classic little black dress that she used for various gallery showings and events. It was knee length and fitted with a deep V-neck and three-quarter sleeves. A black satin belt wrapped around the waist, giving it a little bit of shine and luxury without being a rhinestone-covered sparklefest.

It was classic, simple and understated, and it showed off her legs. She paired it with pointy-toed patent leather heels and a silver medallion necklace that rested right in the hollow between her collarbones.

By the time she shook out the curls in her hair, relaxing them into soft waves, and applied perfume at her pulse points, it was time to leave.

She was anxious as she drove down the winding two-lane highway to Danbury. The fall evening light was nearly gone as she arrived in town. The small square was the center of college nightlife in Danbury and included several bars, restaurants and other hangouts. Lotus was at a small but upper-end location. She imagined it was where the college kids saved up to go for nice dates or where parents took them for graduation dinners and weekend visits.

Julianne parked her convertible a few spots down from Heath's silver Porsche. He was standing outside the restaurant, paying more attention to his phone than to the people and activities going on around him.

She took her time getting out of the car so she could enjoy the view without him knowing it. He was wearing a dark gray suit with a platinum dress shirt and diamond-patterned tie of gray, black and blue. The suit fit him immaculately, stretching across his wide shoulders and tapering into his narrow waist.

Heath had a runner's physique; slim, but hard as a rock. Touching him in that shower had been a fantasy come true after watching those carved abs from a distance day after day. Her only regret had been the rush. Their encounter had been a mad frenzy of need and possession. There was no time for exploring and savoring the way she wanted to. And if she had any sense, there never would be. Last night was a moment of weakness, a settling of scores.

It was then that Heath looked up and saw her loitering beside the Camaro. He smiled for an instant when he saw her but quickly wiped away the expression to a polite but neutral face. It was as though he was happy to see her but didn't want her to know. Or he kept forgetting he shouldn't be happy to see her. Their relationship was so complicated.

Julianne approached him, keeping her own face cautiously blank. She had been summoned, after all. This was not a date. It was a reckoning. "I'm here, as requested," she said.

Heath nodded and slipped his phone into his inner breast pocket. "So you are. I'm mildly surprised." He reached for the door to the restaurant and held it open for her to go inside ahead of him.

She tried not to take offense. He implied she was flaky somehow. After eleven years of artfully dodging divorce, it probably looked that way from the outside. "We've got weeks together ahead of us, Heath. There's no sense in starting off on the wrong foot."

The maître d' took their names and led them to their table. As they walked through the dark space, Heath leaned into her and whispered in her ear. "We didn't start off on the wrong foot," he said. The low rumble of his voice in her ear sent a shiver racing through her body. "We started off on the absolutely right foot."

"And then we filed for divorce," she quipped, pulling away before she got sucked into his tractor beam.

Heath chuckled, following quietly behind her. They were escorted to a leather booth in the corner opposite a large column that housed a salt water fish tank. The cylinder glowed blue in the dark room, one of three around the restaurant that seemed to hold the roof up overhead. The tanks were brimming with life, peppered with anemones, urchins, clown fish and other bright, tropical fish. They were the only lights in the restaurant aside from the individual spotlights that illuminated each table.

They settled in, placing their drink orders and coming

to an agreement on the assortment of sushi pieces they'd like to share. Once that was done, there was nothing to do but face why they were here.

"You're probably wondering what this is about," Heath said after sipping his premium sake.

"You mean you're not just hungry?" Julianne retorted, knowing full well that he had bigger motivations than food on his mind.

"We needed to talk about last night. I thought getting away from home and all *those people*," he said with emphasis, "that you worry about seeing us together might help."

Julianne sighed. He'd taken it personally last night when she asked to keep their encounter a secret. She could tell by the downturn of his lips when he said "those people." He didn't understand. "Heath, I'm not—"

He held up his hand. "It's fine, Jules. You don't want anyone seeing us together. I get it. Nothing has changed since we were eighteen. I should just be happy we finally slept together. Unfortunately, finding you gone when I woke up put a sour taste in my mouth."

"And going downstairs to find you'd signed the divorce papers left a bitter taste in mine."

Heath's eyes narrowed at her for a moment before he relaxed back against the seat. "I signed those last night after you left me on the couch, alone and wanting you once again. I assure you that making love to you in the shower at three a.m. was not in my plan at the time."

Julianne shook her head. "It doesn't matter, Heath. We both know it's what we need to do. What we've needed to do for a very long time. I'm sorry to have drawn it out as long as I have. It wasn't very considerate of me to put you through that. The papers are signed and mailed. It's done. Now we can just relax. We don't have to fight about it anymore. The pressure is off and we can focus on the farm and helping Dad recuperate."

He watched her speak, his gaze focused on her lips, but he didn't seem to have the posture of relief she expected. He had started all this after all. He'd virtually bullied her into filing. Now he seemed displeased by it all.

"So," she asked, "are you upset with me because I did what you asked? Because I'm confused."

Heath sighed. "I'm not upset with you, Jules. You're right, you did exactly as I asked. We filed. That's what we needed to do. I guess I'm just not sure what last night was about. Or why you took off like a criminal come morning."

Julianne looked at him, searching his hazel eyes. Having a relationship with him was so complicated. She wanted him, but she couldn't truly have him. Not when the truth about what had happened that night with Tommy still loomed between them. She didn't want anyone else to have him, either, but she felt guilty about keeping him from happiness. Letting him go didn't seem to make him happy. What the hell was she supposed to do?

"We shouldn't read too much into last night," she said at last. "It was sex. Great sex that was long overdue. I don't regret doing it, despite what you seem to think. I just didn't feel like psychoanalyzing it this morning, especially with our divorce papers sitting beside my cup of coffee."

"So you thought the sex was great?" Heath smiled and arched his brow conspiratorially.

"Is that all you got out of that?" Julianne sighed. "It was great, yes. But it doesn't have to change everything and it doesn't have to mean anything, either. We're attracted to each other. We always have been. Anything more than that is where we run into a problem. So can't it just be a fun outlet for years of pent-up attraction?"

Heath eyed her for a moment, his brows drawn together

in thought. "So you're saying that last night wasn't a big deal? I agree. Does that mean you're wanting to continue this…uh…*relationship?*"

When she woke up this morning, it didn't seem like the right thing to do. It would complicate things further in her opinion. But here, in a dark restaurant with moody lighting and a handsome Heath sitting across from her, it wasn't such a bad idea anymore. They were getting a divorce. The emotional heartstrings had been cut once and for all. If they both knew what they were getting into, why not have a little fun?

"We're both adults. We know that it's just physical. The things that held me back in our youth would not be in play here. So, perhaps."

The waiter approached the table with two large platters of assorted sushi. Heath watched only Julianne as things were rearranged and placed in front of them. The heat of his gaze traveled like a warm caress along her throat to the curve of her breasts. She felt a blush rise to her cheeks and chest from his extensive inventory of her assets.

When the waiter finally disappeared, Heath spoke. "You want us to have a fling?"

That's what she'd just suggested, hadn't she? Maybe that was what they needed. A no-strings outlet for their sexual tension. Perhaps then, she could sate her desire for Heath without having to cross the personal boundaries that kept them apart. He never needed to know about the night with Tommy or what happened during their botched honeymoon. She could make it up to him in the weeks that followed.

And why not? They were still married, weren't they?

Julianne smiled and reached for her chopsticks. She plucked a piece from the platter and put it into her mouth. Her eyes never left his even as she slipped her foot out of her shoe and snaked it beneath the table in search of his leg. His eyes widened as her toes found his ankle beneath the cuff of his suit pants. She slid them higher, caressing the tense muscles of his calves. By the time she reached his inner thigh, he was white-knuckling the table.

She happily chewed, continuing to eat as though her foot had not just made contact with the firm heat of his desire beneath the table. "You'd better eat. I can't finish all this sushi on my own," she said, smiling innocently.

"Jules," he whispered, closing his eyes and absorbing the feeling as her toes glided along the length of him. "Jules!" he repeated, his eyes flying open. "Please," he implored. "I get it. The answer is yes. Let's either eat dinner or leave, but please put your shoe back on. It's a long drive home in separate cars. Don't torture me."

The next few weeks went by easily. The uproar of the move and chaos of being thrown together after so long apart had finally dissipated. Dad was home and doing well under Nurse Lynn's care. Jules had a fully operational workshop with her new kiln. She had three new gallery pieces in various stages of completion that were showing a lot of potential and nearly a full shelving unit of stoneware for her shop. During the day, she worked with Molly in the Christmas store preparing for the upcoming holiday rush. They made wreaths, stocked shelves and handled the paperwork the farm generated. In the evenings, she worked on her art.

Heath had done much the same. During the day, he was out in the fields working with Owen. He'd sent out some feelers for teenagers to work part-time starting at Thanksgiving and had gotten a couple of promising responses. When the sun went down, he worked on his computer, trying to stay up-to-date with emails and other business issues. Things seemed to be going fine as best he could tell.

Most nights, Julianne would slip into his bed. Some encounters were fevered and rushed, others were leisurely and stretched long into the early hours of the morning. He'd indulged his every fantasy where she was concerned, filling his cup with Julianne so he would have no regrets when all of this was over.

He usually found himself alone come morning. Julianne told him she woke up with bad dreams nearly every night, although she wouldn't elaborate. When she did wake up, she went downstairs to work. When she returned to bed, she went to her own room. It was awkward to fall asleep with her almost every night and wake up alone just as often.

Despite the comfortable rhythm they'd developed, moments like that were enough to remind him that things were not as sublime as they seemed. He was not, at long last, in a relationship with Julianne. What they had was physical, with a strong barrier in place to keep her emotions in check. She was still holding back, the way she always had. Their discussions never strayed to their marriage, their past, or their future. She avoided casual, physical contact with him throughout the day. When nightfall came, they were simply reaping the benefits of their marriage while they could.

Given Heath had spent eleven years trying to get this far, he couldn't complain much. But it did bother him from time to time. When he woke up alone. When he wanted to kiss her, but Molly or Nurse Lynn were nearby and she would shy away. When he remembered the clock was ticking down on their divorce.

At the same time, things at the bunkhouse had certainly been far more peaceful than he'd ever anticipated going into this scenario. It was one of those quiet evenings when his phone rang. He'd just gotten out of the shower after a long day of working outside and had settled in front of his laptop when the music of his phone caught his attention from the coffee table.

Heath reached for his phone and frowned. It was Nolan's number and picture on the screen of his smartphone. He was almost certain this wouldn't be a social call. With a sigh, he hit the button to answer. "Hey."

"I'm sorry," Nolan began, making Heath grit his teeth. "I had to call."

"What is it?" And why couldn't Nolan handle it? He couldn't voice the query aloud. Nolan was running the whole show to accommodate Heath's family emergency, but Heath couldn't help the irritation creeping up his spine. He had enough to worry about in Connecticut without New York's troubles creeping in.

"Madame Badeau called today. And yesterday. And last week. For some reason, she must think your assistant is lying about you being out of the office. She finally threw a fit and insisted to talk to me."

Heath groaned aloud. Thank goodness only Nolan and his assistant had his personal number. The older French woman refused to use email, so if she had his personal number, she'd call whenever she felt the urge, time difference be damned. "What does she want?"

Nolan chuckled softly on the line. "Aside from you?"

"Most especially," Heath responded..

"She wants you in Paris this weekend."

"What?" It was *Wednesday*. Was she insane? He held her advertising account; he wasn't hers to summon at her whim. "Why?"

"She's unhappy with the European campaign we put together. You and I both know she approved it and seemed happy when we first presented it, but she's had a change of heart. It's a last-minute modification and she wants you there to personally oversee it. She wants the commercial reshot, the print ads redone—everything."

That wasn't a weekend task. Heath smelled a rat. Surely she wasn't just using this as an excuse to lure him to Paris. He'd told her he was married. She seemed to understand. "Why can't Mickey handle this?" Mickey was their art director. He was the one who usually handled the shoots. Redoing the J'Adore campaign fell solidly into Mickey's bucket.

"She didn't like his vision. She wants you there and no one else. I was worried about this. I'm sorry, but there's no dissuading her. I told her about your leave of absence for a family emergency, but it didn't make any difference to her. All she said was that she'd send her private jet to expedite the trip and get you back home as quickly as possible. A long weekend at the most, she insisted."

As much as Heath would like to take that private jet and tell Cecilia what she could do with it, they needed her account. It was hugely profitable for them. If she pulled out after they had spent the last two years making J'Adore the most sought-after cosmetic line in the market, it would be catastrophic. Not only would they lose her account, but others would also wonder why she left and might consider jumping ship. It was too high-profile to ruin. That meant Heath was going to Paris. Just perfect.

"So when is the plane arriving to pick me up?"

"Thursday afternoon in Hartford. Wheels up at four."

"I guess I'll pack my bags. I didn't really bring a lot of my suits to work on the farm. Thankfully it's only for a few days."

"You need to pack Julianne's bags, too."

"What?" he yelled into the phone. "How the hell did she get involved in this discussion?"

"Just relax," Nolan insisted, totally unfazed by Heath's tone. "When I was trying to talk her out of summoning you, I told her that your father-in-law had a heart attack and you and Julianne had gone to the farm. I thought reminding her about your wife and the serious situation you were dealing with would cool her off a little. I lost my mind and thought she would be a reasonable person. Instead, she insisted you bring Julianne to Paris as well."

"Why would I want to bring her with me?"

"Why wouldn't you want to bring your sweet, beloved wife with you to Paris? It's romantic," Nolan said, "and it would be suspicious if you didn't want to bring her. Between you and me, I think Madame Badeau wants to see her competition in the flesh. What can it hurt? Maybe she'll back off for good once she sees Julianne and realizes she's not just a made-up relationship to keep her at arm's length."

Heath groaned again. He'd never met a woman this aggressive. Had his mother not died when he was a child, she would be a year younger than Cecilia. It didn't make a difference to her. She was a wealthy, powerful woman who was used to getting what she wanted, including a steady stream of young lovers. Heath was just a shiny toy she wanted because she couldn't have him.

"Do you really think it will help to take her?"

"I do. And look at the bright side. You'll get a nice weekend in Paris. You'll be flying on a fancy private jet and staying in a fabulous hotel along the Seine. It's not the biggest imposition in the world. You're probably tired of staring at pine trees by now. It's been almost a month since you went up there."

Heath *was* tired of the trees. Well, that wasn't entirely

correct. He was tired of being cooped up here, pacing around like a caged tiger. If it weren't for the nights with Julianne to help him blow off steam, he might've gone stir-crazy by now. Perhaps a weekend away would give him the boost he needed to make it through the holidays. It was early November, so better now than in the middle of the holiday rush.

"Okay," he agreed. "You can let her know we'll be there."

"Thanks for taking one for the team," Nolan quipped.

"Yeah," Heath chuckled, ending the call.

Paris. He was going to Paris. With Julianne. Tomorrow. Even after the happy truce they'd come to, going to Paris together felt like returning to the scene of the crime, somehow. That's where he'd told her he loved her and kissed her for the first time since they were nine years old. They'd left Paris for Spain, and then took a detour to Gibraltar to elope.

With a heavy sigh, Heath got up from the kitchen table and tapped gently at the door to Julianne's studio. Now he had to convince her to go with him. And not just to go, but to go and act like the happy wife *in public*, one of the barriers they hadn't breached. To fool Madame Badeau, they had to be convincing, authentic. That meant his skittish bride would have to tolerate French levels of public affection. It might not even be possible.

The room was silent. She wasn't using her pottery wheel, but he knew she was in there.

"Come in."

Heath twisted the knob and pushed his way into her work space. Julianne was hovering over a sculpture on her table. This was an art piece for her gallery show, he was pretty certain. It was no simple vase, but an intricately detailed figure of a woman dancing.

Julianne's hair was pulled back into a knot. She was wearing a pair of jeans and a fitted T-shirt. There was clay smeared on her shirt, her pants, her face, her arms—she got into her work. It reminded him of that first night they'd spent together, sending a poorly timed surge of desire through him.

"I have a proposition for you, Jules."

At that, Julianne frowned and set down her sculpting tool. "That sound ominous," she noted.

"It depends on how you look at it. I need to take a trip for work. And it's a long story, but I need you to come with me. Do you have a current passport?"

Julianne's eyebrows lifted in surprise. "Yes. I renewed last year, although I haven't gone anywhere. Where on earth do you have to go for work?"

"We're going to Paris this weekend."

"Excuse me?"

Heath held up his hands defensively. "I know. I don't have a choice. It's an important account and the client will only work with me. She's a little temperamental. I know it sounds strange, and I hate to impose, but I have to take you to Paris with me. For, uh…public companionship."

A smile curled Julianne's lips. "I take it the French lady has the hots for you?"

He shook his head in dismay. "Yes, she does. I had to tell her I was married so she'd back off."

"She knows we're married?" Julianne stiffened slightly.

"I had to tell her something. Rebuffing her without good reason might've cost us a critical account. I had to tell my business partner, too, so he was on the same page."

Julianne nodded slowly, processing the information. She obviously didn't care for anyone outside of the two of them and their lawyers knowing about this. It was one thing for family to find out, but who cared if a woman halfway across the globe knew?

"She's insisting I come to Paris to correct some things she's unhappy with and to bring you with me on the trip. I think she wants to meet you, more than anything. It would look suspicious if I didn't bring you. We're supposed to be happily married."

"What does that mean when we get there?"

Heath swallowed hard. They'd gotten to the sticking point. "Exactly what you think it means. We have to publically act like a married couple. We need to wear our rings, be affectionate and do everything we can to convince my client of our rock-solid romance."

Heath looked down and noticed that Julianne was tightly clutching her sculpting tool with white-knuckled strength. "No one here will find out," he added.

Finally, Julianne nodded, dropping the tool and stretching her fingers. "I haven't seen you look this uncomfortable since Sheriff Duke rolled onto the property." She laughed nervously and rubbed her hands clean on her pants.

He doubted he had looked as concerned as she did now. "I can probably get Wade to step in and help while we're gone. Things are in pretty good shape around here. So can I interest you in an all-expense-paid weekend in Paris? We leave tomorrow. My personal discomfort will simply be a bonus."

Julianne nodded and came out from behind her work table. "I get to be a witness to your personal discomfort *and* experience Paris for free? Hmm…I think I can stand being in love with you for a few days for that. But," she added, holding up her hand, "just to be clear, this is all for show to protect your business. Nothing we say or do can be considered evidence of long-suppressed feelings for one another. By the time we get home, the clock will be up on the two of us. Consider this trip our last hoorah."

Nine

"Did you remember to bring your wedding ring?"

Julianne paused in the lobby of J'Adore and started searching in her purse. "I brought it. I just forgot to put it on. What about you?"

Heath held up his left hand and wiggled his fingers. "Got it."

Julianne finally located the small velvet box that held her wedding band. The poor, ignored gold band had been rotting in her jewelry box since the day they returned from their trip to Europe. They'd bought the bands from a small jewelry shop in Gibraltar. With a reputation for being the Las Vegas of Europe, there were quite a few places with wedding bands for last-minute nuptials. They hadn't been very expensive. They were probably little more than nickel painted over with gold-colored paint. Had they been worn for more than a week, the gold might have chipped off long ago, but as it was, they were as perfect and shiny as the day they'd bought them.

She slipped the band onto her finger and put the box away. It felt weird to wear her ring again, especially so close to the finalization of their divorce. Part of her couldn't help thinking this ruse was a mistake. It felt like playing with fire. She'd been burned too many times in her life already.

"Okay, are you ready? This is our first public outing as a married couple. Try to remember not to pull away from me the way you always do."

Julianne winced at his observation. She *did* pull away from him. Even now. Even with no one here having the slightest clue who they were. It was her reflex to shy away from everyone who touched her, at least at first. He seemed to think it was just him instead of a lingering side effect of her attack. She just didn't care to be touched very much. She wanted to tell him that it wasn't about him, but now was not the time to open that can of worms. "I'll do my best," she said instead. "Try not to sneak up on me, though."

Heath nodded and took her hand. "Let's go and get this over with."

They checked in at the front desk and were escorted to the executive offices by Marie, Madame Badeau's personal assistant. The walls and floors were all painted a delicate shade of pink that Heath told her was called "blush" after the company's first cheek color. When they reached the suite outside Madame Badeau's offices, the blush faded to white. White marble floors, white walls, white leather furniture, white lamps and glass and crystal fixtures to accent them.

"*Bonjour,* Monsieur Langston!"

A woman emerged from a frosted pair of double doors. Like the office, she was dressed in an all-white pantsuit. It was tailored to perfection, showing every flawless curve of the older woman's physique. This was no ordinary woman approaching her sixties. There wasn't a single gray hair in her dark brown coiffure. Not a wrinkle, a blemish, or a bit of makeup out of place. This woman had the money to pay the personal trainers and plastic surgeons necessary to preserve her at a solid forty-year-old appearance.

Heath reluctantly let go of Julianne's hand to embrace Madame Badeau and give her kisses on each cheek. "You're looking ravishing, as always, Cecilia."

"You charmer." The woman beamed at Heath, holding his face in her hands. She muttered something in French, but Julianne hadn't a clue what she said.

And then the dark gaze fell on her. "And this must be Madame Langston! Julianne, *oui?*"

At first, Julianne was a little startled by the use of the married name she'd never taken. She recovered quickly by nodding as the woman approached her. She followed Heath's lead in greeting the woman. "Yes. Thank you for allowing me to join Heath on this trip. We haven't been back to Paris since he confessed his love for me at the base of the Eiffel Tower."

Cecilia placed a hand over her heart and sighed. "Such a beautiful moment, I'm sure. You must have dinner there tonight!" The woman's accent made every word sound so lovely, Julianne would've agreed to anything she said. "I will have Marie arrange it."

"That isn't necessary, Cecilia. I'm here to work on the spring J'Adore campaign. Besides, it would be impossible to get reservations on such short notice."

Cecilia puckered her perfectly plumped and painted lips with a touch of irritation. "You are in Paris, Heath. You *must* enjoy yourself. In Paris we do not work twenty-four hours a day. There must be time for wine and conversation. A stroll along the Seine. If you do not make time for that, why even bother to be in Paris at all? *Non*," she said, dismissing his complaint with the elegant wave of her hand. "You will dine there tonight. I am good friends with the owner. Alain will make certain you are accommodated. Is eight o'clock too early?"

Julianne remembered how late Parisian evenings tended to go. Eating dinner at five in the evening was preposterous to them. "That would be lovely," she responded, before Heath could argue again. The last time she was in Paris, they couldn't even afford the ticket to the top, much less dining in their gourmet French restaurant. She would take advantage of it this time, for certain. "*Merci, madame*," she said, using two of the five French words she knew.

Cecilia waved off Marie to make the arrangements. "Quickly, business, then more pleasure," she said with a spark of mischief in her dark eyes. "Heath, your art director has made the arrangement for a second photo shoot today. It should only take a few hours. While we are there, perhaps your *belle femme* would enjoy a luxurious afternoon in the spa downstairs?"

Julianne was about to protest, but the wide smile on Heath's face stopped her before she could speak. "That's a wonderful idea," Heath said. "Jules, the J'Adore spa is a world-famous experience. While I work this out, you can enjoy a few hours getting pampered and ready for dinner this evening. How does that sound?"

She thought for certain that Heath wouldn't want to be left alone with Cecilia, but this didn't seem to bother him at all. Perhaps her appearance had already made all the difference. "*Très bien*," Julianne said with a smile.

Cecilia picked up the phone to make the arrangements and she and Heath settled at her desk to work on some details. Julianne sat quietly, sipping sparkling water and taking in the finer details of the office. A few minutes later, Marie reappeared to escort her to the spa.

Remembering her role as happy wife, Julianne returned to Heath's side and leaned in to give him a passionate, but appropriate kiss. She didn't want to overdo it. The moment their lips met, the ravenous hunger for Heath she'd become all too familiar with returned. She had to force herself to pull away.

"I'm off to be pampered," she said with a smile to cover the flush of arousal as one of excitement. "I'll see you this evening. *Au revoir*," she said, slipping out of the office in Marie's wake.

They returned to the first floor of the building, where a private entrance led them to the facility most customers entered from the street to the right of the J'Adore offices. Marie handed her over to Jacqueline, the manager of the spa.

"Madame Langston, are you ready for your day of pampering?" she said with a polite, subdued smile.

"I am. What am I having done?"

Jacqueline furrowed her brow at her for a moment in confusion, and then she laughed. "Madame Badeau said you are to be given all our finest and most luxurious treatments. You're doing *everything, madame*."

Heath hoped everything went okay with Julianne. Had he not sent her to one of the finest day spas in the world, he might have been worried about working and leaving her alone like that. He'd thought perhaps that he would need her to stay with him all the time, but the moment Cecilia laid eyes on Julianne, the energy she projected toward him shifted. He knew instantly that she would no longer be in pursuit of him, although he wasn't entirely sure what had made the difference.

It wasn't until they were going over the proofs of the photo shoot several hours later that she leaned into him and said, "You love your Julianne very much, I can tell."

At first, he wanted to scoff at her observation, but he realized that he couldn't. Of course he would love his wife. That's how marriages worked. He tried to summon the feelings he'd had for her all those years ago so his words rang with an authenticity Cecilia would recognize. "She was the first and maybe the last woman I'll ever love. The day she said she would marry me was the happiest and scariest day of my life."

That was true enough.

"I see something between you two. I do not see it often. You have something rare and precious. You must treat your love like the most valuable thing you will ever own. Don't ever let it get away from you. You will regret it your entire life, I assure you."

There was a distance in Cecilia's eyes when she spoke that convinced Heath she knew firsthand about that kind of loss. But he couldn't see what she thought she saw in his relationship with Julianne. There might be passion. There might be a nostalgia for the past they shared. But they didn't have the kind of great love Cecilia claimed. A love like that would have survived all these years, shining like a bright star instead of hiding in the shadows like an embarrassing secret. Perhaps they were just better actors than he gave them credit for.

The conversation had ended and they'd finished their day at work. Julianne had texted him to let him know a car was taking her back to their hotel and she would meet him there to go for dinner. Cecilia had booked them a room at the Four Seasons Hotel George V Paris, just off the Chámps Élysées. He arrived there around nightfall, when the town had just begun to famously sparkle and glow.

Perhaps they could walk to the Eiffel Tower. It wasn't a long walk, just a nice stroll across the bridge and along the Seine. The weather was perfect—cool, but not too cold.

He opened the door of their hotel room, barging inside. He found Julianne sitting on the edge of their king-sized bed, fastening the buckle on the ankle strap of her beige heels. His gaze traveled up the length of her bare leg to the nude-colored lace sheath dress she was wearing. It hugged her every curve, giving almost the illusion that she was naked, it so closely matched the creamy ivory of her skin.

Julianne stood up, giving him a better view of the dress. She made a slow turn, showcasing the curve of her back-side and the hard muscles of her calves in those sky-high nude pumps with red soles. The peek of red was the only pop of color aside from the matching red painted on her lips. "What do you think?"

"It's…" he began, but his mouth was so dry he had difficulty forming the words. "Very nice."

"When I got done a little early, I decided to go shopping. It's a Dolce & Gabbana dress. And these are Christian Louboutin shoes. I honestly can't believe I spent as much money as I did, but after all that pampering, I was feeling indulgent and carefree for once."

"It's worth every penny," Heath said. In that moment he wanted to buy her a hundred dresses if they would make her beam as radiantly as she did right now. "But now I'm underdressed. Give me a few minutes and I'll be ready to go."

Heath didn't have a tuxedo with him, but he pulled out his finest black Armani suit and the ivory silk dress shirt that would perfectly match her dress. He showered quickly to rinse away the grit and worries of the day and changed into the outfit.

"I was going to suggest we walk since it's so nice, but I'm thinking those shoes aren't meant for city strolls."

"Even if they were, Marie arranged for a car to pick us up at seven forty-five. Perhaps we can walk home." Julianne gathered up a small gold clutch and pulled a gold wrap around her shoulders.

Heath held out his arm to usher her out the door. In the lobby, a driver was waiting for them. He led them outside to the shiny black Bentley. They relaxed in the soft leather seats as the driver carried them through the dark streets and across the bridge to the left bank where the Eiffel Tower stood.

The driver escorted them to the entrance reserved for guests of the Jules Verne restaurant. The private elevator whisked them to the second floor in moments. Heath remembered climbing the over six hundred stairs to reach this floor eleven years ago. The lift entrance tickets were double the price, so they'd skipped it and walked up. The elevator was decidedly more luxurious and didn't make his thighs quiver.

They were seated at a table for two right against the glass overlooking Paris. Out the window, they could see the numerous bridges stretching over the Seine and the glowing, vaulted glass ceiling of the Grand Palais beyond it. The view was breathtaking. Romantic. It made him wish he'd been able to afford a place like this when they were kids. Proposing from the lawn had been nice, but not nice enough for their relationship to last. Caviar and crème fraîche might not a good marriage make, but it couldn't have hurt.

They both ordered wine and the tasting menu of the evening. Then they sat nervously fidgeting with their napkins and looking out the window for a few minutes. Pretending to be a couple in front of Cecilia was one thing. Now they were smack-dab in the middle of one of the most romantic places on earth with no one to make a show for.

They'd spent the last few weeks together. They shared a bed nearly every night. But they hadn't done any of that in Paris, the city where they fell in love. Paris was the wild card that scared Heath to death. He'd done a good job to keep his distance in all of this. Julianne's remoteness made that easier. He liked to think that in a few short days, he would be divorced and happy about that fact.

But Paris could change everything. It had once; it could do it again. The question was whether or not he wanted it to. He shouldn't. It was the same self-destructive spiral that had kept him in this marriage for eleven long years. But that didn't keep him from wanting the thing he'd been promised the day they married.

As the first course arrived, he opted to focus on his food instead of the way the warm lighting made her skin look like soft velvet. He wouldn't pay attention to the way she closed her eyes and savored each bite that passed her lips. And he certainly would ignore the way she occasionally glanced at him when she thought he wasn't looking.

That was just asking for trouble and he had his hands full already.

"We have to stay and watch the lights."

Julianne led Heath out from beneath the Eiffel Tower to the long stretch of dark lawn that sprawled beside it. The first time they had been here, they'd laid out on a blanket. Tonight, they weren't prepared and there was no way she would tempt the fabric of her new dress with grass stains, so she stopped at one of the gravel paths that dissected the lawn.

"We've seen them before, Jules."

She frowned at him, ignoring his protests. They were

watching the lights. "It's five minutes out of your busy life, Heath. Relax. The moment it's over, we'll head back to the hotel, okay?"

With a sigh, he stopped protesting and took his place beside her. It wasn't long before the tower went dark and the spectacular dance of sparkling lights lit up the steel structure. It twinkled like something out of a fairy tale. Heath put his arm around her shoulder and she slipped into the nook of his arm, sighing with contentment.

Heath might be uncomfortable here because this was where their relationship had changed permanently, but Julianne was happy to be back. This had been the moment where she was the happiest. The moment she'd allowed herself to really love Heath for the first time. She'd been fighting the feelings for months. Once he said he loved her, there was no more holding back. It had been one of those beautiful moments, as if they'd been in a movie, where everything is perfect and romantic.

It was later that everything went wrong.

The lights finally stopped and the high beams returned to illuminate the golden goddess from the base. Julianne turned and found Heath looking at her instead of the tower. There was something in his eyes in that moment that she couldn't quite put her finger on. She knew what she wanted to see. What she wanted to happen. If this *had* been a movie, Heath would have taken her into his arms and kissed her with every ounce of passion in his body. Then he would have said he loved her and that he didn't want a divorce.

But this was real life. Instead, the light in his eyes faded. He politely offered her his arm and they turned and continued down the path to the sidewalk that would lead them back to the Seine. Julianne swallowed her disappointment and tried to focus on the positives of the evening instead of the fantasy she'd built in her head.

As they neared the river, the cool night air off the water made Julianne shiver. The gold wrap was more decorative than functional.

"Here," Heath said, slipping out of his coat and holding it for her. "Put this on."

"Thank you," Julianne replied, accepting the jacket. "It's quite a bit cooler than it was when we went to dinner." She snuggled into the warm, soft fabric, the scent of Heath's skin and cologne comingling in the air surrounding her. It instantly brought to mind the hot nights they'd spent together over the last few weeks. The familiar need curled in her belly, urging her to reach for him and tell him to take her back to the hotel so she could make love to him.

Despite the night chill, her cheeks flooded with warmth. She no longer needed the coat, but she kept it on anyway. As much as she craved his touch, she wasn't in a hurry to end this night. The sky was clear and sparkling with a sprinkle of stars. The moon hung high and full overhead. After the emotionally trying few weeks they'd had, they were sharing a night together in Paris. She wouldn't rush that even to make love to Heath.

They stopped on the bridge and looked out at the moon reflecting on the water. It was such a calm, clear night, the water was like glass. In the distance, she could hear street performers playing jazz music. Heath was beside her. For the first time in a long time, Julianne felt a sense of peace. Here, there were no detectives asking questions, no family to accommodate, no unfinished art projects haunting her and no dead men chasing her in her dreams. It was just the two of them in the most romantic city in the world.

"Do you remember when we put the lock on the Pont des Arts bridge?"

Heath nodded. The bridge was farther down the Seine near the Louvre. It was covered in padlocks that had couples' names and dates written on them. Some couples came on their wedding day with special engraved locks. Others bought them from street vendors on the spur of the moment, like they had. The man had loaned them a marker to write "Heath and Julianne Forever." They'd put the lock on the bridge and threw the key into the river before heading to the train station and leaving Paris for Spain. The idea was that you were sealing your relationship forever. Perhaps that was why she couldn't fully let go of him.

"I wonder if it's still there."

"I doubt it," he said. "I read that they cut locks off or remove entire panels of the fence at night. It's been eleven years. I'm sure our lock is long gone."

Julianne frowned at the water. That wasn't the answer she was looking for. A part of her was thinking they would be able to walk down to the bridge and find it. That they might be overcome with emotions at seeing it firmly clasped to the fence, never to be unlocked, and they would finally be able to triumph over the obstacles that were keeping them apart.

Yes, because that's exactly what she needed to do when her divorce was virtually finalized. But if she were honest with herself, if she let her tightly clamped down emotions free like she did that night in Paris all those years ago, she had to admit nothing had changed. She still loved Heath. She had always loved him. It was her love for him that had forced her to push him away so he could have a real chance at happiness. And it was her love for him that wouldn't let her cut the cord that tied them together. She didn't need a lock to do that.

Heath had accused her of commitment-phobia, of using their marriage to keep men away. But that wasn't the whole truth. The whole truth was that she could never love any of those men. How could she? Her heart belonged to Heath and had since elementary school.

"That makes me sad," she admitted to the dark silence around them. "I was hoping that somehow our lock would last even though we didn't. Our love should still be alive here in Paris, just like it was then."

Heath reached for her hand and held it tight. He didn't say anything, but he didn't have to. The warm comfort of his touch was enough. She didn't expect him to feel the same way. She'd thrown his feelings back in his face and never told him why. He'd asked for a divorce, so despite their mutual attraction and physical indulgence over the last few weeks, that was all he felt for her. He'd carried the torch for her far longer than he should have, so she couldn't begrudge him finally putting it down. Telling Heath she had feelings for him *now*, after all this time, would be like rubbing salt in the wound.

Instead of focusing on that thought, she closed her eyes and enjoyed the feel of Heath's touch. In a few weeks, even that would be gone. Carrying on their physical relationship after the divorce wasn't a good idea. They were divorcing so Heath could move on with his life. Find a woman who could love him the way he deserved to be loved. Maybe take his mystery woman to the Caribbean. For that to happen, she couldn't keep stringing him along. She had to let him go.

She needed to make the most of the time they had left and indulge her heart's desires. And tonight, she intended to indulge in the fancy, king-sized bed of their hotel suite. She wanted the passionate, romantic night in Paris that she couldn't have when they were young and in love.

Julianne opened her eyes and turned to look at Heath. His gaze met hers, a similar sadness there although he hadn't voiced it. He probably thought they were mourning their marriage together in the place where it started. That was the smart thing for her to do. To appreciate what they had and to let it go once and for all.

She pressed her body to his side and with the help of her stilettos, easily tilted her head up to whisper into his ear. "Take me home."

Ten

Heath opened the door to their suite and Julianne stepped inside ahead of him. In a bucket by the seating area was a bottle of Champagne with a note. Julianne plucked the white card from the bottle and scanned the neat script.

"Madame Badeau has sent us a bottle of Champagne. She's not quite the cougar you warned me about, Heath."

Heath was slipping out of his coat jacket and tugging at his tie when he turned to look at her. "She told me earlier tonight that she could see we had a rare and precious love."

Julianne's eyes widened at him, but he didn't notice. He was too busy chuckling and shaking his head.

"Boy, did we have her fooled. I think she's finally given up on me."

She swallowed the lump in her throat and cast the card onto the table. A woman she'd known less than a day could see what Heath refused to see. "Spoils to the victor," she replied, trying to keep the bitter tone from her voice. "Open it while I change."

He walked over to take the bottle from her. When she heard the loud pop of the cork, she moved the two crystal flutes closer to him and took a few steps away to watch as he poured.

As many times as they had been together over the last few weeks, there hadn't been much fanfare to their love-making. No seduction. No temptation. It hadn't been as frantic as that first night in the shower, but they wanted each other too badly to delay their desires. But tonight she wanted to offer him a night in Europe they'd never forget, this time, for all the right reasons.

Heath set down the bottle and picked up the flutes filled with golden bubbly liquid. His gaze met hers, but instead of approaching him, she smiled softly and let her gold wrap fall to the floor. She reached for the zipper at her side, drawing it down the curve of her waist and swell of her hip. His gaze immediately went to the intimate flash of her skin now exposed and the conspicuous absence of lingerie beneath it.

Julianne knew the exact moment he realized she hadn't been wearing panties all evening. He swallowed hard and his fingers tightened around the delicate crystal stems of the glasses. His chest swelled with a deep breath before his gaze met hers again. There was a hard glint of desire there. He might not love her any longer, but there was no question that he wanted her. The intensity of his gaze stole the breath from her lungs.

Drawing in a much-needed lungful of cool air, she turned her back to Heath and strolled into the bedroom. Her fingertips curled around the hem of her dress, pulling it up and over her head. Her hair spilled back down around her shoulders, tickling her bare shoulder blades. She tossed the dress across the plush chaise and turned around.

Heath had followed her into the bedroom. He stood just

inside the doorway, clutching the glasses in an attempt to keep control. She was surprised he hadn't snapped the delicate stems in half. Julianne stalked across the room toward him, naked except for her gold jewelry and the five-inch heels she was still wearing. She stopped just in front of him. She reached past the glasses to the button of his collar. Her nimble fingers made quick work of his shirt, moving down the front until she could part the linen and place her palms on the hard, bare muscles of his chest.

He stood stone still as she worked, his eyes partly closed when she touched him. He reopened them at last when she took one of the glasses from him and held it up for a toast.

"To Paris," she said.

"To Paris," Heath repeated, his voice low and strained. He didn't drink; he just watched Julianne as she put the Champagne to her lips and took a healthy sip.

"Mmm…" she said, her eyes focused only on him. "This is good. I know what would make it better, though."

Leaning into Heath, she held up her flute and poured a stream of the Champagne down his neck. Moving quickly, she lapped at the drops that ran down his throat and pooled in the hollow of his collarbone. She let her tongue drag along his neck, meeting the rough stubble of his five o'clock shadow and feeling the low growl rumbling in his throat.

"You like that?" she asked.

Heath's arm shot out to wrap around her bare waist and tug her body close. Startled, Julianne smacked hard against the wall of his chest, pressing her breasts into him. She could feel the cool moisture of the Champagne on his skin as it molded to hers. When she looked up, he had a wicked grin across his face.

"Oh, yeah," he said. He took a sip of Champagne and then brought his lips to hers. The bubbly liquid filled her own mouth and danced around her tongue before she swallowed it.

Their mouths were still locked onto one another as Heath walked her slowly back toward the bed. With his arm still hooked around the small of her back, he eased Julianne's body down slowly until she met with the cool silky fabric of the duvet.

He pulled away long enough to look longingly at her body and whip off his shirt. Then he poured the rest of the Champagne into the valley between her breasts. He cast the empty flute onto the soft carpet with a thud and dipped his head to clean up the mess he'd made. His tongue slid along her sternum, teasing at the inner curves of her breasts and down to her ribcage. He used his fingertip to dip into her navel and then rub the Champagne he found there over the hardened peaks of her nipples. He bathed them in the expensive alcohol, then took his time removing every drop from her skin.

Julianne arched into his mouth and his hands, urging him on and gasping aloud as he sucked hard at her breast. Her own empty Champagne flute rolled from her hand across the mattress. She brought her hands to his head, burying her fingers in his thick hair and tugging him closer. He resisted her pull, moving lower down her stomach to the dripping golden liquid that waited for him there. His searing lips were like fire across her Champagne-chilled skin. She ached for him to caress every part of her and he happily complied.

Heath's hands pressed against her inner thighs, easing them apart and slipping between them and out of her reach. She had to clutch handfuls of the luxurious linens beneath them to ground herself to the earth as his mouth found her heated core. His tongue worked over her sensitive skin, drawing a chorus of strangled cries from her throat. He was relentless, slipping a finger inside of her until she came undone.

"Heath!" she gasped, her body undulating and pulsing with the pleasure surging through her. She hadn't wanted to find her release without him, not tonight, but he didn't give her the option. She collapsed back against the mattress, her muscles tired and her lungs burning.

She pried open her eyes when she felt the heat of Heath's body moving up over her again. He had shed the last of his clothing, his skin gliding bare along hers.

A moment later, his hazel eyes were staring down into her own. She could feel the firm heat of his desire pressing against her thigh. Eleven years ago this moment had sent her scrambling. The need and nerves in Heath's loving gaze had twisted horribly in her mind to the vicious leer of her attacker. Now there were only the familiar green and gold starbursts of the eyes she fantasized about.

She reached out to him, her palms making contact with the rough stubble of his cheeks. She pulled his mouth to hers and lost herself in him. Instead of fear, there was a peace and comfort in Heath's arms. When he surged forward and filled her aching body with his, she gasped against his mouth but refused to let go. She needed this, needed him.

Julianne drew her legs up, cradling his hips and drawing him deeper inside. She wanted to get as close to him as she could. To take in Heath and keep a part of him there inside her forever. The clock was ticking on their time together, but she could have this.

As the pace increased, Heath finally had to tear away from her lips. He buried his face in her neck, his breath hot and ragged as he thrust hard and fast. Her body, which had been exhausted mere moments ago, was alive and tingling with sensation once again. Her release built inside, her muscles tightening and straining like a taut rubber band as she got closer and closer. Heath's body was equally tense beneath her fingertips, a sheen of perspiration forming on his skin.

"I've never…wanted a woman…as much as I want you, Julianne."

His words were barely a whisper in her ear amongst the rough gasps and rustling sheets, but she heard them and felt them to her innermost core. Her heart stuttered in her chest. It wasn't a declaration of love, but it was serious. She couldn't remember the last time he'd used her full name when he spoke to her. And then it hit her and she knew why his words impacted her so greatly. When he'd said their wedding vows.

I take thee, Julianne Renee Eden, to be my lawfully wedded wife from this day forward.

The words from the past echoed in her mind, the image of the boy he was back then looking at her with so much love and devotion in his eyes. No one had ever looked at her like that again. Because no one had ever loved her the way he did. She might have ruined it, but she had his love once and she would cherish that forever.

"Only you," she whispered. "I've only ever wanted you."

There was the slightest hesitation in his movement, and then he thrust inside of her like never before. For a moment, she wondered what that meant, but before she could get very far with her thoughts, her body tugged her out of her own head. The band snapped inside and the rush of pleasure exploded through her. She gasped and cried into his shoulder, clutching him tightly even as he kept surging forward again and again.

"Julianne," he groaned as his whole body shuddered with his own release.

With Heath's face buried in her neck and their hearts beating a rapid tattoo together, she wanted to say the words. It was the right moment to tell him that she loved him. That she wanted to throw their divorce papers out the window and be with him. To confess the truth about what had happened on their wedding night and explain that it wasn't a lack of loving him, but that she was too damaged to give herself to anyone. It had taken years of therapy to get where she was now. She couldn't have expected him to wait for her.

But she knew telling him the whole truth would hurt him more than his imagined insults. All the boys carried a burden of being unable to protect her, but Heath most of all. If Heath knew that the end for Tommy had come too late…that he had already pillaged her thirteen-year-old innocence before he arrived, he would be devastated. Their marriage would no longer be his biggest regret; that moment would replace it and he would be reminded of it every time he looked at her.

Julianne wanted Heath to look at her with desire and passion. She didn't dare ask for love. But if he knew the truth, he would see her as a victim. He would know the full extent of the damage Tommy had caused and that would be all he would see. Could he make love to her without thinking about it?

Julianne squeezed her eyes shut and her mouth with them. She couldn't tell him. She couldn't tell anyone. No matter how much she loved Heath and how badly he deserved to know the truth, the price of voicing the words was too high. She'd rather he believe she was a flighty, spoiled little girl who couldn't decide what she wanted and stomped on his heart like a ripe tomato.

Heath rolled onto his side and wrapped his arm around her waist. He tugged her body against his, curling her into the protective cocoon to keep her warm. Even now, without realizing it, he was trying to protect her. Just like he always had.

Heath could never ever know that he'd failed that day.

The drive back to Cornwall from Hartford was long and quiet. Heath wasn't entirely sure what was going on with Julianne, but she'd barely spoken a word since they'd departed Paris earlier that morning. How was it that their relationship didn't seem to work on U.S. soil?

They pulled up at the bunkhouse and stumbled inside with their bags. It had been a long day, even traveling by private jet. The sun was still up but it was late into the night on Parisian time.

Heath was pulling the door shut behind him when he nearly slammed into Julianne's back. She had stopped short, her bags still in her arms, her gaze fixed firmly on the kitchen table.

"What is it?" he asked, leaning to one side to look around her. She didn't answer, but she didn't have to. Molly had brought in an overnighted package and left it on the table for them. The same type of packaging the divorce papers had originally arrived in. That only brought one option to mind. The thirty-day waiting period was up. A judge had signed the papers and her lawyer had mailed them.

They were divorced.

Just like that. After eleven years, their relationship was possibly better than it had ever been and they were divorced. Heath took a deep breath and closed his eyes. He wanted this. He had asked for this. He'd harassed her and demanded his freedom. And now he had what he wanted and he'd never felt so frustrated in his life.

He unceremoniously dropped his bags to the floor and

walked around Julianne to pick up the envelope. It had her name on it, but he opened it anyway. There was probably a similar envelope being held at the front desk of his building, waiting for him to return to Manhattan.

A quick glance inside confirmed his suspicions. With a sad nod, he dropped the papers back to the table. "Welcome home," he said with a dry tone.

"The time went by quickly, didn't it?"

He looked up, surprised at her first words in quite a while. "Time flies when you're having fun."

Julianne's eyes narrowed at him, her lips tightening as she nodded. She didn't look like she was having fun. She also didn't look pleased with him although he had no clue what the problem was.

"Julianne…" he began, but she held up her hand to silence him.

"Don't, Heath. This is what we wanted. I know the last few weeks have muddied the water between us, but it doesn't change the fact that we shouldn't be married. We aren't meant to be together long-term. As you said, we were having fun. But fun is all it was, right?"

Heath swallowed the lump in his throat. That was his intention, but it had started to feel like more. At some point, he had forgotten about the divorce and just focused on being with her. Was he the only one that felt that way? It didn't seem like it at the time. It seemed like she had gotten invested as well. Perhaps that was just Paris weaving its magic spell on their relationship again. "Fun," he muttered.

Julianne brushed past him and pulled her wedding ring off her finger. They were both still wearing them after their weekend charade for Madame Badeau. She placed it on top of the paperwork. "We won't need these anymore."

Even as she said the words, Heath got the feeling that

she didn't mean them. She was unhappy. Her, the girl who slammed the door in his face and told him to move on. When he finally tries, she takes it personally.

"So now what?" he asked. Heath wasn't sure how to proceed from here. Did getting a divorce mean their fling was over? They still had the crush of the Christmas season ahead of them. He wasn't looking forward to the long, cold nights in bed without her.

"I think it's time for me to move back into the big house," she said, although she wouldn't look him in the eye.

"Why?"

"When I spoke with Mom yesterday, she said the live-in nurse would be leaving tomorrow. They were able to move Dad's bed back upstairs since he's getting around well. That means I can have my room back."

"Your studio is out here."

She nodded. "But under the circumstances, I think it might be better if we put some distance between us."

Heath's hands balled into angry fists at his side. It was his idea to move forward with the divorce and yet it still felt like Julianne was breaking up with him all over again. "Why is it that whenever our relationship gets even remotely serious, you run away?"

Her eyes met his, a flash of green anger lighting them. "Run away? I'm not running away. There's nothing to run from, Heath. As I understand it, we were just having some fun and passing the time. I don't know if that qualifies as a relationship."

She was lying. He knew she was lying. She had feelings for him, but she was holding them back. Nothing had changed with her in all these years. She loved him then, just as she loved him now, but she refused to admit it. She always pulled away when it mattered. Yeah, he hadn't confessed that he had developed feelings for her, but what fool would? He'd done it once and got burned pretty badly.

"Why do I get the feeling that you're always lying to me, Jules? Then, now, I never get the whole story."

Her eyes widened. She didn't expect him to call her on it, he could tell. She sputtered a moment before finding her words again. "I-I'm not always lying to you. You know me too well for me to lie."

"You'd think so, and yet you'll look me in the eye and tell me we were just 'having fun.' We've had a lot of sex over the last few weeks, but that's the only barrier I've broken through with you, Jules. You're still keeping secrets."

"You keep your secrets, too, Heath."

"Like what?" he laughed.

"Like the reason why you really wanted a divorce."

Heath had no clue what she was talking about. "And what exactly did I say that was a lie?"

"It may not have been a lie, but you have certainly kept your relationship with that other woman quiet while you were sleeping with me the last few weeks. Now you're free to take her to the Caribbean, right?"

"What woman?"

"The so-called Sweetheart you were gushing at on the phone that day."

"You mean my sixty-three-year-old secretary?" He chuckled, although it wasn't so much out of amusement as annoyance. "I knew you were listening in on my phone call."

"You laid it on pretty thick. Do you really expect me to believe your sweetheart is a woman older than Mom?"

"You should. She likes to be flirted with, so I call her all sorts of pet names. I told her if she held down the fort while I was gone that I would give her a bonus big enough to cover the vacation she wants to take to the beach with her grandkids. Without *me*," he added. "Do you really think I would've pursued something with you while I had a woman on the side?"

Julianne's defiant shoulders slumped a bit at his words. "Then why did you really want the divorce, Heath? You came in here demanding it out of nowhere. I thought for sure you had another woman in mind."

"There's no other woman, Jules. How could there be? I'm not about to get serious with any woman while I'm married to you. That's not fair to her. Just like it wasn't fair to your almost fiancé. You just play with men's minds but you have no intention of ever giving as much as you take. You're right. It's a good thing this was just 'fun' to pass the time. It would be foolish of me to think otherwise and fall for your games twice."

"How dare you!" she said. "You don't know anything about my relationships. You don't know anything about what I've gone through in my life."

"You're right," he said. "Because you won't tell me anything!"

"I have always been as honest as I could be with you, Heath."

"Honest? Really. Then tell me the truth about what happened on our wedding night, Jules. The truth. Not some made-up story about you changing your mind. You were in love with me. You wanted me. The next minute everything changed. Why?"

Julianne stiffened, tears glazing her eyes. Her jaw tightened as though she was fighting to keep the flow of words inside. "Any question but that one," she managed to say.

"That's the only question I want answered. Eleven years I've spent wondering how you could love me one minute and run from me the next. Tell me why. I deserve to know."

Her gaze dropped to the floor. "I can't do that."

"Then you're right, Jules. We shouldn't be married. I'm glad we've finally gotten that matrimonial monkey off our backs. Maybe now I can move on and find a woman who will let me into her life instead of just letting me be a spectator."

"Heath, I—"

"You know," he interrupted, "all I ever wanted from you was for you to let me in. Over the years, I've given you my heart, my soul. I've lied for you. Protected you. I would've gone to jail before I let anyone lay a finger on you. And hell, I still might if Sheriff Duke comes back around. I'd do it gladly. Even now, although I really don't know why. I just don't understand you, Jules. Why do you keep me at arm's length? Even when we're in bed together, you've kept your distance, kept your secrets. Is it me? Or do you treat all men this way?"

Julianne looked back up at him and this time, the tears were flowing freely. It made his chest ache, even as he fought with her, to see her cry that way. But he had to know. Why did she push him away?

"Just you," she said. Then she turned and walked upstairs alone.

Eleven

Julianne sat on the edge of the bed staring at the bags she'd already packed. This morning, she would move back into the big house where she belonged. It broke her heart and made her cry every time she thought about it for too long, but she had to do it. They were divorced. No matter how much she loved him, Heath deserved to be happy. He deserved his freedom and a chance with a woman who could give him everything he wanted.

As much as she wanted to be, Julianne would never be that woman. She would always have her secrets. She would always have a part of herself that she held back from him. Even if she told him it was for his own good, he wouldn't believe her.

After the last few weeks together, she could tell he was confused. It was easy to feel like things were different when they were together so much, but that wouldn't last forever. They'd end up caught in the same circular trap where they'd spent the last eleven years. But she could get them out of it, even if he didn't seem to like it at the time.

He wanted his freedom and she would give it to him.

With a sigh, she stood up and extended the handle of her roller bag. She was nearly to the door of her room when she heard a loud banging at the front door.

She left her luggage behind and went downstairs. The low rumble of male voices turned into distinguishable words as she reached the landing.

"I'm going to have to bring her in for questioning."

"Why? You've asked a million questions. What do you want with her?"

Sheriff Duke was lurking in the door frame, looking larger and more threatening than ever before. "I need to talk to her. We also need a hair sample."

Heath glanced over his shoulder to see Julianne standing at the foot of the stairs. He cursed silently and turned back to the doorway. "Ask her your questions here. And get a warrant for the hair. Otherwise, you have to arrest us both."

"I can't arrest you just because you ask me to, Heath."

"Fine. Then arrest me because I killed Tommy."

Duke's eyes widened for a moment, but he didn't hesitate to reach for his handcuffs. "All right. Heath Langston, you're under arrest for the murder of Thomas Wilder. You have the right…"

The sheriff's voice faded out as the reality of what was happening hit her. Sixteen years' worth of karma was about to fly back in their faces. And to make things worse, Heath had confessed. Why had he confessed?

Duke clamped the cuffs on Heath's wrists and walked him to the back of the squad car.

"Don't say anything, Jules," she heard Heath say before the door slammed shut.

Returning to face Julianne, Duke started his speech again and reached for his second pair of cuffs. She stood silent and still, letting him close the cold metal shackles around her wrists. He took her to the other side of the squad car and sat her there beside Heath.

The ride into town was deadly silent. Anything they said could be used against them, after all. It wasn't until they were led into separate interrogation rooms that the nervous flutter of her stomach started up.

An hour went by. Then two.

She didn't have her watch on, but she was fairly certain that nearly four hours had passed before Sheriff Duke finally came in clutching a file of paperwork. Her stomach was starting to growl, which meant lunchtime had come and gone.

He settled down at the table across from her. No one else was in the room, but she had no idea how many people were gathered on the other side of the one-way glass panel. He flipped through his pages, clicked the button on his pen and looked up at her.

"Heath had a lot to say, Julianne."

She took a deep breath. "About what?" she replied as innocently as she could.

"About killing Tommy."

"I'm not sure why he would say something like that."

"I'm not sure, either. He had a pretty detailed story. If I didn't know better I'd lock him up right now and be done with it."

"Why don't you?"

A smirk crossed the policeman's face and Julianne didn't care for it. He was too pleased, as though he had everything figured out. He was probably already planning to use this big case to bolster his reelection.

"Well, as good a tale as he told me, it just doesn't match

up with the evidence. You see, Heath told me that he found Tommy on top of you and he hit him on the back of his head with a rock to stop him, accidentally killing him."

Julianne didn't blink, didn't breathe, didn't so much as shift her gaze in one direction or another.

"Problem is that the coroner says Tommy was killed instantly by a blow to his left temple."

"I thought they said on the news that Tommy had the back of his head bashed in." She tried to remember what she had seen on television. That's what the reports had said. Only she knew that injury came second. She didn't know if he was already dead by then or not.

"He did. But we don't release all the critical information to the news. Like the hair we found."

"Hair?" She hadn't heard anything about hair, either.

"You'd think that after all these years that any evidence would be destroyed, and most of it was, but we were lucky. Tommy died with a few strands of long blond hair snagged on the ring he was wearing. Hair and bone are usually all that's left after this length of time. It was as though he'd had a handful of a woman's hair in his hand shortly before he died."

"There are a lot of blondes in Cornwall."

"That's true, but Heath has already stated he saw Tommy on top of you, so that's narrowing it down for me."

"You said you didn't believe his story."

"I said it didn't match the coroner's report. And it doesn't. So that made me think perhaps he was protecting you. That made a lot of the pieces click together in my mind. Why don't you just save me the trouble and tell me the truth, Julianne. You don't really want me to charge Heath with Tommy's murder do you?"

"It wouldn't be murder," she argued. "It would be self-defense."

"Not exactly. He wasn't being threatened, just you. It might have been accidental, but his lawyers will need to prove it. There's nothing that says he didn't come up on Tommy in the woods and bludgeon him for no reason."

Julianne swallowed the lump in her throat. She wouldn't let Heath take the blame for this. She just couldn't. He'd always told her it wouldn't come to this, but if it did, he wouldn't be charged because he was protecting her. The sadistic gleam in Sheriff Duke's eyes made her think Heath might be wrong about that. Heath wouldn't spend a single day in jail protecting her. This had all gone on far too long. Keeping him out of prison was far more important than protecting his ego.

"I'm the one that killed Tommy. He…" She fought for the words she'd only said aloud a few times in her therapist's office. "He raped me," she spat out.

Sheriff Duke's eyes widened for a moment and he sat back into his chair. He didn't speak, but he reached over to check his voice recorder to make sure it caught everything.

She took a moment trying to decide where to go from there. "I was doing my chores after school. Same as any other day. The next thing I knew, Tommy was there, watching me. I was startled at first, but I thought I would be okay. Until he pulled out a switchblade and started walking toward me. I ran, but he grabbed my ponytail and yanked me back. I fell onto the ground and he was on top of me in an instant.

"He was so large. Bigger than my brothers. I was only thirteen and smaller than other girls my age. There was no way to fight him off. He had the knife at my throat so I couldn't scream. I kicked and fought at first, but he grabbed a fistful of my hair and yanked hard enough to bring tears to my eyes. He said if I didn't keep still, he'd cut my throat and leave my body naked for my daddy to find me."

Julianne's hands started trembling. The metal of the handcuffs tapped against the tabletop, so she pulled her arms back to rest in her lap. Her eyes focused on the table instead of the man watching her.

"I knew in the pit of my stomach that I was dead. No matter what he said, he wasn't going to let me run to my parents or the police. He would finish this and me before he was done. I tried to keep my focus and ignore the pain. It would've been so easy to tune everything out, but I knew that I couldn't. I knew that eventually, he'd get distracted and I would have my one and only chance to escape.

"I was able to slowly feel along the ground beside me. At first, there was nothing but pea gravel. I could've thrown that in his eyes, but it would have only made him angry. Then I found a rock. It was small but dense with a sharp edge I could feel with my fingertips. He still had the knife at my throat and if it wasn't enough to knock him out, I knew it was all over, but I didn't care. I had to do it. I brought the rock up and slammed it into the side of his head as hard as I could."

Julianne had seen this image in her dreams a thousand times so it was easy to describe even after all this time. "His eyes rolled into his head and he collapsed onto me. I struggled as quickly as I could to push him up and off of me. When I was finally able to shove him off, his head flung back and struck a rock sticking up out of the ground. That's when he started bleeding. I panicked. I kicked the knife away from him and started pulling my clothes back on. That's when Heath found me.

"We kept waiting for Tommy to get up, but he didn't. That's when we realized that hitting his head on the rock must have killed him. There was so much blood on the ground. He told me to sit tight while he went for help. He came back with the other boys. The rest was a blur, but I heard him tell the others that he'd hit Tommy with the rock when he saw him attacking me. There were so many times that we should've stopped and gone to the house to call the police, but we were so scared. In the end, all they wanted to do was protect me. And they did. None of them deserve to get in trouble for that."

"What about the note Tommy left? And all his things that were missing?"

"We did that," she said, not mentioning one brother or another specifically. "We were running on adrenaline, reacting faster than we could think. We hid the body, destroyed all his stuff and tried to pretend like it never happened."

"That didn't exactly work out for you, did it?"

Julianne looked up at the sheriff. He didn't seem even remotely moved by her story. He tasted blood and no matter what she said, she was certain he wasn't going to just close the case based on her testimony. "It's hard to pretend you haven't been raped, Sheriff Duke."

"And yet you waited all these years to come forward. It seems to me like you're hiding something. I think—"

A loud rap on the one-way glass interrupted him. Duke's jaw tightened and he closed the folder with his paperwork. "I'll be back," he said. He got up and left the room.

Julianne wasn't certain what had happened, but she was relieved for the break. It took a lot out of her to tell that story. Whether or not he backed down and dismissed the charges as self-defense, she knew she would have to tell that story again. And again. A part of her was terrified, but another part of her felt liberated. This secret had been like a concrete block tied around her neck. She knew it had to feel the same way to the others.

Maybe, finally, they could all stop living with the dark cloud of Tommy's death over their heads.

They sure were slow to book him. Heath had spent hours waiting for the inevitable. He'd told them he killed Tommy. Certainly the wheels of progress should be turning by now.

Not long after that, the door opened and Sheriff Duke's deputy, Jim, came through the door. "You can go."

"What?" He stood up from his chair. "I can go?"

Jim came over and unlocked the handcuffs. "Yes." He opened the door and held it.

Heath was thoroughly confused, but he wasn't about to wait for them to change their minds. In the hallway, he found several people waiting there. He recognized the woman as Tommy Wilder's sister, Deborah Curtis. Brody had sent them all the background report on her when she came to Cornwall asking about her brother. She was standing there with a man wearing an expensive tailored suit. He carried himself like he was important somehow, like he was her lawyer. Heath froze on the spot. Was she here to confront him for killing her brother?

Another door opened off the hallway and Julianne stepped out with a disgusted-looking Sheriff Duke at her side.

"What is going on?" Heath asked.

Julianne shook her head. "I have no clue. Duke said I was free to go."

The man beside Deborah stepped forward. "My name is Pat Richards. I'm a prosecutor for the state of Connecticut. With the evidence I have, your testimony and that of Mrs. Curtis, the state has opted not to press charges. This situation was tragic, but obviously in self-defense. I can't in good conscience prosecute Julianne after everything she went through."

Heath frowned. "Prosecute Julianne? I'm the one that confessed to killing him."

Pat smiled wide and nodded in understanding. "A noble thing, for sure, but it wasn't necessary. The charges have been dropped. You're both free to go."

Sheriff Duke shook his head and disappeared down the hallway into his office with a slam of his door.

"He disagrees, I take it?"

The prosecutor chuckled. "He fancied himself the hero cracking a huge case. There's not much crime around here for him to tackle, and this would give him the boost for his reelection. But even without Mrs. Curtis's testimony of her own attack, there was nothing for us to go forward on."

"What?" This time the question came from Julianne.

Deborah stepped forward, speaking for the first time. "I want you to know that I don't harbor any ill will against you or your family. You took Tommy in when no one else would and did only what you had to do to defend yourself. I completely understand that. My brother started displaying violent tendencies before he was even twelve years old. My parents tried to control him. They punished him, they put him in therapy. They even considered one of the boot camps for troubled teens. But it wasn't until my father came home early from work one day and caught him… attacking me…"

Julianne gasped, bringing her hand to cover her mouth. "Oh, god." Heath wanted to go to her side, but he resisted. Despite what had happened, she might still be upset with him.

"Tommy didn't succeed," Deborah said, "but he would've raped me if my father hadn't come home. I didn't want to press charges, I was too embarrassed. After that, he wasn't allowed to be alone with me. His close call didn't stop him from getting in trouble, though. He was constantly getting picked up for one thing or another. He even did a few weeks in juvie. Eventually the state removed him from the home as a repeat juvenile offender and I tried to forget it ever happened." She shook her head. "I never dreamed he would try to do it again. I feel awful."

"Mrs. Curtis's story was so similar to Julianne's that there was no reason to believe she wasn't telling the truth. The forensic evidence supported her version of his death. There's not a grand jury that would indict her. Anything that happened after the fact is well past the statute of limitations." Pat looked down the hall at the sheriff's office and shook his head. "Sheriff Duke might not be happy, but the only real crime here was committed by the deceased a long time ago. As much as I'd like to, I can't charge a dead man with second-degree sexual assault."

The words hung in the air for a moment. Heath let them sink into his mind. Pat meant *attempted* sexual assault, right? Attempted. Julianne had sworn that Tommy hadn't… And yet, why would a traumatized young girl want to tell him something like that? She wouldn't.

And then it hit him like he'd driven his Porsche into a brick wall. In an instant, every moment made sense. Every reaction Julianne ever had. Their wedding night…

How could he have missed this? It was so obvious now that he felt like a fool. And a first-class ass. He'd believed what she told him despite all the signs indicating otherwise. All these years he'd been angry with her while she'd carried this secret on her own.

"I'm going to have a talk with the local child services agency. There is a major breach in conduct if they didn't share the information about Deborah's assault with Mr. and Mrs. Eden before they placed Tommy there. They might not have taken him in if they'd known." The phone on Pat's hip rang and he looked down at the screen. "If you'll excuse me," he said, disappearing through the double doors.

After a few silent, awkward moments, Deborah spoke again, this time to Julianne. "Mr. Richards and I were listening in the observation room while you told your story," she said. "You are so much braver than I ever could have been. I'm sorry I wasn't stronger. If I had been, I would've pressed charges or talked to people about what happened and this might never have happened to you."

Julianne approached Deborah and embraced her. The two women held each other for a moment. "This is not your fault. Don't you ever think that. I've kept this a secret, too. It's hard to tell people the truth, even though you didn't do anything wrong."

When Julianne pulled away, Deborah dabbed her eyes with a tissue and sniffed. "You know, I came back to Cornwall to track down Tommy, but I wasn't looking for a happy family reunion. My therapist had recommended I find him so I could confront my fears and move on. He had vanished, but I expected him to be in jail or working at a gas station in the middle of nowhere. This," she said, waving her hand around, "was more than I ever planned to uncover. But it's better, I think. I don't have to be afraid of Tommy anymore. He's never going to show up on my doorstep and he'll never be able to hurt me or my little girl. I'm happy I was able to help with your case, too. It makes me feel like I have more power and control over my life than ever before."

Heath stood quietly while the two women spoke. He had so many things he wanted and needed to say to Julianne, but now wasn't the time. They eventually moved down the hallway, making their way out of the police station.

He was relieved to step outside. It was cold, but the sun

was shining. It was like an omen; Noah's rainbow signaling that all of this was finally over. They no longer had to worry about the police coming after them. It was in the past now, where it belonged.

At least most of it. With the truth out, the papers would no doubt pick up the story. They needed to sit down with Mom and Dad and tell them what had happened before some woman cornered Molly at the grocery store. Hopefully Ken's heart could withstand the news now that the threat of his children's incarceration was behind them.

Heath whipped out his phone to text his brothers, but found that wasn't enough. He needed to call them. He and Julianne both, to share the news. He wished he could give Julianne time to prepare, but the truth was out. They had protected her as well as they could over the years, but now she would have to tell her story. First to her family, then to the public. Perhaps after all this time, the blow of it would soften. He couldn't imagine the tiny, thirteen-year-old Julianne talking to police and reporters about killing her attacker. Her *rapist*.

His stomach still ached painfully at that thought. If he had only come across the two of them a few minutes sooner. He might have stopped Tommy before he could have... He sighed and shoved his hands into his pockets. He already believed he failed to protect Julianne, but he had no idea the extent of the damage that was caused. And by keeping Tommy's death a secret, they had virtually forced her to keep the rape a secret as well, and hadn't even known it. Had their attempt to protect her only made it worse?

The bile started to rise in the back of his throat. She should have been taken to the doctor. To a therapist. She should've been able to cry in her mother's arms and she was never able to do any of that.

His knees started to weaken beneath him, so Heath moved quickly to sit on the steps. He would wait there until Julianne and Deborah were done talking. Maybe by then, he could pull himself together.

After a while, Deborah embraced Julianne again, and then she made her way down the sidewalk to her car. Julianne watched her walk away and then finally turned to look at him. It was the first time she'd done that since they'd all gathered inside the police station. She walked over to the steps and sat down beside him.

Minutes passed before either of them spoke. They had shared so much together, and yet when it came to the important things, they knew almost nothing about each other.

"Thank you," she said at last.

That was the last thing he ever expected her to say. "Why on earth would you be thanking me right now?"

"Thank you for loving me," she elaborated. "No matter what we've said or done to each other over the years, when it was important, you were there for me. You probably don't think so, but the truth is that you would have gone to jail for me today. You've spent the last sixteen years covering for me, even lying to your own brothers about what happened that day. You looked Sheriff Duke in the eye and told him you killed Tommy, consequences be damned. How many people are lucky enough to have someone in their life that is willing to do that for them?"

"That's what families do. They protect each other." He watched the traffic drift by the main thoroughfare for a moment. He couldn't turn to face her while he spoke or he might give away the fact that his feelings for her ran much deeper than that. No matter what happened between them, he would always love Julianne. He couldn't seem to stop. Knowing the truth only made it harder not to love her more. All his reasons for keeping her at arm's length were nullified. But they were divorced. What did that matter now?

"You went far beyond family obligation, Heath."

"Why didn't you tell me what happened, Jules? You could've told me the truth."

"No," she said, softly shaking the blond curls around her shoulders. "I couldn't. You had me on this pedestal. I couldn't bear for you to know how flawed I was. How broken I was."

"As though what happened was your fault?"

"It wasn't my fault. I know that. But it wasn't your fault, either. If you knew, you would've blamed yourself. And you'd never look at me the same way again. I didn't want to lose that. You were the only person in my life that made me feel special. Mom and Dad loved me, but I always felt like I wasn't enough for them. You only wanted me. I wanted to stay that perfect vision in your mind."

"By making me despise you? You made me stay up nights wondering what I'd done wrong. Christ, I *divorced* you."

Julianne turned to look at him with a soft smile curling her lips. "I tried to push you away, but you still loved me. All this time, that was the one thing I kept hoping would change. I couldn't tell you the truth, so I knew there would always be a barrier between us. I kept hoping you'd move on and find someone who could love you the way you deserved to be loved. The way you loved me."

He shook his head. He didn't want anyone else to love him. All he had ever wanted was for Julianne to love him. And the way she spoke convinced him that she did. Maybe she had all this time, but the secret she kept was too big. It was easier to keep away than be subjected to his constant needling about why she left him. But to push him into another woman's arms *because* she loved him? "I still don't understand what you're thinking sometimes, Jules."

"I know." She patted his knee and stood up. "Let's go home. We have some long conversations to have with the family."

He got up and followed her to the street. She was right. And he had one important conversation with Ken in mind that she wouldn't be expecting.

Twelve

It was over. Good and truly over.

Julianne slipped into her coat and went out onto the porch to gather herself. The last hour had been harder than confessing the truth to Sheriff Duke. Looking her parents in the eye and telling them everything had been excruciating. Not for her, but she hated to burden them with the truth.

They had taken it better than she expected. Ken got quiet and shook his head, but his color was good and he remained stable. When it was over he'd hugged her tighter than he'd ever hugged her in her entire life. Molly cried a lot. Julianne expected that she would continue to for a while. Her mother was a mother hen. Knowing that had happened to her children under her watch would eat at her for a long time. Maybe always. But Julianne assured her that she was okay, it was a long time ago, and it seemed to calm her.

As she stepped onto the gravel lot behind the house, Julianne looked out at the trees. She had loved being out there once but hadn't set foot in the fields in sixteen years. The boogeyman was long gone. Most of her own personal demons had been set loose today. She took a deep breath and headed for the north field. That was where she'd been that day. If she were going to face this, she needed to go there.

It didn't take long to find the spot, but it took a while to walk out there. The trees were different, always changing as they were harvested and replanted. There were no monsters in the trees, no men to chase her, but she could feel the change in the weight on her chest as she got closer. While Wade had hidden the body and Brody took her to shower and change, Heath and Xander had cleaned up the scene. The rock she'd hit him with was flung into the far reaches of the property. The pool of blood was long gone. But when she looked, she could still see it all.

That's when the first snowflake drifted past her face. One flake became ten, became a thousand. In only a few minutes' time, the tree branches were dusted with white and the bloodstain in her mind slowly disappeared beneath a layer of snow.

It was a perfect moment. A pure, white cleansing of her past. She tipped her face up, feeling the tiny prickles of flakes melting on her cheeks, and sucked in a deep, cold breath.

Over.

Julianne turned her back to the scene of her attack, putting it behind her with everything else, and started walking in the opposite direction, through the fields. For the first time since she was thirteen, she could enjoy the moment. The snow was beautiful, drifting slowly down into fluffy clumps on the branches. The flakes were getting fatter, some larger than nickels. They would have several inches sticking before too long.

She climbed up the slope of the back property, looking for her favorite place on the farm. Somehow she expected it to have changed, but when she finally reached it, everything was just as she remembered. There, jutting out of the side of the hill, was a large, flat rock. She had come out here to sit and think when she was younger. The household was always full of kids and this was a place she could be alone.

Julianne dusted off the snow and sat down on the rock, turning to face the slope of the property laid out in front of her. To the left, she could see the roofline and lights of Wade and Tori's house over the hill. In front of her was the whole of the Garden of Eden. Her own little paradise.

It was nearing sunset, but the fat, gray clouds blocked out the color of the sky. The light was fading, but she could still make out the rows of trees stretching in front of her. The big house, with glowing windows and black smoke rising from the chimney, lay beyond it. Then the dark shape of the bunkhouse with Heath's silver Porsche out front.

Heath. Her ex-husband. Julianne sighed and snuggled deeper into her coat. With Sheriff Duke's unexpected arrival, she hadn't had much time to process her new marital status. While they had come clean about Tommy, they had deliberately opted not to tell anyone about the marriage. That was too much for one day. It might not be something they ever needed to tell. What would it matter, really? It only impacted the two of them since they were the only ones aware of it. And since it was done…it would only hurt her family to find out now.

But, like anything else in her life, keeping her feelings inside made it harder to deal with it.

Maybe if she hadn't come back to stay in Cornwall she

would feel differently about her freedom. If she hadn't made love to him. If they hadn't gone to Paris together. If the last month and a half never happened she might feel relieved and ready to move on her with life.

But it *had* happened. She had let herself get closer to Heath than she ever had in the eleven years of their marriage and then it was all done. How was she supposed to just walk away? How was she going to learn to stop loving him? Eleven years apart hadn't done it. Was she doomed to another eleven years of quiet pining for him?

In the gathering darkness, Julianne noticed a dancing light coming up the main tree lane from the house. The snow had let up a little, making it easier to see the figure was walking toward her with a flashlight. She tensed. She was at a tentative truce with the trees, but she wasn't sure if adding another person would work. It didn't feel as secure as being here alone.

Then she made out the distinctive bright blue of the coat and realized it was Heath. She sighed. Why had he followed her out here? She needed some time alone to mourn their relationship and deal with a hellish day.

Heath stopped a few feet short of the rock, not crowding into her space. "Your rock has missed you."

At that Julianne chuckled. Even Heath remembered how much time she had spent sitting in this very spot when they were kids. "Fortunately, time is relative to a rock."

"I still feel bad for it. I know I couldn't go that long without you in my life."

The light atmosphere between then shifted. Her gaze lifted to meet his, her smile fading. "Life doesn't always work out the way you plan. Even for a rock."

"I disagree. Life might throw obstacles in your path, but if you want something with your whole heart and soul, you have to fight for it. Nothing that's easy is worth having and nothing worth having is easy. You, Julianne, have been incredibly difficult."

"I'm going to take that as a compliment."

He smiled. "You should. I meant it as one. You're worth every moment of pain and frustration and confusion I've gone through. And I think, perhaps, that we might have weathered the trials. In every fairy tale, the prince and the maiden have obstacles to triumph over and strengthen their love. I think the evil villain has been defeated. I'm ready for the happy ending."

It sounded good. Really, it did. But so much had happened. Could they really ever get back to a happy ending? "Life isn't a fairy tale, Heath. We're divorced. I've never read a story where the prince and his princess divorce."

"Yeah, but they have angry dragons and evil wizards. I'll take a divorce any day because things can always change. We don't have to stay divorced. We can slay this dragon, if you're willing to face it with me."

She watched as his hand slipped into his coat pocket and retrieved a small box. A jewelry box. Her heart stilled in her chest. What was he doing? They'd been divorced for two days. He wasn't really…he couldn't possibly want this after everything that had happened.

"Heath…" she began.

"Let me say what I need to say," he insisted. "When we were eighteen, we got married for all the wrong reasons. We loved each other but we were young and stupid. We didn't think it through. Life is complicated and we were unprepared for the reality of it. But I also think we got divorced for all the wrong reasons."

Heath crouched down at the foot of the rock, looking up at her. "I love you. I've always loved you. I never imagined my life or my future without you in it. I was hurt that you wouldn't open up to me and I used our divorce to punish you for it. Now, I understand why you held back. And I realized that everything you did that hurt me was also meant to somehow protect me.

"You said at the police station today that I was willing to go to jail for you. And you were right. I was willing to take on years of misery behind bars to protect you. Just as you were willing to give me a divorce and face a future alone in the hopes that I could find someone to make me happy."

"That's not the same," she insisted.

"A self-imposed prison is just as difficult to escape as one of iron and stone, Jules." He held up the box and looked her square in the eye. "Consider this a jailbreak."

"Are you honestly telling me that between Parisian jet lag, getting divorced, getting arrested and spending all day at the police station, you had the time to go to the jeweler and buy an engagement ring?"

"No," he said.

Julianne instantly felt foolish. Had she misinterpreted the whole thing? If there were earrings in that box she would feel like an idiot. "Then what is going on? If you're not proposing, what are you doing?"

"I am proposing. But you asked if I went to a jeweler and I didn't. I went to talk to Ken."

Julianne swallowed hard. "We agreed we weren't going to tell them about us."

"Correction. We agreed not to tell them we were married before. You said nothing about telling him that I was in love with you and wanted his blessing to marry you. No one needs to know it's round two for us."

She winced, torn between her curiosity about what was in the box, her elation about his confession of love and how her daddy had taken the news. "What happened?" she asked.

Heath smiled wide, easing her concerns. "He asked me

what the hell had taken so long. And then he gave me this." He opened the hinge on the box to reveal the ring inside.

It couldn't be. Julianne's jaw dropped open. The large round diamond, the eight diamonds encircling it, the intricate gold lacework of the dull, worn band… It was her grandmother's wedding ring. She hadn't seen this ring since she was a small child and Nanna was still alive.

Heath pulled the ring from the box and held it up to her. "The last ring I gave you was cheap and ugly. This time, I have enough money to buy you any ring you'd like, but I wanted a ring that meant something. Ken told me that they had been saving this ring in the hopes that one day it would be your engagement ring. He knew how much you loved your nanna and thought this would be perfect. I was inclined to agree.

"Julianne Eden, will you marry me *again?*"

Heath was kneeling in the snow, freezing and holding his breath. Julianne took far too long to answer. Her expression changed faster than he could follow. At first, she'd stared at that ring like he was holding up a severed head. Then her expression softened and she seemed on the verge of tears. After that, she'd gone stony and silent. Waiting more than a beat or two to answer a question like this was really bad form.

"Yes."

And then his heart leapt in his chest. "Yes?"

Julianne smiled, her eyes brimming with tears. "Yes, I will marry you again."

Heath scrambled to slip the ring onto her finger. It flopped around a bit. "I'm sorry it's too big. We'll get it sized down as soon as we can get to a jeweler."

"That's okay. Nanna was Daddy's mother and I take after Mama's side of the family. We're much tinier people." She looked down at the ring and her face was nearly beaming. "I love it. It's more than perfect."

She lunged forward into his arms, knocking him backward into the snow. Before he knew it, he was lying in the cold fluff and Julianne was on top of him, kissing him. Not so bad, after all. He ignored the cold, focusing on the taste of the lips he'd thought he might never kiss again. That was enough to warm his blood and chase off any chill.

Julianne was going to marry him. That just left telling Molly. Even though he now knew that Julianne had never kept their relationship a secret out of embarrassment, the idea shouldn't bother him, but he still felt a nervous tremble in his stomach. A part of him was afraid to say the words. "It's getting dark. Are you ready to head back to the house and tell everyone?"

He expected her to dodge the way she always did, to make some excuse, to say that she wanted to celebrate with just the two of them for now. A part of him would even understand if she wanted to wait until tomorrow after all the drama of the day.

"Absolutely," she said, smiling down at him. "I'm thrilled to give them some good news for a change."

Relief flooded through him, and the last barrier to total bliss was gone. They got up and held hands as they walked back through the trees to the house. When they came in together through the back door, Molly was in the kitchen cooking and Ken was in the living room reading a book.

"Mom, do you have a minute?"

Molly nodded, more focused on the boiling of her potatoes than the clasping of their hands. "Yes, these need to go for a bit longer."

"Come into the living room," Heath said, herding her ahead of them to sit down next to Ken by the fireplace.

Heath and Julianne sat opposite them. He was still holding Julianne's hand for support. She leaned into him, placing her left hand over their clasped ones and inadvertently displaying her ring.

"Mom, Dad…" Heath began.

"What is that?" Molly asked, her eyes glued on Julianne's hand. "Is that an engagement ring? Wait. Is that Nanna's ring?" She turned to Ken with an accusatory glare. "You knew about this and you didn't tell me!"

Ken shrugged. If he got wound up every time Molly did, he would have had twenty heart attacks by now. "He asked for my blessing, so I gave him the ring. That's what you wanted, didn't you? Saving the ring for Jules was your idea."

"Of course it's what I wanted." Molly's emotions seemed to level out as she realized she should be more focused on the fact that Heath and Julianne were engaged. A bright smile lit her face. "My baby is getting married!" She leapt from her chair and gathered Julianne into her arms.

She tugged Heath up from his seat to hug him next. "I didn't even know you two were seeing each other," she scolded. "A heads-up would have been nice before you dropped a marriage bomb on me! Lordy, so much news today. Is there anything else you all need to tell us?"

Heath stiffened in her arms. He was never good at lying to Molly, but Julianne was adamant that their prior marriage stay quiet, no matter what. "Isn't this enough?" he said with a smile.

"Wonderful news," Molly said, her eyes getting misty and far off as her mind drifted. "We'll have the wedding here at the farm," she declared. "It will be beautiful. Everyone in town will want to come. Please don't tell me you want a small affair or destination wedding in Antigua."

Julianne smiled and patted Molly's shoulder. "We'll

have it here, I promise. And it can be as big and fabulous as you can imagine it."

"This time," Heath added, "I think we need to have a grand wedding with the big cake and a swing band."

"This time?" Molly said, her brow furrowed.

Julianne turned to look at him, her green eyes wide with silent condemnation. It wasn't until then that Heath fully realized what he'd said. Damn it. With a shake of her head, Julianne held out her hand, gesturing for him to spill the last of their secrets. They might as well.

"Uh, Mom…" he began. "Julianne and I, uh, eloped when we were eighteen."

Both he and Julianne took a large step backward out of the blast zone. Molly's eyes grew wide, but before she could open her mouth, Ken stood up and clasped her shoulders tightly. It made Heath wonder if it was Ken's subtle restraining of his tiny wife hidden beneath the guise of supportiveness.

Molly's mouth opened, then closed as she took a deep breath to collect her thoughts. "When did this happen?"

"While we were on our European vacation after graduation."

"You two immediately went off to separate schools when you got home," she said with a frown.

"Yeah, we didn't plan that well," Heath admitted. Even if they'd had the perfect honeymoon and had come home blissfully in love they still would have faced the huge obstacles of where they went from there. They were heading to different schools a thousand miles apart. Not exactly the best way to start a marriage, but an ideal way to start a trial separation.

"And how long were you two married? I'm assuming you're divorced now, considering you're engaged again."

This time Heath looked at Julianne. It was her turn to

fess up since they were married that long due to her own procrastination.

"Eleven years. Our divorce was final a couple days ago."

Molly closed her eyes. "I'm not going to ask. I really don't think I want to know. You think you know what's going on in your kids' lives, but you have no clue. You two were married this whole time. Xander and Rose had a baby I never knew about. And to think I believed all of you were too busy with careers and I might never see everyone settled down!"

"We would've told you, Mama, but we pretty much broke up right after we married. We've been separated all this time."

"I think I've had about all the news I can take for one day, good or bad. This calls for a pot of tea, I think. You can let go of me now, Ken." Molly headed for the kitchen, then stopped in the entryway. "I might as well ask…you're not pregnant, are you?"

Julianne shook her head adamantly. "No, Mama. I promise we are not pregnant."

"All right," she said. "You two wash up. It's almost time for supper."

Molly disappeared. Ken clapped Heath on the shoulder as he passed by. In a moment, they were alone with all their secrets out on the table.

"I think it was better this way, don't you?" Heath asked.

"You only think that because you're the one that spilled the beans."

Heath turned to her and pulled Julianne into his arms. "Maybe. But I am happy to start our new life together with no more secrets. Everything is out in the open at last. Right? You've told me all of it?"

Julianne nodded, climbing to her toes to place a kiss on his lips. "Of course, dear."

Heath laughed. "Spoken like a wife filled with secrets she keeps from her husband."

She wrapped her arms around his neck, a naughty grin curling her lips as she looked up at him. "This *is* my second marriage, you'll remember. I'm an old pro at this now."

"Don't think I don't know all your tricks, woman. It's my second marriage, too," Heath noted. "And last."

Julianne smiled. "It better be."

Epilogue

It was a glorious spring day in northwestern Connecticut. The sun was shining on the farm. The delicate centerpieces of roses, hydrangeas, lilies and orchids were warming in the afternoon light, emitting a soft fragrance on the breeze. It was the perfect day for a wedding on the farm; the second in the last six months, with two more on the horizon.

Molly was absolutely beaming. She'd been waiting years to see her children marry and start families of their own. All of them had been more focused on careers than romance, much to her chagrin, but things had turned around and fast. It seemed like each of them had gone from single to engaged in the blink of an eye.

Today was Brody and Samantha's big day. It was the ceremony that she'd lain awake nights worrying she might never see. Molly had always hoped that Brody would find a woman who could look beyond the scars. She couldn't have imagined a more perfect match for him than Sam.

She had thought for certain that Brody and Sam would opt for a wedding in Boston. He'd promised her a huge ceremony with half the eastern seaboard in attendance, but when it came down to it, Sam had wanted something far more intimate at the farm, which thrilled Molly. That didn't mean a simple affair, by any stretch—this was still Sam's wedding they were talking about. Her new daughter-in-law imagined an event that was pink and covered in flowers and Swarovski crystals.

All of "her girls" were so different, and Molly was so pleased to be able to finally say that. She had four daughters now, and each of their weddings would be unique experiences that would keep the farm hopping all year.

When Ken had his heart attack, Wade and Tori had postponed their plans for a fall wedding. Since Brody and Sam were already planning a spring ceremony, they opted to wait until the following autumn and keep with the rustic theme they'd designed. Xander and Rose were marrying over the long Fourth of July weekend in an appropriately patriotic extravaganza.

And as for Heath and Julianne…they hadn't gotten very far into planning their second wedding when it all got chucked out the window. They'd promised Molly a big ceremony, but when they realized they'd come home from Paris with more than just souvenirs, they moved up the timeline.

Molly stepped away from her duties as mother of the groom to search for her daughter in the crowd. Julianne was sitting beneath the shade of the tent, absent-mindedly stroking her round, protruding belly. The delicate pink bridesmaid gown Sam had selected for her daughter to wear did little to hide the fact that she was extremely pregnant. Although Julianne had sworn she had no more secrets, in only two months, Molly would be holding her second grandbaby and she could hardly wait.

Julianne and Heath had had the first of the weddings on the farm—a small family ceremony while everyone was home for Christmas. It was the polar opposite of today's circus. Brody and Sam had a band, dancing, and a catered sit-down meal.

A new song began and Brody led Sam onto the dance floor. They might as well have been the only people here since Brody couldn't take his eyes off of her. His bride was beaming like a ray of sunshine. Her white satin gown was stunning against the golden tan of her skin. The intricate crystal and bead work traveled down the bodice to the mermaid skirt, highlighting every amazing curve of Sam's body. Her veil was long, flowing down her back to pool on the parquet dance floor they set up on the lawn. She was stunning.

Brody, too, was looking handsome. Molly had always thought he was a good-looking boy, but the first round of reconstructive surgery with the specialist had done wonders for his scars. There would be more surgeries in the future, but Molly could already see the dramatic change in the way he carried himself. She'd never seen Brody look happier than he did right now.

It wasn't long before Wade and Tori joined them on the dance floor. Then Xander and Rose. Julianne took a little convincing, but eventually Heath lured her out to dance, completing the wedding party.

The sight of all of them together brought a happy tear to Molly's eye. The last few years had been so hard with nearly losing Ken, the crippling financial burden of his medical bills and dealing with the police investigation. Even when all that was behind them, Molly and Ken had to work through their guilt over what had happened with

Tommy and how their children had suffered silently for all these years. It had been rough, but the Edens were made of stern stuff and they had survived and become stronger for it. The year of weddings at the Garden of Eden was a fresh start for the whole family.

Molly felt a warmth at her back, then the slide of Ken's arms around her waist. He hugged her to his chest, pressing a kiss against her cheek.

"Look at our beautiful family, Mama," he whispered into her ear.

Molly relished the feel of his still strong arms holding her and sighed with contentment. "It's hard to believe there was a time we thought we might not have any children," she said. "And here we are with a full house. And grandbabies."

"It's better than I ever imagined or could even have hoped for. I think the fairy tale I promised you on our wedding day is finally complete."

"Yes," Molly agreed. "We've reached our happily ever after."

* * * * *

MILLS & BOON®

Power, passion and irresistible temptation!

The Modern™ series lets you step into a world of sophistication and glamour, where sinfully seductive heroes await you in luxurious international locations. Visit the Mills & Boon website today and type **Mod15** in at the checkout to receive

15% OFF

your next Modern purchase.

Visit **www.millsandboon.co.uk/mod15**

MILLS & BOON®

Why not subscribe?

Never miss a title and save money too!

Here's what's available to you if you join the exclusive **Mills & Boon Book Club** today:

✦ *Titles up to a month ahead of the shops*
✦ *Amazing discounts*
✦ *Free P&P*
✦ *Earn Bonus Book points that can be redeemed against other titles and gifts*
✦ *Choose from monthly or pre-paid plans*

Still want more?

Well, if you join today we'll even give you
50% OFF your first parcel!

So visit **www.millsandboon.co.uk/subs**
or call **Customer Relations on 020 8288 2888**
to be a part of this exclusive Book Club!

Snow, sleigh bells and a hint of seduction

Find your perfect Christmas reads at
millsandboon.co.uk/Christmas

MILLS & BOON®

Why shop at millsandboon.co.uk?

Each year, thousands of romance readers find their perfect read at millsandboon.co.uk. That's because we're passionate about bringing you the very best romantic fiction. Here are some of the advantages of shopping at www.millsandboon.co.uk:

* **Get new books first**—you'll be able to buy your favourite books one month before they hit the shops

* **Get exclusive discounts**—you'll also be able to buy our specially created monthly collections, with up to 50% off the RRP

* **Find your favourite authors**—latest news, interviews and new releases for all your favourite authors and series on our website, plus ideas for what to try next

* **Join in**—once you've bought your favourite books, don't forget to register with us to rate, review and join in the discussions

Visit **www.millsandboon.co.uk**
for all this and more today!

MILLS_WEB